Ever the Hunted

EVER THE OUTCAST   EVER THE BRAVE

Ever the Hunted

ERIN SUMMERILL

HOUGHTON MIFFLIN HARCOURT
BOSTON NEW YORK

www.hmhco.com

The text was set in ITC Legacy Serif Std.
Map illustration © 2016 by Jennifer Thermes
Design by Lisa Vega

Library of Congress Cataloging-in-Publication Data
Names: Summerill, Erin, 1978– author.
Title: Ever the hunted : a clash of kingdoms novel / Erin Summerill.
Description: Boston : Houghton Mifflin Harcourt, [2016] |
Summary: Seventeen- year-old Britta Flannery is the outcast daughter
of a bounty hunter who must use her powers to track her father's killer
in a world of warring kingdoms and dangerous magic.
Identifiers: LCCN 2015039038 | ISBN 9780544664456
Subjects: | CYAC: Fantasy. | Magic—Fiction. | Revenge—Fiction. | BISAC:
JUVENILE FICTION / Love & Romance. | JUVENILE FICTION / Fantasy & Magic. |
JUVENILE FICTION / Action & Adventure / General. | JUVENILE FICTION /
Mysteries & Detective Stories.
Classification: LCC PZ7.1.S853 Ev 2016 | DDC [Fic]—dc23 LC record available at
https://lccn.loc.gov/2015039038

Manufactured in the United States of America
DOC 10 9 8 7 6 5 4 3 2 1
4500622195

To my dad,
who accepted my kidney
and, in return,
taught me about sacrifice
and love and healing

Kolontia
SHAERDAN KINGDOM
DRY PLAINS
PADRIN
Jacinda's Well
FENNIT
CELIZE
Lord Conklin
Enat's Home
GREAT CANYON

CHAPTER 1

T O SURVIVE THESE WOODS, A MAN HAS TO BE *strong as the trees,* Papa had said. The memory is a whisper compared to the attention my cramping stomach demands.

I try not to think of him or my trembling legs as I dust my boot prints from the path with a broken branch. Every starved scrap of me begs to stop and hunt here on the foot trail in the Ever Woods. Only the danger of getting caught propels me onward, boots stumbling over rocks and dirt.

Weak as I am, I won't make it through the craggy Malam Mountains to where King Aodren's land edges the lowlands. It's a two-day walk. Two long, grueling days. Spots dance in my vision. Seeds, I need food. Papa's old training spot will have to do. The king's guard, the eyes over the royal city of Brentyn, aren't likely to catch me there. Through a pinched, rocky canyon, the remote site has only been used by Cohen, Papa's former apprentice, and me. A spasm racks my insides, and the decision is made. To the practice clearing.

The sun's halfway to its peak when I stumble into the glade. Heady, sweet pine scents the brisk air. The leaves on the white-barked quaky trees around the nearby lake glow like embers, fiery gold and auburn against the evergreens. The sight is a warm welcome home.

Though starved and here to hunt, I cannot stop myself from finding *our* tree and tracing the carved names: *Britta & Cohen*.

Nor can I swallow the emotions that lump in my throat.

Since Cohen left last year to work for the king and Papa was killed two months ago, I've kept the pressing loneliness mostly at bay, managing it in little pieces. But this morning, it's like isolation up and walloped me in the face.

I swipe a sneaky tear away and ready an arrow to my bow.

My body resembles a freckled skeleton for how thin I've become. Not much will change my paleness, but catching a squirrel or grouse will satisfy my hunger. Something to strengthen me. Later, I'll bag a larger beast. Winter's not far off, and I desperately need a decent kill to trade for lodging. The king's guard will soon seize my land—no, Papa's land—now that my mourning is over.

Bludgers will be pounding on my door in a couple days,

foaming at the mouth over my cozy, one-room cottage. I pull back on my bowstring, testing the pressure, needing to shoot something. Anything. To keep a Malam tradition—home isolation for two months of mourning—I nearly starved, and now must break the law, since no one brought food after Papa died. Never a kindness for me—Britta Flannery—daughter of a Shaerdanian and, therefore, an outcast.

A year before my birth, the king regent closed the border between Malam and Shaerdan. Since then it seems all of Malam contracted amnesia; nobody remembers the good that came from the neighboring country. Once, we prospered from Shaerdan's trade and relied on Channelers' healing salves. Now we shun them for their strange Channeler magic. We fear what they can do.

With a huff, I push down the anger and focus on the hunt.

That's when I discover the print of an elk hoof, two half circles with pointed ends. The moisture puddling inside the tracks reveals that the elk was here recently. My pulse quickens at the promise of a good catch as I stand stiller than a tree to listen for the elk's movement. Birds whistle; leaves swish. All normal sounds of the Ever Woods, but something is off. That something abruptly tugs inside me, and an invisible finger skitters unease up the back of my neck.

I'm not alone.

My eyes ricochet from the branches to the shrubs to the sky, seeing everything and nothing. I spin around, expecting to meet the red coats of the king's guard, and only find pine trees. I bite my lip. Swipe ghostly blond strands of hair out of my face.

Who else could be here?

No one dares hazard a hunt in the king's Ever Woods. Hunting is only permitted where royal land ends near Lord Devlin's fiefdom. That's two days west in the Bloodwood firs or three and a half days south. On a rare day, poaching will get a man whipped or tortured. Most days, death.

I clench my bow and push myself to search for signs of an intruder: broken tree limbs, prints in the soil. It's frustrating to abandon the elk hunt, but *safety ensures survival* — Papa's first lesson.

An hour of combing the underbrush passes before the strange sensation disappears. Which in a way is more unsettling, since my instincts have never led me astray. Perhaps hunting without Papa has me on edge. Perhaps being alone —

A shadow shifts a few lengths ahead.

I dash behind a rotted trunk. My fingers contract and relax around the bow's well-worn grip. Flex. Release. Papa would clap my ear for acting like a skittish girl. *Stay in control,* he'd say. *Focus is a weapon as much as your bow.*

I draw a breath, slow and calm, and force myself to lean away from the decaying wood to get a look.

Whatever I was expecting to see, it wasn't a six-point bull elk. A king of the forest, he struts into the glade. Proud shoulders, sturdy haunches. It takes a beat to remember this elk means my survival. From where I'm crouched, the angle makes for a tricky shot. One knuckle-width too high or low will hit bone or cartilage, seriously wounding but not killing. Torturing, if my aim is off.

I shoot. The arrow thunks deep into the bull's chest, impaling the vitals in a killing blow. The elk starts, jerks to a run, staggering a few steps before his eyes roll white. He thuds to the needle-covered ground.

I stare blindly at the beast, my bow arm falling to my side. A touch of sadness, a trickle of unworthiness beats through me as blackbirds flap out of the branches. An absurd reaction for a hunter, I know. His husky, labored breaths echo around us, to which I whisper shapeless, calming words as the beast accepts death. The life left in the animal struggles, a ravaged soldier fighting his way off the battlefield, having no hope of survival.

My hunter's instinct always recognizes the cusp of passing. *The awareness you possess is a talent only the best hunters develop,* Papa said. Except, how can it be a talent when it's only ever felt like a curse? I give the elk a quick end, slitting his throat.

My grip tenses over the intricate etchings on Papa's dagger, my knuckles a match to the ivory handle. I force the blade to the animal's belly to begin gutting and quartering. Stick to the task. Cut through the fur. Slice the skin. Roll out the innards. I'm good at pressing forward, always moving onward.

While some elk is curing and drying, other pieces roast over a small fire. It's the same way Papa prepared the meat from my first kill ten years ago. He laughed when I took a bite and grimaced from the gamy taste. *Nothing better than this dinner right here,* he'd said. *Because you caught it. Now I know you can do it again.* His praise didn't come as often as his lessons. When it did, I treasured every word.

I chew the last sinewy bite and pull my threadbare blanket from my satchel. The cloak of night cinches around the forest. Chilly air sneaks through the blanket's weave and nips at my arms. And still, the evening is better than any I've had since Papa passed. Stomach sated, I settle onto a bed of needles. If only he could see me now, surviving on my own.

Sleep steals me away in seconds.

I'm standing outside. Behind me, the coarse stones and thatched roof of my cottage are stained bluish black from the night.

Stars sprinkle the sky like salt spilled across a well-oiled table. My hair, which is usually bound in a braid, falls past my shoulders, a veil of pale blond that shines silver in the moonlight.

Where our pasture meets the Evers, something moves. It's the shape of a young man.

My eyes narrow, and then I smile. Since the incident, he's only come once—earlier that day he traveled the half league from Brentyn to visit our cottage. My heart gallops as I force myself to walk to where he stands in the shadows until the darkness swallows me whole. There, his whispery breath breaks the stillness.

Hair the rich color of soil after a rainstorm. Sharp hazel eyes. A face too handsome for the angry scar that mars his cheek. The guilt is overwhelming as my fingers itch to trace the shiny red mark. I want to touch him and tell him how I feel about him. How he owns my heart.

All that comes out is "Cohen, I'm sorry."

The howling wind wakes me. Cohen vanishes, replaced by the gray shaded trunks and the pine limbs stretching above like specters. I curl my legs in tight and cinch the shoddy woolen blanket snug around my shoulders. The dreamt memory has left me disoriented, and it takes two inhales and two exhales to ground myself. To calm my pulse.

When I was twelve, Papa no longer took me on regular bounty hunts for King Aodren. Alone in the cottage, I felt the quietness eat at me. I pretended the creaking woods or my own breaths were other voices. Company to pass the night. Ridiculous, but it helped me fall asleep.

Those old tricks won't work tonight. Not when Cohen's face lingers in the darkness. Always, I see his scar first—an injury suffered weeks before he left. Starting just under his eye, it leads to the strong line of his jaw that's covered in sparse sable scruff, because at eighteen, when we were last together, he was too boyish to grow a full beard. Perhaps that's changed now that he's twenty, two years and a pinch older than me.

I like the idea of an older, rugged Cohen. More than I should admit.

A year and three months have passed since Cohen completed his apprenticeship and became one of the king's court, taking up the title only my father, my grandfather, and all Flannery men before them held. As one of the king's two bounty hunters, Cohen is allowed to travel through Malam's fiefdoms and cross the borders. It's unimaginable to me. I'll never have the chance to leave Malam.

When Cohen left without a goodbye, I hoped he would visit. Except he didn't return; not even for Papa's wake.

Using the heels of my hands, I try to rub him out of my mind. A useless endeavor. Cohen has taken up too much space in my heart and head for the last five years to dismiss so easily. As always, my thoughts turn to his long absence. And I wonder if he never returned because he realized there's no future for us.

As the king's bounty hunter, Cohen is in a league above commoners. Ten leagues above me. Like Papa, he'll be revered for his position in the king's court. He'll be considered nobility and be given lands. And if he chooses, he'll marry the daughter of a lord.

A noble marriage, let alone any union for that matter, is about as likely for me as the king himself proposing. I snort at the idea.

All that came with Papa's honored title, home, and land returns to the king, since Papa has no living relations except me. And I'm ineligible to inherit. Though my parents married in Shaerdan, the law only recognizes unions made before a priest of Malam. Before they could do so, my mother was accused of selling secrets to Shaerdan and killed.

In the law's eyes, I'm illegitimate. To most of Malam, I'm Shaerdanian. But to some, the gossipmongers in Brentyn, I'm a traitor's daughter.

None of that matters to me, though, because like my father, I'll always be a Flannery, and I can take care of myself.

At sunrise, I walk to the crystal-clear lake and splash water on my face. Brisk morning air fills my lungs and prickles my skin. It isn't until I've patted dry with my tunic that a disturbance along the muddy shore seizes my attention. Fresh boot prints. A man's — by the size of them.

I leap to my feet, spinning wildly to search the clearing. Like yesterday, nothing stands out. Nothing more than evergreens and the glassy blue water spread beneath the cloudless sky. Even so, there's no question now.

I'm not alone.

CHAPTER

2

IT ONLY TAKES A FEW MOMENTS TO THROW together my pack and to shove strips of cloth-wrapped elk around my bow and blade. A pile of elk cuts remains on the edge of my camp, but there's no room left in my bag. I groan and curse the leftovers. But I cannot carry it all. Nor can I risk returning.

I glance at the lake. At the boot prints.

An arrow of fear zips through me.

The lucky forest animals will get to devour the remainder. I quickly fasten a gray woolen skirt over my trousers and adjust my tunic, belting it at the waist like the style worn by most townswomen. Balancing the heavy bag on my shoulder, I dart out of the clearing, eyes peeled for any signs of movement in the trees and undergrowth.

Autumn bites the air as I hurry down the mountain.

Brentyn's royal cathedral sits like a stone watchman, its spires snaked in green ivy and piercing the sky. A sullen viol harmony drifts through the stained glass. It clashes with the market sounds: commoner chatter, shouts from traders, creaking carts, cooing church birds. I hide in the cathedral's shadow and smooth down my braid. I'm restless and anxious, as always when coming to town. Today, though, with boot prints on my mind and poached meat burdening my bag, the usual nerves feel more like a bout of winter ague.

Something at the far end of the square has drawn the crowd's attention. People shuffle closer, filling in the square like pigs in a pen when the slop is served. On my tiptoes, I stretch to see what has everyone's interest. My insides twist harder.

A woman is in the pillory, wrists and neck captured in the wood planks. Dried blood clings to her broken lip. Agony is written on her tear-stained and dust-caked face as she shifts her weight from one filthy, swollen foot to the other. A ring of dirt surrounds her—a ritual believed to draw out a Channeler's power.

A farce is what it is. If a woman draws water from a well thought to be dry, she's a Channeler. If she walks through a storm and doesn't catch a sniffle, it's black magic. All the *real* Channelers fled to Shaerdan, where their magic originated, twenty years ago during the Purge.

Channeler magic is devilry in its darkest form, a scourge sent from

Shaerdan . . . Those inflicted must be cut down and their powers eradicated. I read the Purge Proclamation once, found it in Papa's books. The Proclamation didn't start the mutual hatred between Malam and Shaerdan, but it certainly sealed it. In Shaerdan, Channelers are revered.

There's nothing to be done for the woman. The guards will decide her fate. Still, it's challenging to pull my eyes away and to not selfishly worry that an accusation will be made against me now that Papa's gone.

I clutch the satchel's straps, fingernails biting my palms, and search the crowd three times over. Leather coats, earth-colored tunics, blackened trouser cuffs, sweeping skirts. None wear the royal red. The king's watchdogs aren't near the pillory or in the market. For the time being, they're letting the townspeople torment and shame the woman into submission.

While skirting the market, my bag hangs from one shoulder, as if full of feathers and not elk. The last thing I need is questions. I've every right to shop at the market, but no one likes to be seen consorting with the Shaerdanian girl. My trade opportunity is limited to Mr. Tulach, the only merchant who willingly did business with me when Papa wasn't at my side.

A gaggle of children winds around a log, laughing uproariously and singing a tune of Midsummer's Tide as they imitate the maypole dance. I sidestep their play, wondering how it would've been to have so many friends. *You won't trade with Britta? Then I'll take business elsewhere,* Cohen once told a merchant, and never bartered with the man again. Cohen was the only friend I needed.

Mr. Tulach's tent is busy with patrons who are admiring winter blankets and woolens.

"Filth."

It's spoken softly, but the venom in the word snags my attention. I glance up to find two townswomen, woolen brown dresses, full skirts dusting the cobblestones, and arms holding baskets of tubers and carrots. One woman is old, her skin like crumpled parchment, and the other is young and well fed, if not overfed. The two months of isolated mourning come to mind, and my abdomen grumbles in remembrance. Under the women's gaze, I self-consciously smooth a free hand over my ratty skirt.

The older one turns her nose up. "Dirt. Like her mother."

I stiffen. Papa said not to let their words affect me. *Words cannot hurt.*

Besides, the same could be said of her, considering the mop of hair on her head looks like an entire flock of birds has used it for nesting. I cannot react. Ignore them. Biting the inside of my cheek, I force my feet to the side of Mr. Tulach's tent where the leather flaps hide me from the market and those awful crows. It doesn't block the sound, though.

"Their kind shouldn't be allowed here."

"Gods bless the border."

A murmur of agreement then: "Did you know her mother tried to follow the Archtraitor?"

I roll my eyes at the outrageous rumor and the ones that follow about the Archtraitor's blood thirst, the savages he's gathering, his plan to take over Malam. The gossip never changes.

Malam's built on gossip; its towns are pens of sheep. Papa's silly saying makes me want to bleat at the ladies, since nobody really knows where Millner Barrett, the Archtraitor, is or what he's doing now. Once he was captain of the king's guard. Then he opposed the Purge and the border closure before he cut down his own men and fled. His disgrace will never be forgotten. At least, not till he's caught.

Once they leave, I release my grip on the table and quickly straighten the leathers and wools as Mr. Tulach steps to my side of the tent. His attention remains on the passing patrons. He doesn't like for others to see us trading.

"You haven't been here in a while." Mr. Tulach's chin dips in a subtle nod.

He knows I've been in mourning, so I forgo this detail. "I need to trade. I have bull elk for you. A six-point catch. It's fresh—"

"Where'd you hunt it?" He whips around to me, raven braids slicing around his broad back. "Never mind. I don't want to know." His eyes volley to the crowd. "What are you asking?"

The profile of his hawkish nose doesn't alter direction as he waits for my answer.

"You have a connection to a place of lodging in Fennit," I

say, fighting to keep my voice from cracking with desperation. "I need a place for winter."

Mr. Tulach shoots me a questioning look.

Surely he knows about the king's inheritance law. I meet his stare, but when he doesn't yield, I rush to explain, "The king will soon be seizing my cottage."

Mr. Tulach turns away, crossing umber-brown arms. "I cannot take the risk. Not when we're on the brink of war. The guards overlook nothing these days. A bunch of bloodthirsty wolves, they are." His voice drops. "You've known the law your whole life. You must have other options."

Panic presses on my chest, making it difficult to breathe.

Papa said I had a talent for knowing the honesty of a man's word. A sort of heightened gut instinct. When someone speaks the truth, a warm sensation starts in my belly and spreads beneath my ribs. A handy trick, considering it works for lies too, except dishonesty feels like ice on my insides, chilling me top to bottom. I can feel the warmth of his words, the truth of his rejection.

The table's edge digs into my hip as I lean closer. "Please," I say, swallowing my pride. "The other merchants won't trade with me. And I didn't plan on my father getting murdered." The words taste like ash.

He balks. "If I'm caught with your poached meat, I'll be thrown in the dungeon. Or worse. Boys as young as fourteen are being made to fight against Shaerdan. I cannot risk my family. Take your trade and go."

The closed look in Mr. Tulach's eyes, coupled with the warm truthful sensation spreading through my core, crushes my hope. I grit my teeth, sling the bag over my shoulder, and dash from the tent. How will I get lodging now?

The other merchants will have nothing to do with me. Eyes shift away when I approach. Backs turn. It's no different from the first time I went to market without Papa by my side. *Can you not see we're here to do business with you, sir?* Cohen's words were steely.

I've got no business with Shaerdanians, the vendor sneered.

Cohen stepped in front of me. *If she's a Shaerdanian, then you're a jackass.*

It took a beat for the insult to settle on the merchant. By then we were running away. The man's rejection stung, but Cohen's defense soothed the hurt.

If only he were here now.

I'm nearly out of the market when Old Lyman, in soiled rags huddled on the church's steps, whispers a plea from his cracked lips. He lifts his beggar's cup. I don't know why I pause.

When Cohen accompanied me to town, he always stopped to give coins to the poor. *If I were ever in this situation, I'd like someone to extend the same kindness,* Cohen said with conviction, even though a man like him—the chosen apprentice to the king's bounty hunter—would never fall to such misfortune. But that was Cohen, always charitable. Even to those deemed worthless.

I've nothing to give Old Lyman, and so I feel foolish for having stopped. I shake my head, a touch flustered for having dallied at all.

"Kind of ya, anyway, to share yer smile." His words are garbled by the loss of teeth.

Before I can talk myself out of it, I swing my satchel to the side, and, after checking every face in the square, pull out some elk. The portion is small. All I can spare. I press the meat into his dirty palm while muttering an apology for not giving more.

His other hand lands atop mine, trapping me softly between trembling, mud-crusted fingers. "They're lookin' for ya, lass. Guards are comin'. Best go quick."

It takes a beat for his warning to hit me. I jerk out of his grip, mumble thanks, and race toward home.

I'm nearly to my cottage on the outskirts of Brentyn when a whinny and nicker echo behind me. In the distance, the pebbled dirt road hums with the pounding of hooves.

Quickly, I scan for a place to toss the bag. The piles of leaves beside the road aren't ideal, but they're the only hiding spot. Distress snakes through me as I bury my sack, making frantic work to memorize the area before darting back to the path.

Where will I live when they seize my home? Who will take me in?

Dust dirties the air as the riders draw closer. Only then do

I remember Papa's dagger in the bundled meat. I glance at the lump of leaves, hedging on making a desperate grasp for the blade, but time is gone. Six royal guards wearing red coats with gray stripes and the king's emblem — a circular badge with the head of a stag in the center — emerge around the bend.

I tug my skirt lower and run my fingers over my braid, drawing out twigs. When the group trots closer and divides, three riders moving to my left and three to the right, I drop into a small curtsy, as is customary around nobility and the king's men.

A man with a staunch scowl set against weathered skin brings his mare to a stop so that the animal's breath of heat and hay puffs across my face. I stifle a cough and keep my spine tree-trunk straight. The man must be the leader since he has the most stripes on his shoulder. Five in total.

"Britta Flannery." Not a question. "Where have you been?"

"On a walk." My eyes remain forward despite how badly I wish to check the leaves beside the road.

"Is that so?"

His doubt makes me ill. I never know what to say. My usual awkwardness feels like a death sentence as I fumble for a believable answer.

"Perhaps you could explain what that is." His chin jerks to the side where a guard pulls my bag from hiding. *No!* Fear jolts through me.

I stamp the urge to grab the pack and run, and feign indifference. "I — I don't know."

"The bag's marked with your father's emblem." The leader's mouth purses behind a tidy graying beard.

If they see the meat, they'll have evidence I was poaching. "Are you here for my land?" I ask in diversion. Better to give up my home than my life.

"Watch it, scrant," a guard sneers, "that's the captain yer talking to."

Captain of the guard? The condescending tone and crusty expression make sense now. He reports directly to the king. Why didn't they send the lower guards?

On the captain's command, a guard dumps the bag's contents on the road, and strips of meat tumble out with my bow and dagger. I blanch, staring in horror at the elk pieces.

"We came for your father's property. But it appears you've been poaching on the king's land." The captain's voice is cool and eerily calm. His fingers drum against the hilt of his sword for a prolonged moment before his lip curls. "Seize her."

Boorish hands come at me, grasping my shirt and ripping the sleeve as I jerk away. The dagger is all I can think about through a frenzy of elbows and fists. Mine, his, all so I can get Papa's blade. Somehow I free myself of the guards. Maneuver to the pile of meat and weapons on the ground. Push aside the wrapped strips of elk. My fingers find the familiar curve of ivory and—

I'm slammed to the ground. Dirt and rock mash against my mouth.

My arms are wrenched behind me, followed by a kick that

knocks the wind from my lungs. I cough and wheeze, spitting blood and saliva and dust, until the air comes back. The captain plucks my dagger off the ground.

"No!"

The captain grabs my braid and twists my head. "Stop. Or I'll end you here and now. It's my duty to ensure lawbreakers get their due punishment. Poached meat warrants a hanging."

I know he means every word, because sickening warmth spreads in my gut.

I'm boneless as a hulking young guard, maybe a couple years my senior, forces manacles on my wrists and throws me on a horse before climbing behind me and wrapping my waist in an iron grip. Now that the guards have come—now that poaching has made my situation infinitely worse—defeat turns me wooden as the group gallops toward the castle. They've torn the last piece of Papa from me. They've taken my weapons, my bounty, and my father's land. All that remains is my life. Considering the crime, there is no doubt the king's guard will soon have that as well.

CHAPTER

3

AN HOUR AFTER THE GUARDS SNATCHED ME, WE come into full view of Castle Neart. She's a beastly goliath perched in the mountains overlooking Brentyn. Six arms of spires and rust-peaked turrets grab for the sky. Legs of arcading corridors hide behind a ten-man-tall stone skirt trimmed in parapet. In spite of having seen Castle Neart before alongside Papa, the daunting view shreds my courage. I am an ant about to be squashed.

The castle's bridge arcs over a deep, jagged gulch. A dozen rock pillars support wood planks that groan beneath us, a reminder of sheer death below as we cross. It'd be a relief to reach the bridge's end if not for the awaiting reek of excrement. The moat's stench smacks us in the face, only fading after we pass the guardhouse and enter the yard.

Once we're inside the castle grounds, my companion's grip cinches around me, locking me against his body, the bludger. As if I could escape while manacled and weaponless. He pulls the reins to stop beside the others in the yard. Dust curls around the horses' hooves. Only then does the brute guard give me a knuckle's space of breathing room.

The stables are busy. Grooms tend to carriages and muscled steeds, the kind used for heavy cavalry. The guard dismounts and tugs me down alongside him, where I tumble to my knees. Pain zings through my legs, then his thick paws are under my arms, hefting me up. He mutters something that sounds like *Sorry* but couldn't be. A king's guard would never apologize. Especially not to me.

The captain barks an order, and a groom appears to lead the horses away. Red coats flank my sides. Another pushes me forward, farther from the gate, farther from escape, to shuffle over dirt and bits of manure.

Heat pours from the blacksmith's shop, licking at our faces, as we march toward another wall and another entryway —a stone arch over wooden doors. I've never been past this point. Not many are allowed beyond the inner wall. Never imagined it would happen by the escort of guards.

The heat from the smithy dries my throat. Am I marching to my death? With that much evidence, they'll surely hang me. My feet move like they're shod in iron boots.

The archway door groans open into the heart of the keep. I search around in confusion, taking in the crowd of high nobility gathered in the courtyard. There are so many people. Lords and ladies in striking furs and silks, pointed-toe shoes, mushroom hats for men, lace-trimmed veils for women. So unlike my filthy raggedness. Why would the captain bring me here? The guards shove me along the back of the open area, to a passage tucked under carved stone arcading. I still have a view of the gathering as we march under the shadowed arches.

Though Papa was considered nobility, he didn't hold a fief, wherein he could profit from commoners living on his land. He could never afford the finery these lords flaunt. And yet the nobles' attire is nothing compared to the jewels and gold-rimmed crown worn by the young man elevated on the stone steps at the far end of the courtyard. It's a shock to realize that the glittering beacon is Malam's ruler, King Aodren. I've never laid eyes on him, as he does not often leave the castle. Gossip of his youth and golden-haired handsomeness is a market favorite. I see now, not all the chatty crows' rumors are false.

As the guards lead the way through another corridor, I sneak one last curious glance at King Aodren. He is nothing like the man beside him. Lord Jamis, the high lord, who was the king regent before Aodren turned eighteen and took over as crown ruler, addresses the crowd, dropping words like *gathering army, border, Shaerdan*. He has severe features, silver-flecked midnight hair, sharp coal eyes. While the king is thin and reedy, with pale skin, a shadowed gaze that watches with disinterest.

Seeds, a fine ruler he is. Anger and frustration beat through me. Only a few years my senior, he's never wanted for anything in his life. Never been ostracized. Never alone. Never hungry. And apparently he never needs to address his people. Why was Papa so loyal to this spoiled man?

The question slips from my mind seconds later when my escorts stop outside a guarded and locked solid wood door. I realize with a start that this entrance leads to the Dungeon Under the Keep, the kingdom's most secure jail. The captain yanks me forward, despite how stiff my legs have become, as another person unlocks and opens the door. A burly bear of a man, round as he is tall, steps into view, keys jangling against the leather belt supporting his gut.

"Brought me fresh meat, did ya?" The mix of humorless chuckle and chaff cuts the remains of my nerves. I don't even realize I've stepped back until the captain's hand is bruising my arm.

He shoves me through the entry. "She's yours till sentenc-ing."

The door closes, the lock clicks, trapping me in the dim with the dungeon master.

A day, maybe two have passed. The odor in the Dungeon Under the Keep could knock a grown man out. Years of prisoners have used the back of the cell as an outhouse. Too deep a lungful and I'm fighting the urge to gag in this cell that's no bigger than a horse's stall.

I press my eyes shut, struggling with the moans from the other prisoners. It's too dark to see, which forces me to listen to their shuffling and whimpering. A woman nearby mutters something about fire, about her touch being useless, until she starts hacking. Eventually her cough stops, replaced with choppy breathing.

She won't last the week. I wish I didn't know this, but I've known death my whole life, so I know she's slipping away. I rub my raw wrists.

A lantern flickers to life like a cat's eye blinking against the blanketing pitch-dark, illuminating the arm span of the man holding it as he approaches.

"He's ready to see ya." The dungeon master's voice is scratchy, like he hasn't had a glass of water or seen daylight in months—a good match to the unkempt beard that grows like wild wood from his chin.

I stand tall, trying to look formidable despite my tattered appearance. *Weaknesses control you,* Papa had said. "The king?" I think of the lean young man deciding my fate.

"Bullwart, no! 'Tis the high lord." His accent is similar to the tradesmen from Fennit, the town closest to the border. In Shaerdan and in the border towns, the townspeople speak mostly the same words as us, but they have a strange twist to their sounds.

The dungeon master unlocks the cell, holding the lantern

in one hand and the keys in the other. "I'm told yer a feisty one even if yer not much bigger than the wee folk. Be a good girl and ya won't rot like the rest of 'em."

I nod and then glance in the direction of the dying woman. "What's she in here for?"

He tips his head as though he cannot fathom my motive for asking. "That scrant? Crossed over from Shaerdan. She's one of their Channelers."

I think of the woman's mumblings, more curious now.

"She's dying," I say softly, mostly to myself.

"Aye. Good thing. We don't want her kind here." He fits manacles on my wrists and shoves me forward. I'm aware of what happened to the people Papa tracked down. Traitors and spies were always tortured for information and then executed. Channelers were hung. I wish the woman a quick end to her suffering.

"What have ya done?" he asks as we ascend the stairs.

"Poaching."

A grave nod follows. "A crime of death."

I swallow hard and follow him through another door, past a closed room, to the dungeon exit. Daylight pours into the arches and floods the courtyard beyond the arcading corridors, temporarily blinding me, so I'm caught unaware when another guard pushes me through a door and up a winding stairwell of the keep. We pass more guards and walk down another corridor. The interior of the castle is opulent, dizzyingly so. Instead of braided rushes on stone floor, dyed wool rugs lie like puddles of blood on polished granite.

We stop outside a glossed oak door with iron adornments. I catch my ghosting reflection in the shine until two guards emerge, dragging a prisoner. The man is little more than sagging skin on bones. "Please ... don't hang me ... m-my family."

I stare, dismayed as they pull him away, his pleas growing more frantic.

The guard shoves me into the room. "Don't talk unless yer told to," he sneers.

I scowl and take a step away, trying to shake the sight of the prisoner.

One piece of tufted furniture in this study could pay for my land outright. I cannot imagine how much the wall of books rising to the ceiling must be worth. Every speck of dirt and blood on my ruined skirt stands out like pox, making me wish I could sink into the pristine floors and disappear.

"Interested in something?"

My attention snaps to the man I saw in the courtyard beside the king, Lord Jamis. My gaze travels up and up. Seeds, the high lord must be three hands taller than me. He strides through the room and stops at a desk, where he folds into a seat with the grace of a mountain cat. He makes a curling motion with his hand, to which the guard responds by removing my manacles. Relieved, I rub my wrists until I sense the high lord's raven eyes tracking the motion.

"This is my favorite room in the palace," Lord Jamis says. "All this knowledge at your fingertips is exhilarating."

I stand cautiously still.

His long fingers fan out toward a blood-red chair. "Have a seat, Britta—excuse me, Miss Flannery."

Uncertainty rattles through me as I straighten my ruined top, pushing the ripped sleeve over my shoulder, before slowly lowering myself onto the edge of the chair.

"I'd like to express my condolences. Saul was revered around here. As military adviser and royal spokesman, I can say that even King Aodren feels your father's loss." Lord Jamis's sympathy is unexpected, and I bristle, even if it warms me with honesty.

"You must miss him. I'm told you were his shadow." A small smile quirks his mouth, softening the angles of his face. It's as if the thought of me following Papa amuses him. It's annoying. If I only had my bow, I'd show him how pointedly amusing I can be.

"Am I here to talk about my father?" I cringe at the sharpness of my tone.

"Such directness." His eyes flash and I curse myself for having spoken. Elbows on the desk, he steeples his fingers. "Weren't you brought in on poaching?" The lack of ire in his voice should be a relief, though it only increases the tension building between my ribs.

I nod, wishing I knew how to proceed. The last thing I want to do is say something wrong and earn a quicker trip to the noose.

"Your bag held enough meat to hang a man. Or a woman." I hold my breath as he talks. "Did you catch that bounty alone?"

My chin dips again, and in response his eyes crinkle at the edges, confusing me with his politeness. I study his relaxed shoulders and clean hands, willing away the pressure behind my eyes.

Lord Jamis pushes the book on his desk aside and reaches into a satchel, then withdraws a blade. "Recognize this dagger?"

My brows shoot up. The ivory handle etched in elaborate swirls is decorated with a tear-size sapphire. This is not my dagger, though it is a near twin to my blade. The stone is on the wrong side of the hilt, which means this one is Cohen's. How did Lord Jamis end up with Cohen's dagger? Did something happen to —

Unease creeps over my skin and stills my thoughts as Lord Jamis's fingers tap the handle. Once slow, twice fast he pads.

"This weapon ended Saul's life."

Before his implication can register inside, Lord Jamis pulls out a cloak, stained black in old blood, yet still undeniably recognizable. "And this was found with the blade."

"Cohen" comes out on an exhale before I realize his name has passed my lips. *No. No. Not him.* I cross my arms over my waist. I understand what the high lord's doing with this trail of evidence, but I won't believe Cohen's guilty of Papa's murder. Impossible. Cohen loved Papa.

"Someone must've stolen the knife," I tell him. "Finding the weapon or a coat doesn't mean you've found the murderer."

"These belong to Cohen Mackay, and Saul's blood is on both items. This coat was ripped off Mackay, and this dagger" — his long fingers wrap around the handle — "was pulled from your father's back."

I flinch. "But . . . Cohen's gone." I hate how shaken I sound. I take a breath and start again. "He couldn't have done it. Someone must want it to look like Cohen killed my father."

"Perhaps." Lord Jamis's gaze softens into a look I don't see often — pity. "However, Cohen was seen in the same town as Saul on the night of the murder."

"A coincidence," I argue. The boy I knew isn't a murderer. He was a small-town boy who had shown unusual skill with hunting. When my father asked the king regent to find someone worthy to be trained, Cohen managed to earn the high honor of becoming apprentice to the king's bounty hunter. He loved his family so much that he worked tirelessly on their farm spring and summer and then trained with my father every winter. Everything he did was to give his parents and siblings a better life. That's not the kind of person who murders his mentor.

"There are two witnesses." Lord Jamis pauses. He sits so

still, it doesn't even look as though the man is breathing. The weight of his silence is crushing. "Two men who say they saw Cohen murder your father."

Truthful heat crawls through my belly. Breaks me apart.

For the first time in my life, I loathe my body's strange ability. I cannot believe . . . don't want to believe what he's saying. Not Cohen. *Not my Cohen.*

"There has to be an explanation." The words trip out of my mouth. "He couldn't have . . . he'd never . . . my father was like a second father to Cohen." I choke out the last word. No matter how badly I need the high lord's claim to be false, I don't have a good explanation for Cohen's whereabouts, the evidence, or the truth in Lord Jamis's words. Such damning truth.

Lord Jamis frowns. "I'd hoped this would be a relief to know."

A relief? I stare at the blood-red stitching on the chair, sorting through the destruction and shock and fury crashing around inside me. "D-did he admit his guilt?"

Lord Jamis places the dagger beside the book and flattens his palms to the desk. He doesn't need to say anything; his stolid expression says it all. They haven't caught Cohen yet. When it comes to tracking, hunting, hiding, no guard has ever matched my father's skill. No one other than Cohen.

No one other than me.

I take in Lord Jamis's pressed suit and carefully combed hair. To be the right-hand man to the king, he'd have to be educated. Clever. He'd already know the best person who has a chance of catching Cohen is right in front of him. "You want me to track him," I say, shock weighting my words.

"Yes."

I lift my chin, staring at Lord Jamis but seeing nothing. "Why would I do that for you?"

"Your poaching evidence is enough to warrant a hanging, and Captain Omar demands justice be served. It would be a tragedy to see someone of your skill discarded, so I've proposed a trade to the captain, one that will satisfy payment for your crime."

I glance down at the filth on my hands and then back to the high lord.

The angry swoosh of my pulse echoes in my ears. "You want to trade my life for Cohen's?"

He smiles with a hint of pride, displaying a row of large teeth. "Precisely."

CHAPTER

4

LORD JAMIS'S ACCUSATIONS TUMBLE THROUGH me, turning me inside out with doubt and grief and horror. I sit silently as Lord Jamis crosses the room and opens the door to let in three guards. The captain, the same young brute who restrained me earlier and is thick with muscle and built like a bull, and a scrappy fellow whose pinched features remind me of a fox.

Lord Jamis claps the captain on the back. "As the head of my guard, Captain Omar will ensure your safety." He means the *king's* guard, but of course I don't correct him. "Leif and Tomas will also assist on this hunt." The Bull and the Fox. "Once you've found Mackay, they'll return him to the castle."

I meet Captain Omar's stern gaze and wonder if he's pleased with this development, or if he'd rather justice was served by the noose. Nothing about traveling with him or his men has any appeal. Beside the captain, Tomas has beady eyes that shift about, making me think he's the type who would stab a sleeping man. And the bigger fellow, Leif, is too brawny to have the grace a man needs to move silently through the woods. Then again, Cohen isn't much smaller and he always moved like a cat.

Cohen. He couldn't have killed Papa. Could he? And yet, there's no denying the evidence. I crush my fingernails into my palms, needing the distraction of pain.

I pin my attention on Leif. "Three guards are unnecessary and will make traveling harder to go undetected."

Leif shifts his weight, and a frown glances over his mouth.

"The objective is to catch Mackay," the captain interjects in a dour tone, dismissing and sharing his dislike. "You may be considered a good tracker, but you're no fighter. Yesterday should be enough reminder you're easily overpowered."

Yesterday was an exception is what I want to tell him. Then I remember how he responded before to my brazenness and hold my tongue.

"The guards are not optional," Lord Jamis says as he crosses to his desk and rolls out a map. "The kingdom's fiefdoms are not as heavily manned now that the lords have sent their best men to the border. Travel alone would be dangerous. And there's a chance the hunt may take you over the border. You'll need Captain Omar and his men for protection."

"Shaerdan?" I ask, unable to hide my disbelief that Cohen

would flee Malam without the king's consent. He'd be marked as a traitor. Punishment would be torture until he begged for the mercy of the noose. Then again, he's already accused of murdering the king's bounty hunter. What would it matter if he became a traitor as well?

Tomas, the wiry fox-like guard, stiffened when I mentioned Shaerdan. I wonder if he's more concerned about the imminent war or the country's dark magic. He catches me watching him and glowers.

The captain approaches Lord Jamis and looks over the map. His finger punches a spot on the parchment. "We'll leave tomorrow at first light. See that our tracker is outfitted to draw less attention."

Lord Jamis eyes my tangled hair, my soiled skirt, and nods in agreement.

"Maybe the scrant will clean up enough for tasting." Off to my right side, Tomas leers.

Leif doesn't react, but my limbs go rigid. Tomas's comment promises unwanted attention that would lead to his death and then mine for murdering the vile man when he dared touch me. Behind Lord Jamis, Cohen's dagger taunts me from the desktop. It could mean my escape. No longer restrained by manacles, I could easily maneuver around the high lord and swipe it. If I put it to the fox's throat, I could use the diversion to get out of this room. Sprint down the castle halls. Reach the stairwell. But then how would I get past the guards at the gate?

Regardless, I cannot stomach using the blade that ended Papa's life.

Forgetting that plan, I make a note to avoid Tomas as the guards follow Captain Omar out of the study. Another option of escape will present itself. At least, I hope it will.

"A bath and clothing will be brought to the dungeon," Lord Jamis tells me.

I tear my eyes from Cohen's dagger. "I haven't agreed to go."

A confused frown settles over his mouth.

It makes sense that someone in my position, facing death, would agree to his offer, but he doesn't understand that I've already lost everything. Or maybe he does and thinks vengeance is enough to sway my decision. It should be.

"You want me to agree to tracking down my father's killer." It sounds wrong, so wrong to say. "For what? My life for his? What life do I have to return to? The king has my land and my home, so there's nowhere for me to go. Without shelter for winter, I'll be dead anyway. That is, if the captain or his men don't kill me first."

"The captain requested to go as part of the agreement, to ensure you fulfill your end of this bargain. You have nothing to fear if you uphold your end of the deal." Lord Jamis moves behind his desk and stares at me almost sympathetically. "And the other guards will do you no harm. Trust me."

I've never had the luxury of trusting anyone besides my father and Cohen. Though clearly trust has done little for me, seeing as how one of the men I put my faith in is dead and the other an accused murderer. I'm certainly not going to start trusting anyone else now.

When I give no response, he leans forward, elbows on the desk. "Perhaps there's more I could offer as an incentive." He is quieter than before, and the drop in his pitch becomes more ardent, drawing me in. "By law, you cannot inherit your father's land because you were born outside of a legal marriage. But if you find Mackay, I'll grant you ownership of the land and cottage."

Another truth.

I suck in a breath, shocked that I've been able to push him into offering so much. "Impossible. You cannot make that happen."

His smile graces the space above his trimmed ebony beard as he spreads his arms, pressing his hands flat on the desk in a way that widens his shoulders. "I have the power to decide a hunter's bounty. As high lord, I oversee King Aodren's lands. If your cottage is what you want, then I can give that to you."

I'll be able to keep everything Papa left, not just the dagger. I would have a home. *Papa's* home. My home.

My life and my land for Cohen—the offer sickens me as much as it thrills me.

Can I really hunt down my only friend? But that's just it. He isn't my friend.

"The country has been disgraced by Saul's murder. And you've lost a father," he says, drawing my attention back to Papa. "It may be an unexpected payout, but as you said, you'll have no home to which to return. The land is nothing to the king. Mend Malam's pride and get justice for your father, and the cottage will be yours when you return."

Papa was all I had left. My decision is for him. I press my hand to the pain beneath my sternum.

"I'll go."

My washed hair is braided and tucked beneath a boy's cap, which the captain provided, along with trousers and a tunic. Captain Omar informed me I'd be traveling as a boy to draw less notice. Fine with me. Trousers are more comfortable than skirts and, in this aspect, being small-breasted has its benefits.

"Shackle her," the captain tells Tomas as he enters my cell.

I scurry back. "Manacles weren't part of the deal."

"Would you rather the noose?" Tomas sidles around me, pulling my wrists into the iron cuffs. I shake my head and bite back an alarmed squeak when his fingers dig into my arm where it's tender and bruised from the earlier scuffle.

"If you canna find Mackay, the cap'n won't let you go free." Tomas's nasally voice drips with distaste. "Not a daughter of a Shaerdanian."

"Release her, Tomas," the captain clips.

The guard obeys by shoving me out of the cell so that I trip forward, stumbling into Leif's barrier of a body.

Captain Omar tells Leif to escort me out of the dungeon. Just before we reach the door, I hear the captain say, "Tomas, do not overstep your bounds. Next time I'll withhold your food rations. Today you'll tend the horses . . ."

I'm unable to catch the remainder of the conversation once the dungeon door closes behind us. But the little I heard is a reminder not to disobey the captain.

Papa taught that a good tracker always knows the lay of the land. East of here, Malam juts up in jagged, monstrous peaks that stay white-capped all year despite the baking summer. The mountain ridge spans into Kolontia, the northern country where snow and ice rule. Papa told me some of their people live in the crystal caves that tunnel under the northern ridge, while others brave the salty frozen bite of the coast that wraps two-thirds of the country.

Running from the north, the Malam Mountains curve in a southwest sickle to border the Southlands. There, the Akaria Desert's sand dunes ebb and flow like a crawling ocean, and a gorge scars the land as deep as the mountains stand tall.

To the east, the Ever Woods run into the Bloodwood Forest, which carpets the mountains until they crumble into knolls and valleys. With Papa, I traveled along many of the ribboning rivers winding from the mountain glaciers to feed the lowland farmlands. From there, hills of fir, hemlock, and spruce roll into Shaerdan. It's a lush country of suffocating emerald growth. It's rumored that in Shaerdan the rain magically falls without a cloud in the sky.

As we ride, I'm shackled and sharing a horse with Leif. He doesn't wrap a suffocating arm around me like on our last ride together. Still, the uncomfortable lack of space between us is even more apparent when the road rises and falls. Each time I lean forward, Leif pulls me back against his chest. If the captain doesn't hang me, this ride may be torture enough to kill me.

We leave Brentyn, where the royal city is nestled like an animal burrowed for winter in a blanket of green. After traveling at a thundering pace on the main road, we cut off for the southwest mountains, to a route Papa and I traveled often. Only traitors and criminals trying to flee Malam hazard this pass. The terrain is dangerous, the path steep and sometimes slippery.

We stop when we reach the summit, where the path is narrow and overgrown with creeping ground cover.

"Mackay was sighted here two days ago," Captain Omar says. He points west. "I need to know if he's headed toward Lord Devlin's fief."

"I need to be closer to the ground," I tell him. His face darkens and I realize he must think me insolent. "To look for broken branches, prints, any disturbance in the undergrowth," I explain.

The captain gestures and then Leif's off the horse, pulling me to the ground. The sweet pine scent slaps me with memories. Papa pointing out edible berries. Sifting through the forest floor in search of prints. Storytelling around a campfire.

Focus, Papa's voice echoes.

"The manacles?" I lift my wrists.

The captain regards my arms. "Prove yourself helpful. Then I'll take them off."

My raw wrists throb, but I bite my cheek to stop from arguing and scan the bushes for any unusual disturbance. A broken branch, crumpled leaves, limbs bent all in the same direction, hoof prints, hairs, swatches of fabric.

Tomas and Leif trail behind while the captain inspects my every move. Eventually I find a damaged bush with branches bent west. Someone came this way recently. Perhaps two or three days at most. I find it odd Cohen hasn't done a better job of hiding his passage. Still, I'd bet my bow he left these tracks. Hoof prints mark the dirt where the fallen leaves aren't ankle deep, and two strands of coarse black hair dangle from a shrub. There's no forgetting Cohen's black stallion named Siron.

"He's headed this way," I say, ignoring the accompanying illogical twinge of guilt.

"Seeds, she's fast," Leif mutters as Captain Omar views the evidence.

The captain shoots the bull guard a look of irritation before turning to me with eyes that glint with approval. I should feel pleased, but I don't.

"Miss Flannery." Leif clears his throat.

"Britta," I correct him.

"Britta . . . do you, uh . . ." Leif stammers and looks down, so his auburn head fills my view. His neck and ears stain pur-plish red, which draws a hoot from Tomas, who has sauntered closer.

"The brute's trying to ask if ya gotta use the privy."

My face reddens against my will. Besides Cohen and Papa, I've spent little time around men. It takes a second to find my voice. "Seeing as there isn't a privy in these woods, I can-not say."

"We're supposed to keep an eye on ya." Tomas's beady-eyed gaze crawls over me. "Even when you've got personal busi-ness."

My hands curl into fists, missing the curve of my bow. "Well, then, I'll let you know when I need to piss."

Leif's brows rise.

Tomas cackles.

Thankfully we load up and continue the hunt.

The next morning I'm stiff and groggy. It takes another day to reach the end of the Evers where the pines are replaced by the firs of the Bloodwood Forest. The mountains under the crowded firs settle into foothills cut with valleys. Where the black bark trees choke the way, we ride through the river until reaching the flat stretch where logging has left knee-high stumps to wither under the sun. Eventually, after two days, the Bloodwoods dwindle to rockier ground. Piles of boulders lie haphazardly between trees like a giant child's been playing with rocks.

Captain Omar rides up alongside Tomas, who has had the lead during the sun's good light. "Most of Lord Freil's men have left for Fennit. Still, I want the royal colors posted," he tells the fox-faced guard. The guard complies, setting the pole and banner against the leather hold on his horse, so the deep red material flaps as we ride. Lord Freil's men are rumored to be the fiercest in Malam and do not tolerate intruders. For once, I am glad for my companions.

Our search of the valley demands crawling over boulders that block the path. Tracks aren't easy to spot among the rocks, and after an hour my frustration peaks. At first, the sound of Leif's whoop of surprise puts me on guard, thinking he's spotted one of Lord Freil's men. Until I notice he's pointing at the ground. I dart around a massive stone and scramble to his side. A crescent indent is a whisper in the dry dirt.

"Look there, Britta." He beams. "I found one too."

Over the last couple days, he's been kind, even helpful, while the captain remains cold and aloof, and Tomas malevolent. If it were not for his red coat, I might consider the auburn-haired, muscled wall of a man an ally.

The boyish excitement plastered across his oak eyes reminds me of Cohen from years ago, when we were green at tracking, and every discovery was a gift. "Well done." I whisper the words Papa would've told me. Captain Omar turns up to silently peruse the print, and I shuffle away. The man nods once, and Leif's so proud of himself that he lights up like a sunrise.

I drop my chin so the boy's cap hides my frown. I should've found those prints. Fighting the needling worry, I return to tracking, moving quicker than before, telling myself that a couple missed tracks do not mean the captain will think me worthless.

After a while I notice Leif in my shadow, studying my movement much closer than usual. When I pointedly stare back, his teeth shine through a wide grin. "It's Captain's orders to keep tabs on you."

"Can you not do that more than a step away?" I hold up my manacled wrists. "No risk of escape here."

He chuckles, and then his voice drops low so only I can hear. "I'm studying you, hoping some skill will rub off on me."

I smile inwardly at his secret confession and continue searching till finding a wilted yellow flower on a bent narcissus plant.

I point out the find to Leif. He moves in for a closer look and startles me when he props his tree-trunk arm on my shoulder. The unexpected touch, combined with my uneven balance from hunching, sends me sprawling forward, elbows and knees cracking against the rocky ground.

Leif helps me to my feet and mutters a red-faced apology, but not before Tomas notices and tramples the wild flowers to reach us.

"You oaf, that's not how you touch a girl," Tomas says, voice leering. I ignore him and show the tracks to Captain

Omar, who leaves his position beside his horse to study the broken stalk. The captain's approval comes when he pulls keys from the leather satchel at his waist and removes the manacles.

I rub my free arms. If only the captain would throw the iron bands into the stream so I never have to see them again. "Thank you," I mutter, unsure of what else to say.

He dismisses my gratitude with a terse nod. "I've only done what's fair," he says, and then commands the others to move on.

Even though I'm glad for the freedom, so very glad, I turn back to the crumpled narcissus where it rests between rocks in an otherwise cleared glade, something nagging me.

Cohen was never sloppy. Except when it was intentional.

"You're better at erasing your tracks," I said.

Cohen and I had been sitting at the lookout since completing Papa's tracking test. I passed the search portion but didn't do well at leaving no trace.

Cohen traced lazy letters on my arm. "You're better at tracking."

I huffed. "Doesn't matter, if there are no prints to follow. You could take off and I'd never find you."

"Oh, Britt, if I were ever the hunted, you'd find me. Is that what you're worried about? That I'll take off and leave you behind?"

I didn't know how much longer he'd apprentice. He'd reached marrying age and, though it hurt to admit, my circumstances would exclude me. He could have the daughter of a lord.

"*Dove?*" *His hand covered mine.*

I fought the sudden longing that swelled in my chest. "*You've got your family. They rely on you. You're gonna leave sooner or later.*"

"*True. I'll work for the king eventually, but I'll always return.*"

I rolled my eyes. "*You don't know that.*"

He twined his fingers with mine. "*Nothing could keep me away.*"

I study the tracks once more, waiting as the guards move out of earshot.

"Cohen," I whisper to the broken branch. "Is that what you want? For me to find you?"

The last time I saw Cohen, he promised to return the next day. Only he never came back. Why, when the king's guard are after him for Papa's murder, would he leave a trail? Why would he want me to find him now?

As the sunset fades to gray, I'm thankful for the cloak of night. It hides how I worry my lip. I cannot shake the feeling Cohen is leading me somewhere. He must have his reasons. I just wish I knew what they were.

I've no choice but to find Cohen and turn him over.

If only it didn't feel increasingly wrong the closer we get.

CHAPTER
5

O N THE FIFTH DAY WE'RE A WORN-OUT,
soggy-looking bunch from a sudden
downpour that came on earlier. The
sun is balancing on the horizon, a flame bobbing
above the silver arrow-tops of the forested hills
in Lord Conklin's fiefdom.

Captain Omar stops at a pile of horse manure
and then shouts for Leif to set me down to do the
inspection. Dung beetles and crows have ruined
most of the droppings that haven't washed away
from the rain. A portion breaks easily in my fingers, reminding me of how Cohen used to offer
to check dung for me when we tracked together.

"Maybe two days old," I tell the captain before
rinsing my hands in the stream that hugs the low
hill. My eyes are unfocused while my thoughts
wander, always returning to him. Which is why

I don't immediately notice the other side of the embankment, where the dirt has been smoothed, wiped clean of tracks. Unlike the other crumbs of evidence that have led us westward through thorny silver bushes and wildflowers beneath the firs, the cleared area indicates Cohen has turned north.

I frown. Why would he go toward the main road?

Most of Malam's towns are connected by the gravel road that runs east to west like beads on a string. It stands to reason that a person evading the king's guard would avoid the most populated areas of the country.

When Leif ambles over, breaking my concentration, I show him the area across the stream, noticing a partial boot print in the smoothed soil. Why would Cohen clear part of the dirt but not all?

Before I can figure it out, Captain Omar is beside me, keenly studying the ground. "Headed for the main road," he murmurs to himself, a question in his tone about Cohen's change in direction.

The captain stands and tells Leif to set up camp and then turns to me. "Britta, you're going hunting."

I figured one of us was going to have to hunt soon, since our rations are meager.

"How can I hunt when I have no weapon?"

"Watch your mouth," Captain Omar clips.

I press my lips together, frustrated that I always manage to say the wrong thing.

The captain commands me to hunt under Tomas's

supervision. Upon hearing this, Tomas's expression sharpens; he's a starved mountain cat ready to pounce on injured prey. I stifle a shudder at having to be alone with him, keeping a mask of calm on my face as the captain hands over the bow in its quiescent position. How I've missed the comfort of its easy weight.

The smooth bends of the horn-and-sinew recurve bow fight against me until wrangled into place and the string is set. A pluck to test the tension emits a tenor note that captures all three guards' attention. Leif's brows lift like a charmed child's at Midsummer's Tide.

"Seeds and stars, that was fast." Leif's appraisal is short-lived, cut when the captain pulls out my blade and two hands grasp for it at the same time. Tomas snags it for the win.

"You didn't think he meant it for you, did ya?" Tomas says with relish. He tosses my dagger in the air and then catches it, hand bouncing to test the weapon's weight. "I'll use this to keep you in line."

My knuckles whiten around my bow. Tomas's threat will never be anything but empty. I'll never let his slimy hands molest Papa's blade. Especially not against me. The rat guard doesn't know the damage one arrow loosed from my bow can do.

When the captain leaves, I point south. "We should go that way."

"Jumping at the bit, are ya? We're not gonna walk any which way. A little scouting first."

Leif shoots me a sympathetic look.

"Scouting for tracks?" I ask Tomas. I point to the cluster of small pebbled dung a few paces south. "Like that?"

Leif lets out a snort. His broad shoulders curl inward, jerking with laughter. "Looks like a decent place to start to me."

"Nobody asked you, filly. Go bludger off," Tomas goads him.

I nod a silent goodbye to Leif and stalk into the woods.

Tomas trails behind with the grace of a bull stung by a bee. He snaps branches and sets off a cacophony of sounds. I put a finger to my lips and hold out a hand.

"What?" he mouths.

I point to the game trail beaten into the earth. At his bounding pace, he would've missed it. In the dirt there's a cloven print that is two knuckles long. A fawn's print. I wish I hadn't stopped. Papa and I never hunted animals still in their youth. *They've not lived through their purpose,* he'd said.

I suggest we take cover and wait for the animals that will surely be making use of the game trail, since the rain has stopped. Thankfully, Tomas agrees.

Hardly any time passes before the soft pad of the fawn sounds. I hope she's not alone and she's come with a bigger kill. Only, that's not the case.

The thought of killing her doesn't sit right with me, but I consider the situation. She wouldn't be alone unless her mother was dead. Winter's approaching. Without a caregiver, the fawn has little chance, so perhaps a kill is a reasonable choice.

The twang of a bow—

A sudden slice of air—

And the choice is stolen.

A horrible bawl breaks from the animal's mouth as it jumps once and kicks its back legs before darting away. Beside me, Tomas fumbles for another arrow.

"Stop!" I screech. "What have you done?"

He's not looking at me, so I swipe my dagger from his belt and start for the tortured fawn to end the animal's life.

Tomas crashes through the brush, chasing. "Did ya forget how to hunt?"

The entire forest rattles around me. I blink once and then realize the motion is coming from me, shaking with anger and sorrow as I focus on the gleaming red trail.

"Please stay here," I beg Tomas.

He opens his mouth to argue.

"You're too noisy. She'll hear you coming and keep running. If you want to eat before tomorrow, please stop. I'll finish the job."

Resentment flares in his eyes. But he stays.

Daylight is on its way out when I spot the fawn bedded in the grasses. Fear and pain waft from her like smoke from a fire. At the sight of the arrow protruding from her guts and the blood gathering beneath her, shame floods me.

This isn't how I do things. Torture is never how I kill.

I should slit her neck. But my approach would need to be slow and all the while she'd be suffering. I draw an arrow, ready my bow, and shoot the fawn in the neck.

A gush of blood spills across the forest floor — it's a hit to the jugular.

My insides are coated in brackish water, and all I smell is the tang of blood everywhere as I kneel beside her.

"You're pathetic." I look up to find Tomas leering over me. "They said you're the best tracker and hunter in Malam. You're nothing but a weepy girl."

It takes every ounce of control not to notch one more arrow. There's nothing I can say to Tomas that'll release my fury or grief. Without a word, I tear into the woods, leaving him.

I wander through the firs, shooting off the remaining arrows. Each one nails a target and releases a little of my frustration and anger and guilt. I aim and release, until my anger fades away. I'm not absent long. I plan to reach camp about the same time Tomas does, since he'll need to field dress the kill. Except when I return, Tomas is already there.

Captain Omar sheathes his sword with a ringing slap. "Where. Have. You. Been?"

I flinch. The angles in the captain's face are drawn tight. He passes Leif, taking long, purposeful strides to reach me. It was a mistake to leave Tomas. A massive one.

The captain's eyes widen, showing too much whites. "You were told to stay with Tomas." He draws in a breath through his nose and expels it with a puff. "If you're unable to fulfill the bargain made with Lord Jamis, you forfeit your life. Do. You. Understand?"

I can barely get it out: "Yes, sir."

"You directly defied me. There are consequences for dis-obedience."

Leif works the manacles and rope around a nearby trunk and takes my bow and quiver. I'm too unnerved to tell him about the dagger in my boot as he gently pulls my hands in front of me and fixes the iron cuffs on my wrists.

He squeezes my arm and gives me a mixed look — alarm, regret, distress. Then he mouths, "Be strong," reminding me of Papa's advice.

"Ten lashes," the captain says. My only warning.

The whip strikes.

I cry out, unable to hold it in, and stumble against the trunk. The pain and fire and stinging are merciless. *Strong as the trees,* Papa's voice echoes over shallow breaths. I imag-ine he's with me when I lock my knees, shut my eyes, drag air between clenched teeth. I imagine I'm stronger than the crum-bling girl tied to the tree.

The second lash hits.

CHAPTER

6

AFTER THE FOURTH LASH, I FALL TO MY KNEES, nearly unconscious from the agony. After the fifth, the captain stops. "You deserve more, but you have a job to do," Captain Omar says. "Step out of line again, and you'll get your just due."

The throbbing in my back is consuming, the pain too raw to think of anything else.

"It needs cleaning." Leif's voice pulls me back to where we sit beside a stream. He's holding a wet rag in one hand and an herbal balm in the other. I extend my hand, even though the small movement has me wincing and gasping for breath.

"You won't be able to reach," he says. "I can help."

I blink. Surely he's not suggesting I lift my top and let him wash my bare skin. I may not know much about social interaction or friendships, but exposing myself seems inappropriate.

"I won't look. You don't have to worry about me." The tips of his ears are redder than autumn leaves. Well, then, I was wrong. I try to grasp my ripped tunic and end up hissing while spots burst in my vision.

"Let me," Leif urges. "I know you must feel alone right now. But I'm here and — and you can trust me. No one's strong alone. We need each other —"

"Don't . . . Y-you don't know me —" I cut him off, letting rage distract from the pain. What does he know about being alone? He's a king's guard. He doesn't need to worry that he'll never marry. That his home will be taken. That he'll die alone.

"Perhaps not as well as I'd like." His voice turns shy. "But I've seen your strength and cunning and determination. You're loyal. And I know life hasn't been very fair to you."

I let out a snort. But he has my attention.

"My father died when I was nine," Leif continues. "When my ma caught the ague, I was thrown off my horse on my way to fetch a healer. My leg was hurt badly. I couldn't do much for my family. Then someone made me a crutch." He pauses, looks up. "It was your father."

I stare at Leif. Warmth from his words blossoms and spreads through me.

"My ma always used to say, 'It's a good thing to need

others.' It's okay to need my help, Britta. I'm not gonna make you pay for it later."

The leaves of a sapling beyond the stream flutter as a dove emerges and flits away. The sight of the gray puff reminds me of Cohen. *You don't need a lot of friends, just a good one,* Papa said. Back then Cohen was my "good one."

"Go on, then," I whisper.

Leif slowly lifts my shirt upward until my backbone is exposed. He huffs out a breath. I'm about to ask what he sees when the cool press of the rag forces every nerve in my body to hiss. I fist my hands and slam my eyes shut—it's all I can do not to scream.

"You shouldn't waste the grain on the birds." I twisted my hand until my satchel's straps bit into my skin. We had drawn the attention of a few marketgoers milling near the cathedral. Cooing doves pecked the stones just beyond Cohen's reach.

"Give me a couple more minutes." His pleading gaze swung to mine. He jiggled a handful of grain, palm outstretched to lure in the chestnut-colored speckled fowl. None were daring enough to eat from his hand.

A nobleman cut through the crowd, scowling at me. His fur-trimmed overcoat skimmed the cobblestones. My grip on the satchel tightened, even though my fingers were already numb.

"Let's go," I urged. "We've been here too long. Papa will worry."

Cohen sighed. His golden-brown eyes searched mine. Then he tossed the bits to the birds.

On the road that led to my cottage, Cohen looked at the bag of grain in his left arm and then turned to me. "Usually they've gone by now, but this year's been warmer."

"The birds?" I wrinkled my nose.

"They're doves." He shrugged. "They're interesting. Compassionate and loyal."

Skepticism was written across my face.

"Really," Cohen argued. "Both male and female doves care for their young." When I didn't appear interested, he added, "And they mate for life. Shows they're loyal to one another."

A blush rose to my cheeks from his comment. "Guess they're not just dull brown birds."

I hoisted my satchel higher on my shoulder to take the weight off my arms. It was heavy with tubers from the market and new arrows from the fletcher.

"Not all are brown. Sometimes I'll spot a fair one as pale as you."

I rolled my eyes at him. How lovely to be compared to a fowl.

Without asking, Cohen tugged the bag off me and swung it onto his back.

"Didn't ask for your help," I said, bothered that he always felt compelled to take care of me. I may have only been fourteen, but I could manage well enough the months he wasn't there.

"So you didn't ask, but can you not simply accept it sometimes?" He shook his head.

I huffed. "Why accept it when I don't need it?"

Cohen returned the satchel. With the tubers weighing down my arms again, I wished that I hadn't thrown a fit about his help.

"Stubborn as the birds," he muttered under his breath.

"Did you just compare me to the doves?"

He looked at me squarely. "That I did. They wouldn't eat from my hand when I had food for the taking. Like them, you're loyal. Compassionate. But you never want help when I offer."

"Stop offering and I'll stop refusing."

He chuckled. "Whatever you say, Dove."

That night I dream Cohen is bloody and dying in my arms, and I am choking on fear and sobs.

My throat is dry as stone when I wake flat on my front, my entire body sweating and smarting from the pain. I haven't had the nightmare since right after the accident that gave Cohen his scar.

Trembling, I push up to sitting. Captain Omar watches me through the fire pit's smoke.

"She'll need food to help regain strength," he tells Leif, who is loading a pack on the captain's horse. "And give her more balm."

When the captain leaves, Leif hands me a tin of food. Tomas saunters over and I turn away from Leif, who is the one ray of sunshine on this bleak excursion.

"Learned yer lesson?" Tomas's pointy chin juts at me. "Need me to give you another?"

"Shut your gaping hole, you son of a scrant." Leif jumps up. "Stay away from her. You couldn't take two of those lashes."

Tomas lunges at Leif and slams his fists into the bigger

guard's jaw. The scuffle ends before it can truly start when the captain grabs Tomas and yanks him on his rear. I watch, motionless, as Tomas scuttles backwards.

"Told you to leave her alone." Captain Omar's nostrils flare as he pins Tomas to the dirt.

The guard's face purples, but he's got the sense not to say anything.

"No lunch rations for you today and tomorrow." Captain Omar pulls the guard off the ground and drags him to the horses. Their conversation is no longer audible, but a short while later I see pinch-faced Tomas working on grooming the horses and readying them for travel.

"Captain Omar's not pleasant," Leif whispers to me. "But he's consistent and fair."

Perhaps in Tomas's case. Not sure I agree with Leif otherwise.

CAPTAIN OMAR KEEPS THE MANACLES IN HIS satchel the next few days, since I can barely move as it is. After two nights lathered in balm and sleeping on my stomach, the pain is manageable. Leif cannot believe my speedy recovery, but I've always been a fast healer. Which is good, considering once we reach the main road, the captain demands we move faster.

Too soon, I'll have to face Cohen and trade his life for mine. The anticipation is like waiting for the executioner's ax to drop.

Now that we're out of the forest, all around us the farms and fields stretch out in the low-lands like faded patchwork quilts. If I squinted, it would look beautiful. Open space where families grow like corn. Only, the land has grown tired and old. Unattended crops have gone to seed.

"What are you looking at?" The scruff of Leif's rust-colored beard scratches against his uniform as he turns his chin to face me. Leif and Cohen are close in age. I wonder if Cohen grows as much facial hair as Leif. If it makes him seem older, rougher. Shaking my head, I drag my attention back to the fields. "I thought only one man in each family was required to serve in the army. Is the rumor about boys going to war true?"

"Lord Jamis wanted a stronger front, so he asked every able male to report." Conflict underlines his words.

"That isn't what the law calls for." One man from each household appeases the king's mandate. How would a family survive if they lost all the able men in their home?

"A month ago, the king changed the law." Captain Omar's comment catches me off-guard as he rides up alongside us. "Shaerdan's troops are larger than ours." I don't think offering up young boys to be slaughtered is a solution, or stealing a family's livelihood by requiring all men to leave, but I don't say this. "If your Cohen continues on this route, we'll go right through the south end of the war camps."

There's no enmity in the captain's words; still, I hate the way he says *your Cohen.*

He'll never be my Cohen. Not anymore.

. . .

Cohen lies in my lap, his motionless body covered in blood. I hold fast to him, as if my hands might fuse together the gashes that have opened his torso and torn his face. I rock forward and back. Forward and back.

"No, no, no, no, no!" The space beneath my rib cage is hot and full like it might explode. I cannot lose him, my Cohen.

And yet, I know it's soon to happen. I hate that I know when death is near. I can feel the thread left of his once-vibrant presence. He's a drop. A whisper. Cohen's hazel eyes, dim and no longer able to focus, wander as he coughs. Crimson speckles his pale lips.

"I—I never told you." I choke on my words. A sob breaks out. "I love you."

When his eyes close, my grief cuts through the woods. I'd trade my life to save his.

I wake in the dead of the night, skin clammy and cold. In those first moments, the strangest tugging sensation ghosts through me, tiny invisible feet dancing across my back and up my neck. I'm being watched. Pushing up off my front, I move onto my knees and glance around the campsite. To the shadows stained blue in the half moonlight. To the three sleeping guards snoring louder than a sloth of bears.

The same impression hit me in the Evers before I took down the bull elk. Before then, I'd never experienced the sensation. Perhaps the stress of Papa's death, or hunting Cohen, is affecting my imagination.

Even so, I withdraw slowly from my bedroll and stand

while pulling the dagger from my boot, where it's been hidden since the lashing. Two days ago, Tomas noticed the blade was missing, but he doesn't know I have it. The rat guard doesn't want the captain to know he lost the dagger, so he hasn't spoken a word about it.

Movement flickers in the trees, and then the unmistakable crunch of footsteps sounds.

Not my imagination. I suck in a breath.

Casting a wary glance at the dozing captain, I debate what the man will do if he finds me missing.

The fading footsteps snap my resolve. I shove to my feet, ignoring the slice of ache between my shoulders, and run after the intruder—a tall man, my guess by the glimpse of his shadow.

He's too far away to distinguish features. Too quick. I'm barely able to follow his silhouette. In an instant, he darts around another tree, leading us farther from camp. Doing everything possible to keep him in my sights, I push my legs faster, pump my arms harder, but the soreness in my back steals most of the needed grace to dodge trees and shrubs.

And then, quite suddenly, I cannot find him.

My legs slow to a jog. Did he change direction?

A familiar sound—a *whir*—splices the air just before an arrow sinks into the trunk beside me. I dive behind the closest boulder. Forget the healing lashes on my back; a war drum pounds beneath my ribs.

I lack strength and a bow. I shouldn't have followed him. Not alone. How foolish of me.

Some time passes before I'm daring enough to peek around the rock. Except he's gone now.

I kick the sandstone, cursing under my breath, and whip around to find the arrow. It's buried a quarter shaft deep into the wood—impressive for an archer. A wiggling action frees the arrow. The moonlight filtering through the branches provides enough ambient glow to take in the weapon's details. To read the word carved into the metal tip: *Dove.*

My fingers rattle as I run my hand from fletching to tip, knowing he's touched the arrow the same way just moments before.

I spin, searching the woods wildly for him, even though he's long gone.

The scratched word, Cohen's nickname for me, is rough beneath the pad of my thumb.

He missed intentionally.

Nothing makes sense. Not this arrow. Not his tracks.

The last time I saw Cohen was after a mountain cat attacked us in the woods, which caused me to be bedridden for a week and Cohen permanently scarred.

I ran a hand over my hair—a sheet of silver under the stars and moonlight—left down how Cohen liked it. Movement across the pasture caught my eye. It took squinting to make out Cohen's form. When he'd visited earlier, he said he'd come again. My heart leaped at the sight.

Nerves rattled inside as I slipped into the shadows to meet him. After the accident, I vowed I wouldn't wait to tell him of my feelings. Still I worried he didn't feel the same.

The angry line under his left eye socked me with guilt. "Cohen, I'm sorry."

"It wasn't your—" He started to argue but stopped when my fingers twined with his.

"It kills me that you're hurt. I—I care about you . . ."

"I care about you too." Heat from his skin spread through mine.

I summoned the courage to finally admit my feelings. "I—I meant as more than just friends. I have feelings for you. I want to be with you, and I don't ever want to lose you."

His eyes widened, and dark sable swallowed the usual gold flecks.

"Britt" floated out. His head dipped, and he pressed his lips to my cheek, then the corner of my mouth. Soft and sweet. He asked me to wait for him. That he'd return the next morning.

Though confused, I agreed. For Cohen, I'd do anything. Then he whistled for Siron and left.

He didn't come back like he said he would.

Not the next day. Not the following fall to apprentice. Not even when Papa died.

I stare deep into the darkness. *We need each other,* Leif said the other day, but he was wrong, because I don't need any part of this.

I hate the way Cohen makes a mess of my thoughts. Hate

that I'm here in these woods, hunting him for murder. Hate the doubts tangling my mind because they're meaningless next to the truth in Lord Jamis's words.

I snap Cohen's arrow in two and throw it on the ground.

I hate him.

CHAPTER

8

THOUGH KING AODREN HAS YET TO DECLARE the country officially at war, the border town of Fennit is teeming with men in steel armor and chain mail. Tents the color of dishwater line the fields northward. To the west, across an expanse of wheat fields and clusters of wooded areas, pillars of smoke dot the horizon. Enemy camps. Preparing, waiting. Thousands upon thousands of men are here, and yet I'm somehow certain Cohen is too.

"My father never thought it would escalate to this," I tell Leif. "Suspicions aren't reason for war."

Tension between Malam and Shaerdan has brewed for years. Papa told me of a time before King Aodren's rule when a three-year drought decimated Malam's crops. People blamed Shaerdan's Channelers, who used to sell healing ointments all over Malam. Suspicion grew but it didn't spread countrywide till the old king died from a sudden illness after a meeting with Shaerdan's leader, the chief judge. People were convinced Channeler magic was to blame.

"Course not." Leif leads his horse to follow the captain through Fennit's busy market. "But it's like a pot of water over the fire. Eventually it'll boil."

"Sure it'll heat up. Not explode," I argue.

He shrugs. "I heard they're after our ore, too."

I frown. "That doesn't make sense." When commerce had faltered between Malam and Shaerdan, many merchants had been unable to feed their families. The king had been forced to reinstate the ore trade—the one resource that would bring back some of the funds lost when the border closed.

"Their chief judge wants to own a mine in our mountains," Leif tells me. "King Aodren declined his request two months ago. Then their soldiers plundered one of our border towns."

That was right after Papa died and my mourning started. The isolation kept me from hearing this news earlier.

Tomas sidles up to us. "They wanna make us heathens like them and their black magic." He hasn't uttered more than a dozen words since killing the fawn. I mourn the loss of his silence.

"What do you know of that?" I challenge.

"I heard about one. A real whore, cheating on her husband."

I cringe at the word *whore*.

"The old man went fishing with his fellows," Tomas continues, "and his heathen of a wife did some devilry and made a wave as tall as the Castle Neart crash on that boat. Killed 'em all."

He sounds like a gossiping market crow. "Horse dung."

"You snit." Tomas white-knuckles his reins. "What do you know?"

"I know not to believe rumors."

He urges his horse closer. "Better hope Mackay doesn't cross the border. If their army doesn't get you, some Channeler will hear your sharp tongue and end you."

I fist my hands. "Somehow I don't think I'll be the one they find offensive."

"Watch it. The border's dangerous. Anything can happen."

"Nothing's going to happen to her," Leif interjects.

"Not like it'd matter." Tomas smirks. "Nobody'll miss her."

It's a struggle not to react—I refuse to give him the satisfaction of knowing his words have pierced me through. He has uttered one of my greatest fears—that I'll die alone.

The captain shouts a command that ends our conversation. When the captain's horse canters ahead, Tomas follows.

Leif's thick hand squeezes my arm. "It's not true about no one missing you."

But he's wrong.

Tomas's comment is the truest thing in my life. If I died, nobody would miss me.

Leif faces front again, and I feel bad for not speaking. Just like I'm guilt-ridden for not having mentioned Cohen's visit. His arrow is all I've thought about today. It's planted a grain of hope inside, whispering that there's something to Cohen's message. A guilty man would not act so.

It's nothing but a speck of doubt compared to Lord Jamis's truth.

Still, doubt has a way of making quicksand of stable ground.

We enter the first tavern we find in Fennit and chat with the local drunkards.

"Yep. I've seen him." The man's belly rests on the bar like a sack of potatoes. A belch bursts from the man's mouth. I squelch the need to gag. "Told me he'd give me two silvers for information about a woman named Enat."

I advise the captain to visit the clergy first, since they have the best records. If that doesn't pan out, then the merchants might know something. The captain sends Tomas and Leif to inquire with the local lord. Then he accompanies me to the church.

"I don't know where she is." The clergyman folds his hands over his book of Scripture. "Told the same thing to your friend earlier."

"Do you happen to know which way *my friend* went?" The captain grimaces.

"To Barton, the stonecutter. He did business with the old woman."

The captain snaps a brusque goodbye and leaves.

My eyes dart to the door, and I hesitate. "Was Enat a member of your congregation?"

"No." The clergyman gives me a strange look. "She wouldn't have been. She's a Spiriter." My face must show my confusion because his lip curls as he adds, "One of their Channelers."

"I've never heard of a Spiriter." I talk quickly, mindful of the captain's lack of patience.

The clergyman's eyes dart nervously to the door. "A Spiriter is rare. One or two are born to a generation. It's dark magic," his voice warns. "That's all I know."

The clergyman, face pale and with rigid shoulders, stands and ushers me toward the door.

"Can you at least tell me why Cohen is searching for Enat?" Before he pushes me out, a need for answers burns through me. "What does he want from a Spiriter?" I sound desperate now. I don't care.

"I don't know. But there aren't many reasons a man would go looking for a Spiriter."

Before I can ask him to explain, he swings the entry open and shoves me out. The sun is low in the sky, painting the stones of the church a weak shade of ocher. Another day on the way out, and we've not found Cohen. I twist around and breathe a sigh of relief when I find the captain interrogating a stranger on the road.

The moment I reach his side, he turns to me and arches a stern sable brow. "Did you learn anything of value?"

I contemplate keeping the information a secret, but something tells me the captain will see through my lie. "He thought Enat might be a Channeler."

The captain considers my answer, though he doesn't respond. Perhaps he's as confused as me about why Cohen would be after a woman from Shaerdan.

We follow Cohen's trail to the stonecutter, to the healer, and to an oiler, who tells us that Cohen is at a local inn. Lightning fast, we're on the captain's horse and galloping through Fennit.

When the thatched-roof two-story building comes into view, an awareness of something tugs inside. The back of my neck tingles.

Cohen's here.

The captain's gaze whips around, and I realize I've spoken aloud again. I want to smack myself. Cohen may not even be inside, and the captain will think me a fool.

Captain Omar growls out, "Mackay," as he drops to the ground with fierce determination in his eyes.

Cohen isn't in sight, though. Disappointment floods me. I want to see him again. To have one more moment with my old friend before . . . and yet I shouldn't want such things. I'm a traitor to myself. No matter what we were in the past, we are nothing now.

I slip off the horse to follow when the captain spins back. I slump against the mare's leg, putting on a show of feeling faint. He frowns, eyes flicking to the inn door. This may be a chance to escape. Never before has he left me with a horse and no guards around — an ideal situation.

"You stay here." A threat laces Captain Omar's words as he rushes inside.

Eager for an arrest, the man has left me completely unguarded. As I turn to mount the horse, an arm wraps around my waist, pinning my arms to my sides. I yelp and struggle against the strong hold.

"You didn't think I'd let them catch me, did you?"

The familiar husky voice floods my senses. *Cohen.* It takes a beat to realize I'm sinking into his warm embrace instead of combating it. To remember the reason I'm here.

I shove an elbow into his gut. Heel to his foot.

His grunt breathes warmth over my cheek. "Stop moving or I'll knock you out," he growls against my ear. "I swear it."

He loses his grip, freeing my elbow, which I throw back into his face. Hot blood spreads against my skin. I spin to find those hazel eyes that I haven't seen in fifteen months flash, angry and wild. He shifts and manages to get one arm around mine, clamping my swinging limbs against my torso, while one hand smothers my mouth.

He removes his hand, and I suck in a quick breath and cry, "CAP—"

Cohen smacks a cloth over half my face, forcing me to inhale a sickly sweet scent that scorches my nostrils. *Poison!* I squirm, twist, buck. My lungs burn with the desperate need to take a breath.

"Shh, shh," he's saying as spots dance across my vision.

I gasp for air and the world tilts on its axis.

"Sorry, Dove. I didn't want . . ." A fog hides his words.

Everything fades.

I HEAR THE CRACKLE AND HISS, THOUGH I CAN-
not seem to push off the weighty darkness. It's been years since I've woken like
this, half-asleep and conscious at the same time.
Somehow I rally enough energy to pry my lids
open. A blaze dances in a stone hearth. I try to
look around the otherwise dark room, except my
vision is spoiled with white splotches of light as
dull pain hammers behind my eyes. I blink, making out a straw mattress beneath me. A table by
the fireplace. One chair. Curtains over a window.

The last thing I remember was the captain
. . . tracking in Fennit . . . the captain told me to
stay . . . and then . . .

Cohen attacked me.

I push up against the bedding, needing to
stand, and my scars smart from sleeping on my

back again. The remaining scabs create the worst kind of itch that's nearly impossible to reach on my own. Once I've managed to sit upright, the vertical position puts a bright burst of pain behind my eyes. An awful sound like a braying of a donkey slips from my mouth, and my fingers clutch my head. *Boil me.*

"The sleeping concoction leaves a nasty headache." Cohen stands just inside the doorway.

The sight of him knocks the wind from me like the time I fell out of Papa's walnut tree. It was ages before my lungs could fill with air—that same aching breathlessness catches up with me now despite my horrid headache. The firelight glances off Cohen's hair, making his messy brown strands appear sun kissed. His eyes are warm molasses sprinkled with gold dust. His pursed lips . . . The sight unhinges me. What am I doing?

I open my mouth. Close it.

Cohen crosses the room and drops into the chair an arm span away. I'm hit with the strangest compulsion to reach out to him.

"You might want to take it slow." He props his elbows on his knees. His tunic pulls across shoulders that are broader and more muscular than they used to be. It's not the only noticeable change. His beard is fuller, his voice deeper. Not that it matters. He killed my father.

"You put up quite a fight. Not that I expect less from you." His hand strays toward my face. I sit motionless, staring at his fingers.

"No," I croak. "Don't—don't touch me."

His fingers curl into his palm, and his frown looks like disappointment as he sets his hand on his lap. I should be relieved. I am.

My life for his. The deal with Lord Jamis echoes in my head, filling me with doubt and shame. Which makes little sense, considering all the evidence.

"Let me check your head," he says.

I set my feet on the floor. "Don't touch me. I—I will kill you." The words come out because I should be filled with vengeance.

He leans back in his seat. "Yeah, Dove. But not today. You're not in any condition to do much damage to anyone. Nor will you be for another few hours. Give or take. Till then, I'll rest easy." He winks.

Anger fires through me. His arrogance and ease are too much. I reach for my boot where the blade is tucked against my leg and end up listing to the side.

"You're not even standing and you're swaying. Lie down, Dove."

"Don't . . . don't tell me what to do. And don't call me that!" My voice rises and the hammer in my skull pounds faster. I let my hair fall in my face to hide my grimace.

"Always stubborn," he mutters.

Before I know what's happening, he's crouched in front of me, his hands on my arms. His touch makes me spasm. He's too strong and manages to push me on the mattress so I'm lying down on my side.

"Please rest," he says, softly. "At least for a few hours more. Then we'll talk."

To my exasperation, he's out the door before I can form a protest, and my eyelids are drooping against my will.

I'm tired of following Papa through the market, tucking myself behind his wide back as he works his trades. It's tough to stay hidden all the time, but Papa says it's better for me to stay in his shadow so the traders don't say something that will force Papa to draw his sword against one of them. It's a relief to leave the tents of vendors when he steps into the bakery. I hope the baker is in and not his wife. She's horrid and likes to call me names. Her husband, on the other hand, usually doesn't notice me.

Unfortunately, Siobhan, the baker's daughter, stands at the counter beside a tray of steaming buns. My mouth waters. She recognizes Papa and sends him to the back of the store. He flicks his hand out once. His way of telling me to stay.

"Did ya steal those off a corpse?" sneers Siobhan when we're alone.

I resist the urge to tug my skirt down. At one time the material dragged on the ground, now it's a hand span too short to hide the boots that are too large for my feet.

"Only a dead man would be caught in those shoes." She laughs.

Last week I made the mistake of trying to talk to Siobhan. She was huddled in the alley behind the shop, tears coursing over her round cheeks. The kids had been teasing her, calling her stupid and piggish. I approached, only speaking two words before she wiped her face, shot me a hateful glare, and stormed off.

Her laugh is a cackle as I scramble for something to say. The right words never come.

"Don't talk to me again," she says. "I don't want people thinking I'm friends with a Shaerdanian. Or worse, a traitor—whore's daughter."

I flinch, though I've heard it many times before. People said my parents' marriage wasn't real because they married in Shaerdan. Doesn't matter that it was before the border closure. "Don't call my mother that."

"Your momma hated you so much, she'd rather follow the Archtraitor than stick around to raise you."

"Stop!" I lunge at her, knocking her perfect baked goods to the floor.

Morning finds me balled up on the mattress with a blanket tucked around my body. I shake off the dreamt memory and push the hair from my eyes. The door swings open and Cohen walks in carrying a bowl of steaming—is that porridge?

I scramble to my feet, grateful my back pain is nearly gone.

His eyes flick from my hands to my face. "You're feeling better."

He sets the bowl on the table. The porridge is covered in honey and cinnamon, and—stars help me—smells divine. *Stop looking at the food. Stop staring at Cohen.*

"Why'd you find me in the woods? Why bring me here?

What are you playing at?" The words tumble out. I don't even care how frazzled I sound. I want answers. "W-what do you want from me?"

His mouth pulls into a tight line. Against his otherwise schooled features, it's the only sign that he's either displeased or he doesn't have an answer. I've never been able to read him when he isn't smiling.

"Eat," Cohen says. "We'll talk later."

"No."

After a moment of hesitation, he crosses his arms. I wait for him to explain. Instead he has questions of his own. "Did Jamis send you after me? Or Omar?"

"Lord Jamis."

He scoffs. "Perhaps I shouldn't have let you find me so easily."

A scowl pinches my features, covering my chagrin. Truth be told, it makes sense that the wild-goose chase was his plan. Typical arrogance. Cohen was always a little too reckless. A little too self-assured.

A small wiggle of my ankle tells me the dagger is still in my boot. Clearly, Cohen's overconfidence hasn't changed at all. The fool shouldn't have left me armed.

In a snap, my blade's in my hand and pointed at his sternum. "Why did you kill my father?"

COHEN DOESN'T SO MUCH AS BLINK.
He's always had a gambler's face. I could be a mule birthing an immaculately conceived fawn, and he wouldn't bat an eye. Which is why when his foot snakes out and hooks my ankle, it tips me off balance.

Bludger.

I scramble around the bed as he brandishes a knife. On instinct, or years of training together, we both drop into similar fighting stances, circling each other. He kicks the chair out of the way. It clunks against the wood floor. Using the distraction, I rush forward, slicing at his torso. Cohen grunts and jumps back. The best defense against someone Cohen's size and with his strength is distance. I move away, wobbling while fighting to keep an arm's reach between us.

Whatever he drugged me with hasn't completely faded. My head still aches as though it's been trampled by a herd of horses. A groan slips out as I attack. Cohen parries each of my blows with ease. My strength is dwindling faster than I could empty a waterskin. I manage to punch his perfectly straight nose, but at this distance it doesn't do more than draw a little blood. In a flash, he has my arms pinned and my body twisted so my back is held flush to his body.

"Are you done, Britt?" he says, low and clipped.

He's too close, filling my nose with his familiar woodsy scent. I heave to catch a breath. When he steps back to pull me from the corner, I use the amount of wiggle room he's given me to slam a heel back, aiming for his knee. It catches him off-guard and he tumbles to the ground, taking me with him. With every seed of energy left in me, I wrench out of his grip and twist, falling against his torso with my dagger to his throat.

"I should kill you right now," I hiss through labored breaths. Blade to his skin.

His nostrils flare. Then he relaxes and lies motionless, waiting for me to make a move, face impassive, calling my bluff. He knows I'd never hurt him when he's lying there, allowing it. My fingers flex and loosen around the handle. Tighten and release.

I'm a fool.

I scramble away, sliding back on the floor until my shoulders touch the bed, even though this position makes me vulnerable. I suck in deep gulps of air that smell nothing like Cohen.

"Why'd you kill him?" The pain I've locked away for the last two months quakes through me, clamoring to get free. It burns my eyes and clogs my throat. "Why Papa?"

I've never been good at reading Cohen's expression, but his daggered glare isn't complicated.

"I didn't kill Saul." His voice sounds close to a snarl.

So worked up, it takes a minute for me to feel his words. Warmth blossoms in my sternum, pools in my gut, and spreads outward to the tips of my limbs. *Truth.*

Truth?

I lower my weapon. "You—you didn't do it?" My mouth gapes open.

Cohen's fingers graze his scar before wrapping around the back of his head to knead his neck. "I had nothing to do with his death." The warmth in my belly turns into an inferno. *Truth.* "He was like a father to me. I would've given my life for him."

The dagger in my hand could be a yoke for how it weighs me down. Relief. Sadness. Guilt. Shame. I fix my sight on the floor where a nail sits too high. Cohen knew me better than anyone, and I knew him just as well. I should've seen past Lord Jamis's claim.

Cohen's head dips and his eyes grab mine. "You believe me." Not a question.

I nod.

He slips his blade into the sheath at his waist and stares deep into the fire. "I didn't think you, of all people, would believe I killed Saul."

I flinch, though he hasn't said anything I don't deserve. I'm ashamed that Lord Jamis's words were enough to turn my faith in my friend. Lord Jamis must've believed absolutely that Cohen was the murderer.

"Why didn't you say something?" It's hard not to be angry with myself and mad at him for not clearing this up sooner. "You never came back to Brentyn. You missed the wake. You shot at me in the woods. Why?"

"I figured you would know I was innocent," he says. "Come on, Britt. You *know* me."

"But why did you put yourself in danger reaching out to me?"

He groans. "I thought they had something over you. My arrow was a message. So you would know you're not alone."

Not alone. His words slay me.

He moves to where the overturned table lies and stands it upright. I gather myself off the floor and plunk down on the mattress. I should tell him I'm sorry, but the words don't feel adequate.

"Lord Jamis had evidence." My explanation sounds weak. "Your coat. Your dagger."

His neck shows cords of tension. I suspect this information has taken him by surprise.

"Why do you believe me now?" he asks.

Even though we spent every winter together after he turned twelve, I never told him about my ability to perceive truth. It was a shock that Cohen would be a friend to me despite everyone else shunning me for my mother's blood and traitorous actions. My ability remained my secret because I never wanted to risk losing Cohen, not when his friendship was my world.

But I owe him the truth.

"I believed Lord Jamis for the same reason I believe you now," I say, disliking how soft and uncertain my voice sounds. I suppose truth is an easy thing to determine. Not so much to deliver. "I feel something when a person speaks the truth. My body has a reaction." I pause for fear of sounding ridiculous. "It's like a fire in my gut. Warmth spreads through me. I didn't want to believe Lord Jamis, but when he spoke, I felt the warmth of truth."

Cohen studies me in meticulous measure as he would survey the forest during a hunt.

My pointer finger tugs at the collar of my top, needing a breeze. The room is too stuffy. "If you were to lie, I would know that too. A lie feels cold, chilly."

"Are you ever wrong?"

"No. Never."

He doesn't blink. "Apparently not *never*."

I start to roll my eyes and then stop. At least he doesn't think I've gone mad. "Lord Jamis must've been fed wrong information. Maybe it felt like truth to me because he believed the accusation."

I knot my hands in my lap when I realize I've been moving them awkwardly while talking, waving the dagger around like an imbecile. Quietly, lamely, I add, "I wanted you to be innocent. I just needed you to say you didn't do it."

Cohen stands and crosses the room to where the forgotten porridge now lies in a gooey mess on the floor. I watch, waiting for a response, as he scrapes up the breakfast. When he finishes and turns to face me, a dark shadow has crossed over his face. "What will happen when you don't deliver me to Omar?"

I want to hide my face in my hands, but I force myself to hold his gaze. "I was caught with poached meat and the captain was going to hang me. Lord Jamis proposed a trade. My life for yours."

Cohen's face pales. His hand clenches on the bowl of porridge. He stares at me hard, saying nothing for an uncomfortably long stretch of time. "Good," he finally snaps. "I would've done the same."

I recoil, feeling as though he's smacked me. The strangest part about his comment is it registers in my gut with a mix of warmth and cold sensations. Truth and falsehood. What does that mean?

Cohen stands and walks toward the door.

"Where are you going?" He wouldn't leave me here, would he? He took off before and never returned.

"To the kitchen." He gestures to the bowl.

I push myself off the floor. "I traded my life for yours. I confessed that I could sense when someone's telling the truth. Have you nothing more to say?"

"Your explanation is all I wanted."

Perhaps he doesn't believe me. Perhaps he's too angry with

me to care. "Cohen, I'm sorry I kept my secret from you." The apology rushes out.

He gives me a sad sort of smile. "We all have our secrets, Britt."

Cohen returns to the room with two more bowls of breakfast.

"If I promise this isn't poisoned, you have to promise not to stab me in my sleep."

My lips flatten into an amused line.

It takes only moments to devour everything in the bowl. I'm going to need my strength. I'll never turn Cohen in now. There'll be no reprieve for me until I find the real killer and bring him before the high lord. Captain Omar wouldn't allow anything less. And if I cannot produce my father's murderer in exchange for my life, then the captain will have me strung up.

Setting the empty bowl on my lap, I turn to Cohen. "I have a plan."

"Do you, now?" Cohen stands across the room with a half smirk on his face, his earlier anger gone. "I hope it involves trekking west, since you're coming with me to Shaerdan."

"Er, no. Heading into a country that's going to war with ours doesn't sound like a plan. More like suicide. I'm not going to run. I'm going to find Papa's murderer."

His lips quirk. "You've been tracking me from Brentyn to here. Where did you think I was headed?"

"I thought you were dodging the guards." As soon as I've

spoken, I want to retract the words. He clearly wasn't solely evading them. I should've figured as much earlier when his path was too direct. The clergyman mentioned a woman named Enat. "You're already tracking the murderer."

The corner of his mouth turns up more in approval. "There's the Britta I know."

Guilt sneaks up and kicks me in the lungs, stealing my breath. I shouldn't have doubted his loyalty.

"Is Enat the murderer?" I ask.

He crosses the room and sits down beside me on the bed. "Possibly," he says. "Though I don't think so." Cohen explains that he's been following leads to figure out who wanted my father dead. Most people have been tight-lipped. But he has informants listening in on tavern talk who report to him.

"That explains the cleared path and partial shoe print," I say, realizing he must've met with an informant in the woods before changing directions and heading north.

He seems surprised and then pleased. "You always were an excellent tracker. Knew you'd catch me, Dove."

The familiarity of his comment propels me up and off the mattress in need of space to breathe without him nearby. The rush of old emotions is suffocating. He opens his mouth but doesn't say anything, though I'm sure I look rabid for how crazed I suddenly feel.

"I should get going," I tell him.

The only man who has a chance of tracking Cohen or me is the captain. By splitting up, we would make it impossible for the captain to find us both. Together, we're two halves of a massive target.

"You mean *we*," Cohen says in that arrogant way I've not missed at all.

I shoot him a withering look. "No. I'm certain I spoke correctly when I said *I*."

"You have a lot of *I*'s there." He teases as his eyes follow my movement to the door.

"Exactly. So you won't be confused when *I* leave."

He crosses the room in three steps, setting his bowl beside mine on the bed and moving between the door and me. "As it stands, I have more information than you. Your best bet is me. You go with me."

That deserves an eye roll. "You haven't changed a bit. Still pushy and overbearing."

He gives me a tilted smile that does whispery things through every bit of me.

Even if he's arrogant, he's right. "What information do you have?"

"We need to head to the coast of Shaerdan. To Celize."

Oh. Cohen really is going to cross the border, which means going with him will make us both traitors. I've lived my life resenting my mother's choice. Could I really willingly become a traitor? The thought sickens me.

"Why Celize?"

The corners of his mouth tip down, as if he's confused about my question. "Saul was killed in a tavern there."

"He was killed in Celize?" The question is more for myself than Cohen.

Cohen nods, understanding dawning in his caring eyes.

"How?" I whisper.

It's clear he doesn't want to answer by the way his lips form a tight line. When I repeat my question, he concedes. "He was stabbed in the back. Blade went right through the heart."

"Your dagger," I supply, out of breath.

He nods. "I was in Celize on a tip about finding the Archtraitor. His bounty would pay off my family's farm and give my sister a sizable dowry. The night before Saul was killed, a thief broke into the room while I slept. It made no sense to me. I should've woken if someone was in my room."

He hangs his head. "They stole my coat, my dagger, and my money."

I walk to the lone chair in the room and flop down, needing to rest against the weight of the new information. Even though I knew Papa was murdered, hearing the details of his death makes me unbearably sad.

"Britt," Cohen says softly. He pushes off the bed. "I'm sorry. I didn't mean for this news to hurt you. I thought you knew about Saul's death." How can he always read me like a book? He squats in front of me, his hands touching my knees. His Adam's apple rises and falls beneath the muddy-brown stubble scattered over his neck. "I'm sorry if I'm being pushy. You always hated it when I told you what to do. Tell me what you want to know."

"Everything." My reply is soft.

"All right. Saul's last bounty hunt took him into Shaerdan. After he delivered the prisoner to Omar at the border, Saul told him he'd need a week more."

Captain Omar never mentioned he was working with my father. In all the time we traveled together, he could've mentioned it. Hateful man. I see now how someone could've framed Cohen, but it takes a moment to process what he's told me about Papa's death. The guards who came to my door to report Papa's death lied to me. They said he was killed while tracking a criminal.

"How do you know this?"

"It's my business to know these things. Your father's contacts became all my confidants. Many he introduced when I was an apprentice, and after I started hunting, I worked with them often. I'm lucky that some stayed true to me even after the murder accusations," he says, though he sounds anything but pleased with his luck. It must've stung when not all his contacts stayed true. Cohen explains how he spent the first few weeks after the murder gathering information and putting together Papa's timeline while he was in Shaerdan. "Only the other day did I receive word that Saul was searching for a woman," he says.

"And you're certain it wasn't another assignment from the king?"

He shakes his head. "Saul covered his tracks so well, it's clear he didn't want anyone, not the king or the royal guards, to know whom he was searching for."

"Enat." She's a piece to this puzzle.

Cohen's hand squeezes my leg, a confirmation. He stands, moving back to lean against the door. "I don't know why he was searching for her, but when we find Enat, I'm sure we'll find the murderer. Or at the very least, the reason someone wanted Saul dead."

I wonder if he even realizes how he's inserted *we* into his sentences. I figured that as the older sibling of Imogen and Finn, he bossed them around as much as he tried to boss me. When we were younger, Cohen always wanted to take the head position. Even when it led us into trouble. How much trouble waits if I go with Cohen now?

I take in his broad shoulders and crooked smile — the very expression that has always devastated me. In the fifteen months he's been gone, my foolish heart hasn't forgotten a single stitch of Cohen. If not for evading Captain Omar, for this reason, I should say no.

It would be wise to protect my heart. To remember that Cohen left without a goodbye. But all I can think of is Papa saying, *Bravery is a choice that is yours to make. Don't let fear steal your will.*

Something tells me this hunt won't end well.

But since I am a brave fool: "Yes. I'll go."

CHAPTER 11

FOLLOWING COHEN, I STEP CAREFULLY AND softly as we sneak out of the room into a dark hallway.

"Stop lurking, Britt. They're already gone."

I scowl and straighten. Cohen's genius plan entailed hiding directly under the guards' noses. Typical of him. "I wasn't lurking. It's exercising caution."

"Roosters and hens. A fowl's a fowl."

"Something's foul all right."

He chuckles. "They left early this morning. I watched them mount and leave, headed straight for the border. You were too busy snoring to notice."

"I was sleeping. I don't snore."

"Ha! Like a tavern rat, you do. Especially after a night of slugging ale."

He's baiting me, much like he used to, and it shoots a twinge of ache straight through my center. Those days are over, and though part of me might wish for us to be like we were, another dose of his rejection will destroy me, so I keep my mouth shut and follow him to the door.

My bow peeks from the top of the bag slung over Cohen's shoulder. He insisted on packing our weapons together so we don't have to do it later when we meet up with his horse, Siron. I reluctantly agreed with the exception of Papa's dagger, which is in my boot.

"Something for the road." Molly, the innkeeper's widow, steps into the sitting room. A simple apron cinches over her dress, and a cloth-covered basket rests in her hand.

"Thanks, Molls." Cohen hugs the woman.

I stand there, unsure what to do with my hands while I watch them say their goodbyes. I forgot how comfortable Cohen is around people. Or rather, I forgot how much others like him.

"Archers watch the stretch from the town to the border posts," Molly cautions Cohen.

"We're going to head south for the wooded hills to get some distance from the guards. We'll cross there."

I gape at his openness. He is always so quick to trust others, while I trust no one.

Worry is etched into her wide eyes. "The watchmen scour those woods for traitors."

"Fewer watchmen are on the border now that they're needed at the front. One man still stationed to the south is a friend. We'll be fine. Siron will help navigate those woods, and Britt here is the best tracker in both countries."

His comment fills me with pride. I glance up to see him watching me.

Molly wrings her hands on her apron. "You should at least change your clothes once you're in Shaerdan so you fit in. They don't take kindly to our people."

Papa told me they could be a ruthless people. Shaerdan is ruled by a council of judges, led by a chief judge. Kinsmen are fiercely loyal to their local judge. If they see we're from Malam, they may strike first before asking questions. My skin prickles at the thought.

"I've already planned to do so." Cohen taps his pack, and then makes a joke about Shaerdan's awful bright colors.

"Of course, my boy." Molly pats his arm. "You'll do just fine."

It's like she's talking to her own kin. I shuffle away from them, closer to the door, where I'm not as much of an interloper, listening to their conversation.

Molly reaches for me before I can escape, as if she might fold me into a hug. The motion catches me off-guard and I stumble back, flushing a slight magenta all over.

By the gods, Cohen must be mortified by my strangeness. I know I am.

Forcing myself to Molly's side, I give her arm a pat like the one she gave Cohen. I don't want her to think I'm not grateful for her help.

We head south, away from the amassing war, away from the main road littered with guards and soldiers, away from Omar, Leif, and Tomas. As we slink through the wheat fields and grasses at a snail's pace, our movement isn't detectable. It takes hours to reach the hills and woods south of Fennit.

Cohen's horse, Siron, waits for us where the woods grow thick and wild and dark. His black coat is perfectly camouflaged in the inky shadows, with only the flash of his yellow eyes to give his location away. Cohen said whenever he enters a town, he commands Siron to remain in the forest because the horse is too noticeable.

Siron drops his nose, pushing out a thin whinny as we approach. He never cared much for anyone besides Cohen.

After drawing a brush from his satchel, Cohen combs the stallion's body, shoulder to rear. The animal's cocked leg straightens and his ears perk as he measures me and then turns away with an airy snort. Siron was a wild horse, caught in the southlands, where the harsh Akaria Desert makes animals savage. Though Cohen spent months breaking the madness out of the creature, I'm certain there's still much of the wild dunes in his horse.

I wait, allowing Siron one more chance to take in my scent.

"Don't worry," Cohen says, mistaking my pause for

apprehension. It's the first time he's spoken without whispering since leaving Molly's inn. We're far enough away from Fennit now that there isn't much risk in being overheard. I haven't seen others' tracks since we entered these woods.

"Siron can handle your featherweight," Cohen says. "I doubt he'll even notice the difference between you and perhaps an extra bow."

One thing I am not is vain, since I've no misgivings about my appearance. Unnaturally pale, white-blond hair, freckles, bony figure with a hint of breasts; there isn't much to admire, and so there isn't much for Cohen to tease about. Still, I cannot let his jest slide.

"You're certain? I wouldn't want to be the cause for putting the old horse down."

Though his face is out of view, I notice how his shoulders grow rigid. "He's not old."

My grin should be ear to ear, but I know Cohen's bond with the horse is strong. Teasing him is mean sport. "No, he's not," I admit. "Your horse doesn't like me very much. I was giving him time to get used to me."

The conversation flounders as Cohen settles himself on Siron and then offers me a hand. Before I've steadied myself, Cohen clicks his tongue against the roof of his mouth and the beast responds by taking off, causing my arms to flap out like bird wings. I flail and end up grasping Cohen around the waist. His ribs move out and in as he chuckles.

"He's reserved with everyone," Cohen tells me. "When he

was a colt, he didn't have much contact with people, so he needs time to trust others. Know what I mean?"

More so than I'd like to admit.

With the dangers of crossing the border in mind, we fall silent as we ride. We move into a gentle river to hide Siron's prints and continue to weave westward. Just before reaching Shaerdan, Cohen pulls up on the reins and stalls in the water.

I glance over his shoulder, and my hands fly to cover my mouth. On either side of the river, two bodies swing from nooses, one far more decayed than the other. The flesh has decomposed and withered, exposing bones among the corpse's rags. But the other — *mercy* — stinks of fetid flesh. Flies swarm a man's pale body that cannot be more than a couple days old. His commoner clothes, a tunic over simple trousers, are stained in blood from multiple arrow injuries. And by the awkward twist of his feet, it appears they've both been broken. I'd heard rumors about the merciless watchmen — men hired by the king to prevent people from passing through the border. They're paid per person they catch, which makes them a bloodthirsty bunch. The torture they inflict is fodder for nighttime tales. Seems those rumors are true.

"They're meant to scare. You never know when you'll cross one." Cohen's low tone is apologetic.

"They serve their purpose well, then. We best not get caught." I shiver despite the day's heat. Covering my nose to stop myself from heaving, I drop my forehead against Cohen's back.

He digs his heels into Siron, urging him to a run, water splashing against our legs, till we've crossed the border. And then farther. We don't slow until we're a good distance into Shaerdan. We pass a giant tree with a trunk so thick, Cohen and I couldn't wrap our arms around it if we were fingertip to fingertip.

I thought I'd feel different once we entered Shaerdan. That I might notice a strangeness in the forest. This is a country of black magic, after all. But a few hours past the border, nothing stands out as unusual.

The only noticeable change is my increased worry. We're traitors. And now I have firsthand knowledge of what my punishment will be, should they catch us.

"We shouldn't slow down yet." My comment is muffled by Cohen's back.

"We're clear, Britt."

"They could still follow us." The grotesque bodies fill my mind. As well as thoughts of the Archtraitor. My father hunted him for twenty years on order from the king. I've no doubt the captain would chase our hides for that many years, if not more, to ensure justice was served.

Celize is a ten-day trek past the border. We plan on taking six, seven days at most. The first few days are an arduous ride over rocky trails and dense brush. Which is why I'm not prepared when Siron starts down a steep ravine. Cohen leans back and his body mashes against mine, the heat of his back instantly seeping into my front. It's impossible not to notice the way his muscles flex and relax against me as he moves.

I tell myself not to get comfortable. Not to fall back into our old patterns. He'll only leave again.

"Are you all right?" Cohen glances over his shoulder. "Need a break?"

I catch myself about to suck in a deep breath of Cohen's scent. "Ah, no. I'm fine." Good thing he cannot see me blush.

Cohen tugs on the reins and Siron stops.

"Why are we stopping?" The sun sits low in the sky, but there's still enough light to travel.

He glances to the side, eyes raking the landscape as though he's taken notice of something, but then turns to me with a carefree smile. "You were squirming like there's a bug in your drawers."

"I was not."

He shrugs, a simple up-and-down of his shoulders that mocks my comment. "Now's a good time to stop. Siron's been carrying us for three days, and he needs the break. So I say we're done for today."

"We should go on foot, then."

"Only a sliver of the moon's gonna rise tonight. It'll get dark fast. We need to use this time to survey the area." Cohen gives me his usual unreadable look. "And we crossed a stream not far back. I don't know about you, but I'd like to wash up before night falls."

My gaze briefly drops to the sweat mark on his shirt and

then to his full lips framed by rugged facial hair. The sight does something strange and liquidy to my insides. "I'll, um, find the stream."

"Take your time," he says with a soft chuckle.

Does he need a break from my incessant staring? Oh, I'm such a fool. I hurry toward the water.

The undergrowth is thicker here than in Malam, covered in crawling vines and ferns and tiny yellow and purple flowers. I leave rock markers along my way until reaching the stream, which is more of a small river, wide and deep enough for bathing.

I fill the waterskins and drink till full. In the pool's reflection, the grime caked on my face and neck makes my pale skin look brown as bark. After peeling off my clothes and sinking into the cool water, I use the sand from the streambed to scrub away the grime.

It's a relief to be clean once again. The water is a needed reprieve from the long, torturous hours with Cohen. I thought seeing him again would ease the ache inside. Oh no. Having him so close only makes me think of how I'd love to curl into his arms once more.

Cohen lived with Papa and me in the winters, returning to his home in the south of Malam each year for spring planting. There he led an entirely separate life, tending to his parents' farm alongside his brother, Finn, and sister, Imogen. His family was the reason he worked tirelessly, apprenticing for Papa. He wanted to give them a better life.

I cannot fault him for his selflessness. Still, I cannot forget that I don't fit in his plan.

When the time came, he chose a life without me. I'd do well to remember that.

Halfway back to the campsite, a tiny pin of anxiety pricks my chest. It's nothing, really, and yet it stops me in my tracks. I press my hand to my chest, over the seed of unease, sprouting roots that twist and tangle around my lungs and tighten.

I'm suddenly certain of one thing:

Cohen's in danger.

I TAKE OFF RUNNING, SPRINTING DOWN THE GAME trail cut between ferns and clovers as the clang of metal echoes through the trees.

Cohen and Leif are sword to sword. Tomas is on the ground, unconscious, bloody, but not dead — a fact only obvious by the rise and fall of his torso. I don't know what's more surprising, that they've found us, the king's two best bounty hunters, or that Leif and Cohen appear evenly matched.

And strangely, I'm frightened for both.

The scene is madness, swords clashing as I hide behind the trees, scanning for Omar. When he's nowhere to be found, I quietly circle the area. And still find nothing. Siron is missing as well and, with him, my bow.

"Where is she?" Leif's fierce tone freezes me

in place. It sounds foreign, coming from the gentle giant of a man I've come to know. I press myself against a tree trunk and peer around.

Leif advances on Cohen.

Cohen swings his sword in a tight circle that hooks Leif's and sends it back over his shoulder. "Back down, Leif. I don't want to hurt you."

"Where is Britta?"

"Enough," Cohen snarls. "She's not here. Yield. I've no qualms killing you."

Leif never mentioned they had a history. Granted, my purpose on this trip wasn't to make friends with the guard.

The fight continues, weapons clash and cross and swing, until Cohen has the upper hand. Cohen's eyes are flat and angry in a way I've never witnessed. Leif grunts when Cohen's sword slices a clean line through the arm of his shirt. Blood darkens the bold blue material of Leif's Shaerdanian commoner clothing, turning my guts inside out. *Bludger.*

"Stop!" I jump from hiding.

Cohen's chin jerks in my direction. His eyes go dark and flat. He seems furious with me. It's no more than the span of a heartbeat before Cohen's attention returns to Leif, but Leif uses the moment to his advantage and puts space between their swords. I might feel a touch bad for distracting Cohen, if I weren't relieved for Leif.

The point of Leif's sword holds steady as his attention

volleys from me to Cohen. Then back to me. "Britta?" Uncertainty turns the corners of his mouth down.

I'd assumed Captain Omar and the guards deduced my loyalty had switched. I start to explain when my name, sharp as an arrowhead from Cohen's mouth, stops me.

Leif's eyes narrow. It's like viewing cogs click into place as confusion clears and dawning sets in. "You've joined with *him*. Your father's murderer?"

I shake my head, worried he'll think me to be the worst kind of traitor. "No. That's not how it is." Cohen mutters something, but I ignore him. "He's innocent. Lord Jamis was wrong."

Leif guffaws in his funny way, but it's tinged with disappointment. "He's lying." His hand clenches around the hilt of his sword, forearm straining. "He'll say anything to get what he wants."

This isn't the place, nor is this the time, to explain to Leif how I know Cohen is innocent, but I cannot leave it alone. "Someone made it look like Cohen did it. Planted evidence to make him look guilty."

"Britta, please. Don't be fooled by him." Leif reaches out his free hand and then lowers it, and then raises it once more. It's an awkward arm dance, like he's not quite sure how to coax me to him.

"If you go with him, you'll be breaking orders from Lord Jamis," Leif says, gentler now, pleading. Hearing his concern knots my insides.

Tomas moans.

Leif's attention diverts to the injured lump of a guard. "If you do this, I'll have to come after you with force."

Leif's been kind to me when there was no cause for it. In spite of my crime. In spite of who I am.

"I know," I tell him sadly. "But I need to find the real murderer."

His face is pained.

During our exchange, Cohen has slipped away from me and maneuvered close to Leif. Without warning, he slams the pommel of his sword against the back of Leif's head and the guard crumples.

"Cohen!" I gasp, and then scramble to Leif's side to roll him off his back. Before I can set his body right, Cohen's hand seizes my arm. "Let's go," he commands.

"Stop, Cohen. He could choke on his own vomit. I'm just setting him right."

"Why are you pitying him? Whose side are you on?"

"I'm not . . . I just . . . It's not pity," I stammer, unsure of myself. "He was kind to me when he didn't have to be. He's my — my friend. And he doesn't deserve to die."

"I didn't realize you two were friends." Cohen's face pinches in a sullen expression. He stands there for a beat, his flattened hazel eyes switching between Leif and me. I'm tempted to think he's jealous. But he'd never be. Not over me.

He sighs, sheathes his sword, and leans down to help me roll Leif on his side. Once we have the guard situated, Cohen walks away. He thrusts his fingers into his mouth and blows out a sharp whistle. Moments later, Siron appears. After we're both seated and heading for the stream to disguise our trail, Cohen falls into a brooding silence.

"Why are you upset with me?" I ask a safe distance away from the guards.

He twists around in the saddle, his mouth a thin, tight line. "You waltzed into the clearing and announced to the king's guard that you're working with me. I'm not upset. I'm furious."

That was to the point. Clearly not jealous.

I cringe and then glare at him. It may not have been wise to show myself to the guards, but his response grates. "I didn't want to absolve you of my father's murder only to have you arrested for another. Perhaps you should consider your own recklessness."

"You didn't have to run in to save me. Or Leif. I wasn't going to kill the bludger. Now you've sealed your fate."

True, he might not have meant his threat; however, intentions can change in an instant.

Cohen faces forward and prods Siron to go faster, until trees are whipping past us and the spring water is splattering our legs.

The sliver of a moon provides no light to navigate through the forest as we forge westward despite the late hour. Without Siron we'd be useless in the night's pitch-black. There aren't many horses like Siron, with his ability to see perfectly in the dark.

Travel jostles our bodies until we're bruised from banging into each other—it's impossible to prepare for a dip you cannot see. When we reach a spread in the trees, Cohen takes a moment to check our direction from the star patterns in the sky.

His caution tells me he's as concerned as I am. From my time spent with the guards, I know Tomas is worthless at tracking, but Leif's skills are passable, and the captain is highly skilled. We need to make the most of traveling tonight.

When we get to Celize, we won't have much time, if any, to track down Enat and Papa's murderer. I wish I knew why Papa was after her. Hunting her down isn't much different from galloping through the night, blind to the perils ahead. For all we know, Enat could be the killer.

If only Papa had left information, even the smallest clue. I always thought Papa held no secrets from me. How wrong I was.

"You're right. I was reckless." Cohen's voice interrupts my line of thinking. "Earlier in the day I noticed the tracks of three horses, and I guessed it was the guards. I decided to follow them to see where they were headed."

His admission stuns me.

"I sent you to the river so I could assess their strengths and weaknesses," he admits. "But when I overheard Leif mention Omar was gone gathering supplies, I seized the opportunity."

"We could've slipped past them, and they'd be none the wiser." My pitch rises with incredulity. "Only, you decided it would be best to pick a fight?"

"Thought I'd do a little damage and slow them down."

My hands are fists around the back edge of the saddle to keep me from pummeling him, while he doesn't move a muscle. Just sits there, calmly telling me he thrust us into the guards' reach, like we're two farmers discussing a troublesome cow's teat. "Of all the risky things you've ever done, this one" — my breath lances out — "this one could win a gold ribbon at the Midsummer's Tide fair."

"Yeah, Britt. It was foolish." He groans, the sound brimming with pain as if someone's punched him in the gut. "At the time it seemed like a good idea."

A good idea would've been Cohen telling me he'd spotted tracks, instead of making a brash decision. Back when he apprenticed for Papa, he was always bent on doing what he thought was best without asking for my input. Of course the bludger hasn't changed.

I forge on, my frustration spilling out, a barrel of ale with a broken spigot. "A good idea, like the time you insisted we take the extra buck meat to market. You didn't believe me when I said no one would trade with me."

He straightens in the saddle.

"Or the time you went after that wild boar with only your dagger? The healer had to sew up your arm."

"Point taken. I can be brash," he says. "I should've

mentioned the guards' tracks. It was just a shock to see they were so close." Cohen twists to look over his shoulder at me, the moonlight shifting over his brown hair, painting his dark locks blue.

I snort, more irritated with my detour in attention than his excuse, but decide to let the matter go. It cannot be undone.

"That time we went to market with the meat," he says a short while later, voice reflective, "I was thinking of you. You never liked the clothes Saul gave you, and I thought . . ." He clears his throat. The sound snares me, holds me in its trap, transforming me into immobile, breathless prey. "Thought you'd like something new. Something you could pick out. Something special."

His words are water, dousing the fire of my irritation. Regardless of the warnings I've given myself, his confession makes me long for the past. Why didn't he tell me this before? That's the question I want to ask, but instead I say, "What will we do now that they know we're ahead of them?"

"We've got to use the small lead to our advantage. Gain some distance."

"You don't know the captain. I've never met a more devoted criminal hunter. If anything, you surely lit a fire under Captain Omar."

"I know the captain just fine," he says with a heavy sigh, which tells me he agrees with my last comment.

We travel in the darkness, falling into silence, leaving time

for me to think about
nicer for me.

After a stretch, Cohen
it to me. "I should've given t
you changed tunics. It work
traveling with Omar."

I hold the cap in my hands.

Cohen twists even more in th
hand's distance from mine. Silver   his
strong jaw and straight nose. Mesm   the colorless
shadows and highlights on his face, I don't notice his hand
until he brushes a hair from my cheek. His touch sends a jolt
of surprise through me.

"Your hair shines too much," he whispers. "It reflects the
moon. Right now you're a moving torch for anyone to see."
His hand wraps over my hand holding the cap. "You should
wear it."

A tingle spreads beneath my skin until my entire body feels
more alive than it's ever been. No compliment's been spoken,
and yet here I am soaking in his words like a steamed bath. I
swallow a smile, place the cap on my head, and shove my shining hair into hiding.

W E STOP A FEW HOURS BEFORE DAWN.
Cohen offers to take the first watch. He dismounts and then reaches up to help me off. I let him because exhaustion hit me hours ago and his strong hands around my waist are comforting.

"We should both sleep, since neither one of us has rested much in days," I tell him. Leif and Tomas were unconscious when we left. Even if they tracked us, night has fallen, hiding any prints we made before we took to the stream.

"I'm not going to take any chances. I'll keep watch while you rest."

It's clear from the determination in his tone there's no arguing with him. Cohen has never been one to let his mistakes go. He'll do what he must to make things right.

A yawn splits my lips open. "Suit yourself. Wake me in a couple hours."

As I move to make a bed of the pillowy ferns at the base of the trees, Cohen rifles through the satchel of food and pulls out a lone sweet roll, the last of Molly's treats.

"Want to share this?" He drops down in front of me, sitting with his back to a tree trunk. We're close enough that the starlight shows the definition of his features but leaves most of his face in shadows.

"It's yours." I do want a piece, but I feel the need to maintain some distance. The last couple days have almost made me forget why Cohen isn't good for me.

It's difficult to see his expression, but I think he's studying my shadowed face. "We used to share everything."

He tears the roll in two and offers me half. I'm thinking of what he just said . . . how we *used to* be. I wonder if he thinks about how we used to be as much as I do. But if he did, why didn't he come back to me?

"You're welcome," he says, his fingers brushing mine as he hands me the offering.

I bring the roll to my lips to hide how my smile spreads, even though he likely cannot see my reaction. After we polish off the remaining nuts and fruit, I lie down comfortably on my back for the first time since the whipping.

Someone grips my shoulder, and my eyes snap open to the sight of bloodshot hazel eyes. In the midst of the gray morning,

Cohen looks a push away from collapsing. I don't know when the last time was that he had a good night's rest.

"It's been a couple hours." His voice is rough, gravelly. "The sun will rise in another hour."

Stretching, I let out a yawn as big as the Malam Mountains. I'm startled to find Cohen watching me with a strange pull on his face.

I start to question him, but he turns away and focuses on the dirt at his feet. "We should get going."

"What about you? You need to sleep." He looks back the way we came, into Shaerdan's strange vine-strangled forest. Indecision plays across his furrowed brow, undoubtedly related to the captain and the guards. "I won't be able to hold your boulder of a body up if you pass out while we're riding."

His brow quirks. "Boulder of a—?"

"A figure of speech." I flick my hand in the air, dismissing the comment. "Lie down, Cohen. I can keep watch for a couple hours," I assure him, promising to wake him if I see or hear anything. His exhaustion will render him useless if he doesn't get some sleep.

Of course he argues. Fortunately, I'm equally stubborn, convincing him to rest an hour.

I've scarcely settled myself against a log when his breathing slows.

The early sunrays pierce the blue-black shadows and the dew glistens, painting the landscape in vibrant green. Though we've been in Shaerdan a few days, this morning is the first time it truly seems as though I've stepped into a foreign world.

The land is quiet except for the birds. They sing perky soprano notes, intermittently broken with clucks and clicks, unlike the caws heard in the Evers. The trees here are different too. They're similar to the spruce trees in Malam, but these are thicker and grow closer together, like soldiers huddled before a fight. Moss dresses the bark where an ivy-like plant doesn't cling. Plumes of ferns make green clouds across the forest floor.

This land is bursting with life. A current of energy ebbs beneath the black soil and flows into every plant around me. I've never felt this way in the Evers, invigorated by the lush life. The sight reminds me of a time Papa pulled his daggers from their box. The morning light glinted against the sapphire on one handle, throwing a magnificent display of azure sparkles across the wall that captured my attention.

"Do you like this, Britta?" Papa asked.

I nodded, first awed, and then a touch sad because I'd never seen something so beautiful. I was always the girl looking and never having.

"This'll be yours one day," he said. If my chin hadn't been propped on my fist, my jaw would've dropped to the table. He saw my shock and added, "I don't tell you nice things very often, and that's my own fault. But I want you to know, in my eyes, you're more precious than these daggers."

Embarrassed, I lowered my eyes, savoring his words as he contin-
ued to explain how I would earn the dagger by completing training
with the boy who was coming to apprentice.

Now, as the dawn stretches across the tops of the trees, that same sense of awe hits me. I search for movement in the forest, wherein only birds flutter and prattle.

We are alone, so I allow myself one more quick chance to study Cohen, enjoying the view of his messy brown head. If I could erase the reason I'm here, if I could forget the time that's passed between us and how he broke my heart, this sunrise beside Cohen would be perfect.

The rush of air presses against my cheeks and tangles my hair as we ride hard through the plains, where tall grasses swish like river rapids. Crossing them puts us out in the open. Cohen urges Siron to go fast, fast, faster, until the wind washes over me with its whispers of freedom.

Just before we reach another stretch of forest, Cohen glances over his shoulder, takes in my outswept arms, and laughs. "What have you done all this time?"

The break in the silence catches me off-guard; even so, I know what he means before he adds, "While I was gone."

"You first. What have you done?" I ask in diversion, not wanting to explain I did nothing more than what we did together — hunt, train, read — only alone.

"Besides working my body into boulder shape?"

I snort and give him a hard shove in the ribs. "Boulders make great target practice."

"Warning noted." He chuckles. "I traveled. Spent a lot of time in the woods. Mostly I took job after job from the king." His casualness about the time he was away turns the light-heartedness I felt moments ago into something murkier. Makes my innards feel like they've been plucked. I spent those months thinking of him constantly.

"What types of jobs?"

"I hunted spies in court, army deserters. Anything they asked me to do. I've been busy."

I think of the bodies we saw and cringe. Papa hunted people for the king. I don't know why it doesn't sit well with me to think of Cohen doing the same.

"Is that why you never came back?" The question slips from my lips. Papa once told me I needed cheesecloth over my mouth to catch all the words that should stay in.

His spine goes taut in front of me. "Yeah. That's why."

An uncomfortable chill snakes through my gut. Did he forget I'd know when he's lying?

Before I can ask, he stops Siron. "I'm going to give him a break. I'll hop down and walk for a bit."

I start to swing my leg over to follow, but Cohen touches my ankle.

"Stay there. I'm quite a bit heavier than you. Without me, he'll be able to rest."

Unsure of what to do, I remain seated as Cohen walks ahead. I consider mentioning the lie, only then his comment about us all having secrets comes to mind.

I kept my secret for years, so perhaps this time he can keep his.

On the fourth day, we're forced to leave the river when it bends due south. It's taken us in a southwest direction, so we have to head northwest to correct our path. If anything, our indirect route will confuse the guards, leading them off course. Continuing on land, we're no longer able to hide our prints as effectively. Our trek slows in pace so we can wipe the evidence away.

North of the river, the forest thins into grassy hills spotted with firebush and thick cedars that make me think of giants squatting around a camp. They grow wide with stretched-out limbs that hang toward the ground. The sun blazes hotter here than the warmest summer afternoon in Malam. My skin reddens where the cap and tunic don't cover, and sweat drips down my face and into my eyes.

Water is scarce. By the end of the second day on our new course, Siron has hardly had a drop to drink. A horse his size could easily take in thirty gallons a day. I offer half of what's left of my water jug, hoping to take a small edge off the beast's thirst and leave a small amount for me, but Cohen says Siron will be fine—that his desert upbringing has made him more tolerant to dehydration. Tomorrow we'll cut a dead-west course in search of a stream.

Neither Cohen nor myself has been much for talking since our water has dwindled.

Eventually the quiet eats at me. "Did you like being away?" I ask.

His shoulders rise and fall, typical Cohen Mackay non-answer.

"A lot to see?"

He brushes away his footprint and nods.

"Shaerdan is different from Malam." I push, determined to break the wall surrounding his vocal chords. "Warmer and stickier in the woods. Hot as a blacksmith furnace here." My accompanying laugh comes out stilted and quickly fizzles.

After a beat, he surprises me by saying, "Wait till you see the ocean."

His eyes lift to mine as he tells of the first time he saw the great blue. He stood on a hill, overlooking one of the bays and watching the waves, like massive walls, crash on the shore. "I've never felt so insignificant," he says.

"Did you jump in?"

His mouth twists into a wry smile. "I waded in till the water was above my knees. The ocean pulled back and curled up in a terror of a wave. I ran for the shore as fast as I could."

I laugh at the image, amusement bubbling unbidden from my lips.

"You think that's humorous, do you?" His gaze sinks to my mouth, his shadow towering over me as we walk side by side. He leans closer, inclining his head, and every piece of me halts aside from my galloping heart. The most delightfully peculiar thought that he might kiss me runs through my mind. And I lift my chin —

His brow furrows and he pulls back sharply, putting three hands of space between us.

Crestfallen, I have to turn my head to hide the hopeful feeling that's capsized and is sinking to the depths of my stomach.

"You, scared of water?" I muse to mask my foolishness. "Yes, that's quite entertaining."

"In a couple days, you can find out for yourself what it's like." He goes on as though nothing awkward stands between us. "We'll see who's scared."

A shiver runs under my skin. Heaven help me, but I like the idea of going to the ocean with Cohen.

THAT NIGHT COHEN SITS DOWN ON THE BED-
roll where it's positioned parallel to
mine between the firebush. He stretches
out his left leg so it comes knuckles from my
knee. "I told you a little bit about where I went.
It's your turn. What have you done over the last
year?" His voice sounds scratched from having
close to nothing to drink.

I shrug.

"Hunting?" he asks.

I nod.

"Reading?"

Another head dip.

"Did you finish the book about the oceans?"

"You remember that? I don't recall talking to
you about that one." The corners of my mouth

lift, betraying my surprise. "I suppose you thought it odd Papa brought me so many books to read."

"Believe me, that's the last reason I would think you're odd." Cohen's lips curl into the smirk I know so well. "I'm glad he encouraged you. You were always beating me to a pulp, out-shooting, out-tracking, outdoing everything I did. The only time Saul praised my efforts was when you were off reading."

An exaggeration, but it makes me laugh and he smiles in return.

"What about friends? Or suitors? Has anyone been courting you?"

"Who are you, a market gossip?" My tone is light, even though his last question backs my belief that he was never interested in anything more than friendship.

His husky tenor laugh is as lovely as the Midsummer's Tide fiddlers. "Come on," he presses. "I'm just asking. I hoped you had made friends. Someone to keep you company so you were not alone."

Not alone. His words are tiny daggers that pierce my heart, making me ache.

"I worry about you all on your own." That deserves a glare.

"No need to worry about me."

His fingers still, abandoning the artwork they were doodling in the sandy dirt. "Didn't you like it when we went hunting together?"

He knows I did. My gaze drifts to the cedar, hulking beside us like a mammoth watchdog.

Cohen leans forward, inclining his head to the side until I look at him. "It's what I missed most."

"Then why'd you leave?" I ask, wondering if he'll avoid my question again. Needling him about this isn't my goal—I just wish for answers. His quick departure never made sense to me. Papa didn't tell me Cohen completed the apprenticeship until Cohen had been gone a week. Why didn't Cohen tell me himself? Why did he promise to visit the morning after I confessed feelings for him, and then not return? The only explanation is he was so horrified by my admission he couldn't face me again.

His gaze gives nothing away as the silence spreads between us. When I start to say something, he asks, "Do you remember what happened just before I left?"

My eyes land on the scar, a token from our last hunting trip together. His jaw ticks, the only sign he's uncomfortable. I don't remember everything, only bits and pieces. A cave. A mountain cat. Blood.

Too much blood.

Cohen fell through the ground into an underground cave. It was too deep to climb back out, so I searched for another entrance. My efforts were careless—not paying attention to my surroundings, I came face-to-face with a mountain cat. It attacked, and somehow Cohen was there. He threw himself in front of me, risking his life for mine to take on the animal. The bloody struggle knocked me down, and my head hit a rock. Which is why I don't remember most of what happened after. Everything I know was stitched together from Papa's comments.

"You saved my life," I say.

The jaw tick happens again. "That's why I left."

Truth. I hate that his words resonate with warmth and at the same time confuse the seeds out of me.

"What do you mean?"

His brow furrows and he shoves a hand in his hair. "I couldn't watch you suffer . . . not after what happened in the cave. It killed me to see you that way."

I pull my hands into my lap to fist the material of my bright green top. "So — so you left?"

"I should've said goodbye." His face openly displays raw regret that cuts through me. He moves closer, eliminating the space on the bedrolls between us. "I didn't because I wouldn't have been able to leave if I saw you again."

His words are picks and shovels, uprooting the hurt I buried long ago. I feel turned inside out by his confession. I want to wind back time and keep my feelings to myself. If I hadn't met him that night, perhaps he wouldn't have been reminded of my weakness. He would have stayed and apprenticed in Brentyn longer. And then maybe Papa would have lived.

"I'm sorry I didn't say goodbye." His fingers brush my cheek.

I scoot back and clutch my hands together.

Even after Papa told me Cohen was accepted as the king's new bounty hunter, I still believed he'd return to visit. For the first few months, I watched the road, analyzing every second we spent together, rethinking every interaction, every conversation. The unknown drove me mad. A year passed. When Cohen never returned, rejection and loss devastated me.

"It hurt a great deal when you didn't return," I admit. "But it hurts even more to hear you say you left because it was painful to watch me heal. Do not feel guilt over what happened. My foolish actions are the reason you have that scar." My fingers curl into fists as I force myself to be candid. "I never wanted you to leave because of me. Now that you're back, I don't know how to be the friends we used to be."

Cohen's mouth curves into a bleak smile. "That doesn't mean we cannot try."

The lack of water has made my mind sluggish. I consider crushing handfuls of cedar leaves and sucking the moisture from them. My throat is dry. My body aches. My head pounds when the bouts of dizziness break. I cannot imagine how Siron must feel. Mostly, I fear the lack of water will give Captain Omar an edge, and before we know it, he'll be on us.

From afar, the small town at the edge of the dry hills is no more than a brown smudge against the greener woodlands beyond. To me it's an oasis. Where there is a town, there must be a nearby water supply.

Yesterday Cohen managed to siphon some water from the roots of a cedar, but the tree was stingy and didn't provide much. So I don't argue the dangers of being spotted near the town because I know Siron needs the hydration.

The colorful dyed dresses and tunics worn by the towns-people clash against the brown wood construction. As we come down the hill toward the outer-lying homes, the people look like a scattering rainbow. It makes them easy to see. Easy to avoid.

A timber-framed, two-story cathedral marks the center of town. We skirt around the buildings, moving toward the edge of forest beyond the town.

I hear a woman singing, a string of strange discordant notes and foreign words. Cohen does as well and stops beside me, gesturing to drop back. I shake my head. The sound of her haunting melody intrigues me. One woman isn't a threat I couldn't handle. Before he can argue, I draw my bow and fol-low the voice through the woods, leaving him to trail behind.

A woman with long onyx-colored hair pulled into a messy braid sits on the edge of a rock-and-mortar well, singing as she pulls up a rope from the depths below. At the sight of a well, the dryness in my throat doubles at the promise of water. A dog, snow-colored and large as a donkey, sits beside the woman.

With the cap pulled over my hair and my bow at my side, I gesture for Cohen to wait at the edge of the clearing. The woman finishes lifting the bucket from the well before she notices me. I try to keep my eyes from ogling the bucket. "Good day, miss."

The dog lets out a small whine and then lays its head down. His mouth is foamy, which I didn't notice before. He's dying. Does the woman know this?

"You're not from around here, boy." Her voice is friendly, though a touch unhappy as she takes in my cap.

Even so, I worry she'll realize I'm from Malam and notify the town's guards.

"I'm passing through," I say, faking a Shaerdanian accent. Hopefully the dry rasp will assist the charade. "If it's all right, I could use a drink."

She touches the rope protectively. "It's a private well. I've no water to share."

My gaze flicks to where Cohen waits behind a tree. "Please. My friend and his horse haven't had much to drink in days."

The dog lets out a whining whimper, and the woman's face crumples as the animal struggles through labored pants.

"Shh, shh," the woman coos as she gently strokes his head and neck.

My sympathy goes out to her and her dog. There's nothing to be done for him but wait for death. I imagine little more than a trace remains in the animal's life. If anything, he needs to be put out of his misery. Perhaps I can do this service for the woman.

"Would you like—" I stop when the woman glances at my bow and presses her hand to her mouth to muffle a sob. Her anguish somehow marks me, slicing me to the core with surprising compassion.

"He was bitten by a snake and there's venom in his body. He's suffering, but I cannot end him. Not yet." She sniffs.

A venom-crazed dog attack would be bad. I should insist on putting him down. Only my brain's message doesn't reach my feet, and now I'm kneeling beside the dog, wishing to help.

"I'm sorry," I say, for lack of anything more, confused by my own reaction. In either her sadness or shock, she has allowed me to be near her animal.

A tear runs a straight path down the woman's face. "My husband died a year ago, my eldest boy six months later." Her hand lingers, making slow strokes from the dog's head to back. "He's watched over my family, kept us safe. He tends the herd and the chicken coop." She wipes her eyes. "He's just a dog. But to us, he's family."

I let my hands take the place of hers on the dog's head. If the animal's fear and pain were visible, I'm certain it would look like steam wafting off a boiling kettle.

"Even Beannach water didn't help," she says in a choked voice.

"Beannach water?"

"Blessed water."

Must be another Shaerdan custom. For snake venom, an antidote would've been a better choice. I don't tell her this, though.

Usually when an animal is on the edge of death, it's

because I brought it to that point, and so my blessing is one of peace and thanks. A strong, compelling urge to help the dog drives me to act, but I don't know what to do other than offer a similar blessing.

Moving from throat to trunk, my hands sweep in a soothing stroke. Beneath my palms, I sense the strangest bit of darkness, the snake's venom, slithering through the animal's veins. This is insane. And yet I know it's true. I know it'll soon spread through his vitals, a shadow stealing the last bits of light. With every second that passes, alarm rushes through me as he falls further victim to the poison.

My prayer starts like all the others I've muttered over the years, soothing, calming words, but I cannot bring myself to finish the same. The woman's sniffles escalate into full-blown wails. Her misery draws something different from me. They make me want to somehow fight against the venom. My shapeless words turn to a silent plea, asking the weakened life to remain. To be strong. To fight the toxin.

My palms make upward strokes from the dog's torso to his mouth.

Be strong.

The dog quakes and the darkness in his veins moves, leaving me amazed and frightened and baffled. I could be mad. Delusional. But the motion of my hands seems to be drawing the sickness up and out of his body. Numbness spreads from my trembling fingers to my elbows. Little beads of sweat break out across my brow. The well and the woman and the woods whirl around me. I tilt my head side to side to clear the echo in my ears and stop my vision from dimming when all I really want to do is lie down and sleep.

The injured dog is suddenly on his feet, shaking me off. He makes it half a dozen paces before his body racks itself, ribs pushing in and out as he vomits.

The foul stench snaps me out of the head fog. Staggering to my feet, I gag and then dry heave.

The woman appears at my side, sobbing and saying something that makes no sense because the fog returns. She is endless tears over a stream of unintelligible mumbling, and I'm terrified that I've killed her dog.

"I'm sorry, I'm sorry," I repeat as I stumble away, toes tripping over tree roots. Cohen's deep tenor echoes nearby, but it's overshadowed by the woman's chatter. Her words mesh together. I stumble forward. Blink against the splotches overtaking my vision. I am an hourglass, my energy seeping out fast, fast, faster.

I walk into a wall.

"Britta, stop!" The wall is Cohen.

I'm in his arms. Mine flop by my side while Cohen is speaking; only his words slip away before I can catch them.

Warm water trickles over my lips. Down my chin.

Cohen's face hides behind the splotches in my sight.

His grip bites into my arms. It jars me awake. "What's happened? You were at the well. I stepped back so the woman wouldn't see me. Then you're crashing through the trees." He sounds afraid, though Cohen is never afraid. "Where are you hurt?"

Hands start moving, touching.

"Dog . . . needed help," I force out.

This time when the blackness slips in, Cohen cannot keep me from it.

CHAPTER 15

"WAKE UP, DOVE." WARMTH BRUSHES MY ear. The rough curls of a beard graze my forehead before lips press against my temple. Ah, that's nice.

Though I wouldn't mind staying in the dark warmth a moment more, I open my eyes. Cohen is holding me, his face a sliver from mine. I'm limp, boneless. Beyond the haziness, a low animal whine sounds again and again. Disoriented, I slowly take in more of the scene — Cohen sitting on a rock, supporting me with one arm under my back and another under my knees; a whitish golden dog beside us, nudging my leg with his snout; a dark-haired woman a few paces off, waiting with a careful expression.

She's the woman from the well. And her dog. Tail-wagging, tongue-lolling, happy dog.

"You left so quickly." The woman shuffles closer, bucket in hand. "Forgive me for not giving you water when you asked before."

"She needs more than water. She needs rest." Cohen sounds different, strained and angry. I wish I could curl into him more, but my noodle body doesn't respond how I want.

"Aye. My home is close." She points beyond me. "But the Beannach water will strengthen her the most. It's the best way I can help. It will help make her whole again."

I can feel Cohen's reservation in his clenching grip. He must trust her to some extent because he takes the water from her, sniffs it, and then tastes some. After deciding it's good, he cups a handful for me.

Scoop after scoop, he encourages me to drink till my belly is full. My tongue tingles from the Beannach water. Better than what we've drunk out of the streams, each mouthful tastes like drops of honey have been added. The sweetness spreads through my heavy limbs, infusing them with light-ness and strength at the same time.

I glance at the eager blue eyes of the woman, brimming with concern. It makes sense that she's a Channeler. She pro-vides a bucket of her blessed water for Cohen before leaving and returning with two buckets for Siron, which she refills as soon as he empties them.

"The well is sacred to my family." Reverence touches her comment as she gathers the empty wooden buckets by their braided rope handles. "Whenever you're passing through, please drink from it."

Her head dips, thick black hair falling forward as she places a bronze-toned hand to her violet dress just over her heart. "My offer of gratitude. Go well with the spirit."

What do I say to that? I blink at her, mind wading through exhaustion to come up with a response. Cohen scuffs his foot against the ground. I turn my chin to find him staring at me with a strange, almost alarmed expression in his eyes.

"Er, you too." I attempt a small wave that ends up looking like a hand stutter.

Cohen's attention catapults to the woman as she walks away, confusion and curiosity betraying his usual gambler's face. If he's trying to figure out what transpired between the woman, the dog, and me, well, his guess is as good as mine.

A quiet, subdued Cohen saddles up behind me and encases my frame in his arms before clicking his tongue twice against his teeth—a command for Siron to leave. The water has renewed Siron, giving him vigor to run fast, taking us far from the town and the woman's well. We've traveled over a league when I realize the significance in the woman's comment. *"She needs more . . ."*

I twist in the seat to look at Cohen, wide-eyed. "The woman knows I'm a girl. She—what if she talks about us?"

His hands shift to rest loosely on my hips. "We'll be fine,

Britt." I expect worry, but his voice is cavalier and his expression unreadable. It's a reckless move to continue on a westward path. He must know that.

"We don't know her. We should change course." Siron's hoofs clip against the rock lining of a dried-up creek taking us west to Celize, where the land is greener. Over my shoulder, Cohen's face shows no hint of apprehension.

"She told me you helped with her dog." The tone of his voice rises as if he's asking a question. My head is too cloudy from the aftermath to figure out what happened. Perhaps Cohen is equally confused, which is why he's not pressing me for answers. His eyes are indecipherable, telling me nothing of his thoughts. I don't know how it was possible for me to draw poison out of the animal. Before I can explain to Cohen what happened, I need to be able to understand it myself.

"She believes she owes you a debt. She won't betray you to Shaerdan's soldiers or Omar." He breaks my concentration with his matter-of-fact tone, insisting worry about the woman is superfluous. I find myself relaxing. "Besides, Channelers don't speak of their magic to outsiders."

Seeds, I hope that's not the case with everyone. How will I figure out what happened?

Never in my life have I possessed the power to heal anything. Truth and lies are discernible to me, and I have an uncanny knack of knowing when animals are close to death. But healing a dog? Normal girls simply don't heal dogs. It's a mystery. An alarming, confusing mystery.

I wish I knew more about my mother. Papa rarely spoke of her. She grew up in Shaerdan. Was she also a Channeler? A healer? Could the same power run through my veins? And yet, if that were so, Papa would've told me. Wouldn't he?

Control yourself, thoughts and actions. Then you can combat the world. There's no comfort in Papa's words, not today when my mind is spinning and utterly out of control. The farther we travel, the more uncertainty plays tricks on my mind. And Cohen surely isn't saying anything.

The water helped restore some of my energy, but not enough to keep me awake against Siron's drumming tempo. My lids droop, my joints ache, and my head pounds. More fatiguing is the allure calling to my entire body at Cohen's nearness. My gritty eyes close and open, fighting to stay awake; it's all I can do not to meld into him when his large hand strays from my waist to my head, holding me to his sturdy frame. His breath dances against my cheek.

"Sleep, Britt. I've got you."

Distance, my head cries. But my body, a pushover to his warmth seeping into my back, battles me into silence. His spice and woodsy notes drift with me into the dark.

The scene at the well slowed us down. To make up for it, we travel all night and through the next day. Honeysuckle-and-amethyst rain clouds hover over the lingering blaze of sunset from a storm that passed through earlier.

Once the sun drops and the temperature dips, my flesh

bumps up like a chicken's. The tunic I've been wearing for days is too thin, and my weak muscles quiver against the chill in the air.

Cohen mutters a curse under his breath and tugs the reins north. "Padrin's not far off. It's a small forest village, away from the main road. We'll sleep there."

"Shouldn't we stay in the woods?" My jaw jitters. Though the idea of sleeping somewhere warm appeals to me, it would be reckless. It's easier to escape the guards if we steer clear of towns. I can tough it out. A little cold has never hurt me.

"You need a decent night's rest, maybe two." His arm flexes around my midsection.

When I object again, his chin dips closer to my ear, his voice insistent. "We've been in streams and backwoods for five days on a zigzag course to lose them. Padrin is so far from the main road, they'd never consider checking for us there." His proximity muddles my thoughts. Makes me think a night indoors doesn't sound half bad. "If anything, Britt, a day or two there will get them off our scent."

The planes of Cohen's torso down to the muscled ridge of his abdomen tense behind me. I cannot stop another shiver from seizing me. He makes a small noise as if my shudder is due to the cold and I've proven his point. "We're sleeping on a bed tonight."

If there weren't a road leading into Padrin, a traveler might miss the forest-camouflaged town. The shops and homes, the color of mud, sit wedged between thick, gnarled trees. An earthy tang of new rain mixed with lumber and ripe manure masks the air around a pig farm on the far west reach of town.

Bludger, it's terrible. At least the odor works to mask Cohen's inebriating scent. The man's been traveling for days. Weeks. How can he smell so good?

Cohen nudges Siron toward an inn that sits on the edge of the forest. "I know the owner—he's an informant of mine," he explains as we ride along the back to the stable. "He'll alert us to any trouble."

Cohen leaves to make arrangements for rooms while I wait in the stable with Siron, who, per usual, regards me with a casual glance and a snort, though he seems chipper to be out of the woods. Not much later, male voices echo from outside the stable just before Cohen enters with an older man who could be my father's age.

"I'm Kendrick." The man extends his callused hand to me in a handshake and then claps me on the back. "Put some more meat on your bones, lad. You're a mouse compared to Cohen."

I cough to cover my surprise and realize the cap still hides my hair. Even so, the word "lad" rankles. Outside the well, Cohen didn't seem to care that the woman knew I was a girl. If it was safe there, why wouldn't it be safe around his friend? Why didn't Cohen introduce *me* to his friend? I'm probably being ridiculous, but it feels a lot like the stinging rejection of my youth. Cohen was never ashamed to introduce me as his friend when we were younger. In fact, he often stood up for me. So what's changed?

My thoughts are apparently loud enough to garner a questioning stare from Cohen.

I push down my annoyance and give him a subtle headshake, letting him know it's nothing. Since it should be nothing.

"Have you any news?" Cohen asks.

Kendrick's eyes dart to me, and Cohen says something about me being trustworthy.

The man's questioning expression changes to acceptance. "The courier you asked about, Duff Baron, will be in town tomorrow's eve for the Merryluna Festival."

"You're certain?" Cohen's eyes brighten.

"Aye. His mother releases the moonflowers every year into the fountain at midnight. He always comes to watch."

"Looks like I'll be needing to stay two nights instead." The men chuckle while I piece together what's going on. Seems as though this Duff Baron person may know something about my father's murder and will be at the town's celebration. I was going to insist we only stay one night, but if he can answer questions about Papa, it'll be worth sticking around.

The conversation shifts to Cohen's brother, Finn. And a spark of pain shoots through Cohen's eyes.

"Finn's been called to fight in the war. He's stationed at

Alyze, just north of Fennit." Cohen's answer comes as a complete shock, since he hasn't mentioned Finn or his army assignment the entire time we've been together. It floods me with guilt. I've been so bent on finding out why Cohen left that I didn't think to even ask about his family.

"No matter what side he's on, the lad's too young for the war front." Sympathy pours from Kendrick.

He leads us back to the inn, where a young boy and girl come bolting through the door. They're a twisting windstorm of laughter and squeals.

"Mattie. Meg!" Kendrick fixes them with a stern gaze.

Both kids skid to a halt. The girl clamps a little dirt-stained hand over her mouth to stifle her laughter. The boy is less successful.

"Have you gathered the eggs?"

The boy's laughter fades. "Not yet, Papa."

Both children's faces turn repentant as Kendrick gives them a light scolding before sending them on their way.

"Nine and ten years old . . . think they have the run of the inn." Kendrick puffs out a breath of exasperation, but tenderness softens his expression. Reminded of the way Papa used to chastise me and Cohen, I feel a small lump catch in my throat as we follow him inside the inn.

Kendrick gestures to a cozy, torch-lit hallway beyond the kitchen area. "Get some rest. The boy looks like he could use it."

I frown and pad along the plank flooring, following Cohen

down the hall. His shoulders fill the entry as he turns the last door's knob and gestures for me to pass.

"Where are *you* staying?" I ask at the same time he says, "We're in here."

"We're?"

Cohen nudges me forward and closes the solid wood door behind him, sliding the lock in place, before speaking in low tones. "It would've looked odd if the lad traveling with me needed a room to himself."

All right, that makes sense. And yet he could've just told Kendrick I'm a girl.

I look pointedly at Cohen, who somehow seems three times larger in the weak light filtering between the linen curtains, before stepping around him to study the room.

One bed. One chair.

Thankfully Cohen remains behind me, so he cannot see how my eyes grow two sizes bigger. There's no need to feel self-conscious. After all, we've been sleeping by each other for the last week. Even so, my insides could be a gaggle of geese for all the chaos beneath my skin. It takes a moment to shutter my reaction away, then I turn back to face him and—*boil the bludger*—Cohen doesn't appear the least bit affected.

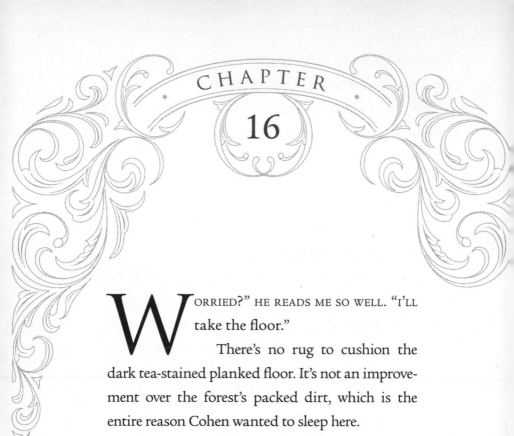

W ORRIED?" HE READS ME SO WELL. "I'LL take the floor."

There's no rug to cushion the dark tea-stained planked floor. It's not an improvement over the forest's packed dirt, which is the entire reason Cohen wanted to sleep here.

"You wanted a bed; you have it," I tell him.

He folds his arms and stares at me, throwing down an unspoken challenge.

I stare back. I once heard the phrase *He who talks first loses*. So when Cohen opens his mouth to speak, I throw a little victory celebration in my head until he says, "This isn't up for discussion."

Mule.

"Exactly," I retort. "My choice is the floor."

A line furrows between his brows. He waves a hand at the bed. "It's more comfortable."

"Which is why you should sleep there."

He grits his teeth. "You're always so stubborn. So pig-headed."

"Pigheaded? Me?" I hit him with an incredulous stare. He has little room to be talking. After all, we're at the inn despite my protests. His head jerks in a sharp nod, like adding kindling to a fire, and my temper flares.

"Britt, you would fight me on a request even if I were taking my last begging breath."

Bloody bludger. I throw my pack on the bed and spin to face him, hands in fists. "You think I wouldn't care that you were dying as long as I was getting my way?"

The fire and frustration in his eyes flicker and dim to something softer. My challenge hangs between us. Cohen's unfocused gaze carries over my head, and I wonder where his thoughts have taken him, though I don't dare break the silence. He just stands there, a one-man island between the door and bed.

"I shouldn't have said that," he says, subdued. "I've no doubt you'd care if I were dying." He coughs the grating from his throat. "Forgive me, Dove. I'm sorry."

His apology doesn't crack the wall I've erected between us; it obliterates it.

Emboldened by his sweet resignation, I glance at the bed that is barely large enough for two people. "We can share. It's only for a couple nights."

His eyes leap to mine.

I feign nonchalance, though I'm thinking and rethinking

and overthinking my offer. The area in the woods we shared was about the same size. It would be no different from sleeping outside, except for the roof above our heads and the soft mattress.

He looks at the bed, then me. His gaze turns molten. "If you're certain."

I look away. "If you make it an issue, then I'll take back the offer. Or if you snore, I'll push you onto the floor. There are enough bears in the woods—"

"You don't want another in your bed." He finishes, matching the cheek in my answer. But his playfulness makes me dizzy.

"Just don't snore," I say in a rasp. I turn away, hiding my face, and remove my weapons, placing them on the floor near the bed. Cohen does the same after he sharpens the blade of his sword and checks the arrows in his quiver. A bucket of warm water and a bar of soap later, I've washed myself clean while Cohen is gone from the room. When he returns, his skin is scrubbed free of dirt and his cheeks are tinged pink.

The moment we both stand on either side of the bed, my nerves come alive again like lightning bugs. I look to Cohen, hoping he'll make the first move. He doesn't so much as blink. Ignoring the commotion buzzing beneath my skin, I climb onto the mattress.

A second later, Cohen drops down beside me. His weight indents the mattress, causing me to roll against his body. His very warm body.

Sucking in a sharp breath, I scramble to the edge of the bed and turn to look at the plaster above us.

Cohen's soft chuckle echoes in the darkness. "You'd think I actually was a bear for how skittish you are tonight."

"It's your odor I was avoiding."

He turns his nose into himself and draws a deep breath. "I smell just right," he says, sounding incensed.

I can hardly stifle my laughter. I open my mouth to tease him more, but before another word is out, the brute covers me with his hulking form. "Admit I smell just fine, Britt."

"Get off me."

"Admit it, or you'll be smelling me all over you the entire night."

Honestly, he smells wonderful. Like fresh mountain air and masculinity and ... I squirm beneath him, hoping he won't notice how flushed I've suddenly become.

Cohen stills. His eyes lose their teasing tilt, darkening till they're brown as bark instead of hazel, as his attention follows an invisible path along the curves of my face until landing on my lips.

His jaw ticks.

"Night, Dove," is all he says before he abruptly pushes off of me and moves away, hugging the far side of the bed.

I lie there, breathless and confused. Was he about to kiss me? Impossible.

I want to smack myself. It's obvious he still sees me as nothing more than a friend or a sister, since he pulled away despite the eagerness painted all over me. I'm such a fool. A wanton, ridiculous fool.

We stick beside the inn until nightfall and then make our way to the market square at the center of town, where the Merryluna Festival is alive with music and dancing under strings of hung lanterns. Laughter is shared and smiles tossed around as we weave through the edge of the packed, cheerful crowd. Ale flows from barrels set on tables beside sweet cakes and breads. The nutty aroma of the fresh loaves reminds me of the time Papa tasked Cohen with a week of kitchen work as punishment for not having prepared his arrows properly before a hunt. Cohen had the last laugh when he baked two loaves of the best bread I've ever had — a skill forced on him by his mother. A smile runs free across my face. I turn to ask Cohen if he remembers, but in the crush, we've been separated.

The top of his brown hair bobs several paces away. I move toward him as the fiddles adopt a brighter, jauntier tune. The onlookers whoop in recognition. Women in full skirts flock to the open area beside a circular water fountain, where they spin circles around men dressed in their finest tunics and coats. Stepping close, then moving away, their dance is a mesmerizing kaleidoscope of color.

I never danced at Midsummer's Tide or Winter Feast; the taunts from others were too much of a deterrent. The few times I went, I left before the fiddles and citterns and drums played in full swing. Now I look around at the awe and glee on so many faces. The desire to be more like these happy strangers beats through me in time to the locals' dance steps.

"Do you want to dance?" Cohen's deep, clear voice catches me off-guard and I jump, giving him reason to release a full, throaty laugh. I turn away from the dancers, embarrassed by Cohen's teasing and, in the same breath, angry with him for making me feel that way.

There's a break in the gathered group where I can escape and wait till we talk to Duff Baron. I weave away from Cohen and out of the festival crowd, passing jugglers and children playing stick games and arm-wrestling men.

Once I'm beyond the throng of people, I stand in the shadows and watch the two women who have a bucket of fire displayed at their booth much like a keg of ale would sit on a tavern table. One woman is tall and lithe, the other short and button-nosed. Curiosity pulls me to step closer, but I remain hidden as a young girl sitting on the shoulders of her father approaches the booth.

The scarecrow of a woman holds her hand over the bucket's flame until a ball of fire leaps into her palm. It makes little movements of bobbing while the woman holds her arm still. Is the fire not burning her?

How does she do that?

I gasp. She's a Channeler. For a moment my muscles bunch in anticipation of the townspeople turning ugly accusations on the woman or red coats swarming over. Instead, the little girl and her father clap and laugh and cry for more. I've forgotten we're in Shaerdan — this woman's life isn't at risk. The woman holding the flame flips her hand over a jar and drops the walnut-size fireball inside. The flickering orb bounces against the glass as the jar is passed to the young observer and her father.

"Amazing," I murmur.

"Want one?"

My attention snaps away from the women. The dark lane Cohen has found me in shadows most of him, so I cannot make out much of his face other than the genuine smile on his lips. For a moment, my mind goes blank.

Then I remember his earlier question.

"No, I don't," I say, even though a jar of Channeler fire sounds like the most intriguing thing in the world.

"Why'd you leave? Weren't you enjoying the music?"

"I didn't enjoy you teasing me."

"What? When?"

My arms cross over my tunic. "When you asked me to dance."

A smile spreads cheek to cheek, his white teeth reflecting the festival lights. "You're upset because you thought I wasn't serious. What if I truly wanted to dance?"

Why is he pushing this? My cheeks grow hot. "Regardless, I wouldn't have danced with you because I'm dressed as a boy. And that surely would've drawn notice."

Cohen's eyes narrow in thought, and then without warning, his hand snakes out and steals my cap so my braid tumbles down my back. "Now you don't look like a boy. Will you dance with me now?"

I make a move to take back the cap, but his arms are too quick. He holds it behind his back and lifts his brows in silent question. As if he honestly wants to dance here in the street.

"You're ridiculous," I say, the *no* evident in my tone. He chuckles and steps closer until I'm completely swallowed by his shadow.

"No one will see us here." His arms spread invitingly.

My entire body tingles with wanting to step forward and drop my hand in his. We should be keeping watch for Duff Baron, not dancing in a back alley. Although Kendrick, the innkeeper, said Duff Baron and his wife don't come out until midnight.

"One dance, Dove," Cohen says. The cottony soft touch of his words bewitches me.

I cannot say no to that. My chin dips in a reluctant nod, and suddenly the fingers of his hand are curling around my hip, and I'm twirling under his arm. He pulls me to his chest and rocks me to the side. Though I've never danced with a partner, Cohen guides me effortlessly around the lane. When the tune changes, we spin to the quick saw of the fiddle until I'm breathless and bursting with joy.

When I peek up at him, Cohen is staring down at me. He pulls my hand into the crook of his elbow and walks to the side of the lane. "A man should always escort the lady back to her seat," he says.

A giggle nearly slips from my lips, which is so unlike me. "I didn't realize you were such a gentleman."

He grins wolfishly. "I don't have to be if that's what you want."

I cannot even think of a response to Cohen's teasing. But it does make me wonder how many other girls have fallen for his charms. Too many, I'm sure. For some reason, the thought is like a bucket of water on a flame.

"Thank you for the dance." My words lack warmth. I pull my cap from his pocket and put it on, shoving my hair underneath it. "Now that's out of the way, we can remember why we're here tonight."

Cohen's smile drops. He doesn't move for a moment as he looks at me, his expression morphing back into something callous and unreadable. Then he gives me a perfunctory nod and, without another word, walks to where the darkened lane meets the festival.

I watch him go, squeals and laughter filling the silence between us, and wonder how I can feel so crestfallen when the choice to end the fun was mine.

At midnight the music stops and the crowd's raucous gaiety dims to excited whispers and anticipation held on bated breath. The gathered people part, allowing an older woman to approach the fountain. The woman's salt-and-pepper hair is drawn into a neat bun. She pulls out a clutched fist of something from her pocket, and then soft *oohs* escape from the onlookers as she opens her fingers and flings a handful of seeds into the water.

The woman shuts her eyes like she's concentrating while faces around the fountain turn awestruck. But I cannot see what they're looking at. I lean from the shadows, stretching onto tiptoes.

Suddenly, emerald vines spring from the water, and twists of white spread into fully bloomed moonflowers. My mouth pops wide open. Another Channeler. The crowd erupts into applause.

Of the little I know about Shaerdan's magic, I remember hearing that Channelers influence elements of nature: flame, wind, water, and land. And, of course, spirit, which the clergyman mentioned. The two women handing out jars of light must be flame Channelers; the woman from the well could influence water. But this woman, I'm not quite sure. Is she also a water Channeler? Or land?

"There he is." Cohen points to a man who is probably ten years older than me, pulling my notice back to the reason we're here. Duff Baron. He's escorting the Channeler woman away from the fountain. There are too many people here. Any moment, Duff and his mother will be swallowed into the crush before we have a chance to talk to him. We cannot let that happen. Cohen agrees to cut through the throng of townspeople while I try circling the crowd.

In the shuffle, I lose sight of Cohen and Duff Baron. Chin

tucked, I stick to the edge of the square, where I'm nearly unnoticeable. When Cohen doesn't return right away, I assume he reached the man, and I wait for him. By the time Cohen comes back, a chunk of festivalgoers have left for the evening, though quite a few remain, dancing and drinking the night away.

"What did you find out?" I ask him while we walk back to the inn.

Cohen glances down at me. "He told me Enat has been in contact with someone from Malam."

"Who?"

"He didn't know. He was given a secret place to drop her letters. Two weeks later, he'd check again and a letter would be there, addressed to her in Celize. He never found out who she was writing to. Almost three months ago, the letters stopped."

Papa died almost three months ago. Surely that cannot be a coincidence. Was Papa the person she was writing to? Who was she to him? It's hard not to feel like a dog on an endless endeavor to catch his tail.

When we return to the inn, my mind is consumed with too many questions, so that the residual tension between Cohen and me is nearly forgotten. He must be in the same frame of mind because as soon as he hops into bed, he mutters, "Night, Britt," and is asleep in moments.

I'm not disappointed. The last thing I want to discuss is our dance at the Merryluna Festival.

But I also am unable to stop thinking of his flirtatious words and wondering what he would've done if I'd flirted back.

Completely cocooned in warmth, I find it nearly impossible to crack my lids open. The bed is more comfortable than anything I've ever slept on. I yawn and rub my eyes, and—

One of my arms is resting on Cohen's chest while our legs twine like vines. My face is smashed into his ribs. And when I lift my head, I find a coin-size spot of drool.

Oh no.

I hold my breath as I carefully untangle myself. Cohen wakes up regardless. He yawns and glances around until he finds me perched awkwardly on the side of the bed.

"Morning." He rubs his bleary eyes, which look darker than usual in the room's pale gray light.

"We should head out." My dry throat makes my words crack.

He stands on the opposite side of the bed and stretches his hands toward the ceiling. A peek of light golden skin shows between his top and his low-slung pants. By the gods, I have to stop staring. *Stop staring.*

I look out the window at the trees beyond the town while Cohen shuffles through the room.

After cleaning up and readying for the day's travel, we gather our weapons and head to the stables. The hour is still early, so neither Kendrick nor his wife is awake. But now that we've heard that Enat is most definitely in Celize, it's clear she's the only person who has answers about Papa's death. We need to find her as soon as we can.

The shuffle of hooves and a snort of air are audible through the stable doors. Siron is pitching a fit about something.

Cohen extends a hand to block my path. "Stay here," he says, and then slips through the door.

I listen for only a moment, and after hearing nothing more from Siron, I follow. Right as I walk in, my gaze lands on Tomas. The sight shocks me still. Until I notice Cohen, unconscious and head bloodied, slumped to the dirt in front of the bludger guard.

"Cohen!" I start for my dagger. Hands seize me from behind. My bow digs between my shoulder blades and my quiver crashes to the ground, spilling arrows across the hay and dirt floor. Frantic, I slam my heel back, nailing my attacker in the shin. I jerk my arms free, but he's quick to grasp them again, managing to seize my left wrist.

With only my right arm free, I throw an elbow back, hitting hard.

He groans. "Britta. Stop."

Leif.

"Stop," he says again, his cheek near mine.

I listen because struggling would do nothing more than deplete me of energy, something I'll need later to figure a way out of this.

The stable door creaks and Captain Omar enters; his eyes immediately seek mine and narrow to slits. He is wearing a brown and gold uniform, which is definitely not one from Malam. "Ready to return to the dungeon?" My muscles contract under his gaze. The daggered look in his eyes is the same expression he wore the night he whipped me.

We're so close to Celize. It's sickening knowing we're going to be taken back. I open my mouth to plead my case, and the captain backhands me. I hear the smack of his hand against my jaw and feel the jolt from the sting, before bitter blood fills my mouth. I cough and shake my head.

"I have enough cause to string you up." Menacing threat darkens his low tone. "The only thing keeping you alive is that Lord Jamis hasn't sent a death order. Give me a reason, and I'll disregard his oversight."

Truth — warmth and nausea mix in my gut. His silver eyes drill into mine, promising pain if provoked any further.

When we're outside the stable, Omar and Tomas drop Cohen to the ground like a sack of potatoes. Tomas kicks Cohen's ribs. I whimper, wanting desperately to stop them, to help Cohen. The sight of the dark blood around Cohen's hairline makes my eyes watery. I blink hard and search for a sign that Cohen is breathing. *Please be breathing.*

Finally, his chest rises and falls.

My relief is cut short, however, when Kendrick walks out of the inn and Omar nods to him. "My word is good. Your son will be spared." His accent holds the perfect Shaerdanian lilt. Omar is a lying, sneaky bludger. Kendrick must've turned us in because he thought Captain Omar and his men were from the Shaerdanian army. He thinks they'll save his boy from service. How wrong he is. Before I can say anything, Leif's hand clamps over my mouth.

"Shh," he whispers so only I can hear. "Don't make it worse right now."

When he releases my mouth, I nod, accepting he's right, that talking now will only get us killed faster.

"I couldn't let them take my son," Kendrick says to me. He is grief and guilt and relief all mixed in one. "Ten is too young to go to war. Tell Cohen I'm sorry. I had to do this." He casts one more glance at Cohen. "I couldn't lose my son."

The rage that filled me moments ago disappears. I cannot hate a man for wanting so badly to save his son that he was willing to trade us.

Leif escorts me toward a carriage that is marked with a brown and blue crest with a gold bird painted above it. The captain must've stolen this wagon from the Shaerdanian army when he swiped the uniforms. Clearly, I underestimated the lengths to which Captain Omar was willing to go in order to find us.

After putting Cohen in the carriage, Captain Omar manacles my wrists and shoves me in as well. One look at Cohen's unconscious body and remorse cuts through me. I should've never made that deal with Lord Jamis. If I hadn't tracked Cohen, he'd be free and clear now, and probably would know who the real killer is.

When the time comes, I'm going to right this wrong.

I'm going to do what it takes to free him.

Once we're moving, the carriage lurching along the rutted roads of Padrin, Captain Omar finally speaks. "I wasn't pleased you slipped through my guards' fingers. That's a mistake they won't make again." As always, there is an undercurrent of bitterness in his tone. He must be furious that I managed to best his men. "You weren't easy to find. It was luck more than anything. Leif remembered Cohen had a friend in this village."

His confession makes me think he wants me to know that Leif and Tomas paid for what happened the other day and I will too. I grit my teeth and focus on the wall of the carriage.

"Perhaps you understand now how far I will go to see that you and your Cohen are rightfully sentenced." The captain pulls out my dagger and twists the ivory handle in his leathered hands. "A nice blade. Good weight. Sharp. Showy." He touches the tip of the dagger to his finger. "I might keep this as a token."

He's goading me, and yet, despite knowing this, watching him fondle my father's weapon enrages me. In a measured tone, I manage, "When this is over, I'll have my dagger back."

"Your dagger? When you betrayed the king, you forfeited the few rights you had, including your property."

My spine could be forged with iron for how straight I sit. Everything inside me rallies to act on my anger, but I need to be smart if I'm going to escape. It's clear the man has a firm sense of what he believes to be justice. My back itches at the memory.

"I would never side with a murderer," I say, hoping to draw on that sense of justice now.

The dagger is in midtoss. Omar catches the handle and pauses.

"I could've led you off course," I go on. "There were tracks I could've overlooked. If my goal was to run off with Cohen, I would've escaped the first night you left me unshackled."

His eyes narrow to slivers, barely containing the man's loathing.

"But I didn't. I led you to Cohen because I believed he was guilty. You must see that. I only went with him because I found out he didn't kill my father."

"You say he's not guilty. Yet you're running away from Brentyn."

"We weren't running away—we were running *to* some-where," I say lamely, not wanting to divulge our secrets. Again, he gives me a look of disbelief. I have to offer something because our only option is to gain the captain's trust. "We were headed to the place my father was killed to find the real murderer. Or, at the very least, clues."

"Celize," he says.

"Yes. And I wouldn't have told you if I were trying to hide a murderer," I add, hammering on the fact of Cohen's innocence.

Captain Omar watches me, his scrutiny fierce and unwavering, like a predator's. Though his expression seems void of the usual dislike, his thoughts are a mystery. A scant seed of hope starts inside; it's an indigo drop of dye tinting a vat of boiling water.

The carriage jerks, jostling us and breaking the man's attention. "Don't speak again unless you want me to gag you."

When night falls, the carriage rolls into the small village Cohen and I avoided before we stopped at the well. Having woken earlier, Cohen has said very little. He didn't so much as grunt when Tomas punched him for moving too slowly back to the carriage after we'd stopped for a privy break.

When he meets my gaze, his dark eyes are heavy with disappointment. No word has been spoken about Kendrick, but Cohen is shrewd and has likely worked out his friend's betrayal. I offer a thin smile in return.

The captain finds an empty inn. When he enters with

Cohen and me in tow, he plays the part of a Shaerdanian soldier as he orders the keeper to give us his largest room.

Tomas manacles me to the bed while Omar and Leif tie Cohen to a chair at his ankles and wrists. Considering the injuries to his head, his night is sure to be hellish.

Later Tomas unties one of my hands and places a meager meal of bread and broth in my lap, while Cohen isn't given anything.

"Eat it," Tomas says.

The rounded loaf would usually set my mouth watering, but it has no appeal. It doesn't sit well with me to eat in front of Cohen.

Cohen must sense my dilemma. "Britta, eat."

Reluctantly, I take a bite of the bread. It coats my tongue like ashes. I chew. Swallow. Think about how to get free.

"You'll listen to the murderer but not me?" Tomas sneers.

I should ignore him, but I cannot let the comment go.

"He is no more a murderer than you are a gentleman."

The back of his hand whips my cheek, snapping my head to the side. I've been hit in the same spot so many times that the skin below my eye socket smarts as if stung by a hundred bees.

Cohen lurches in his chair. "Don't—"

"Shut yer mouth." Tomas points his knife at Cohen. "I'll kill you now."

My eyes meet Cohen's, pleading silently for him to say no more.

Tomas squats in front of me and grabs my chin, pinching the skin between his dirty fingers. "Now you'll talk to me, eh? You liked to think you were above me. The whole time we were traveling together, you didn't have nothing to say to me." His spit flicks my cheek as his hot breath cascades over my face.

My stomach roils. Over the guard's shoulder, Cohen's lips form a thin line and his eyes flash murderously, his once-unreadable expression now a promise of pain for the vile guard.

"You're an ugly thing." Tomas laughs to himself and taps my nose. He angles his body so Cohen no longer has a clear view. I squirm in an effort to gain precious space. "Too much freedom has given you ideas. I should teach you a lesson."

I shudder to think what his *lesson* entails.

His hand travels away from my face and down my arm to my thigh. He squeezes my leg, sending a new slithering alarm through my body. Anxiety presses against my chest, a winter storm encroaching on a cottage, slipping icy fingers through every weak crack. His grip clutches tighter to the point of bruising, and I cannot stop myself from trembling. I hate myself for showing weakness. It's a fight to keep my face a stone mask, hiding the way I want to gag and retch as he touches me.

The door opens. I nearly sigh aloud, never having been so relieved to see Captain Omar.

"What's going on in here?" the captain demands.

Tomas stands up and steps away. "The snit was trying to convince me to let her go."

The captain regards the scene. "I'll take the first watch. You'll have the third."

Tomas leaves the room. The captain tightens my restraints after binding my free hand, takes a seat in the corner, and then orders Cohen and me to sleep.

I've too many aches to doze off, and the night trudges by until sometime during the wee hours, after Leif has replaced Omar, I finally fall asleep. It seems like only a wink later when Leif is waking me, holding two bowls of porridge.

I'm glad he brought something for Cohen. Leif places a bowl in Cohen's lap and unties his right hand. Then he comes to my side, unbinds one wrist, and helps me sit up. He catches my eye, and his face twists into an apologetic grimace.

When we traveled together, I thought he was the bright spot in a dark situation. I thought we were almost friends. Perhaps he felt the same.

"Do you believe me?" I whisper, needing to know if he still thinks I've sided with a murderer.

He nods almost imperceptibly, but I see it. Maybe Leif could help us —

"Leif, come ready the horses," Omar barks from the doorway, crushing my hopes.

Leif pushes the bowl of food closer and leaves the room on the captain's heels. Tomas saunters in, a new bruise shining on the underside of his cheek. A punishment from Captain Omar? If so, it's deserved.

"Noticed that, did you?" His mouth twists into an ugly grimace.

The toe of his boot connects with my leg, just below my knee, and I yelp, surprised. My leg stings, but it's not too bad. It's muted by the sight of Cohen, who's behind Tomas, trapped in his seat, a vein bulging from his neck.

"You're lucky you made a friend of Leif." Tomas moves behind me and jerks the restraint on my left wrist, since it's still bound. The metal cuts into my flesh, breaking old scabs. I bite back a cry. A dagger to the kidney, arrow to the vitals, Siron's kick to his head, my hands around his neck — my mind recites all the ways I'd like to see Tomas perish.

"If he weren't around, I'd have a little more fun with you," the guard says. "For now, I'll just have to enjoy leaving marks he'll never see."

I tense, the image of last night when his hand was on my leg sticking in my thoughts. Tomas steps in front of me, crowding me so his mildew odor wafts around me. He traces my jaw with rough fingers. "And you're not going to say anything because at any time I can and will exact punishment on your friend here. I have to take him to Malam, but it doesn't mean I cannot torture him first."

No.

"Now get up. It's my turn to escort you to the privy," he says with a sickening smile.

Dread seeps into my muscles.

Tomas leans in to unchain the restraints from the bedpost, and panic pipes through me at his proximity. And then realization dawns — his nearness also compromises him, and my right hand is still free from breakfast.

I try to capture Cohen's attention to send a message, only Tomas blocks my view of him. This may be our only opportunity to fight back. If we can bring Tomas to heel before the other men return, we'll have a chance of getting away.

My free hand balls into a fist and, just before Tomas pulls back, I punch him in the nose. Only there isn't enough force to drop the guard.

"Scrant!" Tomas's eyes turn wild as he snakes a handful of my hair and yanks back. "You'll be sorry for that."

I might be sorry for a lot of things, but punching Tomas will never be one of them.

The keys clatter to the floor while Tomas grabs for his dagger. One-handed, I fumble for anything to use as a weapon, and seize the bowl of porridge. He raises the dagger just as I slam the hot breakfast into his face.

A crack sounds.

He roars and releases my hair as the dish clatters to the floor. Blood runs like a waterfall from his nose. There's only so far I can move while still manacled to the bed; scurrying back doesn't get me far enough away. He lands a furious punch to my temple and, I swear to the gods, my eyeball might pop out.

"Britta!" Cohen yells.

I shake my head to clear the pain. *Focus.*

Tomas lunges for me, but I manage to roll away from him, twisting my restrained arm almost to the point of breaking. I pull my knees into my body and then thrust both feet at his chest, hitting him squarely.

The impact causes Tomas to stumble back, trip over Cohen, and fall to the floor.

Cohen tips himself and the chair over like a felled tree, landing on Tomas's torso. The breath whooshes out of the guard. His unconsciousness is sealed when Cohen slams the butt of his elbow against the side of Tomas's head.

My grin stretches across my face like an addled person's. Cohen and I each have only one arm free; yet, we downed one of the king's guards.

"Where did the keys fall?"

"Underneath the bed." Cohen twists against his bindings.

I turn until the edge of the key ring is visible, only it lies out of reach. Right then the locking mechanism in the door clicks.

No! I jolt up. Cohen's eyes meet mine. As soon as Captain Omar enters the room, our lives will be forfeit. We were so close. *So close.*

The door opens.

The captain doesn't walk in.

The woman from the well does.

CHAPTER 18

I WONDER IF TOMAS'S PUNCH BRUISED MORE THAN my face. Surely, I'm not seeing things right. But after a good eye rub, she's still there— with ebony hair pulled to the side in a braid that snakes over her right shoulder, it's definitely the woman from the well.

"I heard about your arrest and came to help," she explains as she rushes to Cohen's side and loosens his bindings.

The truth in her words amazes me. Gratefulness wells up inside, putting a lump in my throat. "Someone told you we were arrested, and you didn't run in the other direction?"

She smiles like I've said something comical.

"Who helps two criminals? We could be murderers for all you know."

The woman unlocks my manacles. "Not you. Your heart is too good."

"How'd you find us?" Cohen asks as he finishes freeing his legs.

"This inn belongs to a friend."

How trustworthy is that friend?

"Promise, you're safe for now," the woman assures me as if reading my mind.

"The guards, they're not from Shaerdan," I say, realizing the additional danger she's put herself in.

She nods. "Aye. Noticed that. The big one doesn't hide his Malam accent well."

True. Leif's faked brogue sounds more like a lamb's bleat and bellow than Shaerdanian.

She steps around Tomas and extends a hand to help me to my feet. "Besides, you needed my help. Doesn't matter where the guards are from."

Not wanting to question her motives any further, I ask her if she passed Leif and the captain on her way in. Even though Tomas has been knocked out, the captain will never allow us to stroll out of here.

She pulls a flask from her skirt. "Sleeping draught."

I stare at her slack-jawed and, at the same time, mesmerized by her cunning as she explains how she snuck a few drops into Leif's and the captain's morning drinks. According to her, both men will sleep for eight hours.

Cohen steps beside me and points a thumb to his chest. "Cohen. This is Britta. We're glad for your help."

"Jacinda." Her blue eyes twinkle. "Happy to be of service."

"You feeling all right?" Cohen asks. I think he's talking to her, only to jump when his fingers feather across my jaw and up to the bruised area on my face.

My lashes lower. "Probably not as bad as I look." After a day's travel and having the crow beat out of me, I'm probably no sight to behold.

"When we get some distance, I'll make a poultice for the swelling," he promises.

My palm moves to the curve of my cheek, where his hand was moments ago.

"I found your horse in the woods. Must've followed the guards. Smart animal. Never seen such a loyal southland horse before," Jacinda tells Cohen, seeming impressed. "He's in the stable now, having a drink."

It's not the least bit surprising that Siron followed his master. If that horse were from Shaerdan, I'd think he had Channeler abilities.

Cohen takes her hand and inclines his head. "I'm in your debt. Thank you for watching out for him," he says, relief coloring his voice, before crossing the room to pick up the manacles. He shoves them on Tomas's wrists and jerks twice to test that they're secure. "I'll go check Omar and Leif. Then we can figure out an escape that won't alert neighbors. Don't want anyone pointing the guards in our direction."

Jacinda goes to drop the key on the bed, but Cohen stops her. "We can find a resting place that'll be a bit more difficult to find. Wouldn't want to make it too easy for them." His mouth tilts in a half smile.

With an expression that mirrors his, Jacinda tosses the iron ring to me. "Sly friend you have there, Britta. I like him. And I certainly don't mind putting a little hurt to those Malam guards. Last night, Lockdell, the village southeast of here, was raided by soldiers from your army. Buildings were burned down. It's chaos in the town square here with all the surviving kinsmen gathering."

"Malam attacked an entire town?" Astonishment raises my voice a notch.

"Aye," Jacinda says gravely. "Not the entire army, but some of your men did."

My eyes dart to Cohen, taking in his flat expression. "What does this mean? Is this the official beginning of the war? Has King Aodren declared it so?"

"Might only be a skirmish," Jacinda says. "I've heard no word of a formal declaration. Still, you shouldn't tarry long in Shaerdan. Judge Auberdeen assigned armies from the coast to meet at the war front. Don't know how long it'll take the kinships to assemble, but as soon as they reach the border, you won't be getting into Malam."

"We'll be returning to Malam soon," Cohen says in a

definite way that causes me to think he has plans other than what we've discussed.

"Anything else you need?" Jacinda's hand squeezes mine.

I'm startled by the gesture, and my arm locks at the elbow. But I don't yank away like I might've done with anyone else. "You've done more than enough. More than anyone else would've ever done."

A genuine earnestness fills her face, dark brows arching over her bright eyes. "After what you did for me, I couldn't look the other way when you were in need."

What I did for her? I still don't understand it. This may be my only chance to ask what happened with the dog. "I could tell he was close to death. And I know I helped him . . . but how?"

"You—you don't know?" Her disbelief sets me on edge.

I step back and cross my arms, torn with wanting to ask Jacinda questions and wanting to leave well enough alone because I'm afraid to know the truth.

She covers the space that I just took, studying my face as she crowds me. "You're not from around here." It sounds like a question, but it's not. And somehow, from an answer I've not given, she appears as if she understands something more than before. "Don't know much about you, Britta, but what you can do is a gift."

My focus drops to my scuffed boots to contain the clash of apprehension and interest jangling through me. "Like—like your gift with the water?" I make myself ask. My heart is a firefly trapped and fighting to get free from the jar of my rib cage.

"Not quite—"

Her answer is cut off by the creak of the door. Cohen looks at both of us and then cocks his head. "You're certain the sleeping concoction will last eight hours?" Oblivious to our conversation, he approaches Tomas's side and nudges the guard with the toe of his boot.

"Aye. Perhaps ten if you're lucky," Jacinda tells him.

"Then we'll plan on riding hard for the next eight hours. Doubt they'll be any friendlier when they wake. Do you have anything left for him? Sleeping draught? Or death serum?"

A smile flashes across Jacinda's face. "Forgot the death serum at home," she says as she pulls a small vial from a pouch at her waist and kneels beside Tomas. "But I've got enough draught."

Cohen huffs out a disappointed sigh. "That's too bad. Thank you once more, Jacinda."

I jab him with my finger. "You don't want to be acquitted for one murder only to be charged with another."

He leads me to the door and throws a glance back at Tomas. "If it were his, I might not mind."

I try to give him a chastising look, but it's broken when I snort a laugh.

Cohen is walking down the hall when Jacinda calls me back into the room. "What you asked about . . . You should be prepared: with a gift like yours, there will be people who won't understand. Won't welcome it. Be careful. Even here in Shaer-dan."

In the little she's said, there's much to be heard.

I cross the room and squeeze her hand. "Thank you for everything."

We claim our weapons from the captain's carriage, where they've been locked away. After slipping my dagger into my boot, I toss the keys into a nearby pile of hay and start to untie the guards' horses while Cohen readies Siron.

"No, leave them," Cohen says.

"If we leave them, it'll only help the guards get to us faster."

The joking side of him gone, he looks haggard from days of not shaving now complemented with purple bruising. "True. But we have to think ahead. Once we find out who killed your father, we'll need the guards to believe us. Not charge us with another crime. Sometimes it's hard to look past a grudge to see the truth. Captain Omar will be spittin' fire when he wakes from the draught and realizes we escaped a second time. Hell, the man will be wanting blood. If we add theft to the charges, Omar will make certain we're both hanged."

"Except they're not really his horses. He stole them and their uniforms. He's more a thief than I am."

Cohen rests a hand on one of the stolen mares, rubbing along the animal's neck. "I doubt he'll see it like that."

True enough.

"Besides," he says, "the guards don't know where we're

headed. These horses are better suited for the carriage. Not a chase. They're no match for Siron's southland pedigree."

That's true as well—Siron is a far stronger and faster horse; however, Cohen doesn't know of the conversation I had with Captain Omar. I chew my lip. Study the pile of hay. "They don't need to track us. Captain Omar knows we're headed to Celize."

Cohen's hand slips from the horse. "What? How?"

"I was trying to reason with him," I explain. "You were unconscious, and I thought they might kill you. I was doing what I could to plead our case, hoping he'd understand, perhaps let us go. Or at the very least, let us live."

His jaw pulses under the wild twining of his short brown beard.

I lift my chin. "I did what I thought was best. Captain Omar is a man of reason. He's bound and determined to see justice served. That's why I explained we were looking for the murderer. It wouldn't make sense for us to go to Celize if you were really a murderer on the run."

Eyes on the stable's rafters, Cohen stretches his neck side to side, and lets out a slow exhale. "I understand your rationale, though not sure I agree with you about Omar. He's delivered plenty of cruelties, regardless of justice."

He reaches out and grasps my wrist. My focus immediately shifts from his face to his hand as his thumb slides over my skin, tracing the raw marks left by the manacles. "This, for example," he murmurs. "He could've kept you restrained without causing injury. He let you sleep in them when they were too tight."

There's not enough air in the stable. My entire body is attuned to the connection where his fingers linger, shooting my veins with liquid fire.

I shrug out of his hold and push my foot back. Then another. "It's nothing. Certainly not the worst the captain's given me." This is said to change the subject.

But then Cohen is in my space, hands seizing my upper arms. "What do you mean?"

The alarm and worry he usually keeps hidden from his tone are bold and bright as Shaerdan's clothing. It traps me in place. His eyes scan my body from head to toe. The attentiveness unsettles, like he can see through me and into me, and everything I don't want him to see.

"Tell me," he urges.

"It's nothing." Scant more than a whisper. "I was a prisoner for a week. Broke a rule. So the captain punished me."

"How?"

Shame at how I was tied up and whipped fills me. I struggle to move away from him, but his fingers hold tight, pressing into my skin. "How, Britt? Tell me, please."

He won't let this go. It's too difficult to look him in the eye and explain how foolish I was to run off after Tomas shot the fawn. Instead, my sight sticks to the knuckles of distance between his toe and mine as I recount the entire awful story. When I reach the end, explaining how the captain gave me only five lashes, Cohen's grip is nearly bruising my arms.

"You're cutting off my circulation," I jest, and pull away from him.

"I—I'm sorry." He blinks. A dark cloud of fury and remorse shifts over his earthy eyes. "I didn't mean to hurt you. Are you all right?"

"I wasn't being serious. Don't start treating me like a weak girl now."

Cohen steps around me and is lifting the back of my tunic before I realize what's happening. I leap forward and cross my arms tightly against my waist to pin the material down. "Are you trying to undress me?" My pitch squeaks up.

He doesn't even seem chagrined. Same old straight-faced Cohen. "May I see?"

I hesitate, fingers kneading the clenched material.

"To make sure it's healed and see that you don't need anything for it."

Perhaps that would be all right. It's not as if I can see behind me. Holding my hands tight to my ribs to keep the tunic in place, I turn around, remaining a statue as Cohen takes his torturous time peeling the material up.

"Dove," he says as though the nickname breaks him. His ragged exhale hits my bare back, enticing a shiver to dance through me a moment before his fingers connect with my skin and make mincemeat of my thoughts.

His hands tremble behind me. "I'll kill the bludger."

The sentiment does flipping acrobatics through my core until he abruptly drops my top.

"It's healing fine," he says with a slight rasp while staring at a spot above my head when I turn to face him.

He speaks the truth; I feel it. Though Cohen cannot even look at me. Is my back that repulsive? His reaction increases my shame tenfold. He must think me a fool to have earned the lashing.

Chin up, I take a big step back and, forcing indifference into my voice, I say, "No need to kill the captain. It's in the past. We should get going and make use of the next eight hours."

Since Captain Omar knows where we're headed, it would be pointless to travel through woods that will slow us down. Our only option is to ride hard and fast to reach Celize.

Siron's energy is high. His power thunders beneath his midnight coat. Hooves pound against the dirt road as trees fly past. I revel in the rush of the wind, knowing that when we stop, the freedom of this moment will be over. Hopefully when we reach Celize, the man Cohen calls Delmar will know where to find Enat. With only eight hours' lead, there's not much time to locate her.

Near dusk, we pass the road that leads to Padrin. Sitting behind Cohen gives me a clear view of the muscles clenching around his neck and jaw. I can only imagine he's thinking of Kendrick's betrayal. Having intimate knowledge of the hurt from losing a friend, I give him time with his thoughts while I focus on the shades of autumn that bleed across the horizon.

But when tension spreads down his shoulders and to his hands, which grip Siron's mane like a lifeline, I take a deep breath and pull my gaze from the sky. My arms wrap around Cohen's back, and, for the first time in fifteen months, I hug my friend.

THE OCEAN IS A ROLLING FIELD OF THE BLUEST crop I've ever seen, filling our view two days after escaping the guards. The sea touches the horizon, swaying and moving like a living, breathing being beneath a lid of white clouds and sunshine. It's possibly the most beautiful thing in this world.

Cohen slips off Siron at the edge of the mammoth trees and motions for me to stay behind as he darts into the open farmlands that spread out before Celize. Leaving Siron, I follow Cohen, regardless. He needs a lookout. The first farmhouse has three rows of clothes strung up in the yard. How many men live here? A half dozen? Hopefully they won't miss a few items.

While monitoring the area for any movement in or around the home, I gesture at a billowing linen seaman's frock, wide enough to fit Cohen. He frowns at the suggestion but snags it quickly, along with a pair of breeches and a jerkin. He grabs similar clothes for me while I keep watch until we're back in the safety of the woods.

The short navy breeches and linen shirt, combined with a blue bandanna to cover my hair, turn me into the perfect shipmate to Cohen's sailor attire. When he steps into full view, jerkin fastened to his taut body and sleeves puffing around his arms, I cannot hold my laughter—it bursts from me like water slipping past a dam, swift and free and explosive. Cohen's eyes lighten, and one side of his mouth tips up as he's carried along in the wave. It only lasts a moment until he straightens his face and makes an incensed sound.

"Stop yer laughing," he says, sounding gruff and serious in perfect Shaerdanian. "I'm warning you, mate, I'll send ye between the devil and the deep."

His ship talk surprises another roll of laughter from me. I salute him as though he were my captain, saying, "Aye, aye, sir," and a full smile cracks his lips.

Together we snort and carry on like we're kids once again, escaping Papa's chores instead of running from the king's guard.

It's a release we both need before heading into Celize.

Great white birds with bright orange beaks swoop on the salty wind, where, beyond them, white-painted clay buildings climb the cliff that faces the ocean. Their orange rooftops and brightly painted shutters remind me of the strange birds.

After we leave Siron, we make our way down a narrow road that winds between buildings. Garments hung from clotheslines flap above us like seagulls, snapping in the wind that beats against the cliffs.

Delmar, another of Cohen's informants, owns a blacksmith shop sandwiched between a stable and other merchant buildings. Stepping out of the quiet street, we enter Delmar's shop. Heat from the forge licks at our faces, bringing with it the smell of steel and sweat. Near the source of the blaze, Delmar, a giant of a man, dripping from the heat, pounds a mallet against something I cannot see. His arms, thick chunks of muscle darkened with a crop of black hair, work to bring the mallet down in consistent timing.

"He doesn't like newcomers," Cohen cautions over the *clang, clang*. His hand briefly touches my arm, a staying gesture, before he moves deeper into the shop. I find a place to rest by the door when Cohen and Delmar step out of view. Though surely they cannot have been gone long, it feels like hours. After a while, the heat plays tricks on me, turning my mouth dry. My tongue swells and I need a drink, but my waterskin is with Siron.

I don't see the harm in escaping for a moment. A little cool air would do me some good. I crack open the door and glance along the road. It's clear, so I slip outside into the ocean breeze. And oh, it's so refreshing. It's tempting to stay there, but the alley next to the stable is a safer choice.

On my way there, I nearly overlook the smithy's neighbor

—a small shop with a sign that looks a day away from falling apart. Something about the dappled peeling green and blue paint hooks my attention. The twisting curved symbols are familiar. My sight narrows. I've seen those overlapping circles before.

Yes, on my dagger.

I pull the blade from my boot and hold the ivory handle up to examine it against the sign. The intricate carvings on my blade match the faded shop sign. What does this mean? Did Papa purchase the blades here in Celize?

I push through the unlocked door.

An older woman with parchment skin and watery eyes glances up from where she's sitting at a table covered in bottles of liquids and tied bunches of herbs. The space around her, crowded with shelves of books and jars of dead things, is infused with the cloying scent of sandalwood and roses.

The old woman squints at me and then at the dagger clenched in my hand. "Something you need?"

"I, uh . . ." My grip, which had closed to cover the carvings, loosens around the handle. "The marks on your sign," I say while keeping my chin down. "What do they mean?"

She doesn't seem ruffled by my sudden appearance in her shop with a dagger in hand. Chagrined at my odd entrance, I quickly slip the blade into my boot and mutter an apology. She points at a chair.

"Oh, no. I cannot stay. I only wanted to know about the

sign." I consider telling her that it matches the etched shapes on my blade, but push the information away.

"Most people who walk through my door are drawn here," she says, and I almost expect her to glance at my ankle where the blade presses against my skin. "Sit. I won't take much of your time."

I take in the skin sagging under her chin and her rounded dress. She seems harmless, so I relax, allowing myself a moment longer. "What sort of shop is this?" My question is light and carries a lilt to hide my Malam accent.

"It's not a shop. It's an Elementiary." The herbs in her hands drop to the table. She dusts her fingers off and then makes a sweeping gesture. "An Elementiary is like a school. Girls come here when they show signs of having the Channeler gift. I offer them guidance and tools. Most feel drawn to others like themselves. That's why you've come, yes?"

Her words pluck specific thoughts from my mind like meadow flowers pulled into a bouquet. The well, the festival fire women, the moonflowers. All of them come together at once, begging questions in an unsettling way.

When I don't speak, she takes a handkerchief from her pocket. The small square is stitched with the same design on the shop sign and my blade's handle. "See the overlapping rings, each different. They represent the four energies that govern our world. Wind and water. Land and flame."

"Channeler energy," I say, mostly to myself in puzzlement.

Why would Papa's daggers have Channeler symbols on them? Did my mother give them to him? Is this proof she was a Channeler?

Her spotted skin stretches over her hand as she reaches for a sprig of rosemary and binds it to a vine the color of eggplant. "Aye. Would you like to learn more about them?"

Yes. Yes, I would. I have so many unanswered questions.

Knowing time is short, I quickly walk between wooden crates, looking over jars of peculiar things. Claws of a bird float in pinkish liquid. A tapestry hangs in the back of the shop, above stacks of books. It's woven with the same Channeler symbols on my dagger, except placed differently. Each symbol rims the edge of a circle like a compass, and in the center is a fifth symbol, the stitching still a shock of blue, considering how old the tapestry appears.

"It was passed down from my grandmother's mother."

I spin around to find the woman resting against a cane. She points at the symbol in the center. "That's the sign of ether. The fifth energy."

"Ether?"

"Spirit."

My mind suddenly latches on to the clergyman's words. "Is ether what Spiriters control?"

She nods. "Channelers *influence* energy. They connect with it differently than others do. For example, a land Channeler could encourage plants to grow faster, stronger."

Like the moonflowers at the Merryluna Festival. So would a Spiriter be able to influence a person's spirit?

"Why haven't I heard about the fifth power? Is influencing spirit, or *ether,* black magic?" I repeat the clergy's words.

"That was two questions." She winks and taps me with her cane. "I'll answer both and then you'll do the same for me. Yes?" She must sense my leeriness, because she smiles, adding, "Harmless questions."

This old lady is crafty. But I want her to answer mine, so grudgingly I agree.

"People don't talk of the fifth gift because it's rare. Ether was the first of all creation, and all natural powers stemmed from it. It's the spark of all life." Although she has one hand holding her hunched form over the cane, she pokes a surprisingly spry finger into my sternum. "Even inside you."

I skip back, distancing myself from the woman's jabbing hands. "Ether is soul?"

"Not just soul. It's energy and intelligence." She flicks her fingers, circling in the air, her gaze clearing as she speaks. "We're energy first, body second. Ether is in every part of the world from rocks to trees to the ocean to all animals."

"I think I understand—"

"Good place to begin. Other people don't try to understand."

I turn away from her wry smile and check the door. "Why would someone call it black magic?"

Her nose wrinkles, skin bunching on her face like a sagging sock. "Ah, ignorance. It's easy to misunderstand what you cannot see. It's been years since a Channeler was accused of black magic. The woman used her gift to heal a small boy."

I chew my lip, growing uneasy. I healed the dog like the woman healed the boy. "And they called that black magic?"

"No, no. Tragedy struck near the same time. The boy's sister suffered an accident. Poor thing passed. That's when people spoke of black magic. A life for a life."

I frown. "Is that possible? One life for another?"

She taps her cane. "Even if it is, it goes against the code of Channelers: Never harm. Our gifts should improve life. Never take. Since Chief Auberdeen declared any act of harm by a Channeler a crime, there have been no accusations of black magic made."

"Who was she?" I ask, need blossoming inside. "Where is she now?"

She *tsks* her tongue twice against her teeth and winks again. "First, you owe me."

Seeds, there are so many more answers to be found, and little time left. If Cohen realizes I'm gone . . . "Go on."

"Who's your mother?" Her question is so plain, almost as if she were asking me about the weather. It catches me off-guard.

Seeing no harm in answering, I say, "Her name was Rozen." Her brows rise, and her rheumy gaze hones in on my face. The sudden attention makes my armpits grow sweaty. I shift my weight. "I didn't know her. She died when I was a baby. And your next question?" I push on, wanting to finish this discussion.

She shakes her head, muttering to herself. "Never mind. I suppose the first question answered the second."

I'm not sure what to make of her cryptic comment. I've stayed too long, even though there's so much more I want to ask. I force myself to thank her and walk toward the door.

"One thing before you go." Her cane clips against the floor as she shuffles back to her table. She pulls a pinch of dried hemlock from a jar and puts it in a small satchel. As she moves on to another jar, she looks over her hunched shoulder at me. "The Spiriter who healed the little boy . . . her name is Enat."

My body freezes in place. "Is that a common name around here?"

"Only one around these parts." She moves on to another jar that releases a potent whiff of musk when she pulls out a pinch of the moss-green stuff. After cinching the pouch's strings, she shakes the contents.

I watch her while my mind tosses over how to convince this old woman to give me directions to Enat's home. She'll think I'm crazy. Or after no good.

When the old woman looks up with the pouch in her left hand, I ignore the urge to fidget with the boy's cap on my head. Despite my plan to share no details, I go on instinct, hoping the truth will earn Enat's whereabouts.

"I've actually come a far way to find Enat," I confess. "I

don't mean any harm. I just need answers about my father, and I believe she has them. Will you tell me how to find her?"

Her curled nails click against her cane. "She's old and doesn't take kindly to visitors" is all she says.

She breathes in deep and slow, thinking. "Odd as it may be, I believe you don't mean any harm. Hopefully, Enat will see the same and not give much trouble." I notice she doesn't say *no trouble*. "Enat lives on the outskirts of the city at the southern end." Her words paint a vision of the path I'll need to follow from the white cliffs to Flat Rock, then east into the Skyward Forest, where goliath trees scrape the sky. Enat's home is hidden in those woods, beyond a tree cave. To my confusion, she gives the unsubstantial explanation: "You'll know it when you see it."

Seeds and stars, a tree cave? I hope she's right.

To my surprise, she hands me the pouch. "Sprinkle this inside the cave under the tree, and it'll show you Enat's home."

There's something to be made of the woman's having mixed the pouch's contents before I inquired about directions to Enat's home. Though perhaps sometimes it's best to offer gratitude instead of wariness. I start to thank her when the slightest prickle along the back of my neck catches me in midsentence.

A moment later, Cohen barges into the shop, his gaze wild till it lands on me.

"There you are." His eyes shift to the woman, and his

mouth settles into a hard, unyielding line, his expression guarded. "We need to go."

Sparing one last glance in the woman's direction, I mouth *Thank you*, and then trail Cohen out of the shop. I'd bet my bow he's not pleased that I left, although he doesn't say as much. Cohen jumps right to the business at hand, lowering his voice so only I can hear as we rush away from the Elementiary. "Delmar wasn't able to give me much — only that Enat lives on the outskirts of the village. He said Channeler magic obscures her location." Frustration tinged with defeat darkens his tone. "I don't know how to get to her now."

I beam at him and hold up the pouch. "Good thing I do."

WE TRAVEL ALONG THE HILLS, HIDING IN
the brush and patches of trees running parallel to the road. Clouds
form in the west, gray beasts that slink away from
the ocean, growling in an untamed approach. If
we move quickly enough, we'll reach Enat's home
before they're overhead.

An hour out of Celize, we pass a group of
uniformed men, geared with swords and bows.
Soldiers headed to war. The clean press of their
coats shows they haven't seen a fight yet. How
soon will that change?

Though we're hidden in the trees, Cohen,
who's taken to sitting behind me, stiffens. At
first I figure he's concerned they'll see us. But the
foliage is too dense and dark.

"Tell me about Finn," I probe once the men are out of sight.

"My ma's beside herself with worry. He's had hardly any training in hand-to-hand fighting. Only what I taught him . . . It isn't enough." Cohen could be a statue for the little he moves; just his low tenor voice and the vibration of his words quaking softly across my back remind me of our proximity. "He's fourteen. Not old enough to be called a man. Though the king wants him to fight like one."

My thoughts shift to the jeweled, lean man I saw in the courtyard that day at the castle. It doesn't seem right that our spoiled leader can force even the young into war. Once the king's orders are given, only the king can retract them. It makes me wonder if our leader's determination will be our country's downfall, causing Malam to lose to Shaerdan's more battle-seasoned soldiers.

"Will your father fight alongside him?" I ask.

"He died last winter."

His straightforward answer socks me in the stomach with guilt. I've been angry with Cohen for not returning for Papa's wake, while I made no effort to find out what was going on with his family. He loves his family dearly and worked tirelessly during his apprenticeship to make them proud. I can only imagine how the loss must've wounded Cohen.

Twisting in the saddle, I turn back to face him. "I'm sorry."

"The ague was too much for him," Cohen explains so matter-of-factly, it makes my heart ache. "Since Finn is the only male at home, he must fight in the war." He cracks the knuckles on his left hand as it lies against his thigh. I notice the movement but give him my silence so he'll continue to talk. "Should've been me. Not him. But I cannot go home to my family or take Finn's place until I've cleared my name."

I know better than anyone the loneliness and pain Cohen must feel right now.

"I suppose it's better to lose your life to war than the guard's noose," Cohen says bitterly.

"You make it sound like Finn has no chance."

"Don't you remember when we were fourteen? Even though we already had a couple years of training, we would've been lost on the war front."

Cohen quiets behind me. I want to plead with him to keep hope, only those words are dashed by the soldiers, determined men in steel armor, who come to mind. It seems if Finn has any chance at all of making it out of the war unscathed, it cannot be more than a sliver.

"I swore to my mother that I'd help Finn if it became necessary," Cohen confesses. "That I'd save him from the war if needed."

My brow furrows. "But isn't that what you just said you cannot do?"

He doesn't answer for a moment. "I won't let Finn get hurt. Right now he's near the front and training. Should the war start and his unit move into action, then I'll have to do something about it."

"What will you do?"

"Whatever it takes." His reply has the cadence of a death march. "I won't let him die."

I've no doubt that Cohen would fight every man on the battlefield to save his brother. Cohen's need to take care of everyone around him is a weakness as much as it's a strength. One man cannot control everything, though. A reality Cohen has yet to accept. I just hope we can prove his innocence first so he's not walking into his execution.

I want to say something that'll buoy him up, give him some fraction of hope. But I've never been the person who believes the impossible to be possible.

"I'm sorry" is all I say, and even then I feel lacking when I mumble the words, "I wish there were something I could do."

"Being near you is enough," he whispers.

His words. Always an arrow to my heart.

I lean against him as he wraps one arm around my waist, our bodies cinching closer together until I'm not sure who is holding the other up.

The early evening is sooty, taunting us with a light drizzle as we enter the Skyward Forest. Unlike anywhere we've been before, these woods are packed with the most massive trees I've ever seen. Ancient, thick, and tall, each one is a mountain.

The trees eat our sounds as Siron maneuvers over the lush ferns. The thick, permeating quiet makes my thoughts feel too loud.

Being near you is enough.

It's all I've thought of since the words left Cohen's lips. Did he mean in that specific moment? Or in general? I turn his sentence over in my head, his words like garden compost, shifting and breaking down until they've fallen apart.

My thoughts scatter when thunder cracks over the forest. Siron snorts and prances. Cohen leans forward and pats the horse as I check our location. Trees like an army of giants stand shoulder to shoulder, blocking our path. A few have low limbs, bent upward like drawn swords. I review the directions from the Channeler at the Elementiary and know we must be close, except I see no cave.

"It must be here somewhere." I shrug in response to Cohen's dubious look, though it's clear he's not satisfied with my vague answer.

Siron continues on, moving deeper into the woods, until once again we meet a line of trees that look like soldiers ready for combat.

"Haven't we been here before?" I swivel and glance around.

"Not possible." Cohen sounds as confused as me. "Siron's been walking a straight path."

In the underbrush dim, it's difficult to make sense of all the shadows. I squint, looking closer, and notice two limbs held upward like swords.

"Look," I squeak. "We have been here before. We're walking in circles."

Cohen takes a moment to survey the forest, his gaze roving

over the plumes of ferns and tree giants, gathering information like he used to when apprenticing to Papa. He mutters a slew of swears. "You're certain she was trustworthy?"

I dig my fingernails into my palms. I felt her honesty, I'm certain of it. "I've no doubts about the woman," I say, my voice louder than intended, feigning confidence that I don't quite possess.

"Then let's take a closer look," Cohen says.

We hop off Siron and start in separate directions to scan the forest. Walking in touching distance from the trees, I weave over and around their sprawling roots while I curse under my breath about the Channeler's cryptic *You'll know when you see it* madness. All I see are shadows and ferns and the rough bark of these mammoth trees, and more shadows.

"What—" A dark stain that starts near the roots of one tree and spreads upward seems to grow bigger as I approach it. My steps cautious, I keep my eye on the black spot as it arcs into what looks like a cave opening.

The soil is soft, dipping inward toward the cave. My foot slips closer and then Cohen appears at my side, his amazement mirroring my own shock. This is the tree cave the Elementiary Channeler spoke of.

Awe trembles through me.

Cohen's fingers slip into mine, clenching tightly as we walk into the dark hole that wasn't there a moment ago. With my free hand, I pull the pouch from my breeches.

"I think this is what we're supposed to do," I tell Cohen,

jittery in anticipation as I tip the contents out, shaking them all over the padded ground.

A held breath passes.

And then light spreads before us, the tree cave turning into a shallow tunnel that opens to a clearing where a massive felled log has been made into a treehouse. A door is notched into a fallen trunk, windows glow with warm golden light on either side of the entry, and a mud-brown brick chimney pokes out the top.

"Cohen! This is it." My comment squeaks out, airy and excited.

His gaze swings from the treehouse to me. "Will you wait here if I ask you to?"

"No way. We stick together."

He mutters something that sounds like *Mule*. "And will you be just as determined to stick with me if she pulls out a sword and attacks?"

I squeeze his hand and smile. "You'll need my defense."

He snorts. "Come on, then."

Siron follows us through the widened tree opening. When we reach the treehouse door, Cohen knocks while I keep my hand on my dagger. When Enat doesn't answer, Cohen's brows lift in question. "Do you think—"

The air slices between us and an arrow thunks into the door. My heartbeat floods my senses as Cohen jumps back and I duck, sucking in a sharp inhale.

"State your business," a woman's voice booms from the woods.

"It was an arrow. Not a sword," I whisper to Cohen. "You were wrong."

Cohen glares at me as he drops low. "Don't be a fool. Now isn't the time to jest."

I ignore his whisper and sidestep out of his reach. Humor aside, we don't have much time, and I need this woman to trust us enough to share her secrets. "We're looking for Enat," I call out. "Are you her?"

"Even if I am, I'm not interested. Get off my porch."

I turn to Cohen with a *What should we do?* look.

"My second arrow won't miss," the woman who must be Enat warns.

Cohen rises from his crouch and touches my arm. "Britta, let's go."

"No." I pull away, giving him a withering, silencing look. We would be fools to give up so easily after we've come so far. "We just need—"

A second arrow zips two fingers' width past Cohen's left ear.

"Bloody stars!" He grabs me, pulling my tunic as he seeks shelter away from the target area. "Britta, come on. We're sitting ducks."

"We cannot leave without talking to her," I plead with him.

"We won't be talking when we're dead."

I rub the back of my hand against my forehead, trying to think of another option and coming up with nothing. "She's our only lead."

Cohen shields us behind a tree to the side of her porch.

He grits his teeth. "Please don't move. Let me try. All right?" Then he calls to the woman. "I'm only asking that you hear us out. A few questions. Then we'll leave."

"Boy, don't lie to me."

Surprisingly, she's guessed correctly. Cohen's words make my insides dip in temperature.

"If you want my help," she yells, her voice gruff and gravelly, "don't come on my land and try to fool me. Your next lie will be the last thing that leaves your mouth."

I put a hand up, stopping Cohen from saying anything more. "Let me."

He doesn't seem pleased, but he agrees. The woman has said enough that I can pinpoint her location. She's in a fortress of wooden slats high in the branches.

"Please," I call out. "Saul Flannery, King Aodren's bounty hunter, was murdered nearly three months ago while on his way to find you. I just want—I mean, do you know anything about that?"

She doesn't answer. Not a single word.

Panic sets in, since she's our only lead to understanding what happened to Papa. Still, we cannot waste time with the guards on our tail and Cohen needing to return to his family.

"Let's head back to Celize and talk to Delmar," Cohen suggests, quietly, consolingly. "Maybe he'll have another lead."

"No." We need her. We would be foolish to leave. Even if she doesn't know who the murderer is, Papa was after her for a reason and we need to find out why. If we turn away now, then Cohen and I have come all this way for nothing.

I cannot give up this easily. Hopelessness wells up inside me.

There is one thing I have left to barter. I unsheathe Papa's blade and hold it on an open palm. A raindrop lands on the forged steel. Another on the sapphire. A steady sprinkle of moisture breaks through the branches and dots the area all around us.

"What are you doing, Britt?"

I ignore Cohen and step into the open, figuring if the woman were going to kill me, she would've already hit her target. It's clear she's a master bow-woman.

"This—this dagger." I hold it out for her to see. "It's all I have . . ." Emotion overwhelms me. But no matter its significance, the blade means nothing if we are captured by the guards and hanged for murder.

"Don't do this." Cohen takes a step toward me. The break in his voice reverberates in the center of my soul, making me stop even though this has to be done.

"It's worth a great deal," I say, pushing my voice to be a little louder. A little stronger. "I can see your windows are in need of repair. Perhaps you could use some supplies before winter."

Pressure builds behind my eyes. I'm suddenly grateful for the steady patter of drops that have begun to fall all around us. Cohen's hand lands on my shoulder. His reassuring touch gives me strength to continue.

"My name is Britta Flannery, Saul Flannery's daughter. If you know anything about my father's murder . . ." I tap my thumb against the sapphire. "I'll trade this for information."

There's a gentle patter of movement, branches bending, a crack, and a few leaves tumble to the forest floor a dozen paces away. Then we hear a zipping sound before a woman emerges on a rope and swings to the ground. She releases her hold and lands in front of us in a crouch.

I stare, unblinkingly, at the older woman as she rises and approaches. A slight limp causes her body weight to shift side to side. She's petite. Not much more than bone and firm muscle beneath wrinkles. Two spirited eyes, the color of the sky after a storm, blink at me from a weathered face.

"Why didn't you say who you were earlier, Britta?" A smile suddenly blooms. "I'm Enat."

I'm so shocked and relieved to see her and hear her answer that it takes a moment to recognize the absence of the feelings I've come to rely on. Her words register no warmth, no chill.

Nothing.

CHAPTER

21

THUNDER CRACKS OVERHEAD. A ZIP OF WHITE light illuminates the small clearing in front of Enat's log home. What does *nothing* mean? Perhaps it has something to do with her being a Channeler.

Raindrops hit Enat's shoulders, her wild white hair, her freckled hands, and she doesn't seem to notice. She's a rock in a slow-moving stream.

Cohen clears his throat. "Britta?" he whispers, waiting for me to say something.

"You really wanna trade me that dagger for information?" Her lips quirk in a sort of challenge.

"Y-Yes."

She snorts. "Keep your dagger, girl. You're gonna need that blade, unless you have another?"

When neither of us answers, she tips her head. "Come inside. We'll talk."

She ambles into the cottage, and it takes a moment to overcome my shock to follow. Cohen keeps a hand on the pommel of his sword as we enter the two-room tree cottage. A table, chairs, and a fireplace fill one room. The other holds a bed.

"Go on, sit down." She gestures to the table as she hangs her bow.

Cohen's wary glance tells me he is just as confused about her shift in attitude. He moves to the chair against the wall. I take the one beside him as Enat sits across from us.

"Briiiitta." She draws out my name, almost like it's a treasure. Her alarming blue eyes hold me in place as she props her elbows on the table and leans closer, poring over my features in deliberate study. "You're persistent if anything. I like that about you."

I shift in my seat and scrape my feet against the floor before settling to cross my legs at the ankle. Should I thank her?

"And resourceful," she goes on. "Somehow you convinced one of Celize's land Channelers to tell you where I live and give you a charm to see your way here."

She doesn't seem angry or irritated. If anything, she seems pleased.

"You're also brave." She glances at the slender bow strung on her wall and then me. "You didn't bat an eye at my arrow."

Cohen grouses about her aim under his breath. Beneath the table, I smack my knee into his and he grunts.

"It wasn't bravery. It was necessity," I explain. "We don't have much time. Cohen's been charged with my father's murder. And we have only an eight-hour lead on the guards who are after us."

Cohen thumps my leg in return, no doubt wary of sharing too much information.

"We need answers." I don't hesitate to say this. Enat is a smart woman, and we would risk losing her assistance if we mince words. "You're our last hope."

She leans back in her chair and rubs her chin as if forming a response, deciding what she'll share.

"I knew your father," Enat says, reluctantly, almost as if there is a catch to her admission.

I search myself for the telling sign of truth and again *nothing*. Cohen must see my frown because his brows rise subtly in question. I give a dismissive shake of my head. It's not something I can explain now in front of her.

Cohen leans forward, eyes catching briefly on mine before he directs all his attention to Enat. "A lot of people knew him, but he was coming to meet *you* when he was killed. You know anything of that? What he was after?"

Trust Cohen to toss caution aside and cut to the point.

Her focus tightens a fraction, lines pinching around her eyes. "You tracked me down. You don't know why?"

"No, we don't," he admits.

"You've come all this way. Surely you must've learned something about me. Any stories of interest?" Enat scrutinizes Cohen like she's testing him. Or toying with him.

"We heard you practice black magic." I blurt out the only rumor I've heard, wanting to prove our efforts despite our knowing scratch about her.

Cohen stares at me. I shrug.

"You have good instincts, girl." Enat pounds a fist on the table and grins. This old gruff woman, I'm liking her more and more. "I'm the type of person who requires a forthright and honest answer, or I'll not deal with you." She looks pointedly at Cohen before she turns to me. "Your father wanted to pay for a spell."

"No." The word comes out before I realize I've spoken. Even if I cannot discern her lie, my internal gauge doesn't need to tell me she's wrong. I knew Papa. He'd never take part in black magic.

"He needed someone to break a curse." She places her elbows on the table and leans toward me.

"You're wrong," I tell her. "My father didn't know anything about spells or magic or Channelers." Papa's stance on magic was clear. *I won't judge what I don't understand, Britta, and I won't ever get involved in something I cannot control, and that includes magic.* The words he spoke about Channelers are ingrained on my memory.

Enat is wrong. She must be.

Her ocean-colored irises sharpen. "It's the truth. Your father wrote letters and left them in a hollowed trunk that was charmed so no one else could take them except a certain courier."

Duff Baron.

"After his first couple letters, when the seriousness of the situation was cause to fear someone might intercept them, I left a charm for your father. Sprinkled on each letter, the charm cloaked the messages. So any intercepted would appear blank."

If I hadn't just walked through a tree where no path had been visible earlier, I'd think she was a loon. Still, her claim blindsides me like the day one of the king's guards informed me of Papa's death.

My eyes are riveted to her as she pries open the bottom drawer of a knotty dresser beside the table and withdraws a box. Reddish wood shows beneath the cracked yellow paint with the remnants of tiny white flowers. The feminine touches on the box don't seem to fit with Enat's gnarled hands and gruffness.

After producing a tiny iron key and opening the lock, Enat withdraws a pile of folded letters.

"The answers you want are here," she says, more subdued now, as if she can tell she's shaken my world, and I need a moment to find balance. She offers a sad smile. It's mixed with other emotions I cannot name. "All your father wrote in the few months before he passed is in this box."

Any hope I was holding that Enat was wrong about Papa vanishes the moment my fingers graze Papa's signature.

Oh, Papa.

Cohen's arm rests on my chair, lending comfort. Enat pushes away from the table and stands. "Take your time" is all she says before she's out the door with her bow in hand.

I'm dazed like walking through a dream as I sift through the correspondences. I read one dated five months ago.

I've checked out the cities that were attacked, and all evidence and accounts from the locals tell me the murders were at the hands of our own men. Shaerdan's kinsmen aren't attacking us — we're attacking ourselves.

Someone in the king's inner circle is lying to him, manipulating him into calling up more troops.

Cohen taps the letter. "I've spent the last year and a half around the king's inner circle. I cannot think of a single man who'd betray the king and go to these lengths to start a war."

Just as Enat said, the letters span three months. Some claim a turn in King Aodren's behavior, that it's become erratic. That his decisions make little sense. Papa thought King Aodren's health was declining due to some kind of magic. He had dropped weight, no longer spoke at court, and spent long hours in his private chambers. Mentions of the war scatter the pages, as well as the king's brash decision to call on boys as young as fourteen to serve in the army.

As I browse the stack, following the familiar curve of

Papa's scrawled handwriting, Cohen's statement rings in my head — *We all have our secrets.*

Rage surges through me, a sickle cutting me to the core, sharp and swift. I can hardly stand to read the letters, let alone hold the truth of Papa's lies to me in my hands.

How could he have kept so many secrets? I'm overcome with the urge to rip the letters to hundreds of little pieces. To shred them until they're unreadable.

Anger burns hotly in the backs of my eyes and threatens to spill down my face, but I hold it back.

"Britt." Cohen's hand rubs my back, coming to rest between my shoulder blades. "You don't have to read them all right now."

"The captain is on his way to Celize." I force myself to open another letter, but I have to pause and bat a traitor tear off my cheek. "Maybe he's already reached the city. We don't have the luxury of more time."

I want to ask him why he isn't shocked by Papa's mounting pile of secrets. Just thinking the question pricks me with such ugly, uncomfortable feelings, it's better to push them away.

"Cohen, did you know Papa was writing to Enat?" I wonder aloud.

His face twists with confusion. "If I knew that, we wouldn't have come all the way to Celize. Why?"

"No reason. I'm sorry." I rub my arms, which have chilled from the gentle rainstorm echoing outside the cottage. "Papa never mentioned a thing to me." My throat clogs. "It's over-whelming to read it all now. I don't understand why he didn't . . ." *trust me.*

When I had no one else, after Cohen left, I always believed I had Papa. And now this discovery takes that truth and taints it, making me feel like I only ever had a ghost of my father.

Cohen's hand moves to cover mine. His thumb traces my fingers, then dips and rises over my knuckles. "He trusted and loved you more than anyone in this world. Don't do that. Don't think you were anything less."

"I won't," I lie. "I just . . . I'm angry with him," I admit. "He should've told me."

A glint of something I don't understand flickers in Cohen's eyes. There, and then gone. He sits taller in the chair. "He must've had his reasons. Let's keep reading. We'll figure this out."

I nod glumly and flip to the next letter, dated four months ago.

I snuck in to see the king and found him unconscious today . . . When he finally opened his eyes, he was disoriented. His words were nonsense. He said a woman's voice was in his head.

I asked about the attacks and the war, and he knew nothing of it.

The confusion in his eyes was real. I believe him. He doesn't know the country is headed to war.

The last letter, dated three months ago, reads:

The king addressed the nobility and inner circle. He was a differ-ent man from the one who woke in his chamber the other day.

I suspect something darker is at work on him.

I believe he's under the control of a Spiriter. It's been years since I saw it, since before Rozen left us. When he talks, his eyes look glazed. It's a sign his spirit has been taken over.

And if I'm right, whoever is controlling him is pushing our countries toward war. Thousands of innocent people will die if the bind isn't broken. Will you, can you, help me?

Seconds, minutes, hours—I don't know how long I sit and stare at his writing. My thoughts volley to the glimpse I caught of King Aodren, the tall and lithe young ruler. I'm dumbfounded that someone could take control of him like he's a carriage to be driven.

Papa was a shrewd man, with far greater knowledge of our world than I possess. He was painstakingly dedicated to the king. Even though he was old enough to be the king's father, they had a friendship. Papa, more than anyone, would've known the truth. Even though it pains me to read his words now, I believe them.

Enat's door swishes open and she enters, bringing with her the fresh scent of rain and the musty odor of these woods.

"Are there no more letters?" I ask.

"No. That's all of them." Something about the downward drop of her gaze makes me wonder if she's lying.

"Who is controlling the king?"

"Likely the same person who killed your father. And I have no answers to that."

Disappointment floods me, washing away the hope that

our search was at an end. Though she gave us more information than we had before, we still don't know who killed Papa. The guards are probably already in Celize. If we don't turn over the murderer, then the captain will have us hanged. "You're certain there are no more letters?"

"No more." I may not have my internal judge working, but there is something off in her tone.

"Do you know anyone else he may have met with in town?" I press. "He was murdered in Celize. There has to be someone who knows something."

"I know your father was certain the person controlling the king was in his inner circle or one of his guards," she says. "A Spiriter has to be close by for the bind to work."

That leaves us with six men to choose from in his close circle of advocates, and twenty-four guards. Thirty is too many to track down. We need to narrow the list somehow.

"Why push the country to war? That's what we need to figure out," Cohen says, fist rapping against the table. "If we know who would gain the most from a war, then we'll slim down the pool of probable murderers."

All this mention of Papa and his death makes me feel loosely stitched together. I cross my arms around my waist. Despite how angry I am, if there was ever a time I wished Papa were alive, it would be now. He could help me see through the confusion.

"There are those in your country who would like to see the ports of Shaerdan fall to Malam," Enat says. "You're a rich country but stuck between the mountains and Shaerdan. Without ports to open trade with the islands and the great lands north, you have no gains. You're forced to pay taxes to Shaerdan on all your ore."

"Are taxes and money reason to start a war?" I lift my chin, working through her rationale.

A sardonic laugh falls from her lips. "Men have gone to war for less."

I glance at Cohen, thinking of the conversation we had earlier about his brother. His expression is placid as the smooth surface of a river, though certainly something more is churning beneath.

"Where do we go from here?" I ask.

Enat reaches for the letters and gathers them into a stack. "It's been many years since I concerned myself with what goes on in that town, but there's a man who may know something." She taps the folded papers into a neat pile and places them in the box. "Millner Barret."

Cohen straightens in his seat, his expression cracking and shock showing through. "The Archtraitor?"

"The very one."

"My father's enemy?" She must be jesting.

She shakes her head and a smile curves her lips. "They weren't enemies. Millner was one of your father's closest friends."

I FEEL LIKE THE WIND HAS BEEN KICKED OUT OF me by this little old woman. "How can that be? Papa searched for the Archtraitor for years and couldn't find him. He's a rebel and a murderer."

"You're telling me the story your papa told the king."

Shaking my head, I form a protest on my tongue just as she continues. "Your father and Millner worked together long before the king and his inner circle closed the border. After the drought and the old king's death, people were afraid. They were convinced Shaerdan was the cause. Aodren was a wee thing, so his inner court took over and the king regent stepped in to lead. Channelers were hunted, and the border was closed.

"Millner was the only member of the inner court who disagreed. He refused to hang the Channeler women who were brought in. Eventually, he spoke out. That's when guards were sent after Millner, and his family was tortured and killed.

"Your father helped him escape —"

"That is a lie," I cut her off.

"Settle your feathers, girl." Enat's gnarled knuckle taps the table. "Millner's escape shamed the kingdom because he turned a lot of heads. People questioned the new laws, and many fled the country."

"But if my father helped Millner, why would he then hunt the Archtraitor's followers?"

"He didn't. Some he helped escape. He would guide them to Millner. Your father only hunted criminals who deserved to be hauled back to Malam."

I run my fingers over the table's ridges while my mind is caught on the bodies that hung beside the river near the border.

"What about the guards who often traveled with Papa?" I ask. Surely they would've known Papa was meeting the Archtraitor.

"You do not give your father enough credit."

She's right. Papa was crafty. He taught as much to Cohen and me. The trait was a necessity to maintain his position as the king's bounty hunter.

This room is too small, too tight. I need to leave. I want to shoot arrows until I cannot move my arms. I want to run. I want Papa to come back and explain why he never told me any of this. Why I'm sifting through stacks of secrets when he once claimed we had no secrets between us.

"Millner's eyes and ears are the shadows of Celize," Enat says. "The man deals in secrets like you hunt game. The only problem is he's quite unapproachable."

"More than you?"

She snorts. "Perhaps not. Though after your father was killed, Millner practically holed up in a cave and hasn't come out since." She goes on to explain that we'll have to contact another man who will then talk to the Archtraitor. If Millner is willing, he'll then meet us at a specified date and time.

It feels like a step back, before we've had a chance to take a step forward.

Or maybe it seems that way because of Papa's deception. Because the little I had in my life isn't what I thought it was.

The forest is darker than the ash in Enat's hearth. A crack of thunder shakes her small home, and the soft patter of rain echoes through the window. She offers for us to stay the night, and we gladly agree.

Enat places two blankets on the table and then hands a bar of soap and a rag to Cohen. "The storm isn't bad yet, so you should wash up now. Walk past the outhouse a dozen paces and you'll come to a well. The water's warm."

"Warm?" Cohen's question mirrors my surprise. Another enchantment, perhaps, like the cave tree?

"A hot spring flows beneath this land on the south side. I have two wells. One for warm bathing water, and another, on the north side, for drinking and cooking. Take the lantern beside the door. These woods get awfully dark."

Cohen thanks her and leaves.

I move to take the blankets from the table and set them on the floor for Cohen and me. We brought in our belongings earlier, so I shift my pack beside one blanket to rest my head on later.

"You need anything else?" Enat asks.

"No," I tell her, not wanting to take any more than necessary. The blankets and the roof over our heads are more than we expected from her.

She eyes the bedding and then leaves, going through the doorway into her room.

The box of letters remains on the table. When she doesn't return, I take out a few and read the lines once more. The shock from earlier is gone; a hollow ache has taken its place. Papa was all I had. How did I not know any of this? Why didn't he tell me? I would've never betrayed his secret.

"I bet you'd kill to have one of those wells in Brentyn in the winter." Cohen's voice pulls me back. I quickly put the letters away and spin around and—

A drop of water clings to a dark brown lock of hair that frames his scarred cheek—his newly shaven cheek. I haven't seen him without scruff or a beard since he was fourteen. He does not look fourteen anymore.

"There's a washtub in here, Britta." Enat interrupts from the bedroom doorway. For the second time in a few short moments, I wake from a trance. "Storm's picking up. You'll be more comfortable cleaning up inside."

"Really, I'm fine," I say. "You've already offered to let us stay. This is too much. I'm fine going outdoors, and I've never shied away from a storm."

"You got so much dirt and crust on you, it's gonna take a soaking to get off." She points at my mud-stained clothing. My protests die when she insists. She has a point. I look better fitted to spend the night in a pigpen, so perhaps a long soak is best.

"Come, I'll help you draw water to fill your bath." Enat's as stubborn as me and also oddly caring. Which I don't mind.

I follow her to the well. The moon cuts through clouds and forest, dimly lighting our way. The canopy of branches and leaves is thick enough to keep the rain to a trickle.

At the well, we sit on the edge of the rocky circle and draw two buckets of water. Steam wafts up from each bucket. I dip my hand into the first, wanting to test the warmth.

"Is it magic?" I ask, slack-jawed at the temperature.

She chuckles. "Only one of nature's mysteries. It's why I put my cottage here. Not many people know about the water."

I study her for a moment, waiting to feel the touch of truth in her words. And once again, no impression comes.

"What's that look for?"

"Oh, nothing," I mutter, cursing inwardly. My face always gives too much away.

She takes the bucket and the lantern and leads the way back toward the cottage. After dumping my bucket in the wash bin, I return to the well, noticing Cohen's absence beside the fireplace. The low murmur of voices sounds in the darkness. I'm nearly to the well when I see Cohen reaching for the two buckets Enat has pulled up.

He starts toward me. "I thought you could use a hand."

"Oh?"

"So you can get to washing all that dirt and crust off." He repeats Enat's words with a crooked smile. *Right.*

"You didn't have to," I mutter.

He doesn't respond as he passes, his scent, soap and woods, trailing behind. The strangest desire kicks through me to follow him, to draw in a lungful of air and hold it.

I shake my head clear and consider smacking myself.

Wait until Enat passes me.

Then wait another fifty breaths.

I'm immersed in the steaming hot bath when a knock sounds at the door before it cracks open. "Britta?"

Even though it is only Enat, I jerk my arms protectively over my body and sink lower so only my knobby knees show in the candle's glow.

"I forgot to leave a drying cloth for you," she says as she slips inside.

My eyes bug out. Never in all my days has someone walked in on me bathing.

"And these were my daughter's belongings." Enat holds up the bundle in her arms, oblivious to my discomfort.

She shuffles to the pile of rags a few feet from the tub and wrinkles her nose. "Yours are filthy and need repair."

There's no arguing with that; still—

"Mine are fine," I protest. "I don't need anything more."

"I know you're likely a girl who doesn't take things from others, but the dress is no good to me. It would please me if you took it." Her voice trembles as she shuffles closer to the tub. Enat wrinkles her nose at my trip-worn clothes. "It is a better disguise than the tunic you've been wearing. You'll look like one of the kinswomen. I'd appreciate it if you took it off my hands."

She doesn't give me a chance to turn down her offer. She leaves with my stolen sailor clothes in her arms.

I wash the dirt and blood away. The well water seeps into my skin and warms me to the bones. Even in the dim lighting, my fresh-scrubbed skin shines freckled-pink when I step out of the tub.

Hesitantly, I touch the dress's fine cloth and groan to myself. I cannot walk out wearing this. If the cinched waist weren't off-putting, the skirts alone pose too much of a tripping threat. It'll fit strangely, and surely the fabric, all soft and shiny, will irritate. In Malam, only a person of nobility would dress in something so finely stitched.

I scan the room, hoping for another option. Unfortunately, besides the towel, there's nothing else to wear. The horrible, badly blue, trimmed and trilled dress that's staring me down like an animal on the hunt is my only option. Resigned, I grab the garment and shove my arms through the sleeves that smell faintly of lilacs. My nose itches. The collar rubs against my skin, and the thin shift beneath the floor-length skirt scratches my legs.

When I finally leave the room, I'm afraid to meet Cohen's gaze. Afraid he'll think me silly and laugh at my appearance.

"Ah, I knew it would fit." Enat stops chopping carrots and smiles. "You're just about my daughter's size. You look lovely."

Cohen turns from where he is sharpening his knife beside the fireplace. His eyes sweep over the length of my damp hair lying across my shoulders and darkening the ocean-blue dress with each drop.

"Dove." His Adam's apple bobs in his throat as he swallows.

I shift my weight, forcing myself not to tug at the ridiculous dress. My hands go to my waist, where the dress clings to my form, only Cohen's eyes track the movement, making me cringe inwardly when his attention lingers. I fold my arms, and his gaze jumps to meet mine.

"When did your hair get so long?" His voice is tree-bark rough.

My fingers run through the tangled ends. I'm overcome

with the oddest conflicting desires — that he would quit looking at me and that he would never stop.

"I, uh, don't know . . . I didn't have a brush and haven't cut it in a while. It's so long." I huff my annoyance when my hand catches in a snag. "I should just cut it. It'd be easier to travel as a boy."

"No." His sharp response startles me. I drop my hands, leaving my locks to look wild and untamed.

"We won't be traveling much longer. And you won't always be pretending to be a boy. You should keep it long."

I know, without a mirror, my clean skin is pink, and not just from the scrubbing. The clatter of pots and pans is a reminder that Cohen isn't the only person in the room. I turn to see Enat tossing cut vegetables into a pot.

"Do you need water for supper?" I ask. "I can run to the well."

She wipes her hands on a well-worn apron. "If you're willing to go out in the storm, I won't stop you."

I've taken a half-dozen steps outside when the door opens behind me.

"I'd ask if you need help, but I know better than that." The delight in Cohen's gold and brown earth-toned eyes is barely visible in the thin moonlight that breaks past the storm clouds and treetops. "Mind some company?"

I'm a fool because all I can think about is touching his jaw. *Is it as smooth as it looks?*

"I suppose I could tolerate it," I choke out.

Cohen's mouth lifts on the left side, and my knees weaken. I miss him. I miss how he always made me laugh. I miss how I could be myself when we were together. I miss that crooked smile.

"So, what do you think of Enat?" I ask as we walk. The rain patters gently around us, catching my shoulder, my nose.

He shrugs and pulls the bucket from my hands before taking a seat at the well's edge. "She knows more than I expected."

"And?"

"And she's going to get us in to talk to Millner Barret. That's more than we had before. In the end, Saul gave his life for the king. I'm . . . well, I'm honored I was able to work with him, learn from him."

The pride that fills me is followed by warmth from the truth in his words.

"Do you think we can trust Enat?" I push the length of wet hair over my shoulder.

He glances up at me from where he has sat to lower the bucket into the well. A few raindrops hit his cheek before he wipes them away. "We've had our fair share of bad luck on this trip, but she's different. I think we can trust her."

"You sound so sure."

"You never trust anyone, Britt. And I understand why. It's not like you've had many opportunities to exercise your trust in others. But I have a gut feeling about Enat."

I consider asking him what his gut was telling him when

we pulled into the inn at Padrin, but decide to keep the question to myself.

"I'm not sure what I think of Enat. There's something different about her," I say. Some water sloshes from the bucket as he pulls it to the top of the well, plinking against the depths below.

"Besides her hiding in the woods and shooting arrows at anything headed in her direction?" He huffs out a short laugh.

I roll my eyes.

"Tell me." He reaches out and grabs my hand. His touch makes any reservations roll belly-up. "What's different about her?"

"You know how I know when someone's being honest?"

"Yes." His hand squeezes. "What happened?"

"I cannot tell if she's speaking the truth or not. I've asked her a few questions, and I didn't feel anything when she responded."

I don't even realize I've lowered my gaze until Cohen's callused fingers guide my chin up so he can scan my face. "You asked her a question and felt nothing at all?"

"Exactly."

"How is that possible?"

I give him a look. "I don't know."

"Was she being vague?" His fingers leave my chin. "For this to work, doesn't she have to give a specific answer?"

"I think so."

"You think?"

"This thing, it's a little different with everyone." *Mostly you,* is what I should say. *Everyone else registers about the same.* "I noticed it when she was talking about King Aodren. I figured then it was probably me, until I asked her about the well water. When she spoke, I didn't feel anything. It's her. She's different somehow."

"That's strange" is all he says, and a line forms on his brow as he stares off. He runs his right hand over his face. Up and down, up and down, stuck on the track of his scar. I'm caught by the mesmerizing motion until lightning flashes, and one, two, three seconds later the thunder answers, a great grizzly bear roaring into the night.

"So, do you still think we can trust her?"

He nods. "Yes."

"You're so certain. You're always so confident." I wish I had the same conviction. I suppose if Enat wanted to hurt us, she would've. I've no doubt she's capable. That's a testament to her character.

"You trust her enough to meet with Millner?" I ask.

"I do," he says thoughtfully.

Lightning cracks across the sky again, and in the burst of colorless light I notice how close we're sitting — the width of the bucket separates us. I lower my gaze from his, but it catches on his lips. Then noticing the slow movement his throat makes as he swallows, I eventually drop my focus to my lap and the space between us.

"Then I suppose I do too," I whisper, and stand up.

Cohen lowers the bucket of water to the ground before rising and reaching for my arm. "Britta." His voice is deep. Throaty.

His eyes have darkened to the color of the earth after a rainstorm. "Yes?"

"Don't go yet."

"I wasn't, I—"

"I thought about you," he says, frowning, then sighing. I would give anything to know what he's thinking right now.

"You did?"

"When we were apart, you were always there in my mind."

Every nerve in my body zings with awareness of his truth as well as his proximity, muddling the remaining intact portion of my thoughts. I should remind him he left over fifteen months ago and never contacted me. I should step back. But . . .

I want very much to pursue this moment.

He touches my cheek. Heat dances beneath my skin as his fingers slip around my head. His hold is gentle and careful and confusing.

His thumb runs lightly across my lower lip. "Britt, tell me this is all right."

His plea is nearly drowned by the rush of pulse that beats a deafening rhythm in my ears. The rain increases, pelting our skin, and the wind sings around us. Instead of ducking away, I rise up on my toes, scared, and, at the same time, so full of want.

I hear him whisper my name once more before his mouth is on mine. *Oh stars.* My lips are frozen beneath his as shock and logic wage war — this is everything I shouldn't want. Still, I don't care. He kisses me gently at first, and then not so much when my lips respond. His hands clutch me to him; the firm spread of his body presses against mine. I can taste the mint leaf on his lips. His tongue. Flames shoot through my limbs and burn my heart, erasing every single thought in my head except for the sweet awareness of Cohen. Of our needy kiss.

My fingers are possessed, tracing up his neck to twist in his hair. A moan escapes his throat. *Oh my*. It's the most alluring sound I've ever heard.

All too soon his mouth leaves mine and I gasp in objection.

He lets out a husky breath, and a second later my embarrassing protest dies when his lips wind a trail down my throat and back up, moving along my jaw until his breath fans the hollow behind my ear.

"Britta? Cohen?"

Cohen jerks back, eyeing the blue-black shadows around Enat's home and then me as if waking from a dream. Disoriented by the sudden disconnection of our kiss, I trip toward Cohen, but he rights me with both hands on my shoulders.

Enat calls our names once more.

"We better go," he says, squeezing my arms. He turns and moves toward Enat's voice, but just before he's out of sight, he looks back and gives me a tipped smile.

I touch my swollen lips as the rain falls. And stand there, drowning in disbelief.

What. Was. That?

IN THE MORNING, THICK MIST CURLS THROUGH the trees and blankets the forest ground. I watch as Cohen rides away on Siron, wisps of white furling around the black beast's legs like the clouds are carrying him away.

Cohen is leaving for the city to speak with Delmar again. Enat says he's a trustworthy kinsman and is the one who will, in turn, contact Millner Barret and set up a meeting. Cohen argued to go alone because the guards are looking for both of us. Disguised and on his own, he could slip through town easier than if we were together.

Part of me is grateful for the time away from him. Last night I hardly slept. Every time Cohen shifted in his sleep, I was acutely aware of his movements and his slow and steady breaths, despite our being on opposite sides of the room. Hours passed. I tossed and turned and thought about the kiss in the rain. About Cohen. About what'll happen next.

I fear I've made a terrible — wonderful — abysmal mistake.

After Cohen is pardoned, he'll leave to help his brother in the war, or he'll return to hunt for the king. I cannot fault him for his allegiance, but I fear he won't want to be with me. After all, he left me once before. Losing him again will crush me.

Even if he stayed and wanted me, how could we ever be together? Cohen's duty to his family comes first. Any ties to me will be a stain on his reputation, which could possibly have negative consequences for his mother and sister. When we were younger, he bloodied a few noses when boys teased him about being my friend. Now that we're older, a fistfight won't bridge the divide between our two stations in life.

When Cohen returns, I'll explain that the kiss was a one-time incident, a lapse in judgment to satisfy my curiosity. It meant nothing.

The excuse rattles through my head as I sit beside Enat's warm-springs well. The heat rising from the ring of stone contrasts with the cool clutches of mist, and I find myself shivering, despite the ridiculous dress pinching my skin.

I fold my arms tight to my body. I'm uneasy about talking to Cohen, but what vexes me the most is that Cohen will already realize he made a mistake.

"You have that look on your face again. What are you thinking?"

I jump to standing, startled by Enat's comment. She breaks through the mist with two empty baskets in each hand.

I tug at my collar in a futile search of comfort. Blasted dress. "I was thinking about all that's happened." It's not exactly a lie. I want to be honest with Enat, considering all she's shared with me.

"Ah." Her brilliant blue eyes soften into a sympathetic look. "You've been through a lot. Your father's death. And now this trek through Shaerdan."

I say nothing, letting her make her own judgments.

"Come, then." She raises one basket. "I could use your help. I'm short on dried herbs. And the storm's likely blown down seeds and bark gnarls. Wouldn't mind gathering some of those; then I don't have to climb for them later."

"Do I need my bow?"

Her head tips to the left. "Not likely, but it's always good to be prepared. Why?"

"The last time we were in the woods together, you used me for target practice." I smirk. "Just wondering if I should be ready for that."

She barks out a laugh. "Does that wit ever get you in trouble back home?"

"More than I'd like to admit."

"Hmm . . . to keep you on your toes, I'll grab my bow before we head out."

This time I laugh. Enat is exactly what I need to take my mind off Cohen.

"Are the clouds often this low?" I ask as I follow her.

"This?" She points at the mist, parting around our knees. "This is the morning fog. It comes in and leaves again by noon."

"I didn't notice it the other day."

"We don't get fog every day, but enough to keep the trees happy. It keeps them strong. They are ancient, you know."

I nod my head. "I've never seen anything like them."

"Some say they're the first trees the gods planted for us. That's why they are strong and resilient. Even fire has little effect on these beauties."

It seems appropriate that Enat lives here. I don't know much about her, but I think about how she's able to protect herself and how she is the person Papa turned to for help. She's like the trees, strong and resilient.

We spend a couple hours gathering herbs and seeds before returning to the cottage and laying them out to dry. Enat takes the two bark gnarls and breaks them in half. She whittles the centers with her blade until she has a pile of wood grindings.

"What's that for?" I ask.

"The inside of the gnarls can be used for many purposes, a pinch to sweeten tea or even to put out a fire, since the trees are resistant to flame."

"Is that what you're going to use it for?"

She pauses, looking at me reflectively. "No. The grindings of a bark gnarl along with a pinch of chiandra can also be used to slow a person's heart."

My hands stop over the split chiandra that I've been placing on a board to bake in the sun. "And why would you need to do that?"

My question goes unanswered as thumping hooves echo through the trees. My heart's rhythm scrambles to match the beat at knowing Cohen is near. I almost feel a pull toward him. His kiss will likely never leave my thoughts.

Cohen and Siron come barreling into the clearing in front of Enat's home. At the sight, a fluttery sensation dances from my shoulders to my shins.

"The guards are in the village." Cohen hops off Siron. "They're still posing as Shaerdanian soldiers, and they've spread word that two Malam fugitives are hiding there. They've placed a bounty of a year's wages on our heads."

CHAPTER 24

"WHO KNOWS YOU'RE HERE?" ENAT appears at my side with a bow in hand.

"I spoke only with Delmar." Cohen shoves a hand through his hair. "He knew I was headed here, but he'd never betray my trust. The only other person is the woman Britta spoke to at the Elementiary. Is she trustworthy?"

Enat relaxes. "If that's all, then you're safe here. No one can enter my land without a counter-charm. Astoria can be a gossip, but she's loyal to the kinsmen and judge of Celize. She'd never betray me to royal guards from Malam. And Delmar would never betray a trust."

"The guards can be persuasive." I try to make my point without questioning her judgment outright. "If Astoria's already known as a gossip, she'd be an easy target for them."

"She won't talk." There is finality in Enat's tone. "This isn't the first time someone's come knocking on her door looking for me. Channelers have an understanding. We don't cause one another harm, and we don't put each other in harm's way."

"Even if they're not going to talk to the guards, there's a chance someone else noticed us." Papa taught me to always be prepared. Though we were careful, we're still putting her in danger. She must see that. "Anyone could've seen the direction we were headed. Not all the kinsmen will be loyal. We've already been ousted by a kinsman from Padrin."

"That's true, but since leaving Padrin, we've been cautious." Cohen looks at me and then turns to Enat. "Celize was empty when we left, and we didn't cross anyone on the road. I doubt we were seen."

"We cannot assume that," I say. "Our only defense is to act as though we've been noticed and prepare accordingly."

Enat scoops up the drying chiandra and puts the seeds into her basket. "Even if someone saw you, it's difficult to travel through these woods. You're safest here. But you should probably stay away from Celize for the next few days until your guards move on. Although most men are loyal to Judge Auberdeen, there are a few who haven't been happy with his decisions."

"What? No." We cannot stay here. They know we were

looking for Enat. They'll come after her first. "Our being here puts you in the middle of our mess."

"Britta's right," he says. "You've done enough for us. We're leaving."

Enat could rival Cohen for best stone-like expression. She pauses over the berries and seeds drying in the sun. "Nowhere safer than here. Only a handful of people know the route to my home. And like I said, the magic in these woods makes it impossible to find without a counter-charm. Setting up camp elsewhere would be a mistake."

She's right. We would've never found her if Astoria hadn't given us directions and the herb mix.

"I know the layout of my land like every lump on my old-lady body." She winks at the horrified expression I make. "I know the best vantage points. You're better defending yourselves here." She has a point there, even if she's made it ineloquently. "They won't find us. But for the sake of arguing that they will, if they come, it'll be more excitement than I've had in years. Could use a good fight. I haven't had decent target practice in a while."

I wouldn't want to be on the other end of her arrow. At least not again. Enat is as formidable as Captain Omar, with a touch more of madness. Perhaps it's her brashness that makes me forget her bent body.

Cohen looks at me, his face full of silent questioning. When I shrug, he answers for us both. "All right. Britta can stay here while I head into town." My mouth pops open. That wasn't the answer I was expecting. "We need to keep an eye on them so we know what they're up to. Stay one step ahead of them. I'll return once I have more information on the guards' plans."

"No." Belatedly realizing how loud my opposition sounded, I wrinkle my nose and start again quieter than before. "Cohen, you cannot go alone. How would we know if they catch up to you? If something happened?"

He points to Siron, who is busy eating foliage. "I've just returned from traveling alone. I'll be fine going alone again."

"There's more of a threat now. If I'd known there was a hefty bounty on our heads, I wouldn't have agreed to you going alone earlier. It's too dangerous. Too many unknowns. Right, Enat?"

His forehead creases, his eyes shifting between me and Enat. "You really think I'd let them catch me?"

Always willing to take unnecessary risks, always daring to take chances. "Regardless, it's safer to go together. You know that. We'll have more than the guards to worry about now. You need someone to watch your back."

"I don't need you to come."

I pretend his words don't hurt. "We were trained by the same man. Have you forgotten *Safety ensures survival?* We both go or we both stay."

Enat steps between us. "Britta is right. There's safety in

numbers. I'd tell you to stay, but it makes sense to find out what the guards are planning. Once you do, though, I expect you both back here."

I smirk, humored by how almost maternal she is being.

Cohen grunts, not pleased with the development.

It is midafternoon when we leave, and the fog has lifted. By the time we reach the outskirts of Celize, a sliver of a moon hangs in the cloudy sky. The darkness works well for us, making it easier to move into the city unseen as we seek the whereabouts of the guards.

I pull out the hat and cane I brought from Enat's home and hand both to Cohen.

I scoop up some mud. "Here. You should dirty your face. It'll help with the disguise."

He rubs the dirt on his cheeks and arms until he has a vagabond appearance. Still, he's too striking. I worry the disguise isn't enough. As we move into Celize, a few houses on the outskirts have lines of flapping clothes out to dry. Before Cohen can protest, I grab an oversize green tunic and hand it to him.

"Wear this. It'll help."

"Stealing again?" His mouth quirks. "I thought we were trying to avoid a hanging."

"Borrowing, not stealing. You need something that doesn't look like you."

He pulls it on and then flaps his arms to the sides, playing with the excess material. He groans. "I look like a lad playing in his father's tunic."

"A wee vagabond lad," I correct, though he's anything but that.

"I don't want to hear those words out of your mouth ever again." He glares and puffs out his chest, drawing a laugh out of me. "Will you be all right up there?" He points to the line of houses. When I tell him yes, his expression sobers. "If there's trouble, use your bow. I'll be back as soon as I find out where they're lodging."

He hesitates and I can tell he's worried for me, because that's Cohen. He always needs to make sure everyone else is well. "Go now," I urge. "I can take care of myself. Stop wasting time."

With a nod, Cohen heads for the first tavern, while I climb the trellis to the roof. There I crouch in the shadow of a chimney. Three stories above the street, the spot provides a raven's view of the surrounding city blocks. The murmur of voices echoes from conversations below.

A lot like hunting, I wait patiently, scrutinizing every movement and listening for anything pertinent. The waves are too loud and make it nearly impossible to gather any information. So when my legs start to cramp, I abandon my first spot and sneak along the connected rooflines, keeping low, until I find another chimney shadow with a better view.

The time passes slowly. And hours later, when most of the

kinsmen have retired for the night, I still haven't gleaned any-thing useful.

A whistle pierces the night — Cohen's sign.

Hopefully he was able to get more information than I was. Moving from my hiding spot, I shimmy off the roof onto a tree and work my way down, slowly, silently, till my feet touch the ground. Thankfully, Enat returned my tunic and trousers for this excursion. I can only imagine how difficult scaling a tree would be in a dress.

Cohen and I agreed to meet at the edge of the village, close to the cliffs where the forest thickens. Though we may be near town for a few days, it's safer to stay in the woods each night, where we would draw less interest than if we'd stayed at an inn. Sticking to the shadows, it takes some time to sneak unseen out of the city and to our hiding place.

When I arrive, he isn't there.

I wait for him to come and begin pacing the woods when the seconds tick by too slowly. Perhaps the whistle belonged to someone else. Perhaps —

Someone grabs me around my waist.

I screech and then twist to elbow my attacker, when he chuckles. It's Cohen. I relax into his strong, warm hold for a moment before ducking out of his grip.

"Got you." He grins at me. The sight of his wide smile steals my breath. I punch him in the gut. He takes the hit, folding over at his waist, and continues laughing silently. I wish we were always like this.

"Did you find anything?"

"They're staying at the Silver Eel Inn." Even though my eyes have adjusted to the forest's canopy of darkness, when he moves back, it's hard to see him clearly.

"What are they doing? When are they leaving?"

"I overheard mention of an ambush a few days ago. Half a troop of Shaerdanian men were slaughtered. From what I gathered, the chief judge and inner court have issued a call to all soldiers to report to their patrols. Since Omar is posing as a soldier, he won't be able to sit still at the Silver Eel for long. Not without drawing suspicion."

"But we don't know how long they'll risk staying in town. Surely they're counting on the bounty to entice someone to talk." At the thought of Captain Omar finding us again, my back itches, remembering the bite of the whip. "You really think they'll be pressured into leaving?"

"I do."

"You thought we were safe in Padrin," I tell him.

He blows out a breath. "I thought we could trust Kendrick. Though I don't fault him for what he did. He was thinking of his family. I cannot say I wouldn't be tempted to do the same if I believed it was the only option. I suppose then you're right to worry; the right incentive can turn any man into a liar."

I think of my motivation in agreeing to hunt down Cohen and turn him over to the guards. And shame sneaks up on me at the thought. Motivation is a dangerous tool.

"Where should we camp?" I ask, needing a change of subject."

I glance up to where the trees have parted way to the stars and draw in a steadying breath. I haven't been alone with him since the kiss by the well, and I'm not sure how to broach the subject of what happened between us, so I gesture for him to lead the way.

We hike farther into the woods, where Siron meets us. I nearly jump when he passes; he's an ink blot on black parchment. We travel until we can safely light a small campfire and no one will see it from the road.

The forest floor is thick with soft ferns that will make a good bed pad. While I'm flattening some ferns for myself, Cohen drops down next to me and works on his own spot. After he's done, he pulls a small loaf of bread from his satchel, breaks it into pieces, and hands one to me.

As we eat, the silence grows barbs and claws, scratching away the easiness between us. It makes me long for the time when we used to be able to sit together in comfortable quietness.

"Britt." The soft sound of my name on his lips brings goose bumps to my flesh. "About last night . . ."

I open my mouth. Close it. Open it, ready to give him an excuse for why it happened, but change my mind because, regardless of what I thought earlier, I very much want it to happen again.

"I shouldn't have kissed you."

Oh.

Never have I been more grateful for the darkness and shadows that cover us, for it cloaks the humiliation burning across my face. It masks the swift pain that burns in my eyes. I press my lips together.

I shouldn't have kissed you. His words sweep any notions I might've had about him, or us, and push them to the furthest, unreachable corner of my mind.

Foolish, foolish heart.

"I'm glad you said something," I say lightly, hoping to sound relieved, and praying he cannot hear the strain in my act. "I don't even know what I was thinking. It was an exhausting day, and I wasn't of sound mind."

"Right." He doesn't say anything for a long moment.

"Yeah, I'm glad we talked too," he finally adds. His confirmation cracks my chest and makes me feel like I'm shattering into a million misguided pieces.

CHAPTER
25

THE NEXT MORNING I'M WARM AND BLISS-fully comfortable until I peel my eyes open and find myself curled into Cohen. Inwardly, I groan, frustrated to find us so close again and angered because his embrace feels so good. *Boil him!*

I remain still, working out a way to extract myself with minimal humiliation as dawn crawls across the forest floor, grayish light slipping between the shadows of the trees.

Cohen stirs. Yawns, but doesn't wake.

Slowly, I shift out of his hold until I'm an arm span away. A breath sifts between his lips. I study the thick lashes on his cheek to check that he's still asleep, and then I turn away, unable to suffer the sight of him because it slams me with a slicing dose of rejection.

Cohen didn't say anything I hadn't already planned on saying. Even if he didn't think kissing me was a mistake, what would I have done? After this ordeal is over, he'll return to his family or continue bounty hunting, and I'll go home. He was made for greatness, to be an esteemed man in Brentyn, to one day have a beautiful wife and family, to be accepted at court. Even if the high lord gives me Papa's land and cottage, I'll always be the daughter of a Shaerdanian. I cannot change who I am.

Cohen and I could never be right for each other. No matter what my heart wants, our partnership is inevitably going to disband. It would be a mistake to let myself think otherwise.

I lie down and shut my eyes, hoping for a few more minutes of rest to settle my thoughts before we start the day.

"Britt," Cohen is saying moments later, or what feels like only seconds. "Wake up."

I push my eyelids open to discover the sun is higher in the sky than before, the gray light and shadows pushed back by the day's brightness. A yawn slips out as I stretch, hardly believing I slept.

"Time to go." Cohen stands up and tugs his bag over his shoulder. He gives me a look that screams impatience, like he's irritated with me or something.

I grumble, lurching to my feet. "Give me a moment."

He doesn't say anything more as I dig into my satchel for a water skin. After swishing out the stale taste in my mouth, I take a long drink and then splash the remaining water on my face. My morning cleanup is just about finished when the forest comes alive with the flapping of hundreds of birds. A flock lifts up and out of the green tops, sweeping overhead and continuing southward, away from Celize.

Cohen and I share a look, his sharp eyes mirroring my sudden alertness.

Any awkwardness between us is forgotten as we fall back into our old natures, prepared to defend. My dagger is unsheathed and in my hand, my bow and quiver slung across my back. Cohen's fingers rest on the hilt of his sword. He appears casual, though he's anything but relaxed. I know him well enough to know he's as ready as a nocked arrow. I take the first step, moving toward Siron, when Cohen's hand flicks out, palm to me.

"Stay," he mouths.

Then he continues stealthily toward the origin of the birds' movement.

I stare at his back, angry and irritated he doesn't grasp that we're in this together. If he thinks I'm going to stay here and wait for him, he's sorely mistaken. Let the fool think he can manage on his own. I keep him in my sights as I follow. We haven't gone far when I hear a low rumble echoing from the east. Cohen stops a dozen paces ahead of me, having heard the noise as well. Whatever is making the racket is far enough away; we're in no immediate danger.

It's then that Cohen turns around and notices me. His

eyes blaze and then taper into dark beads as he crosses the space between us in a blink.

He moves so close, I'm tempted to step back so I don't fall over, but his mouth lowers to my ear. "I asked you to stay."

The ache, stirred by his nearness, gets shoved into a neat little box. Then I slam the lid on it. "You didn't *ask* anything."

His breath against my skin is tormenting. "I'm sorry. Will you please stay?" His voice is barely more than a sliver of sound. When I don't respond, he changes his approach. "I can go alone and stay out of sight. It's safer that way."

It isn't safer for us to split up, not when there's a bounty on our heads and the entire town could be on our trail. When will he accept we're better off watching each other's backs? I put my hand on the center of his chest and push him back. Cohen's pulse hammers beneath my palm while his face is stone-like. I'm certain he's about to argue, but surprisingly he nods his agreement, and then turns and continues toward the rumble in the distance while I walk alongside him.

As we travel toward the road, clanks and grunts and whacks fill the air. We scale the trees beside the road, about a quarter league from the city, to discover the source.

More than a hundred soldiers in brown and blue uniforms move eastward along the packed dirt and rock route. Shaerdan's emblem, a blue and gold bird, whips around a flagpole, carried by men covered in partial chain mail. I wonder if they'll make the two-week trek to the border in that garb. It won't be easy. Some soldiers, polished and clean, travel on horseback, while others tend carts and march. The men, some with faces younger than mine, pass by, and I find myself wondering how many will suffer in this pointless war.

Wagons filled with armor and weapons, food and tents, pass one after another. The last three wagons are loaded with pieces of wood and metal, tied together in a way that resembles a giant insect. Catapults. In my lifetime, war has never come between our countries, and so I've never seen the damage a catapult can cause. Even so, I don't doubt it will be destruction on a grand scale.

Dust kicks up in the wake of the soldiers, swelling to a massive cloud, an apparition following the men until they're specks on the horizon. Papa risked his life to break the Spiriter's bind. Which means his death will be for nothing if there's war.

The soldiers are no more than an afterthought when Cohen nudges my arm and starts back toward camp.

I started this journey in part for my land, but mostly to avenge Papa. He was all I had, and I cannot accept that he was simply erased from this world for nothing. No, he died for a reason. I realize now, if I'm truly going to avenge his death, discovering the murderer isn't enough.

Cohen and I return to Celize to monitor the guards. If they decide to head back to Malam, we'll want to follow them once we find Papa's murderer. We'll be able to stick to the main roads. It would take a week off of travel.

"The guards have seen you dress as a boy," he says, and then plucks a bonnet from a clothesline on the outskirts of town. "If you wear the dress Enat gave you and put this on to cover your hair, they'll walk right past you."

Cohen moves into my space to put the bonnet on my head. He takes his time tying a bow beneath my chin.

I rush to look at my reflection in the window of the next cottage to hide the way my heart leaps.

"They'll still see my braid." I spin around when he approaches. "My hair is too white not to notice."

"Your hair isn't white. In the sun, it looks lighter, but it's definitely blond, pale blond. Either way, the bonnet will cover some and you can rub a mud and berry mix on your braid to darken the color."

I roll my neck, refusing to think of his observation. It means nothing more than he noticed my hair is blond. *Pale blond.* When we find a shaded corner, I pull Enat's dress from my bag and change. Cohen stands a few paces off, guarding my location. I crouch to pick up some mud and mix it with the berries Cohen had picked up. After making a thin paste, I work it through the part of my hair that shows. Once I'm ready, I tap him on the shoulder.

He turns around and his brows rise. "You—you look fine."

While I changed outfits, Cohen rubbed dirt on his. I stifle a smile. "What will your disguise be? Pig farmer?"

"I'm a beggar." He pulls a frayed cap from his satchel, places it on his head, and then bows forward, morphing his entire posture.

"The point of a disguise is to look different than you usually do."

"Amusing," he deadpans.

Like the night before, we split up, this time planning to meet at noon outside the stone church at the south end of town.

I head toward the guards' inn to chat up the housemaid. Walking in plain sight is disconcerting. I have to keep reminding myself to stop fidgeting with the dress. To take smaller steps. To smile instead of scowling. I'd give anything to trade the bonnet for a bow and arrow.

I'm a block away from the inn when Captain Omar and Tomas appear ahead.

I suck in a sliver of oxygen. I try to judge the amount of time till they reach me — two minutes at most — while scanning the road for a hiding place. There are no outlets, not enough people on the street to hide in a crowd, and no open doors. Reaching for one that may be locked would draw attention.

Up ahead, a flower cart sits on the east side of the road. It's not quite half the distance between them and me. I head there, eyes down. I try to act interested in the flowers as the guards approach.

When they pass, I say a silent thanks.

"Anything for the lady?" the vendor says.

I shake my head, not wanting to speak aloud, since the guards aren't far enough away. The vendor purses his lips and turns to another customer. When the guards are out of sight, I continue to the inn.

The housemaid is in the kitchen. She looks up, alerted by my footsteps. Her hands pause on the pot she was scrubbing. "Need a room?"

In my best Shaerdanian accent, I say, "No. My mum runs the tailor shop down the way. I was wondering if you had any customers who need mending done."

"Hmm, don't think so."

I hold back a frown, though somewhat irritated she's not falling into my trap. "Oh, Mum thought you had a full house." I try again. "You're certain nobody needs some mending in the next day or so?"

"Not this week. We haven't had much business, what with everyone called off to fight. We do have some soldiers staying here while they're awaiting an assignment from the chief judge. They haven't made a peep about needing a seamstress."

"Some soldiers were headed east earlier this morning. Are they part of that group?" I hope the comment fishes the answers I'm looking for.

Her eyes go round. "Oh, you saw men leaving already? Oh my. Perhaps the soldiers will be leaving soon, then."

If she only knew the guards weren't soldiers from

Shaerdan. "I'll tell my mum you had no tailoring that needed to be done."

"Will you stop by again?" She's friendly in a way girls have never treated me. It almost makes me want to linger. "Perhaps we'll have more work for you in the winter months."

A door opens and closes in the inn before heavy footsteps fall on the wood floor. Through the opening that separates the kitchen from the dining room, Leif's reddish hair is distinguishable. He stops at the table and places a bag on top. Dress or no dress, I've no doubt he'll recognize me if he notices me. Not wanting to risk speaking, I shrug in answer to her question and then move toward the kitchen's back door.

"What did you say your name was?" she asks, before I'm clear.

I shove my clammy hands into my dress pockets and silently plead for Leif to be gone. I slowly twist to face her so only my profile is visible to the dining area. I don't dare look in Leif's direction to see if he's still there. This way, he won't be able to see my entire face. By the gods, my accent better be believable enough.

"My name's Essa." It's all I could come up with on the spot and immediately regret as my response pricks through me. It's too close to Enat.

Waving once more at the maid to end the conversation, I force my feet through the doorway. My muscles are screaming to run, flight instinct taking over, though I don't risk making any quick movements.

"Wait."

Twenty steps are all I've taken before Leif calls out behind me.

I could run for it, except the chase would draw too much attention. Pleading is an option, not that it did any good the last time.

My hands are in knots as I find myself praying that he won't realize it's me, that this costume will be enough. If my nerves weren't wound so tight, I'd laugh at myself. It's hard to believe I'm this girl, clean-faced, wearing a dress and a bonnet, and pleading with the gods like some fool.

Twisting slightly, I drop my chin so the bonnet shades my face. "Yes, sir?"

"The girl said you work for the tailor."

I nod.

"I'm looking for a woman named Enat. She frequent your shop?"

I shake my head, itching to run. Relax. *Focus is a weapon as much as your bow.* "No, sir. I don't know her." I keep my accent true to Shaerdan.

He doesn't answer, nor does he leave.

The moment stretches for excruciating ages, and my lungs burn from the breath I'm holding. He must know it's me. Panic fires through me, lighting a blaze in my feet till they're shifting and ready to run.

"Thank you, miss," he says finally.

Shocked and relieved, I resist the urge to glance back as I hurry away.

Only when ten blocks are between us do I slip into an alley, check to see I'm alone, and then suck in deep breaths. Crescent marks of blood bubble to the surface of my palms where my nails dug deep.

That was too close.

A N OLD CHURCH RESTS ON THE EDGE OF THE cliff at the south end of town. Cohen meets me in the cloisters, and then, before either of us speaks, he has me follow him into the garden. When we're tucked behind a row of towering hedges near the cliff face, with only a short-stacked wall separating us from the edge where violent waves crash below, he's ready to talk.

"It's better here." Cohen's mouth is at my ear because it's too loud to hear him otherwise. The longing to press closer to him twists me up inside. I want to punch myself for even considering it.

"Delmar said the Archtraitor's agreed to meet at Enat's home in the morning."

Millner's possession of a charm to enter the tree cave speaks of Enat's trust of the man.

"He said Millner wasn't surprised that Enat wanted to speak with him," Cohen says. Up till now the hunt for Papa's murderer felt like we were chipping away at a glacier. What a relief it is to know we're on the verge of an answer. "Millner knew we were in town."

"How?"

"The guards have been talking to everyone." The warmth of his breath cascades over my ear, clashing with the brisk wind from the ocean. I suppress a shudder and try not to focus on how our proximity makes me feel. I consider mentioning the run-in with Leif and decide against it. Leif didn't recognize me, so it's inconsequential.

"Delmar also mentioned that Omar and his men are leaving town tomorrow."

Cohen moves back so I have a view of his face. He doesn't look pleased about the development. He glances toward the horizon, where whitecaps line the deep blue ocean. "Omar isn't the type to go on a wild-goose chase. He likes to lay a trap. You told Omar you wanted to prove I'm innocent. So Omar knows you'll return to Malam. That's where he'll wait."

I watch the seagulls fighting against the wind as they make their way closer to the cliff. I feel like I'm one of them, fighting against my position in life, fighting against the solitude, and now fighting for my freedom.

The breeze whips my hair across my face as I strain to hear him over the crash and boom against the cliff below. "I thought you'd be happy to hear they're leaving."

"He isn't headed to Malam just to wait us out." Cohen's tone sounds dark, if not a touch troubled. "That army we passed this morning was headed east. There's a rumor that the chief judge has declared war, whether King Aodren is ready or not. He's even sent word down to the Akarians in the southlands, asking to join forces."

"I thought only barbarians lived in the Akaria Desert. Why would the chief judge look to them for help?"

The grave set to Cohen's features tells of his thoughts. "Barbarians don't fight fair. The chief judge must be betting on that. Regardless, the guards are headed back because the war is definitely starting sooner than we realized."

Cohen holds my gaze for a moment and then looks over my shoulder, but not before a rare glimpse of emotion passes over his hazel irises. A hint of fear.

We're careful as we leave Celize, moving fast to erase our tracks until we reach Siron in the woods. Cohen runs his hands down the beast's mane and shoulders, once, twice, three times before turning to me. It seems like he has something on his mind.

The horse blows out a breath and moves before I reach his side, leaving his owner and me face-to-face.

"Do you think the war could really be stopped?" I ask, thinking about the letters to Enat and all that Papa risked.

His boot digs the dirt. "Possibly."

I fist my hands in the long folds of Enat's blue dress. "I've been thinking about it," I confess. "I want to finish what my father started." Papa died trying to break the bind on the king to stop the war, and it feels like my duty to see it through. After all, I've come this far.

Cohen drags in a long breath and looks up to the sky, exposing his neck. "It's too dangerous."

I almost laugh at him but manage to stop myself when I realize he's serious. Danger or not, doesn't he realize this is the best way to save his brother and the thousands of other young men being sent to their deaths?

I've no clue what's going through his head. It's one thing to return to Malam to prove Cohen's innocence. It's another to find a way to free the king and convince him to end the war. It cannot be done alone.

"Now that the army is moving, we have to act fast," I say encouragingly. "We should plan to return to Malam within the week."

"We don't have that much time." He turns away and clicks for Siron, but the suddenly stubborn horse won't come over. "If Omar and his men are already headed back to Malam, there must be some truth to the rumor. War could start as early as the chief judge's letter reaches the front. My guess is

Omar will try to beat the declaration party to warn Malam troops."

He's right. I pull the bonnet off my hair and start picking at the flecks of dirt left in my braid.

"I'll meet with the Archtraitor tomorrow," he confirms. "Then we'll leave. I made a promise to keep Finn safe, and I won't break it, even if everyone in Malam thinks I'm a murderer. Still, I'll give you one more day, Britta."

"Nice to see you made it back." Enat stands beside the woodpile in front of her cottage with a basket resting against her hip.

"That almost sounded like a welcome." I hop off Siron and lift the skirt of the dress so it doesn't drag in the mud as I approach her.

She snorts. "Better than the arrow."

"Ha. So true." I point at the basket. "Where are you off to?"

"When I went out a few days ago, the thistleberries weren't quite ripe. I'm hoping they'll be ready today."

The conversation with Cohen is on my mind as I watch her walk into the woods. Even if Millner identifies the murderer, we will still need her to break the spell on the king. Which, based on Papa's letters, I'm assuming she can.

"Could you use some help?" I ask, and then gesture to the dress. "I could change quickly."

Her brows lift, showing her surprise at my offer. She waves

me toward the cottage. "Go on. I'll wait for you. Company would be nice."

Without hesitation, I rush inside the treehouse and into Enat's room to strip off the blue garment. Once my breeches and tunic are in place, I hurry to her side, sparing a small wave at Cohen, who has made his way to the woodpile.

Enat doesn't talk as we weave between giant tree trunks and over tangled roots. By the time we stop beside a prickly bush, the inside of my mouth is raw with how I've been worrying my lip. After the kindness she's shown us, the thought of asking her to come to Malam, and possibly risk her life by using her Channeler gifts to save the king, doesn't sit well with me. And yet, I must ask. There's no other way to break the bind on the king.

She points at a nearby bush covered in tiny red berries. "This is chokewood. The leaves are good for making a healing tea, but the berries are poisonous."

"So don't eat them?"

"You're like me, impudent to the core."

I laugh at her assessment. I wouldn't mind being more like her. She's witty and strong and agile, as well as wicked with a bow.

"Gather the greener leaves from the bottom of the plant and pick these." She plucks an arrow-shaped mushroom from where it's tucked beneath the chokewood bush. "Find me when you're done," she says.

Ask her. Ask her. Ask—

Enat ambles away. I curse inwardly and set to plucking leaves and mushrooms. She has to go with us; if only I knew the right words to ask.

My fingers are knuckle deep in black dirt when Enat returns. "If I hadn't already met you, I'd think you were a shy little thing. Since I know better, tell me. Why are you so quiet over here?"

I snort. "Just busy picking the leaves." I wipe my hands on my pants and drop the last of the mushrooms into the basket.

"Busy is an understatement." She points at the bush where it's glaringly bald. My cheeks redden. "Have something on your mind, Britta?"

I glance up, knowing now is the time to ask. Our immediate departure tomorrow doesn't provide the luxury of putting off this request, not when Cohen's frantic to reach his brother. I flick my hands, shaking the tightness out of my fingers and releasing my reservations in asking this task of her.

"Will you . . . can you tell me about Channelers?" Seeds, I'm a coward.

"I'm willing to talk to you about Channelers, but tell me this: Do you want to learn about Channelers, or are you asking me how to break the curse on Malam's king?"

"Both," I admit truthfully.

H ER LIPS PRESS INTO A WRINKLED LINE. She moves to my side of the bush and begins plucking berries, her curled fingers working methodically. "All right," she says finally. "Since they go hand in hand, I can do that."

My hands go still over the leaves, relief singing through me. Her response makes me realize how much I want to know about Channelers. Learning how to break the bind is the cream on top. Ever since I healed the dog, I've been curious about what happened. If what I did is related to a Channeler gift, Enat may finally have some answers.

She examines the bush beside me. "It's a rare thing to have an ability. Most Channelers would never use their ability to hurt another. That doesn't mean it isn't possible. When it does happen, it's called black magic."

The clergyman said Enat uses black magic. Though she doesn't seem the type to hurt another, even if she's all bluster.

"Most Channelers would never attempt to use their power to harm because when a gift is used wrongly, it changes the Channeler. On the inside and outside. It's called black magic because it stains a person's heart and mind, changing their heart's intent and warping them into someone or something else." The lines around her eyes deepen as she looks down at her curled fingers.

"So Channelers use their connection to nature to help people? Like a water Channeler makes Beannach water?"

She snaps leaves off a small bush that grows at the base of the massive redwood. "You know of Beannach water?"

I weave the story of what happened beside the well, explaining how I healed Jacinda's dog and then suffered from a strange temporary exhaustion.

"You're a lucky girl." Enat nods thoughtfully. "Jacinda's ability to create Beannach water is rare."

I don't know what's more shocking, that Enat is familiar with Jacinda, or that she has no reaction to my story.

"So if a water Channeler can influence water, then a Spiriter can influence people's spirits?" I ask, forging on.

"I suppose you could say that."

"Since you're a Spiriter, can you break the other Spiriter's bind on the king?"

Her blue-eyed gaze turns upward to the pine needles before returning to me. "I haven't done it before, but I believe I can. If close enough to the man. It's a spell of proximity."

"Then will you come to Malam with us and try to break the curse?" A sharp prick of pain in my finger makes me realize my grip on the bush is too tight. I flick the thorn from my skin, cursing silently.

Enat gently sifts through the berries in her basket. It feels like years passing in the moments before she speaks.

She meets my gaze. Hers is steady and strong. "I'll go."

I let out a sigh, washed with relief. Cohen will be happy he waited one more day. Though Enat's willingness to go doesn't guarantee Finn's safety, it's a step in the right direction. Now all that's left to do is talk to the Archtraitor. If he can identify the murderer, we'll be headed back to Malam to declare Cohen's innocence and stop the war.

"I've twice as many berries as you, and I'm nearly three times your age," Enat says with a laugh as she looks into my basket. "Maybe we should talk less and pick more."

I groan my protest, though I don't mind at all; little of my life has been spent around women like Enat. The needles at the tops of the trees glint like fat emeralds in the afternoon sun, shimmering above as I follow her with a full basket on my arm.

Moving nimbly, Enat crawls over a tangle of roots that skirt a moss-painted trunk. "You should know the majority of Channelers have only a hint of the original ability. Most are not like Jacinda."

I scramble around the tree and fall into step beside her. Papa once bred a horse and a donkey to get a mule, and though it's a crude thought to pop into my head, it makes me wonder about Enat's magic.

"Could two Channelers marry?" I ask. "And create stronger offspring?"

Her foot pauses midstep over a root arching out of the ground, and a donkey-esque guffaw of a laugh bursts from her mouth. "Marry? No. Channelers are always women, since the gift is passed through the maternal line."

It never occurred to me women are the only ones with the gift. But of course that's the case. Still, my question is too funny not to laugh. I join in her chuckling until tears leak from her eyes.

After wiping her face and restoring some order, she adds, "We all have blue eyes."

Hers are the deep cerulean of the ocean, unlike mine, which are pale blue, a sister shade to frost. *Britta, your eyes are blue like the jewels, blue like your mother's.*

I almost laugh once more at the whirl of my thoughts, though unlike before, the humor is eclipsed by uneasiness sliding around beneath my skin. I want to scratch the feeling away. Two weeks from turning eighteen, and it seems as though I may not know myself at all.

It's growing more evident every day that Papa kept one more secret from me.

My fingers rub my sternum where an acute spot of grief grows.

I never questioned why I could discern the truth in others, because Papa explained it as gut instinct. I even figured my knack for knowing when an animal is close to death was hunter's intuition. But I cannot explain away how I healed the dog without considering the possibility that magic was involved.

"When I stopped at the Elementiary in town," I find myself saying, "that woman, Astoria, thought I was a Channeler. Me, a Channeler." I chuckle. Wait for the scoff. Any response to confirm the shopkeeper was out of her mind. Nothing comes. Just as I feared . . . and anticipated.

When Enat doesn't say anything, I push myself to continue. "I think I might be a Channeler, even if I can't explain how it's possible."

I never intended on trusting this woman who was a stranger days ago, and now here I am, fully waiting on her answers. Even if I cannot feel the warmth or chill from her words, my instincts tell me she's someone I can believe. She's someone who will tell me the truth.

Trust is a delicate thing, so easily broken and not so

effortlessly repaired. I spent years alone, guarding myself until my ability to trust others was reduced to a pile of splintered pieces. It's as though I'm sweeping all those shards together to ask one question: "Do — do you think I'm a Channeler?"

She stops just ahead of me and turns around, a faint smile curving the wrinkles around her mouth. "I'm certain you are. Can you guess which type?"

"A — a Spiriter?"

"Correct."

WHEN I WAS NINE, I FOLLOWED PAPA INTO a store where beautiful glass orbs were on display. Somehow, I bumped a delicate ball off the table. I remember it was as if it were happening in slow motion; and yet, to my horror, I couldn't stop the orb from hitting the ground, where, on impact, cracks spread across the glass, breaking it into countless pieces.

I'm the glass ball now, falling slowly and shattering into conflicting emotions.

Shock. Anger. Hurt. Confusion. Relief.

Seeds and stars, not just any Channeler, but a Spiriter? I rub my hands over my face and shove my fingers into my hair until my scalp twinges.

"Have you nothing to say?" Enat watches me with a touch of guarded curiosity.

"I feel like I should've known. I should've figured it out before now." My arms drop to my sides.

Her expression softens. "Oh, Britta, this knowledge is passed down from mother to daughter. And even then, you should know, it's rare. And not often spoken about because many fear what Spiriters are capable of. The gift only runs through a few bloodlines in Shaerdan. A handful of women in each generation possess this power, though not all have the full gift of being able to sense energy in all things and to manipulate and restore that energy.

"Your mother passed on when you were a wee baby, and your country has shunned magic. It's understandable that you didn't know."

Hearing her explanation of what a Spiriter is only makes me wish I'd learned this information years earlier. If it's passed from mother to daughter, then my mother kept it a secret. She must not have told Papa. When I think of all I never learned because my mother chose to return to Shaerdan instead of raise me, anger ignites inside me.

"I hate her," I think aloud, my voice full of sharp edges. "My mother left me alone in Malam. And because of her and my father's lies, I knew nothing." Part of me wants to say I hate him as well, but those words could never pass my lips. It's easier to blame the parent I've never met.

Enat's hand strays from her side and rests on my clenched arm. "Hate's a strong word, girl. It is one thing not to fathom the reason for her choices. You can be upset with her and your father for not telling you the truth. But don't hate her."

I glare at the dirt. "I should've known something was different about me. What a fool I am." This conversation started as an exploration and has now turned to bitterness.

"Don't say that. Girls your age have had training. They've been told about their abilities since they could crawl. You didn't have anyone to tell you."

"I had my father. He could've told me, though I suppose he didn't . . . he must not have known." I peer up at her as hope rises inside me, easing my anger toward Papa.

Enat links her arm through mine. "I cannot answer for him. Though I'm sure if he withheld anything, it was to keep you safe. If people knew what you are, you would've been in danger. Fear is bred of that which we don't understand. You would've been executed."

I remember the many times others ignored me at the market. Or when they didn't overlook me, instead throwing hateful comments in my direction. "Still, I was an outcast," I say, though it's leagues better than death.

"Our lives are, like these woods, ever changing. Nothing is static. And so you cannot count on an easy, carefree life to always remain that way. Or a harsh existence to stay the same. Life can get better. Or life can always become worse. And then you die." Enat smiles ruefully. "Don't reflect on the negative. Think about all the positives in your life."

She's right. And I'm a brat for having pitched a fit at all.

"I wish ..." I'm not sure how to finish. I want so many things my situation cannot yield. I wish to be more than what I've been. To be free of the past. To understand and embrace who I truly am. But mostly, "I wish I could have one more chance to talk to my father." My whisper is lost in the wind that kicks through the trees, their shuffling leaves the only answer back.

Enat adjusts the basket on her hip, trailing her fingers from the berries to the mushrooms. I watch her, remembering the clergyman's comments about the rarity of a Spiriter. In that moment, details stand out on Enat that I hadn't noticed much before — her faded freckled arms, her narrow frame, her sapphire eyes.

My mouth goes dry as dirt. I lick my lips, though the effort produces no moisture. "Enat, are you—?" I clear my throat, fighting to keep panic from my expression. "Are you my mother?"

She lowers the basket, her gaze losing a touch of focus for a beat.

"No, I'm not." I note a twinge of disappointment in her eyes.

Oddly, the look is mirrored by my own remorse. I accepted my mother's death years ago, so it's utterly moronic to feel bereft now. Still, I wish her answer had been different.

"Of course." I ignore the strange ache and shrug. "How

silly of me . . . I saw that we both have blue eyes and light hair and . . ."

"Britta."

"Yes?"

Her left hand contracts around the handle of the basket as she takes a small step toward me. "I — I am your grandmother."

A sputter and a gasp break from my mouth, leaving me gaping at her. "You — you're my grandmother?"

She slips her hand through my elbow and tugs me close, which is as good as an embrace when it comes to Enat. "Welcome home, girl."

A hysterical bubble of laughter bursts from my lips. I've never felt so tumultuous inside. So happy and at the same time so wronged. I don't know what to do with all the angry and frustrated thoughts directed toward my father. If I have a living, breathing grandmother — someone else who would accept me, love me — why, then, would Papa keep me from her?

Why would he leave me alone in Brentyn to fend for myself? If he knew her to be a Spiriter, wouldn't he have known the same of me? Or at least suspected as much? The question leads my mind into a dark and hollow place, where vicious thoughts are hungry preying wolves. Recoiling from them, I dig my toe into the soft dirt and turn my chin to face Enat.

"So, you really, really are my grandmother?" The question begs to be asked once more just to be sure.

Enat lets out a cackle of a laugh, a rusty rumble that she's let loose a few times now and that sums up her coarse mix of kindness. "Britta, we are so much alike, it amazes me you didn't see it before. Yes, I am your mother's mother. You're my flesh and blood. Now let's head back and I'll make you some lunch while we talk, because I've no doubt you're brimming with questions."

Cohen is chopping wood outside the cottage when we walk out of the forest. He must've been at it for a while, since sweat marks his shirt in a dark V. He stops the ax and waves. I might as well be tied to a flock of birds for how his smile eases an invisible weight from my shoulders.

"You were gone for a while, so I chopped wood," Cohen tells Enat as he tosses another one onto the stack, where it thuds against the others, causing a few to tumble out of the neat pile. "And then some."

She appraises his split logs while I struggle to stop myself from appraising the woodcutter. "Good. It'll keep for winter."

I lift my basket and grin. "She's a taskmaster."

"As demanding as Saul?"

"Close." I glance at Enat and marvel, once again, at our connection. I have to shake my head to stop myself from gawking at her. *My grandmother,* the thought, one I never imagined having, makes my body fill with joy. However, the rush isn't enough to drown out the sadness for all the years missed out on knowing her. The dueling emotions are turning me mad.

When Enat takes the basket into the cottage, I start toward

Cohen to tell him everything I just learned. He'll be pleased to hear Enat's willing to go with us—something I'm overjoyed about now that I know who she is and that we will have over a week of travel time to spend together. I wonder what Cohen will think when he finds out she is my grandmother.

"It took three hours?" Cohen drops the ax.

His detached, cold manner stops me midstep. "Appears so. Everything all right with you?"

"It's been a long day and"—he rubs his shoulder and up his neck, so it's obvious something's gotten under his skin— "I've been thinking. We need to discuss our return."

"All right," I say quietly, swallowing my confession of how the last few hours rearranged everything about myself and my life. Turning away, I move toward the house when Cohen's hand, callused and warm, wraps around my wrist.

"Wait. Don't go in yet. Tell me about your talk with Enat. You seem . . . different."

I *am* different. Knowing there's someone who understands me and is just like me, even related to me, changes everything. It upends my world and, at the same time, grounds me. It mixes me up with so many differing emotions, I can hardly see straight. Still, "Enat can break the bind" is all I say.

"Really? She's willing to come with us?"

"Yes."

Cohen follows me into the cottage. "Good. Now we just have to talk with the Archtraitor and then we can leave."

"Hopefully." I shrug as I slip through the door.

Enat sits at the table, busily sorting berries, leaves, and mushrooms into separate piles. Her warm gaze finds me and she smiles, a look that's contagious.

"Britta?" Cohen fixes on my silly grin.

Avoiding his curious gaze, I force myself to act natural. "Need a hand, Enat?"

"I could use some water." She juts her chin toward the bucket by the door. "Fetch a pail from the well out back, will ya?"

The trip to the well and back is quick. Enat and Cohen are talking when I return; the deep notes of their voices echo through the door. I'm about to go inside when Cohen says something too clear to miss: "You told her. You should've let her go without knowing."

"I had every right. I did what I thought was best."

There's a loud thump. Startled, my hold on the bucket loosens and water sloshes down my legs. Cursing, I smack the water droplets away before entering Enat's home to find Cohen rigid as a board with fists at his sides and Enat standing beside the table, her eyes are slits directed at my travel partner. Then the scene breaks, and both of them resume talking as though things weren't tense a moment earlier. As if they could hide the argument from me.

"What were you talking about?" I set the pail on the table. "Cohen?"

He shifts his weight. Straightens his tunic. Looks at the

ground. A seed of unease lodges between my shoulder blades as I recall the words he spoke.

"What did you mean when you said, 'You told her'?"

"Britt." He gives a small, pleading shake of his head.

The emotions he usually excels at taming run with abandon across his features. Apprehension. Remorse. Guilt.

"I didn't—" he starts. Stops and narrows his eyes on Enat, before shaking his head and looking up to the ceiling.

I'm confused. My scrutiny jumps from him to her. Then— in the space between two heartbeats—everything clears.

"You knew?" My voice a squeak.

"Britt, listen, I can explain." Each word from his mouth could be a boulder for how it flattens me. "I didn't want you to find out like this." His tone is soft and gentle and pleading like I'm some damn horse to be tamed. He reaches for me. I rear back.

"The girl had a right to know," Enat says.

He ignores her, peering at me. "Britt."

I pull my lips between my teeth and blink until my eyes stop stinging and his towering height is in sharp focus. I won't lose it in front of him. "How could you keep this from me?"

"I couldn't tell you. I promised your . . ." He doesn't have to complete the sentence for the pieces of this puzzle to fall into a complete and devastating picture. After all, I already suspected Papa knew. Just couldn't bring myself to believe it till now.

"You promised my father," I finish for him. It doesn't need to be a question, for his speechlessness answers loud and clear. Fingers digging into the hard planks of wood, I steel myself against the edge of Enat's table. "How long have you known?"

His hand strays to the scar, tracing it like always, only this time there's a noticeable shake of nerves in the movement of his fingers. "Since before I left."

My snap of a gasp echoes in the otherwise silent room as his confession strikes truer than a blade to my heart. Cohen knew who I was—what I was—and left me alone in Brentyn. His words eviscerate me.

Unable to stand in the cottage and face him, knowing how he's held secrets about me, truths about me that I should've known first, I charge out of Enat's home, tumultuous emotions seizing control of me like I've never known. I'm a blizzard, a thunderstorm.

Enat's bow is laid up against the side of her home. It occurs to me how similar we are, though the moment is too bittersweet and tainted to appreciate it. I grab the weapon with its full quiver and charge out of the treehouse.

Before I can reach the edge of the trees, a door slams behind me and even before he speaks, I know it's him.

"Britt, please." He sounds small and lost. Though I've never heard Cohen like this before, I cannot yield to him because my heart is bleeding pain throughout my entire body. My lungs cannot draw air. My throat aches from dryness. Pressure builds behind my eyes. I blink rapidly to keep my face dry, knowing that if he moves any closer, he'll see the wake of his destruction. What I need most is to just get away.

I hold up my hand. "Don't—please don't come closer."

"Talk to me, then."

"No. Let me go," I say so quietly, it's a wonder he can hear me at all. He must, however, because he doesn't follow as I swing the bow over my shoulder and dart into the lush, thick forest.

I STRING ARROW AFTER ARROW, LETTING THEM fly into the trees in this remote corner of the forest. Aim and shoot. Again and again. Twang and thunk until the quiver is empty, and then, after gathering what's reachable, I start again.

Know how to protect yourself, Papa said. *You have to be strong. Strong as the trees.*

I shoot, shoot, shoot, arrows landing into the knot of a tree, the rough curve of bark, a leaf as it floats toward the forest floor. Birds squawk and flap out of the treetops.

Strong for what? Papa taught me to track, hunt, fight, survive; never once did he prepare me for his lies. His betrayal weakens me more than any foe. And yet, even though my anger at Cohen and Papa eats at me, I feel as though I should just forgive Papa because he's gone. Except then I remember that he kept Enat from me. This wonderful, somewhat mad, quirky woman who is my flesh and blood was held out of my life. And for what? So I could be alone? So I could be mocked?

Papa's actions make no sense. I want to hit something, hurt something, and at the same time I want to lie down, curl up, and cry.

A branch snaps behind me. I spin around, surprised to find Siron of all intruders, and lower my bow.

"What do you want?"

His ears perk to my savage and rough voice. Once he crosses the clearing, his nose drops to my hand, nudging with gentle pressure.

"So now you're my friend?"

The felt of his lips tickles, softening the tight ball of despair inside me. I'm so chock-full of wild emotion — I could be the beast and he the animal tamer.

"Why'd he do it, boy?"

Hot breath puffs from Siron's nostrils as he moves around me, chewing at ferns. He remains close as I return to shooting, gathering arrows, and shooting some more. The shadows multiply, daylight pushing into dusk as the forest quickens with the chattering of squirrels and, eventually, the need to fill the trees full of arrows fades.

When I'm done, Cohen's loyal horse is still here. Not sure why he stayed, I move to his side and run my hands over his muscular flanks and through his coarse raven mane.

"He hurt me," I say to Siron, my forehead dropped against his sturdy shoulder. "And I don't know how to forgive him."

"Please say that isn't true."

Spine snapping straight, I back away from his horse as I lift the bow, taking aim. "You shouldn't be here, Cohen."

With his body leaning against a tree and arms crossed, his notice flicks to the point of my arrow and back to my face. "You going to shoot me?"

"I'm considering it."

He sighs through his nose. "Guess I deserve that."

I lower the bow. "Explain yourself, Cohen. Make sense of this."

"I was only doing what Saul asked. I—"

"Stop. Please stop." I don't want to hear that Papa knew I had other family. Or that he shared such secrets with my best friend. I've been battling those emotions since I wandered into this area of the forest, and hearing them from his tongue only scrubs salt into the wound. "Don't speak of Papa. Right now I need to know why *you* didn't tell me when we arrived in Celize."

"I swear I didn't know who Enat was at first. I had an idea, but Saul never told me her name, only that she was still alive. And he said she was a Spiriter. After we arrived, I confirmed my suspicions. I would've told you, but your father—"

"My father is dead!"

Cohen's jaw tightens against his placid expression.

"You couldn't have told me when Papa died? I was alone.

I had no one. Nowhere to go. What did you think I'd do when the guards came for my home?"

He has the decency to look wounded, shoulders curling forward around his frame. "I thought you might trade for lodging. I — I never wanted you to suffer. I gave Saul my word." His eyes plead with me as he says this, though I'm not sure what he wants from me. His hands have a slight shake as he pulls them together. "We were protecting you."

"Protecting me? Did you even wonder what I would do during mourning? Who would bring me food? Cohen, I nearly starved. The hunger got so bad, I could count most of my ribs. How could I have traded for lodging if I'd died?"

The realization settles in and puts a haunted look in his gaze.

"I ran out of food and couldn't make it out of the mountains, so I was forced to poach. Captain Omar caught me and that is why I had to make this deal or hang from the noose." All my frustration and anger forge the iron in my voice into a blade. I want my words to cut and hurt him as he's done to me. "Is that what you and my father wanted?"

"Oh gods, Britt. I didn't . . . I didn't think. It seems so obvious now, but I swear, it never entered my mind. During those months, I was too focused on finding who killed your father. I didn't sleep. Barely ate, for that matter. I know it's not a good excuse, but it's the truth. I . . . I'm sorry."

I turn away, torn between yelling at him and calling him a fool.

"Please, believe me." His voice catches. "If I'd remembered, I would've come. It was a stupid, terrible mistake, and I will forever be sorry."

Even if he's apologetic for leaving me alone in a time of mourning, it doesn't take away from the plain truth that he has kept my heritage a secret from me.

I wave off his apology.

"Did you not trust me to keep my own secrets? You should've told me what I was capable of. Enat is strong and capable, and she has this ability that I know seeds about. And I—I know nothing about myself."

He gives me a pleading look. "You're strong and capable as well. Hell, you're more capable than anyone I've ever met." His earnestness works like a balm, soothing my anger. Cohen crosses the space between us—and bloody curse me to the devil if I don't want him to come even closer. My pulse pounds and aches and bleeds hurt throughout my entire body.

"This isn't how I wanted you to find out," he whispers. It's a choppy sound, broken with sentiment I don't understand. What's he holding back? Are there *more* secrets?

"How *you* wanted me to find out?" I repeat, anger remembered. "You could've told me anytime and you didn't. You . . . I—I trusted you." The strain in my voice gives away my heartache. "You're my *only* friend."

His head drops, so I'm forced to stare at his unruly mess of roasted-chestnut brown hair.

"For everything, I'm sorry." His words are gravelly and rough. "I swear by the gods I didn't want to leave you last year. Every day has been agony for me. Saul asked me to go. No, he begged me, saying it'd be safer for you."

I shake my head, denying his accusation because I cannot take one more secret about Papa, even though heat is pooling in my gut. Horrid truthful heat. "You had just saved my life. Why would my father ask you to leave?"

He lifts his head. The raw passion in his eyes and on his slackened mouth pierces me.

"What do you remember of our last hunting trip together?" His voice dips into a rasp.

It's always bothered me that I couldn't remember all of it. When I don't answer, he urges me to try. I wrinkle my brow as my focus shifts to the last time we hunted together. Nothing more than vague memories, random pieces like swatches of fabric that don't fit together, comes at first. I remember a hole in the ground . . . Cohen falling . . . a mountain cat . . . and blood.

Too much blood.

I frown, no longer wanting to continue this conversation.

"I shouldn't have left the path," he says. There's an urgent cadence in the way he speaks. It sets me on edge. "I wanted to find a faster route, even though you told me not to go. The mountainside was dangerous after the spring landslide, but I didn't listen, and I fell through a hole into a cave." Images form in my memory gaps as he tells his story. "There was a vine I could've used to climb out, but I didn't want to ask for help. Light was coming from the far end of the cave, so I told you I'd find my way out. You, of course, said I was absurd because you could see the vine too."

That's right. I'd rolled my eyes at him. Called him a bludger.

"When I'd fallen into the cave, I dropped my bow and couldn't find it." He waits, watching me and allowing time for my mind to catch up, and as it does, more unease creeps in. My breath turns shallow as he continues. "I wasn't prepared for the mountain cat. I didn't have a chance to block it before it attacked. I barely remember the struggle, mostly just the pain. Gods, it was terrible."

Forgotten cries echo in my head. The bow drops to my feet as I shove the heels of my hands into my eye sockets, pressing against the horror crawling out of the corners of my mind:

Cohen lying in a pool of red, unconscious and barely breathing.

Tattered skin.

Exposed bones.

His teeth gleaming through a gash in his cheek.

Red, red, red everywhere.

"I heard you cry out." His voice vibrates through me — he's crossed the clearing and is pulling my hands from my face as he speaks. "I was struggling to breathe, and still I was worried for you. I thought you'd been attacked also. We were both going to die, and it was my fault."

My eyes won't shut; they're frozen against the avalanche

of nightmarish memories. The scar on his face has been there this entire time and I never questioned it. Never put more thought into the sort of savage attack that would mar his skin. I thought it was the price he had paid to save *my* life.

"I was searching for the cave opening when you screamed. I'd never heard you sound like that." My voice doesn't sound like mine. "So — so pained." His fingers slide from my wrists to my hands, clutching them tightly. "I found my way in and saw your blood. You were still beneath the cat, that massive beast." What's left of the saliva in my mouth is dust. "I — I remember now, taking it down. One arrow to the vitals, one to the neck."

A shudder racks my body as the overwhelming images, in perfect lucidity, play in my mind.

"It was too late, though," I recall softly. "Wasn't it?"

There's carefulness in the way he nods.

"You were bleeding." Each word I utter is a thread stitching the story back together and simultaneously pulling me, unraveling me. "There was too much . . . and — and I tried to help. I put my hands on you. Your heart beat once . . ."

Everything turns to stone inside and plummets, the vivid and harrowing truth knocking me harder than a horse hoof to the chest. I can scarcely breathe.

"I watched you die, Cohen."

DO YOU KNOW WHAT HAPPENED NEXT?" A touch of uncertainty lingers in his question, anguish in his watchful eyes.

"I think I prayed for you," I admit with a grimace, knowing how strange the confession sounds, especially from me, the last person who'd attend Sunday service or kneel at the stone of the royal church's altar. And yet I remember that in his final moment, I would've paid any price to save him. Would've given my heart, my blood—anything to let him live. "The next thing I remember is Papa leaning over my bed, lathering my neck with that nasty fever rash poultice. After that, nothing. It's strange how I can recall the cloying scent of his poultice. And not much else," I muse aloud.

Cohen reaches for his neck. He catches me

studying him and promptly drops his arm to his side. His expression may not give much away, but I can tell from his body language he knows more.

"Tell me what happened next."

He shuffles back a few steps, his eyes drawn to the ground where his boots push through the creeping groundcover to the near-black dirt below. When his gaze lifts to meet mine, I can see the shift to acceptance, as well as pain. Whatever he's about to tell me is a great burden on him.

"When I woke, I felt like I'd been chewed up and spat out." His words are rough but he pushes them out, determined, even though it seems like he's in pain. "There was blood on my clothes and in the dirt, and my shirt was shredded. I'd seen enough death to know that much blood loss would kill me, so I tried to find my wounds and cover them."

His boot stops its restless gouging in the dirt. "All that blood, Britt, and there were no scratches or cuts anywhere. It was the strangest thing. Beneath all of it, I had scars . . . like the attack had happened months before, not moments."

His fingers slide across my cheek and I jolt, startled by his touch because I'm so lost in what he's saying.

"I found you at my side, pale and cold." He whispers cracked words. His hand gently cradles my cheek, and his eyes glisten as they peer into mine. "Your heartbeat . . . It was so slow, I was certain you wouldn't . . ."

Siron nudges Cohen with his nose until his master relents, patting the beast. When the horse moves away, Cohen continues. "I carried you home. Your father called for a healer. She asked too many questions, though. I told the healer you were attacked by a mountain cat. Only you had no wounds or gashes or anything, while I had this." He points to his face. "Nothing sounded believable. So Saul made up a tale that we'd been out in the woods earlier and crossed paths with a mountain cat. He said I was confused about the attack date. I had jumped in front of the cat to save you, but in the scuffle you fell hard. Saul told the healer we sent for her because you'd taken a turn for the worse."

He blows out a breath, eyes searching the sky, the ground, then my face.

"That doesn't explain why my father asked you to go away."

"Don't you see? You healed me, Britta. Completely." His arms fly out to his sides, palms facing forward, stretching his tunic across his torso, as he retreats a couple steps. "If I stayed, you'd want to know what happened. I wanted to tell you, only Saul forbade me because it was too dangerous for you. You know what happens to Channelers. If word got out and someone accused you, you'd have been thrown in the pillory at the very least, if not tortured and hung."

It's infuriating to know Papa asked my friend—my *only* friend—to leave me, and yet his argument makes sense. It seems every week there is a new woman shackled in the market square. Still, bitterness coats my tongue as I ask, "How long was he going to keep the truth from me?"

"I don't know. He said it was better, no, safer, for you not to know."

"And so you simply left?"

He lets out a harsh scoff of a laugh. "Simply? There was nothing simple about my decision. I couldn't sleep or eat for days. I didn't want to leave. But I"—his chin drops and his eyes crinkle together—"I couldn't lie to you. In the end it was easier to leave."

I want to believe what he's saying, except I'm too incensed, too hurt from the confidences kept behind my back to retreat. I make a sour face. "Easier? Is it easier to lie to me from far away?"

The tiniest frown tugs the corners of his mouth down and then disappears when he lets out a frustrated growl. "Yes, you could say that."

A small prick of pain accompanies his candid answer.

"People notice oddities in Malam. Someone would've asked questions about the attack. With me still in Brentyn, there were more opportunities for people to see us together and speculate. If I was out of the scene, it would be more likely that the town gossips would forget. I had to leave."

"You didn't *have* to leave," I say with weak conviction. A gust kicks through the trees, scattering pods and leaves around us, and infusing the air with an earthy, woodsy tang. In the past, the scent of the outdoors brought quietness to mind when my thoughts were turbulent. Today it does little to soothe the parts of me that are ravaged inside. I tuck a freed hair back into my braid and wait for him to respond.

"Yes, I did. I couldn't stay near you. You are . . ." He pauses, mulls over his thoughts, and then adds, "Noticeable."

I roll my eyes.

"It's true. You've always thought the townsfolk pay you no attention, but you're wrong. They watch you *because* you're different." I cringe and he waves a hand. "When the healer threatened to talk, Saul knew I had to leave town to lessen the chance of gossip. You must know, I'd do anything to keep you safe." Cohen steps around my side to rub Siron's nose. "Do you remember the night I met you in the woods?"

It was the first time I'd seen him since the accident and the only time he visited before he left. Of course I remember. Long after Papa had retired for the night, an invisible tug pulled me from bed and out of the cabin. Cohen was waiting in the trees. When I woke earlier that day, Papa explained how Cohen had risked his life to save me. I accepted Papa's story easily.

Embarrassment and shame kept me from confessing my memory loss.

The need to touch Cohen, to verify he was all right, coursed through me until I reached out and placed my hand on his arm. On contact, everything in me relaxed.

That night was the first time I confessed my feelings to Cohen.

He pulled away, saying he had to leave and that he'd return the next day.

Only he never did.

I've relived the memory countless times, searching for a missing clue to make sense of why he'd go away without saying goodbye. All this time, I believed he was angry with me for being the cause of his pain, his new disfigurement. And wondering if my admission of caring for him actually scared him off.

Cohen's fingers glance over mine, pulling me back to the present at Siron's side.

"The moment you touched me, I knew I'd made a mistake in meeting you. I wanted to stay, and not just for a few minutes. Seeds and stars, Britt, I wanted to hold you and never let go. It felt like I was ripping out my heart when I walked away that night. But it was necessary. I left because I didn't want to put you in danger. Not again. Not after you'd healed me. I left to keep you safe."

I pull my hand from his grip, needing space, and suck in a great big gulp of air as I walk away.

"I almost killed you." Cohen rounds Siron and follows me a half dozen paces through the clearing. "You saved my life, and you almost died in the process. I'm not sorry I left. I'd do it again to protect you. I'll always do what I must to protect you. I am sorry, however, for hurting you. Never wanted that."

The angst in his voice clears away the last remnants of my anger. Both the new anger at finding out he'd kept my heritage a secret, and the old anger at his abandonment that I hadn't even realized I'd been holding on to. Cohen and I are not so different—we both left Malam for the other. Except his reason was to save me. Considering the deal I made with Lord Jamis, how can I be furious with Cohen? Any remaining anger ebbs within me.

"You risked yourself for me," he says pleadingly, brokenly. "Why'd you do it?"

He deserves my honesty no matter how raw it leaves me. "I loved you," I confess. "I would've given my life for you."

His golden-brown eyes widen. "You loved me?"

"Yes." I stare at the prints in the dirt that define our time here.

"What about now?"

My sight lifts to his, and all that fear from before rushes back tenfold. Despite his explanation for leaving, the cowardly voice inside my head begs me not to answer. Of course my feelings haven't changed, only deepened.

I purse my lips and make up my mind to just say it. Just tell him.

But he steps in, slicing the space between us. "I felt the same way then." His tenor could be mistaken for a bass, if it were louder than a murmur. "Feel the same way now."

My breath hitches.

He comes to me quickly, drawing me against him with sudden force that makes my pulse skitter. His lips and nose crush my hair. "Britt, I love you. Then and now. Please say you still feel the same?"

"Cohen" comes out airily.

He moves back enough to look down at me, hope and worry wrinkling his forehead.

"Even now," I say. "I love you."

The answering smile that spreads across his face could rival the dawn. This man. The things he does to me.

Ducking his head, Cohen kisses my cheek, my nose, the corner of my smile, and when I cannot wait a moment longer, he murmurs, "I love you," once more against my lips as his mouth slants over mine. His hands clutch my back as he cinches my body tighter against his. His lips are soft, though his kiss is full of hard desperation. Different from our first, this kiss is full of hunger and need and forgiveness.

THE ARCHTRAITOR ISN'T THE MASSIVE THREAT
of a man I thought he'd be. He's squatty
and round, with dimpled cherry cheeks
that plump like fall apples when he smiles, which
he's done often in the short time since he arrived
at Enat's home.

It's not quite midday as we all sit around
the table. After Cohen and I returned from the
woods last night, we prepared our weapons and
packs for travel, so we're ready to leave.

"You're the Archtraitor?" Cohen asks the visi-
tor.

The jauntiness slides from the man's face.
"That's one of many names, though I like Mill-
ner. Sounds better and it rolls off the tongue.
Also, Millner doesn't attract the king's guard like
Archtraitor," he says, chuckling, "so I prefer it."

"Millner it is, then."

The chair creaks as Millner leans back, clasping his hands over his belly. "Let's get to this, shall we? It wouldn't be good for me to be caught in this area of the woods. But I owe you a favor, and you know I'm good for it." He finishes the last bit while aiming a knowing glance at Enat.

"You know what they want." There's no nonsense in Enat's response. "What can you tell them?"

Millner shifts to face Cohen and me. "You tell me what you're looking for and why, and I'll see if I can help you out. Yes?" He grins.

I openly stare at the man, confused as to why anyone would believe this man could evade my father for years. How did this portly figure earn the legendary Archtraitor status?

Cohen taps my knee under the table. It's his way of putting the reins in my hands.

"Enat said you knew my father, Saul Flannery," I explain. "He was murdered here in Celize, and Cohen was accused of it. The king's guard are after us, and if we're caught, Cohen will be executed. We're looking for the murderer."

A broad smile sweeps across Millner's round features. "I knew Saul. Salt of the earth, he was. And if I could, I would've given my life for his. To think, most people in your situation would've run. You're a mighty impressive girl, trying to track down the killer of your father when you have the guards knocking down every door looking for you. They put a nice bounty on your head."

"Which is why we're here, talking to you," Cohen reminds him.

"Yes, well, I'm not sure how much help I can be to you." The fleshy skin beneath Millner's chin shimmies like a turkey gobble when he speaks.

I frown.

"Now, Britta." He pats his belly. "I have an idea of who murdered your father—I'm just not sure how much it'll help you with the guards. See, the night of the murder, a friend of mine was at the same tavern as your father. Lucky for him, he was taking care of some other business." His face reddens and he coughs, as if I'm naive to what else happens inside taverns.

"Was he with a wench?"

Millner lets out a hearty laugh. "You're smart. Not afraid to speak the truth. I like you. You remind me of your father."

"Yes, well, I'd like *you* more if you could just give us a name." I flash him a wry smile.

He chuckles. "Bear with me. I'm getting there. So this friend of mine just happened to be coming into the tavern through a hidden door when your father was killed. He had the wits to back right out that door before anyone saw him."

"And where'd he go?"

"To me, of course."

Millner has lost his seeds. I cross my arms and lean back. "Your friend saw a man killed, and then told no one but you?"

"Aye. Smart man, my friend. Information like this could've cost him his life."

Even though his words register true, I'm still skepti-cal. "Please, don't leave me in anticipation. What did your friend say?"

"The man who killed your father was wearing the king's emblem on his coat."

I let out a frustrated sigh. "Cohen and I have already deter-mined that the only person who likely killed Papa was one of the king's guards or one of the men close to him. That doesn't help us."

He clucks his tongue. "Patience, Britta. I wasn't finished. Citizens of Celize aren't subjects to King Aodren, but some still fear his reach, as well as the men who serve him. In a busy tavern, there should've been a dozen witnesses. Do you know how many there were?"

"Two," I answer, remembering what Lord Jamis said.

"Two. So you see, people are afraid to talk."

He has a point. "Do you have a description of the guard?"

Millner chuckles. "Just like your father—"

"A description?" If he compares me to my father again right now I might consider taking him back to Malam as well.

"Older man, dark hair, tall, with a solid build."

"That description matches a number of guards." Cohen steals the response right off my tongue.

There is a slight mischievous glint in Millner's eyes as he leans closer to me. "I suppose I should also add that the man's coat had five stripes. Do you know who wears five stripes on his uniform?" He sits up tall, gleaming triumphantly.

I know exactly whose coat he's talking about. "Captain Omar," I say, though hardly able to believe it's true.

"Aye, Captain Omar."

Did the captain really kill my father? Why would he accompany me on a hunt to find an innocent man? Perhaps his motive is to pin the murder on someone else. The truth of what Millner is saying warms me through, but the realization of his words shocks me to my core.

Perhaps Captain Omar needed me to lead him to Cohen so he could take Cohen's life as the man who murdered the king's bounty hunter. Such a devious move would leave the captain free of suspicion. It would even elevate him to the status of a hero. What would the captain gain from Malam and Shaerdan going to war?

"Now can you see why the truth won't do you much good?" Millner's question pulls me from my thoughts.

I groan inwardly at his perceptiveness. He's right. The truth only complicates matters. Two days ago I was certain finding the murderer would solve most of our problems. Now there is an entirely new set of obstacles to face.

How will we convince the high lord that the captain of the guard is guilty? There's no chance the testimony of an unnamed man, told from the mouths of two escaped criminals, will stand against the evidence.

Someone knocks on Enat's door.

A mouse could scurry across the floor and it'd sound like

the padding of a bear for as quiet as we all become. Enat is the first to rise, pulling a blade into her hand.

"Relax. It's just my girl." Millner waves at the weapon Enat has pointed toward the door. "You won't need that."

"Why didn't you say so?" Enat sheaths the blade and welcomes in a girl with hair so dark, it looks like the blue-black of a moonless night sky. She is about my age, with blue eyes set against tawny skin and rosebud lips.

"I didn't expect to see you here, Lirra." Enat pats the girl on the shoulder. "Could've warned me you were coming."

The girl smiles, a gentle curve that levels when her eyes scan the room and stop on Cohen and me. "And miss surprising you?" she says to Enat. "Never."

Enat grumbles a response, to which Lirra laughs. Curiosity and, if I'm being honest, a little jealousy seizes me. I've only just discovered Enat is my grandmother. But I want to have a relationship like the one Enat shares with Lirra. Suddenly, I feel like I've been pretending my entire life. Acting as though I don't care when people say unkind things to me. Acting like it doesn't matter that no one wants to be my friend. Acting as if I'm not lonely.

"Lirra, meet my granddaughter." Enat points in my direction. "Speak freely around her and her friend, Cohen. They can be trusted."

I try not to flush at the compliment. How silly I was for worrying that Enat wouldn't want others to know of our connection. Hearing her say I'm her granddaughter fills me with a warmth of a completely non-Spiriter kind.

"Hello." Lirra waves at me. Her eyes linger on my face long enough that I know she's studying me, perhaps comparing me to Enat. Her attention makes me acutely aware of my knobbiness and dirty hair. Before we leave for Malam, perhaps there'll be time for another bath.

"I didn't know you had a granddaughter," Lirra says. "I thought you said your daughter died years ago."

"She did," Enat answers, her tone turning abruptly cold. I spare her a glance.

"It's nice to meet you, Britta." Lirra extends her hand, and I reach out and take it.

"Lirra," Millner interrupts, "did you see anything?"

She retreats. "Yes, Papa. The men dressed as soldiers for Shaerdan left today, and a rider on the road was carrying a black flag."

For the first time since he entered this house, Millner's expression takes a grave turn.

"What does the black flag mean?" Cohen asks.

"It means there must've been another skirmish at the front," Millner explains. "The black flag is raised when men have died. Lirra, go on, what've you heard?"

"Thirty men from Shaerdan were killed. One troop left two days ago, but today the council decided one from Celize isn't enough. They're calling all able men to fight. I also heard that the chief judge is traveling to the front with members of the inner court. They're asking for a meeting of our countries."

"Interesting." Millner taps a finger to his lips. "Still, the meeting won't put an end to the war unless Shaerdan submits to King Aodren."

"It could prolong the start of the war," I say.

Everyone turns to me. Well, except for Lirra, whose eyes must be broken because they're stuck on Cohen.

"Maybe once our countries have met," I continue, *and the bind is broken,* "the king will see it's better for both sides to withdraw."

"Retreat?" Millner's mouth pulls into a grim pinch. "Malam will never retreat, not until she has control of Shaerdan. Your king's advisers are greedy bastards. They want our seaports, and they're ruthless enough to murder a hundred thousand men to get what they want."

Lirra puts a hand on her father's arm, and his shoulders drop in acquiescence.

"So you don't think a meeting between our two countries will matter." I rub my temples. "Then what should we do?"

"Cut your losses and remain in Shaerdan." Millner relaxes back into his chair and folds his arms over his belly. "It'd be a fool's errand to return and try to prove your innocence. You're up against the captain of the guard, who has witnesses and evidence. Who do you think the high lord will believe?"

Cohen, who's been mostly silent this entire time, leans

forward. "I cannot stay here. My brother will die if I don't get to him before the war starts. Regardless of Captain Omar, I'll be returning to Malam."

"And what do you think will happen when you get to him? Didn't you used to be the bounty hunter's apprentice?" Millner's words are sharp. "You should know if you take the boy away from his company, he'll be charged with treason. A bounty will be put on his head."

Cohen pushes out of his seat and strides away from the table. "So you're suggesting I let him die? Leave my family behind?"

"You're only outside of the boundaries now because you've been on the run." Millner fixes on him with a hard stare. "But you haven't been free, have you? You had the king's guard chasing you clear across Shaerdan. I can assure you that won't change once you have your brother in tow. I've been hiding and running for nearly twenty years. I know what it's like to have the king out for my blood. Is that what you want?"

"I know the risks." Cohen glares at Millner. "Doesn't change my decision."

Millner shakes his head and sighs. He turns to me. "What about you? Think you'll be free to return to your grandmother's house after you accuse the captain of the guard? The closest you'll come is hanging from a noose at the border. You won't be coming back here ever again, I can promise you that."

I hadn't given much thought to returning.

"I have to try. My father's death won't be in vain." My gaze flicks to Enat, who is watching me carefully. The idea of losing her sends me into a panic. There are risks I hadn't considered. The day I was brought to the dungeon, a woman was there. The dungeon master called her a Channeler. She was dying. I imagine Enat in that woman's place, and my body chills as if the ague is coming on.

Millner's point hits the heart of my fears. What if we return to Malam and the guard catches Enat and accuses her of being a Channeler?

I've made a grave mistake. Enat cannot go to Malam.

ENAT IS BENT OVER THE SMALL WOODEN TRUNK in her room, withdrawing a cloak from the box as I lean against the door frame. Since Millner and his daughter left an hour ago, I've done little more than think about Enat and the dangers awaiting us.

"It's much colder in Malam. Here the temperature stays close to the same all year. But in Malam, where we have to travel through the high plains and mountains to reach Brentyn, it'll likely be close to first frost. This should be enough to keep warm." She pats the material, wool that is the same shade as heavy clouds before a rainstorm.

"You won't need it if you teach me how to break the bind," I say.

She turns to me with a sideways glance. "Why do you want to know that?"

My response has run through my head a hundred times, and still it catches on my tongue. I clench my fists and push myself to say what needs to be said. "It's too dangerous for you to go. You could show me what to do, and I'll do it." Even though I want her to come, it would be selfish to allow it.

"No. I've already given you my word. I'll go." She stands and shakes out the cloak so dust particles dance off the material into the slant of fading window light.

"Enat, there are too many dangers. Crossing the border won't be easy. But if you come, you'll have to cross it twice. Who knows what awaits us when we get to the palace. You're risking your life."

She *hmms* to herself as she inspects the cloak but gives no further acknowledgment to my comment.

Cohen chooses this moment to duck his head into the room. "I've checked over the horses, and they're ready."

"Willow hasn't ridden east before," says Enat. "Did you make sure to pack an extra blanket for her?"

"Yeah. What about the other horse? Acorn?"

"Aspen," she corrects. "He'll be fine, though an extra blanket wouldn't hurt. Especially if we hit a storm head-on. This time of year, the fall weather in Malam tends to rage before winter."

It's been almost a month since I left Malam. It amazes me

how easily I've overlooked my country's season change. Being here in the warmth and lush forests has been a nice reprieve. Now it's time to return to frost and rocky mountains.

"You can remain here and not have to spend weeks traveling to Malam and back." I try approaching the subject again as soon as Cohen leaves the room. "There's no danger if you stay."

"Britta." Enat's voice is lower, pensive. "Even if you learn what it takes to break the bind, you don't have experience. This task is no easy thing. It'll take a great deal of concentration and know-how. And without experience, well . . ." She doesn't need to finish the sentence—I already know. Without experience, I wouldn't be able to do it. I look away, embarrassed for thinking I could learn.

Her wrinkled hand wraps around mine. "Now, listen, girl. I knew the dangers when you first asked me to go. Knew what I was getting myself into."

I hadn't given the risk to her a second thought when I asked her to go, a fact that fills me with remorse. Enat tugs me to sit near her on the bed with the cloak between us.

"I'm an old woman. That doesn't mean I'm not capable; it just means I've lived my life and had my adventures. One thing I haven't had in quite some time is a family. We've just met, but I'm not going to let you waltz in here and waltz back out. This is my choice. I'm going with you, my granddaughter."

Oh, how the sound of that pleases me.

For the first time since we met, Enat's short frame and weathered skin no longer seem rugged. The hunch of her shoulders and deep lines around her eyes and mouth make me see her years. Frailty beneath strength. When she squeezes my hand, I wish I could quiet my unease about the dangers ahead.

"It's going to be a tough journey," I say, hoping she'll reconsider and hoping she won't. "Cohen's convinced we'll need to travel day and night to reach Brentyn before the captain. Traveling in a pair makes it hard to stay inconspicuous, so traveling in a group of three will be near impossible."

"Careful, Britta." She clicks her tongue against her teeth. She presses a threaded needle into the fabric and begins a pattern of stitches. "I might start thinking you enjoy that boy's company over mine."

I snort, and the tension between us evaporates.

Clearly, there'll be no changing her mind.

I pick up the other end of the cloak. Papa may not have taught me how to be the best seamstress, but it doesn't mean I cannot fix a seam.

"Can you tell me about my mother?" I ask while mending.

Enat's fingers pause over the fabric. "Talking about Rozen reminds me of times I'd rather forget."

The slight tremble in her fingers jitters down through the thread. What happened back then that she'd want to forget?

The door slams, breaking my trance as Cohen enters the

house, bustles around, gathering supplies, then leaves. All the while, I sit there struck by Enat's words.

Her needle moves in and out of the fabric. "Rozen was close to your age when she left home — her first time working at her Elementiary in Padrin." As her hand moves steadily over the fabric, her story spins a memory to life before me. A chance meeting between a sweet Channeler and an eager young bounty hunter. A summer of courtship whenever Saul could stop in Padrin. A girl who returned home in the fall desperately in love.

"He wrote and asked for her hand in marriage." Enat's fingers stray from her handiwork, her usual purposeful touch now a flutter of movement as she swipes a hair from her forehead. "Rozen was elated. She asked him to come here to meet me and to marry under these trees. Only, the day came and he didn't arrive. She waited for him for a month. When he didn't come, Rozen was heartbroken."

If not for the courtship and proposal, her story of friendship and heartbreak could be mine.

"But they must've married at some point," I add, urging her to continue.

Enat's eyes turn watery. "Rozen needed space to pull herself back together. She packed up and left for Padrin to work at the Elementiary. That's where Saul found her another month later."

She stabs the needle into the fabric and pauses. *Please don't stop.*

My own heart is clenched in compassion for my mother, my curiosity burning through me. "Where was he? Why'd he make her wait?"

"King Leon died a week before Saul was set to leave. His passing was unexpected. Whole country went into mourning. And a panic. In a matter of days, those fool men in the king's court sent out a proclamation saying that Channelers caused the king's death and were to be swept from the country. A bounty was offered to any who would turn someone in for witchcraft."

The Purge Proclamation. The lasting effects provide nightmare fodder to any woman or child who passes the pillory on market day. Seeing battered women trapped in the wooden planks, feet surrounded by a ring of dirt, was awful enough that I never gave further thought to how bad it must've been in the beginning. I sit utterly still, not wanting to shatter the picture her words paint of the hysteria that swept through Malam. Neighbors turned on neighbors. Families were left motherless.

The king's inner court took over for Aodren, a two-year-old when his father passed, and motherless, for she died giving him birth. No one could enter or lawfully leave Malam for two months of mourning. Two months of hunting Channelers.

"Those were dark times." She sits with a heavy set to her shoulders. "Women were accused, tortured, and hung, while a few lucky ones managed to flee. But eradicating Channelers from Malam wasn't enough. The inner court closed the borders."

Hovering on the edge of my seat, I reach out and touch her hand, and she responds with a watery smile and then begins sewing again.

"Millner never talks of it," she says. "The pain is too much."

"I heard he was once the captain of the guard."

Her head bobs as she pierces the wool with her needle. "He was the king's right-hand man. Did you know they were close friends? When King Leon died, it was like losing a brother to Millner." A shock, considering the infamous status of enemy he wears now. "Many people thought Millner would act as a spokesman for young Aodren. Step in as king regent, since Aodren was the last of the royal line."

Defecting to Shaerdan after holding such an elevated station must've been a shock to the entire country. The reason Millner has been called the Archtraitor seems clearer now.

"I know he spoke out against the Purge and the border closure," I tell her. "And he was imprisoned because people listened and rallied against the new laws."

She snorts. "Aye, they listened, but he wasn't imprisoned right off. First, guards were sent to his home. They beat him and tied him so he couldn't move as his wife was tortured before him. Can you imagine that? Seeing the brutalization of your loved one?" The insides of my mouth turn briny as she continues. "The guards dragged Millner outside and then set his house on fire, with his unconscious wife inside and their sleeping babe." My sharp intake interrupts her. Gods, the man lost his wife and child? His cheery face pops into my head and baffles me. How can he be happy after he's suffered so much? The ruthlessness of Malam's inner court staggers me, and yet I've seen traces of their cruelty all my life.

"Only after slaying his family did the guards throw him in the dungeon. The next day they put Millner in the pillory, as a cautionary example to those who would defy the laws." Enat's mouth twists into a grim smile. "But he escaped."

No one simply escapes the pillory. He must've had help. "My father?"

She shrugs. "I believe so, but Millner will carry that secret to his grave. Saul was tasked with finding Millner. When he went to Shaerdan to hunt Millner down, it was only by luck that your father bumped into Rozen in Padrin and had a chance to explain why he hadn't come."

Enat's stitches are tight and uniform, not a single one different from another despite the gravity of the conversation. If anything, her speed has increased while we talk. She pushes and pulls through the material in mechanical movements.

"What happened after he explained?" I ask.

Her gaze remains fixed to her fingers. "Young, and desperately in love, they married at a church in Padrin that evening and left for Malam the next day."

Stunned, I forget about the needle and gouge my pointer finger.

"Ouch!" I hold up my wounded digit. The danger of my

father's trek and the passion of his and my mother's actions ring so untrue to the pragmatic man who raised me. He taught me to value caution and control.

"Your father bribed a friend who was a watchman to help them past the border. Another friend claimed Rozen was a distant cousin and had no Channeler connections. And one more person testified that Rozen had spent summers on his farm and should be considered a countryman of Malam. Those lies were enough for Saul and Rozen to be allowed a quiet life in Brentyn, but not enough to rid her of the Shaerdanian stamp."

"So, like me, she was an outcast?"

"I can see you've taken it in stride." Enat winks, and my short chuckle clashes against the dark tone of the conversation.

"Aye, she was," Enat continues. "Which is why it was difficult to find a priest of Malam who would marry them. No one wanted to aid a Shaerdanian. No one wanted to be accused of treachery like the Archtraitor."

She draws a breath and holds it in her lungs, before letting it slowly out. A minor tremble runs through Enat's hands. Something inside her has grown restless, reminding me of the way Papa's horse used to pace in the stall before a bad storm.

"Rozen sent letters to me through the one trusted watchman. She was with child. On her small frame, her belly grew large quickly, drawing speculation from townspeople. She was too big too fast. They whispered of Channeler magic. When she delivered, there were ... complications. Yet Rozen didn't die in childbirth as others would've in the same situation, so the healer claimed Channeler magic."

"Didn't my father's position protect them?" His title has protected me and kept me from the pillory.

"To some extent, but Rozen was afraid. She wrote, asking me to meet her at the border." Enat's skin pales to an ashen color.

"Why?" I press.

"She wanted me to take your power away. So you could live without fear in Malam."

My frown sinks deeper. "Is that possible?"

"It's nearly impossible, but, on a baby who doesn't know how to resist, it might've worked. Only a Spiriter can give another Spiriter her power. But once it's done, it is permanent. That is the only way, for if a Spiriter takes another's power, it changes the Spiriter in dangerous ways."

I have no words. Having only just learned of Channeler heritage, the loss of power doesn't sound so different from what I've known. And yet the thought of someone taking away my power draws a visceral cry within me that screams, *No, no, no!*

She must be sensing the hint of dread. "I would've never done it," she says. "Never would try, not that it would've worked. But I would never allow you to give it to me either, for fear you would go too far and lose all that you have. What we have is too rare. You must treasure it. Of all Spiriters, our bloodline is the strongest."

It makes me wonder how much of the gift I possess. But my mother's story still hangs unfinished.

"That day, your father had you in his arms as they approached the border pass in the hills south of Fennit, where his friend stood post as a watchman. Rozen rode ahead, checking to see if the way was clear."

Enat abandons her stitching, as a far-off expression masks her face. I shouldn't press her. I should tell her it's all right, she doesn't have to finish. Except the words don't come out. I want to know, *need* to know the rest of my mother's story.

"There wasn't supposed to be two watchmen." Her voice is an earthquake. "Your father noticed them and called for Rozen to fall back. But she was too close to the border, too far from Saul, and the new watchman, too eager to do his job, took aim without asking questions. His arrow struck under her shoulder before she saw it coming."

We sit silently on the bed, both of us leveled by her story.

All these years I've harbored ill feelings for my mother. And now all that remains is deep shame. She didn't leave us. She wasn't a traitor. My hands fist against the sudden surge of emotion. I am furious with my father. How could he withhold so many truths? He allowed me to believe my mother was nothing more than the terrible names the townspeople have slung at me for years.

I feel bereft, like my mother has just been taken, and sympathy for Enat, who lost her daughter nearly eighteen years ago.

Grief and anger clog my throat, making it difficult to swallow. "What I said yesterday about hating her, I'm sorry about that. I don't hate her. You were right. I didn't understand."

Her hand closes over mine, lending strength and sympathy, when I should be the one offering condolences to her. "No need to be sorry, my girl. You have the truth. Now you know of her sacrifice."

She resumes stitching, working until the cloak is finished and the seams are strong. Once she folds the garment and places it between us, I struggle with what to say to take this pain away from her. Unable to let go of my own heartache, I stop trying to search for the right words and, instead, wrap my arms around my grandmother and lay my head on her shoulder.

COHEN SLEEPS BY THE FIREPLACE WHILE I share a room with Enat. His faint airy snores are barely audible over Enat's rustling. She is sorting blankets to decide which ones to take to Brentyn tomorrow. I watch her, wondering what our travels will bring.

I didn't come to Shaerdan to find the truth of my heritage. Though I cannot say I've forgiven Papa for the secrets he held, his reasoning makes a little sense. Now that the truth is out, I cannot ignore the gift inside me. To survive, to protect myself, knowledge is essential.

"Will you teach me how to use my ability?" I ask Enat while she folds a rainbow-colored quilt. Her hands are still over the brightly pieced fabric as she glances up.

I throw my hands up. "I promise I'm not looking for a way to keep you out of Malam. I need to know what I'm capable of. The only two times I used my gift, I didn't have a clue what was happening. So, will you help me?"

Seeing her folds aren't lined up correctly, she shakes out the blanket and starts again. "You're certain? You want to learn how to channel the spirit, even though you're headed to a country where it's illegal?"

"Yes."

She smiles and tightly creases the fold of her quilt. "Then on our way to Malam, I'll teach you."

Once we're under way, each of us on a different horse, Cohen says, "We'll hold out on resting until it's absolutely necessary. We want to cross this land as quickly as we can."

We keep to the forest and grasslands that fall north of the main road, careful to stay out of sight. Cohen takes the lead, while Enat and I trade off the rear position as we make the most use of riverbeds. There's no telling where the captain and his men are. They may have headed back to Malam, but Cohen believes they may also be lying in wait for us.

I watch Cohen as he splashes through the stream ahead. Thoughts of him run endless circles in my head until the guilt of thinking so much about Cohen quells them. Whatever is happening between us is not as important as the task ahead. I have to keep reminding myself of this.

Thankfully halfway into the second day, Enat begins her lessons. Her work keeps me busy and takes my mind off Cohen and the danger we're heading toward.

"A Spiriter can sense another's energy." Enat's crooked finger points at my horse. "Take his spirit, for example — you can feel it hum beneath you."

I put my hand on Aspen, unsure what to expect, and I'm a little disappointed when nothing happens.

"Close your eyes and try to feel what's stirring beneath his body's movement."

When, once again, all I detect is Aspen's body, I grow irritated. "Maybe I'm too old to learn," I suggest, well aware that my frustration is obvious.

"Could be." She waves her hand at me. "Seventeen is ancient."

"Almost eighteen," I correct.

"Almost. Still, it takes practice and patience. Two things you've not yet tried."

Later that evening, when we stop so the horses can rest, Cohen tugs my tunic before I can follow Enat to the stream.

"What are you doing?" I ask, surprised by his gesture.

"That's the question I should be asking you." Though his expression gives nothing away, his tone is short, conveying his irritation. "You're trying to learn how to be a Channeler like her."

I frown. Why is he upset? "Yes. I asked Enat to explain how my ability works."

"Bloody stars," he mutters.

"Cohen, what does it matter?"

He stares at me, the blanket dropping away from his gaze to show pain and fear flickering like gold flecks in his hazel eyes. "It's dangerous, Britta. I left you because your father didn't want anyone to know you had this power. If you learn this now, you'll draw attention to yourself. I cannot stand aside while you make a target of yourself."

"That's not what I'm doing," I protest. "That's ridiculous."

He moves closer until his wide shoulders block the light. "I know you, Britta. You'll test its limits. And what will happen when someone in Brentyn catches you?"

I take two steps away from him, maddened by his sudden involvement. "You left me alone for fifteen months, making the decision to *protect me*. You never asked me what I wanted. Learning my gift is what I want now, and you cannot expect me to walk away."

A vein pulses in his neck. "I'm telling you this is a mistake."

My brows shoot sky-high at his arrogance. I turn on my heel and stride toward the stream where Enat has gone to wash up. There's space for me to sit beside her, where she's kneeling on the soft grasses that curve over the bubbling brook. I set to splashing water over my dirty face.

Enat holds out a rag for me. I take it, mindful of the ease between us, a level of comfort experienced only around Papa and Cohen. If anything, my connection to her only increases my frustration with Cohen. Would he truly see me abandon this gift passed to me by my only living blood relative? The idea of doing so distresses me more than the threat to Channelers in Malam.

Enat runs her hands over a patch of wildflowers, a ribbon of purple that winds through the grass along the stream's edge. "Ready to try again? With the experience you've already had, you'll grasp your ability in no time."

I check back to see if Cohen is standing in the shadows. Though I know he isn't, because I can no longer sense his eyes on me or my hyperawareness of him that usually registers when he's near. His absence doesn't feel right between us; it grows like guilt that has a way of settling in my bones. During our younger years, Cohen always stood up for me when other children teased me. He was my protector. In his own way, he's still trying to protect me. I wish he could understand that I've finally found somewhere I fit in. Something I can belong to.

"Enat, why can I not feel if you're honest or lying?" Turning back to my grandmother, I need a distraction.

"Can you sense when others are honest?"

My answer in the positive has her eyes glinting with appraisal.

"When others speak, their energy is livelier, so it's easier to detect," she explains. "A truthful word puts the body at peace, while a lie grates against a person's mind and energy's need for harmony. That's why you can sense the truth or lies in others. But with me, you cannot because Spiriters innately have stronger control over their own energy, and so it's not free flowing for others to detect."

She straightens, the lines around her eyes tightening as she frowns. "I wouldn't lie to you, Britta. Is that something you're worried about?"

"No." I hand her the washrag. "Just curious."

"You've already shown you can feel the energy from plants and animals. If you can focus on how you do that, you can learn to control your power and call on it when you want."

The dog felt two breaths from death, just as all animals near death have shown a near-tangible discomfort. I realize now, the many times hunting in the past, as well as beside the well with Jacinda, that I was listening to the animals' waning energy. Despite the danger of being found out as a Channeler when we return to Malam, I need to understand this gift. If anything, to gain more control over when to act and when not to.

I stretch out beside her along the bank and reach for her hand. She smiles at me, pleased with my offer. Cupping my hand in hers, she places her other hand on top so we're palm to palm.

"You need to trust in yourself." She nods at me, giving me the approval to feel for her energy like I tried with Aspen. "For that matter, it'd do you some good to trust in others as well."

I huff.

"Quiet all your thoughts," she commands. "Think past my skin to the energy beneath."

Closing my eyes, I shift my focus only to where we're touching.

Rough pads of skin. Curled fingers.

A heartbeat throbs at my fingertips — mine. Then another, a soft pulsing slower than the first, stands out — Enat's. My confidence and determination surge. I focus on the slower beat until something more seems to hum beneath my touch, a slow and steady buzz coming from deep beneath her skin. In awe, I listen to it as it vibrates to my core.

Her triumphant smile gleams at me when I open my eyes.

"Well done, Britta."

CHAPTER 34

FOAMY SWEAT DRIPS IN GREAT GLOPS DOWN the legs of Willow and Aspen, accompanied by their usual sweet smell. We've ridden them harder than ever before to cross the open plains, where, away from the cover of the forest, we'd be easy pickings if anyone was after us. Siron, though, doesn't look taxed at all. Upon entering another span of dense woodland, we slow down and seek out a stream from which the horses can drink to replenish all the water they've lost.

Cohen passes out rations of bread, dried venison, and the berries Enat gathered earlier. Once we've eaten and filled our waterskins, we continue on foot so the horses can go a stretch without having to carry our weight. We haven't gone far when I stop to kneel at a patch of tiny yellow flowers.

"We don't have time to linger." Cohen walks back to me. The horses steal the moment to graze and sniff the wild buds.

"I won't be long. I just wanted to pick some of these blossoms," I tell him, which is not a lie.

He grunts and moves ahead.

I scoop out the flower, roots and all, in a protective ball of dirt, and then in a deft move, I snap the stem.

I study the broken stem. Delicate veins run from the base of the stigma to the curved tips of the flower. A soft trill of energy dances beneath my fingertips.

I jump. And then laugh. The power in the plant ebbs against my palm. It isn't strong and it's diminishing. I remember stroking the dog, feeling his energy follow my motions. I run my finger from the spread of the petals downward while imagining that each stroke straightens and mends the plant. And then it happens, and I'm slack-jawed, staring at a straight green stem, no longer bent. It's perfect and wonderful and —

The petals curl inward and the yellow diminishes into a sickly brown.

Panicked, I rack my brain, remembering what happened with Jacinda and her dog beside the well. I pinch my eyes shut to focus on the exact sensations I experienced after my fingers sank into the dog's fur. The feeling of coaxing the poison *out* of the animal comes to me. I wonder if doing the opposite now will help the plant. Can I push energy *into* a living being? It must be possible, since I had to have done something similar to save Cohen.

I run my fingers along the stem up to the browned top, picturing my fingers as a pail of water, dripping liquid energy. A slight tremor overtakes my hand. My fingers numb and a cold tingling sensation eats its way across my palm and up my arm as the flower transforms before my eyes, swelling with color and blossoming open in full, vibrant life.

Transferring the plant to my other hand, I shake out my sleeping hand and grin ear to ear.

Enat nudges me with her elbow.

"I knew you'd figure it out," she says with pride. "You're more powerful than you know, girl. Inside you there's strength you don't even realize. You're something special."

My chest hitches and then expands.

"Remember that," she admonishes with a warm expression.

Eyes lowered to the healed stem, I tuck her words inside, treasuring them. "I will."

It's close to midnight when we stop to skin and eat the rabbits that were an easy catch along the route.

"How's your hand feeling?" Enat asks.

Cohen looks up, meeting my gaze for the first time since I worked with the plant. It's funny to me that for years he was so hard to read, and now the frustration and worry are plain in his hooded eyes. Though seeing any speck of hurt in Cohen's expression makes me wish Enat hadn't said anything, even if I cherish her concern.

"It's fine." An overt display of twisting my hand right and left is for Cohen's benefit as much as it is an answer to Enat. I need Cohen to see that healing didn't tax me.

"Good. What you felt was minor. A little numbness, a little tremor. But it won't always be that way."

I cringe. This is exactly what Cohen doesn't need to hear right now.

"Think about when you healed Jacinda's dog," she continues, not noticing my discomfort. "The plant needed drops compared to the amount of life force you extended to the dog. To whom, I gathered, you gave a substantial amount."

Cohen stands and walks to the horses without throwing another glance in our direction. I want to ask him to come back, but I know he's haunted by what happened over a year and a half ago. This division between us is enough for me to forget my dinner, despite the gnaw of hunger clamoring through me.

"Transferring energy weakens you until you can naturally refuel through rest and meals," Enat explains. "Sometimes it'll only take a day's rest. Sometimes longer."

"Will my strength always return?" I face Enat once Cohen has slipped out of sight around the far side of the horses.

Her focus drops to her hands, curled around her bowl. "If you haven't given too much of your own energy away, then yes. You have to understand: you're offering your life force, the fuel on which you survive, to others. We're not called Spiriters merely because we can sense the energy in others. We're called Spiriters because we give that part of ourselves away."

Despite the heat of the campfire, goose bumps break out across my skin. I wonder if I gave Cohen almost all my energy. Now his apprehension makes more sense.

"That . . . that sounds so selfless." I push the last bit of rabbit meat around my bowl.

Cohen tosses a bone into the fire, startling me by his return. "There's no one more selfless than you, Britt," he says, offering a small truce of a nod.

No one talks for a while. I think of what Enat's told me, and how she said she saw my mother die.

"Did you not have enough energy to save my mother?"

Enat's chin jerks up, her blue eyes a little more watery than usual. "There were other circumstances," she says, and when a question forms on my face, all she adds is "It was too late."

We travel south to avoid towns and roads. The crisp air, cool nights, and jagged peaks lining the horizon mean that we are near Malam. The border is only a day or two away.

As the daylight fades, Cohen is even quieter than usual — no doubt worried for his brother. He rides ahead, so I have a clear view each time he kneads his neck. His promise must weigh heavily on him.

But what good will come of Cohen rushing to Finn's aid? He'll still be a criminal. He'll be on the run for the rest of his life, and he'll have to take Finn along with him. When both Mackay men are marked as traitors, Cohen's mom and sister will be outcasts. I suppose we could be outcasts together, though I wouldn't wish the life I've lived on them.

Our only recourse is to continue this mad pace to Malam, plead Cohen's innocence to the high lord, and turn in the real killer, Captain Omar. Then we can go about breaking the king's bind.

I pray, for Cohen's sake, that there will be enough time.

When we stop for the night, I approach Cohen with a waterskin. "I just filled this. The brook was chilly, so the water will be refreshing."

He drinks from the skin, and when he's done, he wipes his mouth with the back of his arm. "Thank you, Britt," he says, quietly. Vulnerability and worry lighten his eyes. I wish desperately there were something more I could do to help. I tell him as much.

While Enat busies herself with the fire, Cohen twines his fingers with mine. "It'll be all right," he says, as if I'm the one who needs convincing.

If only his words didn't turn my insides cold.

WHEN I WAKE THE NEXT MORNING, MY face is wet and I'm curled into a tight ball beneath my blanket. I long for the days I woke up warm and comfortable beside Cohen's muscular body. The shadows of the forest are quiet, as a slow, steady misting of rain breaks through the branches above.

Covering my head, I scramble up and hastily pack my belongings. Enat rouses from her sleep with a yawn and a grunt. She puts a hand above her eyes as she looks up, surveying the movement of the gray clouds visible between treetops, and then turns to me with a frown.

"A bad storm's coming," she says. "We need to get a move on if we want to gain some ground before it's on top of us."

I dust off my hands on my trousers. "I need a moment to clean up. I'll be quick."

"Go on, ready yourself. I'll wake the bear," she says with a smirk.

A foreign-sounding giggle bubbles out of me. I smack a hand over my mouth and turn on a heel to find the stream.

I scrub my face and hands in the chilly water, noting the temperature. Perhaps it's the charge in the air—like restrained lightning rallying for a strike—that nauseates me at the thought of crossing the border. The image of the strung-up bodies is not a sight easily forgotten. We've already decided to bypass Alyze and Fennit by traveling through the mountains, because there will be fewer guards to watch out for.

Still, there are too many dangers ahead.

Once we reach the castle, Cohen will navigate the secret passages to Lord Jamis's study so we can present him with the truth about who really killed my father, and then we'll go to the king's private chambers, where Enat will break the bind. Not the surest plan, but it's all we have. What I fear most are the risks we'll face after we cross the border. I've no friends in Malam. Certainly anyone aware of the bounty on my head will not hesitate to aid the king's guards. One of my biggest worries, however, is for Enat, that she'll be in harm's way.

If anything happened to her, it would devastate me.

Like I have every day since we left Enat's home, I scan the forest for a sign of another, though I'm certain Captain Omar would've surely struck by now if he was pursuing us. Nothing stands out in the light drizzle.

Before we head back to camp, a noise over the usual gurgle of a stream sounds somewhere up ahead. It's Cohen — my gut tells me so. The anticipation of being alone with him turns my skin into a net of butterflies. We've had little time with each other when Enat isn't around. Before we reach Malam, I want a moment between us to clear the frustration.

Though I'm the Channeler, it feels as though he holds his own power, the draw of him leading me upstream, where the water curves around a jut of land. It is as though he has an invisible rope tied to my heart. I find him, on the river's edge, wearing only his trousers as he makes a stack of small stones.

Drops of water linger on the powerful planes of his back, while a few trail the indent of his spine. My mouth turns bone-dry. There's so much smooth skin, I almost don't notice the faint scars, shiny slashes starting at his shoulder and disappearing beneath his arm. He turns, and I'm caught in the spell of silvery marks that crisscross over his torso and shoulders and abdomen. His body is scarred, but it is also perfection.

Seeds and stars, it should be illegal for him to go shirtless.

Cohen's cleared throat shakes me from my gawking daze. "Good morning, Dove."

I duck my head. "Morning, Cohen."

"Did you need something?"

I press a rock deeper into the damp soil with the toe of my boot. "Will you always hate my gift?"

His lips part as though his answer is ready to be spoken, and then he closes his mouth and frowns. After a beat he says, "That's not how I feel. I'm in awe and grateful for your gift daily." He closes the space between us and lifts my chin. "These scars are a gift. I'm grateful for them as much as I am for your Spiriter ability. But I'll never be fine with you putting yourself in danger. You're taking a huge risk. If anyone finds out—"

I press my hand over his mouth.

His lips press against my palm in a gentle kiss, and though we've not reached any sort of understanding, it's suddenly impossible to think with him so close. And shirtless. And dripping. Cohen tugs me against his smooth, hot, perfect skin and folds his arms around me. I wind my hands around his back, feeling the damp uneven ridges of flesh and wanting him even more.

The sky growls, warning of the storm coming our way.

Cohen's expression clears and he abruptly steps away. "You should get back to camp."

I leave, feeling as frustrated and unresolved as when I approached.

The horses work furiously to outrun the storm at our heels. The wind sweeps through the narrow canyon, pushing tree limbs to and fro, and howling through the landscape like a legion of specters as rain pours in solid sheets. We cannot stop and look for shelter because of the threat of flash floods. We're forced to climb out along the path that hugs the rocky wall.

I keep my chin down, urging Aspen onward in Siron's wake.

"We're almost there," Cohen yells, his words barely audible over the buckets of rain cascading off the rocky cliff beside us.

A bright light slashes the sky, illuminating the fissure of land leached of color. Three heartbeats later, thunder booms.

Aspen startles. She rears up, pawing the air in her nervousness, and then crashes down, darting forward dangerously close to the drop-off. I fight the reins, tugging and urging her to safety before another break of thunder scares her.

Thankfully—oh mercy, thankfully—she obeys.

Once we're tucked in safe beside the rocky wall, I rest my hand on her mane and take steadying breaths for the both of us. I'm getting better at sensing energy, and Aspen's zips fiercely beneath her skin as rain pelts my hair and face, drowning the calming words on my lips.

I wipe my eyes and search for the others.

Cohen halts a dozen paces ahead. I twist in the saddle—

A blast of light crashes into a dead tree directly beside where Enat is sitting on Willow. And then everything happens alarmingly fast and, at the same time, unnaturally slow—the tree bursts into flames as Willow rears back, throwing Enat to the ground; she lands with a thud and doesn't move; the horse charges forward, skimming the edge of the ravine and tumbling off; then a crack sounds in the eerie stillness, and the torched tree starts to fall.

A panicked cry echoes around us before I realize it's coming from me. I leap from Aspen and I'm racing down the path toward Enat, arms and legs pumping to propel me forward. The tree hangs over her prone form, spitting embers as its dried limbs are consumed in hungry flames. The rain is no match for the inferno.

I see the flash of gold and white right before heat skims my face, but I don't let myself give it another thought as I throw myself onto Enat, wrap my arms around her, and tug so we both start rolling down the path. One, two, three times, I yank her beneath me and over me, moving us as far from fiery death as possible.

When the edge of heat wanes, I stop and lie panting beside Enat.

She groans.

I reach around the back of her head, in search of injury, and find sticky wetness matting her hair. I press to stop the bleeding.

The familiar buzzing sensation hums beneath my palm. I concentrate on the vibration to find where she's weak. I can feel the lack of energy near her head wound.

She does not so much as move as I bleed my spirit into hers, the motion natural now, filling her need and healing her wound.

. . .

When I wake I'm alone, in a cave, kept warm by a small fire set in a ring of river stones.

I cast a sluggish glance around and groan when my aching neck and back protest the movement. I roll myself to sitting right as Cohen steps from the shadows and drops down beside me.

Without warning, his arms are around me, clutching me to him as his face falls to my neck. Nose pressed to the hollow beneath my ear, Cohen drags in a deep shuddery breath.

"Cohen?" A croak. My throat grates like I've eaten hay.

He pulls back, his hair a mess. Shadows linger on his face, bruising the skin under his eyes, despite the light of the fire.

"We found a cave," he says. His gaze drifts to the craggy curve of the walls, the packed-dirt ground, the far reaches of the cave where blackness resists the firelight, before returning to me. The last time we were in a cave together, only one of us was able to walk out. Morosely, I wonder if he's thinking about that now.

I swallow, trying to pull saliva over my throat. "Has the storm let up?"

"Hours ago."

I wince. He doesn't have to say more. We're here, wasting critical time, because of me. Because my ailments are holding him back from helping Finn.

"Is Enat all right?" I ask.

"She's doing well, considering."

"The tree was falling . . . and she was unconscious. I had to help her. I didn't think it would take so much out of me, I just needed her to be safe." The cracked words tumble out. I don't realize how much his approval matters to me until he remains silent.

"Cohen? Say something."

His arm crushes my shoulders against him. "I want to yell at you not to do something like that again because I'm afraid I'll lose you. But then, at the same time, I'm proud of you."

My lashes flutter closed. His praise, something I've rarely heard before, is a balm.

"Every time you put yourself in danger, I feel like I'm suffocating. I cannot stand to see you harmed." He stares down at me, his gaze intense. "You misunderstood me when I said I shouldn't have kissed you. I thought I pushed you too far, too fast. So I let you go. I didn't think you were ready for us. Whereas I knew one kiss wasn't enough."

I want him to clarify the meaning behind his words, but in the next moment Cohen leans in, and I cannot move or blink or breathe. He wets his lips and then lowers his face closer, closer to mine.

"Every time I kiss you," he says, his breath tickling my mouth, "I want you to know that this *is* what I want. Make no mistake, Britt, you are all I think about. You have been since the day we first met, since we first started training together, since I saw you stand strong in the face of so much opposition around you. You are all I need. You are all I will ever want."

I gasp, and his mouth steals the sound as his lips cover mine.

Enat opens the pouch of herbs and seeds that dangles from her belt and puts a pinch into a cup of stream water. "It's not Beannach water, but this chiandra tea will help you regain your strength."

"Thank you." My gaze roves over her, scrutinizing her movement as she hands me the drink for signs of weakness or pain.

"Don't thank me, girl." Enat sits back and frowns. "I should scold you for wasting your energy on me. You could've hurt yourself. Or worse, you could've given too much of your energy away." I start to argue, but she silences me with her upheld hand. "Don't waste yourself on an argument. You've been sleeping for nearly two days and could probably use more."

"I barely feel tired." Time is not a resource we can spare. "I'm fine," I insist, stretching out my legs and sitting taller.

She eyes my movement and shakes her head. "You're determined is what you are. You're lucky, girl, that we heal quicker than others." Enat notices my head cocked to the side and explains, "I know you've much to learn, and yet I keep forgetting how much. We weaken and age like everyone else, but our gift helps us naturally absorb energy that helps restore us to a healthier state."

"I thought taking another's energy is wrong or, at the very least, dangerous. Like black magic."

"Aye. It's both when a Spiriter forcefully takes energy"—Enat's fingers curl into her hand—"or controls it, like in the case of your king. But there's energy all around us that is, in a sense, given to you. It's in sunshine and wind and water and the food we consume."

I reach out and squeeze her fist. "Well, then, you shouldn't worry. I spend enough time in the woods to reenergize myself daily. Did I heal you enough that you can break the curse?"

She twists and stretches her back. "Perhaps better than I was before," she says with a wink. "Don't do it again, though. Spiriters do not heal each other. Healing those who do not have our gift will make you physically weak. But when healing another Spiriter, there's the chance you could lose your power."

I tuck my chin, taking stock of my energy level. "Have I lost some of my ability?"

She waves a dismissing hand. "No. My ailments weren't the type to siphon any power from you. You'll be exactly as you were once you get a little more rest."

"There's no more time to rest," I say. "Now that I've slowed us down, we'll have less time to find the Spiriter."

Enat exchanges a look with Cohen, who is cooking quail on the fire, a silent agreement. "You'll at least eat first," she says. "Besides, we won't have to search too hard to find the Spiriter. It's likely she'll be close because that is a requirement for maintaining the bind. If we need to subdue her, I brought the chiandra tea mix. After she drinks it, her heart will slow and put her into a sleep that lasts a couple hours. Then all I'll have to do is sense the two energies and work at unwinding them."

I think about what she's proposing and what she's just warned me of. Siphoning power. "Is there a possibility she could take your gift?"

"No. You cannot take someone's gift."

Even so, there are too many ways in which this mission could go wrong. "What if we cannot get her to drink the tea? Or, worse, what if we cannot find the Spiriter? Is there another way to break the bind?"

Her gaze follows Cohen as he steps outside the cave. She knots her hands, similarly to how I wring mine when I'm uncomfortable. "A bind will break if one of the energies is too weak to hold," she says. "That's the only other way."

The only time I've felt weak energy is when something is dying. My chin makes a sharp jerk up. "You mean, if one of them is dying? Are you saying you could break the bind if you hurt the king or the Channeler? Bring one of them close to death?"

Her gaze drifts to the side. She unfolds her hands to press them flat against her legs, pressing until the blood leaches from her skin. "Near death is not my preferred way to break the curse, as there are too many risks. But, yes, it is a way to break the bind."

I scrunch my face up. "I thought . . . that is, you said we don't heal other Spiriters. So you would kill her?"

"It would have to be the king."

Panic burns the rest of my thoughts to ashes, leaving only fear for Enat. If she was to wound the king and then heal him, she would surely get caught and charged as a Channeler. Even though her actions would be helping the kingdom, there's no doubt in my mind that the Purge Proclamation would prevail and she would be killed.

"No. It's too dangerous," I say.

Her arms, shoulders to the tips of her fingers, visibly relax. "Aye, there are many risks involved when healing someone who is mortally wounded."

"That's not what I meant."

She offers a wan smile. "Well, then we must find the Spiriter when we reach the castle. Once she's in sight, I'll break the bind before she realizes what's happening. Only if she fights the unraveling of her magic will we need to subdue her with the tea."

Though I haven't seen Enat use her gift, I'm certain she's a force to be reckoned with.

Once we've eaten the roasted quail, we travel all through the day and into the next night, bringing us to the Evers and hours from Malam's border.

T HE SILENCE OF THE BIRDS WAKES ME.
Someone is here.

I slowly rise, hand on my dagger, and leave the warm blanket behind to step into the frigid morning. Enat and Cohen are sleeping as I quietly slip the dagger into my boot and grab my bow.

I walk farther from camp, hoping the energy pulsing around me will give some clue.

The light shifts ahead.

I crouch, grasping for my bow and notching an arrow. The rough bark of a pine tree jabs into my back as I draw a slow inhale, hold it, and then let it out while I monitor the woods, waiting for my target to make his appearance.

A dozen paces north, a man moves around a tree. His steps are marked with the sure carefulness of a trained hunter. Any question of who this man is dies the second I see the royal stag on his uniform. A watchman.

The guard heads straight for our camp, drawing closer to Enat and Cohen than I am. Panic zips through me.

I slide my right foot forward, adjusting my weight to my front leg to gain a better defensive position.

The man stops. Looks around. Cocks his head in my direction.

I cannot let him get any closer to Enat and Cohen, who are sleeping and unprepared for a fight. Shaking off the nervous tremors in my hands, I raise the bow. The tension releases with a twang. My pulse hurtles through my veins as I take in the scene: the arrow piercing the guard's coat, pinning the material to the tree, and the surprise flooding his face. I pray I haven't made a grave mistake in sparing this man's life.

His hands fly into the air as he searches the trees for his attacker. "I mean no harm to you." His voice wobbles.

Harmless isn't an accurate descriptor for a border guard. My mother's story is proof of that.

"I'm looking for Cohen Mackay. Are you with him?" His words echo through the trees and warm me with their honesty. I am immensely more wary than seconds before. Of course he's looking for Cohen. All the king's guard are searching for the alleged murderer, but I'd serve myself up to another mountain cat before I'll turn Cohen over.

The guard must think I've left because he drops his hands

and twists to snap the arrow. Before he is completely free, I shoot another, catching the man unaware as the arrow slices through the material at his shoulder, possibly nicking skin. Instantly, the man freezes.

"I—I—I got your message." His face is gray as his wide eyes zip from limbs to the needled groundcover. "I meant what I said about meaning no harm. If you don't wish to be known, leave now. I won't follow. There aren't many travelers through this pass, and . . . and yesterday I came across a sign from my friend. I thought you were him or with him. If I've made a mistake, let's both walk away from this as strangers. Please. I've a family."

I bite my cheek, debating what to do next, but the verity of his words stops me from walking away without making myself known. "Who left you a sign?"

He jerks toward the location of my voice. "Cohen Mackay. Is that—are you Britta Flannery?"

He knows me.

"He's my friend," the guard says urgently. "He left signs so I'd know he was passing through. I'm here to give him news."

I cannot get over the stag and stripes on his coat. "You're one of the king's guards."

"I am," he says. "Though I'm here now not as a guard, but as his friend."

Before I can answer him, my neck prickles, sensing Cohen's nearness.

"Britta?" Cohen whisper-yells. He cuts through the

undergrowth, directly for me, his steps only slowing when he has me in sight. His shoulders relax. "What are you doing over here?" he asks, at the same time the guard says, "Cohen."

The tension snaps back into place over Cohen's features; his body coils like he's ready to pounce. His gaze darts to me, to my bow, and then around the woods in search of my target.

"Cohen, it's me, Bernard." The guard jerks against the arrows, breaking them.

"Bernard! You found my tracks," he says.

"You left tracks?" I'm stunned I didn't notice. I cannot afford to miss anything out here.

He turns back, tilting his head to the side. "Yes."

"You didn't tell me how friendly the bounty hunter's daughter is." Bernard smirks as he saunters closer. I lift my bow and draw another arrow. I'm down to my last three. The two I wasted on Bernard are useless because he destroyed them in the effort to free himself. He sees me pulling the arrow to the bow and pauses.

"Dangerous words for almost having had my arrow in your back," I tell him. "Perhaps instead of jesting, you should just get to business."

"Britt," Cohen warns.

My nostrils flare in irritation. I lower my bow and slide the arrow back into the quiver. Bernard's eyes fix on my position as though he's waiting for me to leave. I remain planted on the forest floor, my refusal to be in the dark anymore. I'm relieved when Cohen shakes his head at Bernard.

The guard's mouth twists like he's swallowed a tub of pickles. "Fine. There isn't much I have to report. Rumor has reached the front that Shaerdan has sent a declaration of war. With or without the king's response, they're going to attack. Your brother's unit has been called to go to Meridian."

"When?" Cohen's voice is shy of a whisper.

"They left at sunrise," says Bernard.

"I don't understand." Cohen shakes his head, his face darkening. His hands grip his hair, pulling it at odd angles. "Why? Why'd they send them out?"

I cross the distance to him and put my hand on his arm, hoping the contact will ease his distress somehow.

"They'll be surrounded," Cohen says, horror lining his words. "Shaerdan has set up camp in Meridian. The bulk of their army is there. Why would the king send such young and green soldiers there?"

Bernard's expression twists in compassion. His hands stray to the new hole in the arm of his jacket. "I'm sorry, Cohen. I don't know why they're going. Word is they're meant to be part of the first strike. That's why I came to tell you."

I'm new to warfare, but I understand enough to know *first strike* isn't promising. Not for a boy of fourteen. The border town of Fennit was littered with tents and campfires and weaponry. Moving a massive group doesn't seem feasible. Unless the entire group isn't headed to Meridian.

"How many were sent?" I ask.

Bernard stops playing with the two arrow marks, and his

eyes cut to Cohen. "Er, I been told it was only his unit. Two dozen men in all."

I don't notice Enat's approach until she's standing beside me. "Those men are going to Meridian to lay down their lives. They'll be a bump in the road to the Shaerdanian army. It's a shame."

Cohen remains silent.

There is no way to break the bind on the king as well as save Cohen's brother. Not when his brother is marching to his death. Time is up.

Leif said, *No one's strong alone. We need each other.*

I bite the inside of my lip, considering a new plan. If Cohen continues into Brentyn with me, there's a good chance Finn will die. Cohen wouldn't be able to live with himself if he let that happen.

It will be a struggle to continue without him but not impossible.

"You should go." My voice shreds through the padded sounds of the woods.

Cohen blinks out of his stupor and stares at me, emotions uncharacteristically clouding his face. "What do you mean?"

"We're hours from the border. You have enough time to get to Finn if you go now. Who will save Finn if you don't?" He shakes his head, but I won't let him talk. "You gave your word to your mother."

"I gave my word to you as well." His words are spoken like

a growl. His eyes flash ready with an argument. Can he not see there is no way to help us both? If he won't choose, I'll do it for him.

"Listen to me." My fingers whiten around my bow. "Enat and I will go on to Brentyn. I'll disguise myself in the dress and bonnet like in Celize so no one will recognize me. When we get to the castle, Enat can help me discern where the guards are. Then together, we'll find our way to the king." It may not be entirely sound, but it's the best plan I have.

Cohen sweeps his head side to side so chunks of sable and molasses-brown hair fall across his brow. "No. No way. There are too many risks. You cannot go into the castle blindly. You'll get caught."

I set my bow and arrow down and cross through sage bushes to reach him. "I have Enat. Finn needs you. If you don't help him and he dies, you won't be able to let that pain go. I know you, Cohen. You are loyal and true. You would never forgive yourself." I take in a great gulp of cool mountain air to steady my rapidly beating heart. "If you live the rest of your life blaming yourself for Finn's death, we won't ever be happy together. And . . . and." My voice is small. "I want that. I want to be happy with you."

He drops his chin to the top of my head. "I want that too. But what if this doesn't work?"

"It will work." I rest my hands on his chest. "It has to."

Cohen steps away from me. Now that we're no longer

touching, I can see how ravaged his face looks, smudges lingering beneath his eyes and worry lines creasing his brow. "I cannot leave you."

If only the consequences of his choices weren't so devastating.

What I don't tell Cohen is how scared I am to watch him go. He left me once and didn't return. But this decision isn't about me. It's about his family needing him. "You cannot leave Finn out there alone," I say.

Cohen slams his hand into the nearest trunk. "I know." His shoulders slump. "I know, Britt," he repeats, quieter, subdued. Cohen looks off into the distance, pain and indecision flickering across his face like the dance of a flame over darkness. Out of the trees, Siron slips between us, a black cape covering his owner.

"How will you cross the border?" Cohen's voice is so quiet, I can barely hear him behind his big horse. "The guards—"

"I am the only watchman in this section of the woods right now," Bernard interrupts. "I've adjusted the other men's schedules so no one is to come near my post for hours. If they travel quickly, they'll be fine getting into Malam."

If what he says is true, our only obstacle now will be traveling from the border to the castle. I'm grateful to Bernard for his help.

"Enat and I will be careful," I tell Bernard.

With a hand on Siron's neck, Cohen moves so he can see me. His face is anguish and worry and anger. He sighs, and the sound nearly breaks me because I know he'll leave. And I want him to go. But fear reminds me that any goodbye may be our last.

Cohen will come back.

It won't be like last time.

He'll return to me.

"This isn't goodbye," he says, as if he can read the niggling doubt in my thoughts. "I'll find Finn and then I'll meet you before you reach the castle. Promise, Dove. In three days' time, meet me at our tree in the Evers."

Hope floats inside me. Everything will be fine.

"Three days," I confirm. "And you'll come back to me."

He releases Siron and crosses the distance between us, clutching me to his muscular frame. My arms circle his waist while his wrap my shoulders in warmth. "I will always come back to you." His nose presses into my hair as he plants a soft kiss on my temple. "Trust me, Dove."

It doesn't take long for the men to load up. It's much quicker than I anticipate.

What seems like only moments later, Cohen is riding away on Siron.

I wave and then turn my head so he cannot see the emotion in my eyes or the errant tears that trace my cheeks. Cohen said he will return, and I believe him. I do.

We ride hard for two days to put space between the border and us, only slowing when the climb from the lowlands steepens. Frost covers the leaves on the forest floor and the white-capped mountains in the distance. We're lucky the snow hasn't covered this pass.

"You love that boy," Enat says from where she sits behind me as we both ride Aspen into Malam. It's a statement and not a question, but I find myself nodding.

"Yes," I whisper.

"I'm glad. He's a good man and good for you. When this is all over, you should marry him."

I smile, enjoying the daydream sparked by her comment.

A hundred birds whoosh out of the nearby trees and flap away in a massive cloud of black wings. The hairs on the back of my neck rise. Aspen whinnies and canters backwards, fear turning her haunches rigid.

"Hush," I whisper soothingly as I pat her neck while scanning the forest for the source of the birds' movement.

And then I hear it — not so far away, a rhythmic pounding vibrates the forest — horses. Two, possibly more.

Enat grips my waist. "We have company. Let's go."

Digging my heels into Aspen's side, I urge the horse into a sprint, skirting the origin of the birds' flight. The forest flies past, gravel and dead leaves spattering outward in the urgency of our plight. Enat curses, and in my periphery a shadow breaks from the trees, matching our frantic pace.

Tomas appears to the south.

"Stop!" Captain Omar's command thunders over the pounding of hooves around us.

We cannot be caught. The captain, Papa's murderer, will

surely not let us live to see the high lord. Enat hunkers down, lowering her head to my back, and commands Aspen to go faster.

Behind the captain, Leif breaks out of the trees. Three against two aren't terrible odds. I push Aspen as fast as a Southland horse.

Captain Omar cuts northward. "Stop now!" he yells. "Or I'll spare the hanging and slice you through now."

His threat is terrifying because it's true. Every word.

"Keep going," Enat says, though stopping isn't even a consideration. She twists in the saddle, pulling her bow over her head, and—

I feel the thwack before I see the arrow embedded in Aspen's neck.

The horse screams, rearing back so quickly that Enat and I tumble to the forest floor. I shake off the blow and scramble to my feet. Aspen advances a few steps, flailing her head side to side as she lets out a horrible cry.

I rush to Enat's side to pull her up when I see her bow is snapped in two, the pieces sticking awkwardly out of a low shrub. Scattered along the ground among the crush of fallen leaves are two arrows.

My arrows!

I reach for my quiver and notice my bow is missing.

I scramble through the leaves, grabbing up arrows while searching. The guards surround us, with the captain being the first to dismount.

Where is my bow?

Aspen has fallen a dozen paces away, and though she's not dead yet, her blood loss is a pool of black, staining the rocks and dirt. *My bow!* It's attached to the saddle.

"I should kill you here and now," Captain Omar says. He's behind me. The other two guards are at the sides of the clearing.

"Go now!" Enat yells.

I bolt forward, arms pumping, to move me faster to my weapon. Vaguely, I catch the shouts of the other men, but my focus blocks out the details of their words. A ring of steel echoes behind me just as my fingers find purchase on my bow.

I spin back to face the guards with an arrow notched, feathers softly brushing my fingertips. Only, the scene doesn't make sense.

Omar's bow is pointed in my direction, though his attention is on Tomas. The weasel guard has his sword drawn against Enat. Everything seems to slow like it did the night of the rainstorm. Leif rushes in my direction. For a split second, my attention diverts to him — and that's when I hear the cut.

Blade against skin. A short gurgling gasp.

"NO!" I rage, the scene slamming into me in regular time. My arrow is slicing the distance before I even realize what's been done, flying true to nail Tomas between his shoulders. For the first time in my life, I've aimed and shot at a man to take his life. The guard tips to the side and falls next to Enat, who is somehow still standing.

Her eyes roll, showing an unnatural amount of white. A terrible bubbling echoes out of her throat. I sprint to her side, not caring what the other men in the forest are yelling, and wrap my arms around her body to lower her to the ground. I cover her neck with my hand, pressing, frantically trying to focus on her remaining energy.

It's not too late. It's not.

Her energy whispers beneath my hand, ripples on an otherwise still mountain lake, fading fast. I pinch my eyes shut, demanding the panic to settle so I can focus as I start to push my energy into her. Just like after the lightning storm.

The touch of her hand on mine . . . oh mercy. Her bloody, bloody hand has me snapping my eyes wide open. "No," she mouths.

And I know what she's telling me, but I cannot—no, I will not—accept the command. "No," she mouths again, fainter this time. "Find . . ." A gurgle. "Her . . ."

I don't understand what she's saying. Find her? Perhaps the Spiriter? Maybe it's the madness of pain that's causing her to speak nonsense.

"Let me do this," I plead. My eyes sting. My throat aches. "I can make everything right. You were never supposed to get hurt. I—I never wanted anything to happen to you."

Enat has moments left. My voice breaks as hot tears run down my nose and stain her beautiful wrinkled cheeks.

"Please. Please let me help you."

The tiniest movement of her head shows her disagreement.

"No, Enat!" A sob crawls out of my chest. "You're all I have left."

Her free hand lifts, ever so slowly, swaying until landing on my face. It's a miracle she can move at all. Her energy is but the last clinging seed on a cottony dandelion. I want to tell her not to move. To hold still. But her lips part, and I can see she's trying to say something, so I am motionless for the both of us, my heart blackening and breaking and crumbling inside me.

Pain and regret swell in her cerulean eyes.

Her lips make a weak movement. "Love . . . you."

"I love you," I say, frantic for her to hear me as a final breath escapes and her stained hand falls to the ground.

"No!" A keening, high-pitched and tormented, resonates from deep within me as I clutch her body to mine. The color of her skin turns ashen, and her lips pale to white. The life force that once made her vibrant is gone, and in my arms is the husk of my grandmother.

"No, no, no, no . . ."

Captain Omar's bow lies at his side as he watches us. Red, red, red, covers me because of him. I hate him. He took my father's life and has now assisted in stealing Enat's. The anger and pain inside me morph into something blackish and terrible that makes me want to slay more than just one man today.

I seize Enat's sword and lurch to my feet in the blink of an eye.

"You murderer!" I scream at him as I rush to attack.

Pain explodes in the back of my head, and then I'm

tripping forward with the weight of the sword. Lights dim and the leaf-littered ground rushes upward.

The ground is rocking, and I think I'm going to be sick. The blackness spins and twirls me around mercilessly. I roll to my side and vomit.

"Rest," someone says.

"Clean her up," another orders.

Voices echo like they're spoken through a pane of glass. I'm too exhausted to care. I let the darkness steal me away.

WHEN I WAKE, MY FACE IS PRESSED against a cold stone floor, and a thick stench of piss and dung assaults my nose. Ah, the dungeon. I gag and then groan, as there's nothing left inside to retch. Couldn't they have simply killed me?

A dull pain pounds in my skull as I push off the ground and sit upright. I reach back, gingerly touching hair matted with blood.

I've no recollection of how I got here or why my body aches like a horse has trampled it. All I remember is Enat and then nothing.

In the weak dungeon light, I stare down at my soiled clothes. Dried blood—Enat's blood. Her death replays in my mind, and grief floods out of me in sobs that rack my entire body.

I only just found Enat. Just discovered she's

my grandmother. Two weeks ago I stood in her home and argued about going on this trip. It doesn't seem fair that she's gone. She only came to Malam because I asked. How foolish of me to think I could save the king. Or stop a war. That I could finish my father's work. Or help Finn. How could I have been so arrogant?

Ignoring a bowl of food that's been placed beside me, I grab the cup of water and sip it down over my ravaged throat. I cinch my ruined shirt tight to my body and hug my knees, welcoming the solitude of the dungeon.

Someone's touching me, putting cool pressure on my forehead. I thrash awake to find Leif crouched in front of me, holding a bucket of water and a rag. The sight of his uniform hits me with an unbidden vision of Tomas swinging a sword at Enat. I flinch and scramble back against the stone floor to the dank corner.

"Britta, I'm sorry about . . . about what happened," he says mutedly. "It wasn't my intention. I was following orders, and if I'd known . . ." He drops his chin. "I would have done something, Britta. I'm sorry."

I don't care a whit about his intentions. "How long—?"

"A day is all. You slept for most of it." I wasn't going to ask how long I've been here. I meant to ask how long before they hang me.

He holds a cup for me to take.

"We're alone," he says while I drink. I glance up in question.

"The dungeon master is a friend. He's allowed us a moment to talk."

I'm sitting in this rotting hell waiting for my name to be called so they can march me out to the yard and hang me. What's left to talk about? I ignore him.

Leif looks over his shoulder, then back to me. "Do not give up," he says pleadingly.

"You should leave," I croak over a gritty throat.

He stands. "Your time is short, Britta. Is this how things will end for you? Is this what you want? Or what she would've wanted?"

"What do you know of her?" I stare at him stonily. He has no right to talk to me about Enat.

"I know you loved her," he says, and I turn away, needing the darkness to dull my pain. "Life hasn't been easy for you. But there are people who care for you and are willing to help. You're a fighter, Britta. That's why I let you go in Celize. I knew you would find your father's killer and make this situation right. Don't give up now."

I rest my chin on my arms and stare blindly into the shadows that echo with moans and clanks until Leif leaves.

The door at the top of the dungeon stairs creaks and then clangs shut. Anger sweeps through me, and yet, as furious as I am, Leif's comments plague me. He let me walk away in Celize. It's a shock that might amuse me if my entire soul wasn't black.

Cohen's still out there with Finn. If he hasn't already, soon, he'll reach our tree and know something is wrong, but if he comes for me and the guards catch him, he'll be hanged.

I grip the roots of my hair, welcoming the biting pinch.

To survive these woods, a man has to be strong as the trees.

If Enat were here, I'm certain she'd fight. I didn't believe her when she said I was like her. But I want to be. I want so badly to be like my grandmother that I push up off the hardened grime when Leif returns with a dish of gruel.

"So you saw through my disguise?"

A faint smile registers on his lips.

"When you were here earlier, you said not to give up," I say, my coward voice shaking. "Can I trust you to help me? Answer me aloud."

His eyes work back and forth over my face. "Yes, you can trust me."

Truth. I have never been more grateful for the warmth under my skin.

"I want to escape from here," I admit, feeling winded like I'm teetering on the edge of a precipice. "When I was caught with . . . with Enat . . . we were on our way to the castle for two reasons. First, to tell the high lord who the real murderer is. And second, to break the spell on the king." I explain everything we know about a bind on the king and the war.

When I finish, Leif's brows are drawn together.

I glance over the top of the bowl as I eat the terrible-tasting mush. "I know it sounds mad, but if what you say is true, that I can trust you, then you must trust me as well."

He blows out a breath. "I've had some suspicions about the king's behavior and recent orders. This is just a lot to take in. Do you know who's controlling the king?"

"I think so," I say, purposefully evasive. Once Leif finds out about the captain, I fear his loyalty will stand in the way of him believing me. Or at the very least, it'll keep him from helping me escape.

"Tell me. If I'm going to help you, I need to know my enemy."

I don't want to tell him. Though he's right, he needs to know. "It's the captain," I say quickly, spitting it out before I talk myself out of it. "He killed my father and is likely working with the Spiriter controlling the king."

Leif pulls back to look me in the eyes, his expression full of shock and doubt as his hands wrap firmly around my shoulders. "You're certain?"

I tell him about the Archtraitor, the murder at the tavern, the witnesses, and the captain's coat. Leif rocks back on his heels.

"You believe me?" I hold the bowl in my lap, unable to finish the last half. A herd of elk could be thundering through me for how my heart beats with hope.

"Yes, I believe you," he says. "So if the captain is truly controlling the king, it's my duty as the king's guard to protect him, which means I must do what I can to break the bind."

I'm so relieved by his answer, I could kiss him.

"I have a plan," I say. "And it requires my death."

LEIF RETURNS A COUPLE OF HOURS LATER WITH Enat's leather pouch.

"Where's the boiled water?" I ask Leif after he pushes the pouch through the iron rungs.

His eyes cut to the side. "By the door," he whispers, and then darts back, his face shifting into a stoic mask a moment before a guard approaches from the depths of the dungeon.

A scowl shows through the guard's greasy beard. "What are you doing here, Leif?"

"Just checking the prisoner," Leif says coolly.

The guard turns and, after noticing me, presses his bulging belly up against the bars of my cell. "So what, you hunted down the scrant and now you get special privileges?"

"If by privileges you mean I have to smell her rotting carcass when I throw dinner at her feet, then yes." Leif chuckles and makes another comment about how disgusting I am. It's slightly mortifying to hear, even if it's an act.

The guard must have accepted Leif's excuse because he leaves after muttering a few more unsavory comments. I'm relieved to watch him go.

"Sorry about that." Leif returns with the cup. "I, uh, didn't want him to think I was showing you any kindness."

"Are we clear? No more guards will be coming down here?"

"Only Jorgan, the guard who was just here, and the dungeon master. If your diversion works, they'll both be occupied and you'll have your escape if you wake in time."

The promise sounds bittersweet.

"The body bearers usually come at night. I—I'm nervous for you. Have you tried making this herbal brew before? What if you don't wake till tomorrow?"

I press my lips together. The day in the forest when I found out I was a Spiriter, Enat had me gather these leaves. While we were traveling, she said if they're crushed and steeped in water with bark-gnarl grindings, they make a sleeping concoction. There are so many ways this plan could fail. "Enat said the effects only last a couple hours. Once I drink the tea and it takes effect, my heart will slow, and I'll look dead. You'll have to move fast. I don't want it to wear off before the dungeon master has taken me out of here."

I sort through Enat's pouch and find the leaves, grind them between my fingers, and then drop the pieces into the liquid. I have no idea if I used the right amount. For all I know, too little might not do the trick and too much could kill me. I pray it works. It's the only way to get out of this dungeon.

"Where will I wake?"

"There's an area at the far end of the dungeon where the corpses are placed until the bearers come. They'll put you there. I would have the guards take you elsewhere, but that would be suspicious. I promise I won't let the bearers take you away."

"Yes. I don't want to be buried alive. Will you be there when I wake?" The words jitter from my cracked lips.

"I'll check on you and try my best to be there. If I'm not, I'll make sure the dungeon master's keep just beyond the dungeon door is open so you can grab your belongings. Once you're in the courtyard, find the north hall. It'll take you right to the high lord's study."

"You're sure it'll be clear?"

Leif reaches out and takes my hand. The warmth of his fingers is such a contrast to the dank, chilly dungeon. "I'll make sure of it. Even if I have to create a diversion."

All I can do is nod.

Clearly, I'd be a fool not to acknowledge the many possibilities in which this plan could fail. But in the short time left before the war begins—before Cohen realizes I'm not at our tree and is then possibly caught and hanged for murder—this is the only plan I have. Regardless of the risks, it's what I must do for Cohen and myself. And for Enat and Papa.

"Thank you." I push the words out past the hard lump in the back of my throat.

The bitter brew lodges in the back of my mouth, and it takes gagging to get it all down. Leif's eyes are pinned to me, studying my face as if the effects will take place instantaneously. I open my mouth to tell him to stop staring when the metal bars blur before me.

"I think it's work—" My lips fumble over the words that catch on my tongue. The cell's bars spin around me. I shut my eyes and fall under the tea's hold.

I should be grateful for the dungeon odor. The moment it burns my nostrils, I'm certain I'm alive. Hopefully the plan has worked and the dungeon master has fallen for the ruse. An uncontrollable shiver works through me, dragging me the rest of the way from sleep. I move to stretch when my hand hits something cold and solid.

Eyes wide open, I take in my surroundings. Beside me, partially covered in muslin, the corpse of a man is surrounded by the smell of death. I bite my lip and scurry away. Yep, the plan worked.

Only the small crack of daylight coming from the door at the top of the stairs provides light in which to orient myself. I'm in the dungeon, but not in a cell. I rise on unsteady legs. Where's Leif? What should I do now?

I consider waiting and immediately ignore the notion. The

corpse stinks. The dungeon master could return at any time. Or the body bearers may come. Down here there's no way of knowing what time it is. Or how long I slept. I have to act now.

The blaze of daylight beyond the dungeon is nearly blinding. I squint and blink and then slip into an adjacent door of the dungeon master's keep that's been left ajar, wherein I find Papa's dagger. Holding the handle once again gives me a push of confidence.

As my eyes accept the light, I scan the courtyard. A group of men stand a dozen paces away, with their backs toward me, shouting and jeering at a commotion. A glimpse of auburn tells me Leif is in the middle of the action. Perhaps this is his distraction.

It's time to move.

Adrenaline pumps through my limbs as I dart across the corner of the courtyard from the dungeon door to the stairwell that will take me to the north hall, praying no one will see me. I scurry beneath the arcading and stumble into the door that leads to the stairwell. The brew isn't entirely out of my system. It makes my legs hard to command. Luckily, the stairwell is empty, stirring a little remorse for having doubted Leif. Taking the steps as fast as I can manage, I enter the north hall in no time.

The corridor is long and marked with more than a dozen doors that I recognize from my time here before. Though the hall is vacant, my steps stay light and soundless, only pausing once to allow time for my tea-fogged head to clear. When my fingers are wrapped around the high lord's shiny doorknob and no guards are in sight, I finally breathe a sigh of relief.

I've made it all the way here. Unseen.

Now all I have to do is convince Lord Jamis of the captain's guilt.

I crack open the door and slip inside.

CHAPTER

39

S EIZE HER."
Captain Omar's icy command stokes a blaze of adrenaline in me, enough to shake off more of the tea's haze. His glare is sharpened with shock and fury. No doubt he thought me dead. I scramble back and pull my dagger from my boot. I turn to go back out the door when two guards rush to my side. I cannot give up now. As I rise, my elbow lifts up and slams into one guard's nose. He grunts and I punch again, hearing a crack of bone. The second guard reaches for me, but the point of my dagger slows his advance.

With his blade unsheathed, his slashing moves are swifter than I've the energy to combat. I'm still too foggy to think clearly enough to fend him off. Stinging heat zips down my arm.

The bludger's cut me. Beads of blood break out across my skin as I trip back for space. Our fight has turned me around so I'm in the middle of Lord Jamis's study.

The two guards hunker into fighting-ready positions, one glaring over a bloody nose and the other shifting closer with his blade pointed at me. Beyond them, the high lord sits behind his desk watching the scene unfold.

Where's Captain Omar?

A quick glance over my shoulder and I freeze.

The point of Omar's blade is pressed into Cohen's neck. *Cohen.* Crimson drops blossom at the point of contact. Enat's final moment pops into my vision and just as quickly vanishes. My skin turns to brittle leaves at the sight of Cohen, captured by the man who killed my father.

"No." I find my voice. "Cohen, what happened?"

"Hand over your weapon or he dies now." Captain Omar's command allows no option for Cohen to speak. Instead, Cohen stares at me hard with an equal look of apology and fear.

I spin to face the high lord, my eyes pleading for his mercy.

"Now!" Omar yells.

I jump and rip my gaze away from Lord Jamis. My fingers shake with fury as I deliver Papa's blade to the bloody-nosed guard, who sets it on the desk.

The guard tugs my wrists behind my back, and a wave of unexpected dizziness hits. Blood stains my tunic and slithers down my arm from the gash near my shoulder. I shake my head to clear the pain.

Defeat kicks through me.

"This isn't how I imagined us meeting again, Miss Flannery." The high lord finally speaks. Like the first time we met, his tone is formal and composed in such an elegant way it makes me take stock of my filth. He crosses the room, coming to stand by his desk in nearly the same pose he held when we first met. The irony that I'm in the man's study with Cohen by my side isn't lost on me.

"Did we not have a deal?" He steeples his fingers.

"We—we did," I say.

"You were promised sovereignty and the ownership of your father's cottage if you led my men to capture Cohen Mackay. Was this not our agreement?"

"Yes." I grit my teeth together. I want to tell him more, explain who the real killer is, but the guard has my arm twisted in restraint and a blade pressed into my side. If I say anything, he may slide the metal between my ribs before I can finish my sentence.

"And yet you led my men to the town where Mackay was hiding, and then you teamed up with the very man I contracted you to capture. You consorted with the enemy and assisted in his escape." He pulls the matching dagger out of the desk and sets it beside mine in a controlled manner that reminds me of the peace before a winter storm. "When you stood in here and agreed to the deal, was it your intention to deceive me, Britta?"

I shake my head. "No, sir, I—"

"I hope not. You see, I don't like being made a fool." His left eye twitches.

This conversation is spinning out of control. If it continues, my fate along with Cohen's, and possibly now Leif's, will be the noose by this time tomorrow. I cannot let that happen. "I — I can explain," I plead.

Lord Jamis cocks his head to one side, jerking like a falcon. "Explain? What could you possibly say to excuse such grievous acts? On top of poaching, you've now committed treason and aided an accused murderer. Please do explain. I'm sure it'll be amusing."

My throat closes up. He won't be sympathetic to my plea. He won't believe me if I tell him the captain's the murderer. My problem lies in the proof, of which I have none.

"Go on, girl." The guard prods my shoulder with his blade. I arch my back to scrape more space from him.

"I . . . I, uh, left Captain Omar and went with Cohen because I found out he's innocent," I say, wincing at the wobble in my voice. "I went to find the real murderer."

Lord Jamis stares at me blandly. Behind me the guard mutters his disbelief, though thankfully doesn't press his point with the blade.

The high lord seemed kind enough to suffer my presence when we first met. I pray he'll listen to me now. Revealing my Spiriter abilities may be suicide, but there's no other way to prove Cohen's innocence and the captain's guilt.

My time is up and there are no other options. For Cohen, I must do this.

"You sent me to find my father's killer, and I went because I believed you when you said Cohen was a murderer. I believed you because I can tell when someone is speaking the truth."

"That's a lie." The outburst comes from Captain Omar. His hand is gripped on the pommel of his sword. I glance from him to Lord Jamis, whose eyes have widened a fraction. A good sign.

"It isn't a lie," I forge on. "When someone tells the truth, I can feel it."

"Interesting." Lord Jamis taps his fingers together before pulling them behind his back. I'm surprised no one in the room has called me a Channeler. "How can you stand here and argue that you have the ability to tell the truth when you say you believed me, and now you're saying I am wrong?"

"When you said Cohen killed my father, you must've believed what you were saying. And because you *thought* you were telling the truth, I felt it. I can prove it. Tell me something that I wouldn't know the truth about. And I'll tell you if you're honest or not."

"And how do I know you're not merely good at guessing?"

"I don't know," I admit with a frown. "But you can keep testing me. I assure you I will get it right every time."

Captain Omar mutters beneath his breath as the high lord appears to be considering my offer. I take note of the grip around my wrists. The guard has slackened his hold.

"Did you know that I was once a skilled hunter like your-self?" Lord Jamis asks. "Your father and I trained together."

This isn't the type of comment I'd expected. First, because it is true. And second because it's personal. Lord Jamis does not strike me as the type of man to let many people close to him.

"Truth," I say.

His brows lift in appraisal.

"She guessed." Omar moves between the high lord and me. "She's lying to save him."

I rip free of the guard and dart forward. "No! You killed my father." I point at the captain. "*You* turned evidence over to Lord Jamis to set Cohen up. You even tried to silence everyone, but there was one witness you didn't silence. He saw the five stripes on your coat. Only *you* wear five stripes."

The other guards move behind me. Captain Omar puts out his hand to stay them. "You accuse me? You fool girl," he hisses. "Saul was my friend. I didn't kill him. But I will kill his murderer."

Truth. It licks through me, a fire blazing through my body.

My arm drops, weighted by the instant proof in his words. "You're telling the truth."

"Captain Omar is right," Lord Jamis says briskly. "You've had quite the performance. I've seen pitiful men go to great lengths to save their neck. This, however"—he gestures in the air to me—"is the most elaborate of all ploys."

"No, I'm not lying. Please. I can prove it."

"We've seen enough of your proof." He waves the two wait-ing guards to seize me.

I scurry around a chair. "I'm not lying. The witness saw the captain's coat. I don't know how to explain what happened, but Cohen is innocent. He doesn't deserve—"

Someone's arm snakes around my waist, hand clamping over my mouth. I twist and thrash my legs, realizing one of the guards managed to get behind me.

"You asked to wear my coat," Captain Omar says, the cadence of his words eerily slow.

I pause my fight, confused by his comment, only to find he's not looking at me. Lord Jamis holds his attention.

"You asked for my coat and I gave it to you," the captain says.

Lord Jamis takes a step away from the desk. "We can discuss this later."

If the guard's hand weren't clamped to my mouth, my jaw would be on the floor. Lord Jamis had the captain's coat. I think back to my first meeting with the high lord and turn over everything he said. How he displayed the evidence and led me to accuse Cohen. He never answered me when I asked if he believed Cohen killed my father. He identified the murder weapon and then pushed me into believing Cohen's guilt by saying there were two witnesses. But he never spoke the words.

Lord Jamis killed Papa.

"No" is Captain Omar's immediate response. "We will discuss this now. What were you doing in Celize three months ago?"

"You already know we were there to discuss peace." Lord Jamis shakes his head, as if this conversation is ridiculous.

The guard holding me must be confused by the turn of

conversation as well because he freezes as I stare at the man who must be guilty. I need Lord Jamis to say it. I need to feel the confirmation.

Omar opens and closes his hand over the hilt of his sword. "I found the dagger beside Saul's body, which was suspect. After all, why would anyone leave behind something so valuable? But why would Cohen also leave his personal coat? He isn't foolish enough to leave evidence about."

"I do not know," Lord Jamis says, and a slight chill brushes through me.

"You were almost as good as Saul at tracking and taking down a kill. I used to be envious of you two. I would've never believed you could kill him."

Lord Jamis moves around his desk. "Omar, I've done nothing. Let's end this."

His confession's too vague to warrant a full reaction, but his words add to the cold in my gut.

"What reason could you have to kill him?" Omar's words are clipped with barely concealed fury. "Guards," Omar commands with the slightest tip of his chin. Forgetting me and Cohen, both guards abandon us and move in on Lord Jamis.

"Stop this now." Lord Jamis's face shadows. "You will leave my study and recompose yourself. I won't speak to you on this matter again."

Captain Omar unsheathes his sword, and his tone is as sharp as his blade when he says, "Answer now. Did you kill Saul?"

"I did not!" Lord Jamis rages back.

Ice blasts through my veins. I gasp at the intensity of his lie.

Omar's eyes ping to me and back to the high lord. My reaction is all the proof Omar needs. "I think your little bounty hunter would tell me otherwise."

In a blink, Lord Jamis has a sword in hand. A ring of steel echoes through the room as weapons clash. With the guards distracted, I snatch the two daggers off the desk and rush to Cohen's side and cut his ropes. He wraps his free hand around mine, pulling me to his body as he hobbles us both toward the door.

"You're hurt," I whisper the moment we're out of the room.

He grunts, but the sound is laced with pain. "I'm fine enough for now." His words are labored and his breath is short.

I survey his body and notice a stain of dark blood along the side of his tunic. A stab wound? "You're hurt. I need to fix you."

He leans in and presses his lips to my temple. "No, not hurt. Remember, built like a boulder."

I hate that he's jesting at a time like this and yet love him for easing my panic, if only by a hair.

"This is your one chance to be free of the guards," he says. "They'll notice we're gone and come for us soon enough. You may have given them your father's murderer, but they'll still be after you for confessing you're a Channeler."

He's right. I start to explain it was the only way, but he silences me with a short kiss. "Let's go, Britta."

WE RUN-LIMP DOWN THE NORTH HALL to the end opposite the tower. Before we turn the corner to the king's chambers, the guards rush out of the high lord's study and charge in pursuit.

"I'll hold them back so you can get in." Cohen pushes me around the corner and down another hall toward two gold-lined doors.

"I cannot leave you out here—"

His look is withering. "You have no choice. One of us needs to fight off the guards. The Spiriter may already know we're here. The bind needs to be broken now. Can you do it?" His eyes search mine.

He's right. I am weak and so my feel on the energy in the room beyond isn't telling other than it's clear someone is close. I need to find the Spiriter and draw on her energy until the bind breaks.

"Yes." I pass him a dagger.

"Go now." He shoves me toward the door. My heart flinches in pain, beating hard like it's counting our last moments.

One beat.

Two.

Three—

I slip inside the king's chambers, wary of whom or what I may find. After stealing a quick moment to sweep through the chamber, I find no Spiriter, only a body-lump in the middle of a mammoth bed. A blue, maroon, and gold carpet paves the way to the bed like a game trail in the forest, leading to where the king is sleeping.

He has golden hair neatly combed around a regal face. A young face. Then I remember he is only three years older than me.

For a moment I fear I'll wake him, but since he's under the Spiriter's bind, I don't think he'll rouse. I tentatively place my hand on his chest and hone in on the sluggish movement of his energy. Where Enat's felt like a busy hive of bees, the king's energy is a barely crawling snail.

I move from his side and hurry around the perimeter of the room in search of another door or passage. The Spiriter must be here somewhere if she's controlling the king.

"Show yourself," I call out.

When no one appears, I return to the king's side and press my eyes shut, listening for the buzz of energy. The king is the only person I detect at first, and then as I push further, I can sense Cohen's energy as well as the guards', and then others' around the castle. Then among everyone's hum, I can faintly detect another, similar to Enat's swarm of bees. It's the Spiriter.

Her specific location, however, is too difficult to determine. In a castle this size, targeting her location is like trying to distinguish one tree in a forest. Which means finding her, with the guards just outside the door, isn't possible. The high lord's arrest doesn't mean we're free from the captain's wrath. Especially after my confession.

I bite my lip.

The weight of the weapon in my right hand seems to grow and magnify until my arm drops. Enat said the only other way to break the bind is to bring King Aodren to the edge of death. I stare down at the dagger, my pulse swishing through my ears.

This has to be done. It is the only way to stop the war. I may not get another chance.

A swell of disquiet rolls through me, but I tamp it down and focus on having done this before. I healed Cohen. I can do it again.

The quickest way to bring him to his death would be to cut him as I would any prey. A quick slice down the thick vein on his neck. My hand trembles and shakes as I press the point of the blade to the stretch of skin between his rough beard and robe. First, his skin shows resistance. The tip sinks in and warmth spills out, staining his clothing, the bed, and my fingers.

The sight turns the air in my lungs to frost. It's too much like Enat's death. So much so, it's nauseating.

The energy depletes from his body like sand shifting through an hourglass, until only a few pieces remain. It's slow at first and faster in the end. Just when I fear I won't know the moment to begin pushing my energy into his, the loss of life slows.

His torso jolts. The weak energy pulsing from him is different than before. Less subdued. Less trapped. It's no longer sluggish. Now the small remainder of his energy is a wounded bird, struggling for flight.

And I know: the bind is broken.

A bubble of relieved laughter escapes as I splay my fingers against his silk shirt and imagine a ghost hand of my soul reaching out and grasping his. The desire to help him wells up stronger than at any other time I've healed. The moments beside the well seem like nothing compared to the pull I feel now.

The hourglass has been flipped.

I slump to the bed and allow myself to rest beside him so my fingers will remain in contact. My life, tiny grains of energy, slips away, slow initially and then increasing in speed. Shortness of breath comes first. Then tingling hands, arms, legs, feet. Later sharp pain shoots through my limbs until eventually all those sensations fade into a hollow ache that spreads throughout my body as the king's energy revives, swelling beneath my palm.

Because I mortally wounded him, his body needs to regain quite a bit of strength before his life is no longer at risk. If left too weak, his recovery could be compromised. I keep filling him, draining myself, until it's impossible to hold my head up.

The door hinge squeals.

Footsteps click against the floor.

"What are you — no." Cohen's unmistakable timbre makes me stir.

"Cohen." A labored pant is all I can manage.

"Britta, stop. You have to stop." I pry my lids open to gaze at him once more. I see how he winces as he lowers himself so that we're eye to eye and my hand is wrapped in his, over his heart. He's badly hurt. It brings tears to my eyes because I won't be able to do anything for him.

"I'm. Sorry." My words are punctuated by the labored breath it takes to push them out. Spots dance in my vision.

His hand tightens around mine. I can see him squeezing even if I'm too numb to feel it. "Take it from me."

He's already too weak. If I draw energy from him it could kill him. "No," I manage.

"You can't leave me." Emotion thickens his words and chokes him. "I need you. Don't you see?" His breath washes over my face as he leans in and presses his lips to my nose. My cheek. My forehead.

My own energy stutters.

"Please take it all from me. I give it to you. Just live."

Though there cannot be more than ten breaths remaining in my lungs, I do what he asks. I allow the energy zipping beneath his palm to flow into mine. His energy tangles with mine; my heart, my soul, my mind gratefully absorb his gift like water to the desert ground.

I don't know how long I soak it in, but I fear it's too late. I don't even have the strength to lift my head. Focusing on his face as it dances on the cloudy edges of my vision is as difficult as shooting an arrow at a spinning target.

A ragged breath sounds. A choking cough. The king stirs under our combined hands.

My vision slips in and out.

Cohen's skin loses color. I've taken enough to pull me out of the pit of death, but perhaps not enough to take me from the edge of the cliff. Either way, I'll not take his life. I squeeze his hand once more to let him know we're done.

"Cohen," I try to say, but only my lips move.

Blackness crowds my vision and draws me into its grasp.

I'M DEAD.

It's the first thought that comes to mind, though the pain playing mercilessly with every muscle suggests otherwise. Grit cements my eyes shut. After a few tries, I somehow manage to crack them open without the use of my hands, which I've discovered are helpless against an unknown weight.

A few more blinks and I'm awake, lying on a bed, smothered in blankets beside a lit fireplace. A familiar worn book lies on the stone hearth. My book.

This is my cottage. My home.

I struggle to free my arms from the mountain of covers.

"Don't do that." A young woman moves into

view. Her midnight-black hair falls over her shoulder as she leans closer to the bed, inspecting me. I'm too weak, too worn, to mind.

"Who . . . are . . . you?" My voice is a rusty hinge. She hands me a cup of warm broth. I gag on the drink, which tastes like dirt and flour. In addition to the woman's disheveled hair, shadows linger beneath her eyes. "You don't look so good."

"Ha." A smile flickers across her thin lips. "I look a league better than you, so watch your mouth. Besides, you've slept for almost a week while I've watched you night and day," she says, and then coaxes me into taking more sips of the broth. My stomach manages it somehow, and as it settles inside me, it has a subtle strengthening effect. "We didn't know if you'd make it. You gave us quite a scare."

"Pardon me, but who are you? And what happened?" Pieces of memory fill my head. The castle. Lord Jamis fighting Captain Omar. King Aodren's blood. And then Cohen taking my hand. "Cohen," I whisper, when my thoughts settle on an image of him wounded and pale beside me. "Where is he?"

She chuckles. "My name is Gillian. I am one of King Aodren's healers. And I sent your Cohen away. He needs his rest too. Course, he's doing better than you. Other than a sword wound that needed to be patched, he just needed sleep. He wasn't getting any over here with how he kept a hawk eye on you. Finally he listened and returned to the castle to catch up on his rest. We would've kept you there as well, but Cohen insisted you would heal better here."

Relief and confusion come together at once. "Why would he go to the castle?"

"So he could rest." She runs a cloth over my forehead. "Perhaps you should close your eyes and sleep some more."

She doesn't understand, and I do not have the energy to explain. I heave out a sigh. "How long have I been here?"

"Six days."

Before I can ask more, a knock sounds at the door. Captain Omar ducks his head in with Leif at his side. Alarmed, I move to grab my dagger, only to discover my body isn't responding. My movements are creaky and so painful, I give up and fall back against the bed.

Gillian places her hand on my head, holding me down. "Lie back."

"How is —?" Captain Omar stops in midsentence when Leif interrupts: "She's awake."

"She woke moments ago." Gillian leaves my side and approaches them. "I won't allow ya to upset her. She needs her rest."

"That's not on my agenda for today," says Captain Omar before he steps around the healer. Leif remains by the door.

"I'll speak with him," I volunteer before she pushes him out, knowing what must be coming. He knows I'm a Channeler.

Gillian moves around him and thrusts another cup of her brew in my face. "Drink this first," she says.

When the cup is empty, Captain Omar pulls a chair beside the bed. He looks different from the last time we spoke. A few more cuts, bruises, and a little less vengeance blazing in his eyes.

"I know you're recovering, so I'll make this brief." He nods to Gillian before turning back to me. "First, I wanted to say Enat's death wasn't my plan. Tomas acted rashly, and he deserved the end he received."

I don't know what I expected, but it wasn't that. I lower the cup to my lap, focusing on the final dregs to keep my sadness at bay. I never imagined I could lose so much.

I dare to meet Captain Omar's eye. "What does this mean for me?"

"Tomas acted without my command, thus any injury he sustained from a defensive attack is his fault." Even as he says this, I can see lines deepening on his forehead, as though it pains him to grant me amnesty. "As far as the law is concerned, you acted in defense of the king. You also had an agreement with the high lord, which the king has agreed to honor. You found your father's murderer and are now absolved of your crimes."

I blink. "Absolved of my crimes?"

"You're free to go and live your life, Britta."

Any relief to be had is at odds with the pain of Enat's

passing. In spite of the freedom he's offering, I cannot muster anything more than a grimace. He'll forever be connected to Enat's death.

"What about my—"

"I know what you did to save the king." The captain cuts me off. "And no one is accusing you of anything more than tending to King Aodren." He gives me a knowing look. "Understand?"

He's completely turning a blind eye to my Channeler ability.

"You're a smart girl, Britta. I think you understand me just fine. You risked your life for him and this country. Your actions were honorable." He shifts beside me. "And . . . and I am here to apologize."

Never in a thousand years would I have expected such a confession from Captain Omar. "Pardon. Did you say you needed to apologize?"

"Yes." His answer is scant more than grunt.

"Am I dead?"

"Britta, don't give the captain a hard time," Leif warns without conviction. "He's already here, groveling at your bedside for his many, many mistakes and misjudgment of your character, failures that might possibly have brought more harm to the king. Don't make it any worse."

Omar's face purples. Leif laughs.

"You know about the Spiriter, then?" I ask Captain Omar, allowing the change in conversation.

"Yes, which is another reason I've come to talk to you. Lord Jamis is charged with your father's murder as well as treason against the king. He's detained in the dungeon but has refused to speak to anyone, despite our persuasion. We don't know who he was working with. Do you?"

"No," I tell him. "She wasn't in the room. Though she couldn't have been far. For her bind to work, she would've had to be close. I could sense her somewhere in the castle. I would've searched for her if I could have pinpointed her location."

He strokes his beard. "Interesting."

"If that's all, Captain Omar and Leif, the girl needs her rest." Gillian takes my cup.

The door creaks open, and Cohen appears in the doorway with Siron's shadowy form behind him. His sudden appearance is such a pleasant surprise, it takes me a moment to realize I didn't *feel* his approach. The horse lets out a saluting snort, which makes me smile. The sight of Cohen, healthy and strong, fills my heart with such peace and happiness.

Captain Omar stands. "I was just leaving," he tells Gillian, and then faces me. He clears his throat. "I wanted to say thank you."

My lips part in surprise. "You—you're welcome."

Before the captain leaves, Leif moves to my side. "I'm glad you're all right," he says with a bashful smile. "I just came to tell you that anytime you need me, I'll be here for you."

"I couldn't have done it without your help," I tell him. "I'll always consider you a friend."

He blushes. "You deserved that and more."

When Leif leaves the cottage with the captain, Cohen steps forward, and two things I hadn't noticed a few minutes before steal my thoughts—his disheveled hair and haunted eyes.

"Britta." He says my name almost reverently as his eyes sweep over my face.

"I thought you went to the castle to sleep."

A half smile plays on his mouth. "I did take a small nap, but I'm restless without you near. And even more restless when I see Leif at your side." He frowns and I laugh. "I'd rather be here and exhausted than anywhere else."

His words put a lump in my throat. "I didn't know you were welcome to sleep at the castle."

"That changes after you help save the king's life."

Is that so? I wonder. I glance around my cottage and hope that my life is done changing. I'm happy right here.

I shift to the side of the bed. "There's room for two. Perhaps then we can both get some rest."

He drops down beside me, maneuvering his arm beneath my head so I'm curled into his body.

"Tell me what happened after we split up in the woods," he says.

I explain about the captain's attack and Enat's death. When tears trail down my cheeks, he kisses them away and then smiles so sweetly at me, I temporarily forget my heartache.

"Bernard and I made it nearly to Finn's camp when we were overcome by a group of guards," Cohen says. He goes on to tell how the captain set up the entire trap. Finn may be in the king's army, but he was never in danger of being moved to the frontline. The captain, who hoped to flush Cohen out of hiding and anyone willing to help him, spread those rumors.

I'm tempted to spend time thinking of all the ways we could've done things differently. How we might've spared Enat's life. But one thing Enat taught me is to stop living in the past and look toward the future.

Gillian crosses the room to the fireplace and adds a log to the fire before excusing herself and leaving Cohen and me alone in the cottage.

"All that matters is you're here with me," I tell him.

Cohen presses his hand to his chest. "I don't think I've ever heard such sweet words out of your smart mouth."

"I promise not to make a habit out of it." My smile mirrors his.

He takes my hand and adds pressure. "I should be thanking you. You saved my life."

"We did it together."

"Together," he murmurs into my hair. "I like that."

I do too. I look into the crawling flames. The wood crackles and pops as the fire licks its edges, until it's consuming the log. We're bathed in glorious heat.

Gillian returns a short while later and drops into my

father's chair. She pulls out her knitting. I curl up against Cohen's sturdy frame, intoxicated by the feeling of peace in my home.

"How long do you think she'll stay?" Cohen whispers mischievously to me.

"It could be days or weeks. I don't know. She seems tenacious."

"Then she better get used to me kissing you and taking advantage of your immobile state."

My eyes widen at the warmth in his warning while he grins down at me.

"I almost lost you." He draws a strand of hair away from my cheek and leaves his fingers resting against my skin. "After the guards caught me and brought me in, I was certain Omar would have my head before I ever saw your face again." His playful smile fades as his eyes lower to my hands in my lap. "I never want to lose you."

"Lose me?"

"I won't lose you. You're mine, and I'm yours. And if I have to take on the world to make it so, I'll do it."

His truth burns hot inside my chest, taking my breath away.

He inclines his head, his lips a whisper away from mine. "I love you." The vibration of his words sends shivers to my toes. There's no one else who has this sort of hold on me. Which makes me feel like everything in my world is finally right.

. . .

Before sunset, Cohen leaves to meet with Captain Omar to make a strategy to hunt down the mysterious Spiriter who was controlling King Aodren.

He isn't gone long, though. No more than an hour has passed when I feel the tiny pull inside. The tingling awareness that Cohen is nearby. It's odd how much stronger the sensation is, compared to the last few weeks, which makes me wonder if there's something more to my hypersensitivity to Cohen than just the anticipation of seeing him.

I breathe out a sigh of relief knowing he's returned, only to be surprised when he knocks at the door. Strange. Papa's cottage has always been his second home, and Cohen always felt comfortable entering at will.

Gillian leaves my side to answer the door. When she pulls it open, I look up with a wide smile painted across my face.

Only, a crown set on rich golden hair seizes my attention. My expression vanishes. "King Aodren?"

"I heard you woke, and I couldn't wait any longer to see you." He ducks into the room, suddenly making my cottage feel small and filthy in comparison to his bold maroon cloak and polished boots. His face looks healthier and fuller than when last I saw him.

"I wanted to come sooner, but I knew you needed time to recover," he says. "I had to meet the girl who risked her life for me."

Every word he speaks makes perfect sense, and yet I cannot wipe away the puzzled expression on my face. His presence has me so arrested, I don't notice Cohen enter until he's taken a knee before the king. Which is also when I realize I didn't sense Cohen's return at all.

My wide-eyed stare catches King Aodren's gaze. "Please accept my humble gratitude," he says. "I want you to know that you are welcome at the castle whenever you're feeling up to moving. I would enjoy sharing tea with you and talking." He tips his chin in a regal nod and then leaves. I stare at the door, surprised that I can sense him move farther away. And baffled by my body's reaction: Why do I want to follow?

"Britta?" Cohen says. "Are you all right?"

I snap out of my daze and take in Cohen. Why don't I feel a pull to him anymore? The man I love is no longer the one I'm connected to. Though he's here with me now, I cannot help but feel panicked.

"Dove?"

"Yes, I'm, uh, fine," I say, fighting back my shock.

I suppose now I'm the one with the secrets.

TO BE CONTINUED

Acknowledgments

Writing a novel is a trek. Over craggy mountains. During a blizzard. In slippers and sweats. I would've never made it without the following people:

My gratitude to my mom, who told me I could be anything in life and, like Saul, taught me to press on; and to my dad, whose wanderlust inspired me to dream of other worlds.

Mark, my greatest champion and the most patient man I know, thank you for pushing me up the hill. To my children — cyclones of laughter, curiosity, tears, joy — may you know your potential is out of this world. To my siblings, who have put up with my wild notions and still claimed me as family.

Sarah Landis — editing wizard and literary therapist — my deepest gratitude goes to you and the team at Houghton Mifflin Harcourt for giving me a publishing home. Thank you for your buoying praise and your skillful eye.

Josh Adams — agent extraordinaire and slayer of skepticism — your guidance and unshakable faith have made all the difference. Kathryn Purdie, thank you for guiding me toward the agenting light, sitting on my couch, and cleaning my book mess. Elana Johnson, I'm honored to have you as my friend. This book wouldn't be here without you. You gave me direction on my raw ideas and, when the time came, wrote my query.

Jessie Humphries, one of my best friends, thank you for reminding me to have positive thoughts, for cutting up magazines and handing me glue to make a vision board, and for endless laughs.

My heartfelt thanks to Peggy Eddleman, my writing ally, whose compassion and kindness are boundless; to Rob Code, amazing critique partner and idea bouncer; and to Jason Manwaring, Jaime Kirby, and Julieanne Donaldson for years of support. To Cecilia Carter, who read aloud to me and helped me through the tough scenes. To Marta Tyler for her romance prowess that breathed life into Britta and Cohen. To Leslie Pugh, who cared for me while I was in recovery and believed in this book. To Danny Wilcox for his master strategy. To Finn Bjarnson for his generous nature and inspiring music.

For their encouragement and amazingness, sincere thanks to Ally Condie, Sara Larson, Stacey Ratliff, Caitlyn McFarland, Nichole Giles, Emily King, Katie King, Taffy Lovell, Tammy Merryweather, Erik Bayles, Alecia Bales, Rahul Kanakia, and Emily Hammerstad.